Praise for *The Candy Store*

Poague's vibrant characters and piquant period details make for an entertaining voyage into the past. An engaging, bittersweet saga about finding a place to belong.

Kirkus Reviews

I quite enjoyed *The Candy Store*, it was a lovely exploration of the trials of growing up, fitting in and finding a place in the world… All in all, a really great book, and one I'd recommend to anyone.

Belle M., Independent Reviewer

Reading *The Candy Store* was like savoring a bittersweet chocolate bar that has a surprise twist in flavor at the last bite. The novel was a delicious combination of sci-fi, time travel, historical fiction, and romance. I highly recommend *The Candy Store*. It is the perfect novel for teens looking for a story packed with love, friendship and adventure.

Estrella Salgado, A LitPick Reviewer

This novel was a blast from the start until the finish. The relationships the characters had with each other were crafted extremely well, and I was very impressed. It is clear the author put a lot of effort into making both the setting and the characters lifelike. Even though I never lived in the 20s or even the 80s, I felt like I was able to briefly be a part of those eras and have fun with characters that were having the time of their lives.

Hailey Karter, A LitPick Reviewer

The candy store is the centerpiece around which the story revolves. Although this is the story of Jett's life, it is also the story of a generation as seen through the many lives that become a part of her story. An important part – the backdrop – of the novel is its historical content and the social settings of the time, clearly conveyed and interesting in itself. The author writes with perception and with insight into human nature. Characters are finely honed, universal, typical of their generation, and convincing in their individuality – a good ending with a bit of subtlety.

Robert Krueger, author of The Children's Story, About Good and Evil.

THE CANDY STORE

THE CANDY STORE

Is destiny determined by the future or the past?

MICHELE POAGUE

THE CANDY STORE Copyright © 2015 by Michele Poague.

This book is a work of fiction. Names, characters, businesses, organizations, places, events and incidents either are the product of the author's imagination or are used fictitiously. Any resemblance to actual persons, living or dead, events, or locales is entirely coincidental.

Cover design by Michele Poague

Bent Briar Publishing LLLP
214 W Calle del Estribo
Sahuarita, AZ 85629
roseliterary@aol.com

ISBNS
978-1-942665-00-7   HC
978-1-942665-01-4   SC
978-1-942665-02-1   EPUB

Printed in the United States of America

First Edition: August 2015

10 9 8 7 6 5 4 3 2 1

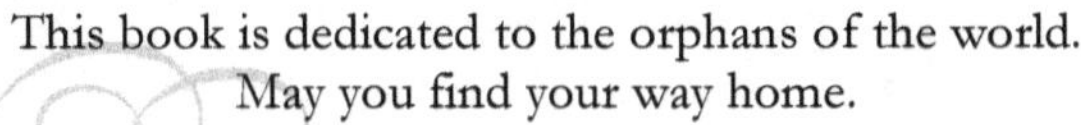

This book is dedicated to the orphans of the world.
May you find your way home.

PROLOGUE

A shivering hotel maid huddled beside a large black dumpster near the red brick wall of the Oxford to avoid the biting October wind. A day's worth of soiled linens sat in a rolling laundry cart at her feet. In her hand, she clutched a letter from the U.S. government. Her eyes burned as she read the words again. The form letter from the U.S. government, printed under the raised eagle, informed her that her brother, one of the 40,000 Marines President Johnson shipped to Vietnam the previous April, had died while searching for Viet Cong near Da Nang. Margret hated the war. By July, the U.S. military presence had increased by an additional 125,000 men and the monthly draft numbers had doubled. This morning,

Margret's youngest brother had received his draft notice. It wasn't turning into a good day for her.

Pulling a red and white pack of Marlboro cigarettes from her apron, she watched the Reliable Linens truck slowly back down the alleyway. Thursday marked the last day of her workweek, and she was almost done for the day.

As the big white truck rolled to a stop, Margret thought she heard a baby cry. Stomping out her cigarette, she peeked around the corner of the building toward the street. She saw no one. Returning to her heavy basket of linens, she waved to the driver. Again, the high-pitched sound of a baby's wail beset her, clearer and much more insistent this time. Again, Margret looked up and down the alley, but the laundry driver was the only person in sight.

She rolled the cart toward the van. "Cold enough for you?" she asked him. "That wind is a bitch today."

"I've seen worse days," he said, taking the laundry from her. "Hey, can I bum a smoke?"

"Sure. Do you hear that?" She asked, tapping out a cigarette and handing it to him.

"Sounds like an unhappy kid."

"You hiding something, old man?" She grinned as she peered into the cab of the vehicle.

"Not me. Not the daddy type." He lit the cigarette and inhaled deeply. "Thanks for the smoke. I'm trying to quit."

Margret grinned. "Only smoking ohpees now?"

"Ohpees?" the older man asked.

"You know, other peoples' cigarettes."

"Oh."

Another shrill scream flooded the alleyway. This time both of them turned toward the dumpster a few feet away. They ran and threw open the lid.

"Oh my God," Margret shrieked. "Who would do such a thing?" Among the rubbish in the oversized trash bin lay a newborn green-eyed baby girl. The poor thing was naked and blue from the cold.

"That's brutal," the driver whispered, staring at the squalling infant. "She can't even be a day old. Good thing we were here to find her."

"I swear, she couldn't have been there ten minutes ago." Grabbing a clean-looking white linen tablecloth from the truck, Margret scooped the child up, wrapping her as best she could. "I just can't imagine what was going on in her mother's mind. She's such a beautiful child." The painful shrieking quieted when she hugged the infant to her chest, rocking her gently.

"You're going to be alright now," Margret said to her charge. "There are lots of people in this world who will love you. Don't you worry none."

As Margret carried the abandoned baby past a small transistor radio in the hotel kitchen, she heard the clear and gentle voice of John Lennon singing, *Yesterday, all my troubles seemed so far away.*

CHAPTER 1

It's been said that history repeats itself. Consider the women's suffrage movement at the end of the nineteenth century and the Women's Liberation movement of the 1970s. Certainly there were similar women who had similar thoughts and did similar things; similar yet not the same. Time plays tricks on us. To a child, a year feels like an eternity, while the same year passes in a heartbeat for the person nearing the end of life. It's actually quite annoying how too much or too little time can take a bad situation and make it just a little bit worse. As an orphan, abandoned in a dumpster the day I took my first breath, I'm no stranger to tough situations. I spent my early years in and out of orphanages thanks to the foster care system. Although I don't know exactly when my life began to spin out of control, I'll start this story in the middle of October 1981.

It was my sixteenth birthday, and I was sitting on a high-back wooden bench in Union Station. In my lap were brochures from several schools. My eyes ran down the list: Adams State University, Arapahoe Community College, Colorado University at Boulder, Denver University, Metropolitan State, Denver Institute of Art. I sat there for a long time wondering how I was going to pay the tuition.

There it was. The Colorado Institute of Art offered a Bachelor of Arts degree in Culinary Management. I read the class information paragraph for the tenth time in as many minutes. The wooden bench was hard, and my McDonald's Happy Meal wasn't making me happy.

My goal was to complete both my GED at Emily Griffith Technical College and get through an art program within the next two years. A culinary arts degree would land me the kind of job I needed to get on my feet, at least. The big question, how to come up with the thousand-dollar tuition I needed to get started?

Earlier that day, after turning in my application at Emily Griffith, I had walked up and down Fifteenth and Sixteenth Streets looking for work. My part-time waitressing job didn't pay much and I only had ten dollars left from my last check. Although I wasn't scheduled to work again until the following Tuesday, that was actually a good thing because the regular exposure of the White Spot increased my chances of being recognized. Dodging Social Services, and most recently, a detective from District 2, made holding a steady job difficult.

I also needed a new place to live. The Rescue Mission had been fine for the past couple of months. The missionaries were nice enough and they didn't ask a lot of questions, but it wouldn't be long before someone found me there.

My stomach churned as I remembered the school interview. I don't mean to be hard to get along with, but sometimes my mouth engages without consulting my brain. I made up a fake address because I didn't want the admissions assistant to know I was staying at the Rescue Mission. I guess I was a little sensitive. She had been cordial enough when she asked for my parents' names, but I took offense. Reading my name from the application, she had asked, "Jett Margret Oxford. What an interesting name. Is that Oxford, like the hotel down the street?"

"Yes," I'd said, sharper than I'd intended. I didn't tell her why I used the hotel's name for my own. I had changed my name many times over the first sixteen years of my life. Not having a birth certificate meant I could be anyone I wanted to be. Jane Doe was written on the police report, but the nuns who first took me in called me Mary Margret after the hotel maid who discovered me the day I was dumped. Personally, I always felt I should have been named something exotic, like Cher or Twiggy. Until recently, I'd had bleached blonde hair and an ID that said my name was Madonna J. Monroe. A good ID and new hair color made it easier to hide in plain sight, and calling attention to myself with a name like Madonna wasn't a good idea right now. I liked to change my middle name on occasion, sometimes using Marilyn, Malibu, or Mykala. Today, I chose the name of the woman who found me behind the Oxford Hotel in 1965.

I had to discover my true name for myself. Six years ago, while I lived at the Denver Children's Home, the administrators regularly lined us up like stray dogs at the pound and people would come by to look us over. Sometimes they would ask us questions, but mostly they would talk about us as if we weren't standing two feet in front of them. One day, a thin woman with a pinched face and too much gold jewelry came to pick out a child. She wore a leopard fur coat with matching leopard pumps. She was looking at the tiniest ones, not interested in a ten-year-old. As she glanced over me, she said to the round, red-faced man beside her, "Look at that jet black hair."

At the time, I didn't know what "jet black" meant, so I looked it up. Black jet stone was created by pressure during the decomposition of wood. *Cool,* I thought, *I'm under pressure.* Jet stone is a form of coal, known as lignite, which becomes electrically charged when rubbed with silk or wool. *Cooler still.* Jet stone was often used for rosaries, for mourning jewelry, and in magic rituals. *Coolest of all.*

The interview was short. It may have been my imagination, but I thought the woman disapproved of me and was glad when I got up to leave. Before I left, she said, "Have your parents sign the application and bring it back. We'll need their financial records to determine your tuition."

"I have no parents. My finances are listed on the second page."

"How old are you?"

"Eighteen today," I lied. "Like it says on the application."

She nodded and filed the papers in a folder.

When I left the school, I wasn't in the best frame of mind to be seeking work, which is why I ended up sitting on a stiff wooden bench at the train station without a clue what my next move was going to be.

I shouldn't have spent money on a Sony Walkman, but music had always been my escape. Cranking up the volume, I bobbed my head to the pounding beat as Joan Jett wailed, "*I love rock and roll.*" Joan Jett was my newest idol, tough as nails and smart as hell. The Blackhearts were quickly nudging out REO Speedwagon as my favorite band.

I was sitting on the bench, minding my own business, when the ticket master looked over at me, frowning. Ignoring him, I returned to eating my lunch, nibbling on the last of my fries. The lobby was bathed in the gray light flooding through the two-story-high arched windows. Union Station was pretty dead on this cloudy afternoon. There wasn't much call for train travel these days. Across the room were two men on another bench playing cards. Judging by their loose-fitting clothes, I thought they were probably homeless. They never looked at the train schedules. I looked at the schedules all the time, wishing one of the many destinations was my own. Union Station must have been a madhouse when train travel was the primary means of transportation. I only hung out there because it was warm and, on most days, no one bothered me.

Today was different. The cop in the corner was watching me intently. Half a dozen signs around the old building said *No Loitering* and this was the third time I'd been here in a week. He strolled over to the two men playing cards and asked to see their tickets. It was time to go, before he had a chance to ask me for an ID. The last thing I wanted was for Social Services or the police to find me.

Throwing my paper sack in the wastebasket, I headed out into the icy October wind, wishing there was enough money in my pocket to afford a taxi. The Rescue Mission was only eleven blocks away on Twenty-Third Avenue and Lawrence, but it was beginning to snow, adding more crap to a pretty crappy day.

Down the street, on the right, was the Oxford, Denver's oldest grand hotel and my namesake. With its red brick, intricate window moldings, and beautifully arched windows all along the fourth floor, the hotel looked out of place in this modern age. Back in its heyday, the Oxford boasted a separate dining room where gentlemen could eat privately while conducting business. It was the first of its kind, with a pharmacy, a Western Union office, a library, a barbershop, a restaurant, and a sophisticated saloon. It was like a city within a city. In recent years it had fallen into disrepair. Although the antique oak furniture, marble floors, and elegant carpets were worn, I'd always been drawn to the place like most people are drawn to a car wreck.

Recently, the hotel had closed for a major renovation, and I felt lost. The Oxford was the only thing that connected me with the woman who gave me life. Before it closed in 1979, I used to walk the lobby and peer into the dining rooms where, like a wealthy old woman in her diamonds and pearls, the linen-covered tables sparkled with expensive glassware, china, and real silver service.

From the north side of the street, I watched the workmen hanging Art Deco panels in the corner bar. I'd heard the Cruise Room was going to be exactly the same as it had been in the early thirties, with panels, carved in bas-relief, celebrating toasts from around the globe, including one portraying Adolf Hitler, swastika and all.

I stood there several minutes, wondering if my mother had been a guest there in 1965. Did she have a Brandy Alexander or Pink Squirrel in the Cruise Room? Did she eat breakfast in the east dining room, or was she just another homeless woman passing by?

I imagine my mother looked a lot like me with curly black hair and big green eyes. I'm only five-foot-three, so she probably wasn't a tall woman. Then again, maybe I have my father's eyes or his hair. Just one more of life's little mysteries.

Wrapping my heavy red woolen coat tighter and tying the wide belt helped to block most of the bitter wind. My coat was like an old friend. Given to me when I was twelve, it was missing two big black buttons and was about a size too small for me now. The big fake-fur collar kept my ears warm and the long wool covered my knees. It was an obvious reject from the seventies; surely I'd seen this same coat on Mary Tyler Moore.

Clinging to the north side of the street allowed the high-rise buildings to block the most formidable gusts. It was starting to snow harder as I stopped in the doorway of a little shop. The curved sign etched into the window said *Watson's Candies* in a beautiful antique script. The three-tiered window display paraded an exhibition of chocolate candies and cookies so beautifully crafted they made my heart flutter. Dainty Monarch butterflies of sugar graced the five layers of an elegant wedding cake. Marshmallow and coconut snowmen ice-skated on a silver platter. Caramel candied apples reminded clients that Halloween was only a week away.

I was about to walk away when I saw it. In the lower right-hand window, propped up by a tray of chocolate truffles, was a hand-written sign. HELP WANTED.

Excited, I opened the door. Thinking it would be a perfect place to work while I earned my culinary arts degree. Maybe I would learn to make those darling candies, too.

The tiny bell on the door tinkled gaily as I stepped inside. Immediately, I was dazed by the smell of hot chocolate and fresh cookies. I took a deep breath and savored the heavenly scent. The display cabinet looked like a piece from a Hollywood movie set. A large, mechanical brass cash register sat on the top of a display case made of oak and beveled glass. Inside, a cheery assortment of chocolate-covered cherry cordials, almond caramels, hazelnut truffles, peppermint patties, and vanilla cream fudge tempted the senses. A pair of corner display cases with beveled glass on the sides, golden brass trim, and curved glass doors held candied fruit, lollipops, and coconut bars, each confection more delectable than the last. On the counter next to the register was a bowl of tiny sugar flowers with a note that invited me to taste them. I didn't hesitate.

The confectioner was gifted. Every incredible treat had a signature W or a tiny sugar flower.

"Hello," I called out. "I'm interested in the position you advertised in the window."

"Just a minute," a man shouted from the back. "I'll be right out."

Gazing out the window at the swirling snow, I waited. In the window's reflection I saw an old man shuffle out from the back of the store. When I turned around, he dropped the box of taffies he'd been carrying and the little waxed-paper-wrapped candies spilled haphazardly across the wooden floor.

"I'm so sorry," I said. "I didn't mean to startle you."

He stared at me with intense Paul Newman blue eyes. "Oh, my word!" he stumbled over his words. "I don't—it can't…"

I was getting weirded out by the way he was looking at me. Thankfully, an equally old woman came into the room tucking whips of white hair under a plastic shower cap. Like the old man, she looked to be about eighty.

"It's okay, Henry," she said. "I told you she was coming." She patted his hand lovingly.

The old man didn't look away, and I was starting to feel sorry for him. Dementia can be so cruel. Maybe he didn't like strangers.

He mumbled, "I know you told me, but I never really . . . "

"Yes," the woman said hastily. "I know, darling. Why don't you go check on the candied apples while I help this young lady?"

Looking at me like I had boogers hanging out of my nose, he said to the woman beside him, "That's why you put up the help wanted sign."

The old woman reached up and fondled the necklace that hung from her deeply wrinkled neck. It looked quite old. Tiny, intricate swirls of silver filigree held a rectangle-cut clear crystal. On closer inspection I could see the sides of the stone bowed gently, resembling a cushion. It was beautiful. I'd never seen anything quite like it.

"It's been a long time," she said. "I wasn't sure she'd come. Remember what I told you? Now, I need you to let me take care of this."

I didn't understand what the two old coots were talking about, but I wanted to get back to the reason I was standing there. "You were, like, maybe, expecting someone else?" I asked. "I'd really like to work here. I'm going to attend Emily Griffith's GED program and, like, go to culinary school. This would be so, like, right up my alley."

The gray-haired man took a hold of my hand and smiled. "We would love to have you. We need some young blood around here."

EWW. Please don't let him be a letch. I gently pulled my hand back.

"Slow down, Henry. She doesn't know you yet." The woman reached into a small file box and drew out an application. "I'm sorry about Henry. You can call me Jay. Henry, stop staring at her. Can't you see you're making her nervous? Now, please. Go check on the apples like I asked."

"Sorry, Jay. You know how forward I can be." They laughed at some unknown joke. With that, he left the room, but not without staring at me all the way to the door. There was definitely something wrong with the guy.

"My name is Jett, Jett Oxford." I said, proud of the name I'd chosen. A jet could take you places. Only recently, Joan Jett had also freed my inner desire to revolt. "I don't know anything about making candy, but I learn fast."

Without giving me the application, she smiled widely and said, "Welcome, Jett. We usually start baking before dawn. If you would like, I have a room upstairs you can use. It's small, but it's warm, and you won't have to worry about buses or taxis. Denver can be a dangerous place for a young lady using public transportation at three and four in the morning."

I couldn't believe my luck; a job and a place to stay. Henry was a bit strange, but Jay was totally cool.

Using the last of my money, I took a taxi to the shelter to pick up my meager belongings. It wouldn't take much to pack a few articles of clothing, my favorite banana clip, some mascara, and the linen tablecloth the maid had wrapped me in the day she found me.

I'd met a few people at the shelter, but Penny is the only one I was going to miss. She was quiet, almost morose, but she was smart and looked after me, even when she didn't need to. She had lost her husband in a drunk driving accident. They had both been drinking and her husband had tried to talk her out of driving, but she'd insisted because it was her car. The Mercury Capri went off a bridge into the Platte River. Although she could have asked for welfare, I believe she lived at the Rescue Mission as a sort of penance.

She was lying on her cot, reading *Sophie's Choice* by William Styron, as I gathered my few belongings.

"A detective came by today. He was investigating a shooting that went down last summer. Said he was looking for a young girl, maybe sixteen or seventeen, little over five feet, and blond. Goes by the name Madonna."

"So, like, what did you tell him?"

"Nothing," she said thoughtfully.

"Thank you, Penny."

"So what's up? This got something to do with the way you looked the day I found you under the Washington Street Bridge?"

"Paisano."

"Your old boyfriend? The one who cut you up last summer?"

"It was only one cut."

"On your cheek!"

"You can hardly see it now," I said, folding my spare pair of jeans.

"You think he's got something to do with this detective?"

I shook my head. "Last I heard he got time for possession."

Penny stared at me. "So what is this shooting he's looking into? And how *did* you get the cut and the black eye?"

I let out a long sigh and sat on the bed across from her. "I wasn't willing to do what he wanted me to do."

She nodded. "And?"

"So, like, I had been living with a foster family on the west side when my foster dad got all touchy with me. I met Paisano at the rec center at Barnum Park. He was so cute and sexy. He said I could crash at his place for a few days if I wanted to get away."

"How old is he? Old enough to have his own place I'm guessing," Penny said, now sitting on the edge of her cot.

"He must be about twenty or so. Anyway, I was staying at his house when he made this deal with a couple guys from the north side. When he told me I was part of the deal, I refused. He threatened to kick me out. I told him I didn't care and he punched me in the stomach."

"Good Lord!"

"The guys from the north side said they didn't want a girl who wasn't willing and they would be good with an extra fifty for the stuff. After the guys left, Paisano was really pissed off, coming after me with both fists. He had me down on the couch, hitting me. That's how I got the black eye. I knew whenever he met with dealers he kept his .38 between the cushions."

Penny's eyes popped. "You didn't shoot him, did you?"

"No. He hit me a couple more times and then got up. I pulled the gun out and pointed it at him. He laughed and said I didn't know how to shoot a gun. His wallet was on the coffee table next to the plastic-wrapped kilo. I made a quick calculation and shot the bag of coke."

"You shot his cocaine?"

"Yeah, the table was glass and a piece of the table hit me in the cheek. Paisano was so upset about his coke, he didn't see me grab the wallet. I backed toward the front door and told him I'd kill him if he came after me. For good measure, I shot the coke again."

Penny shook her head. "I can't believe you did that."

"Well, I didn't have the guts to actually shoot him. I just needed a distraction to get away. So there was, like, enough money in the wallet to get a box of hair dye, a big hat, and sunglasses. I was hiding under the bridge when I saw you."

"You were a mess that day." She looked sympathetic. "But if you didn't shoot Paisano, how did the cops get involved?"

"Someone probably reported hearing gunfire. When the cops pulled up, they probably found Paisano trying to pick glass out of his coke. A friend told me he went to jail that night."

"I'll bet that seriously pissed him off."

"Yeah. Hopefully he's locked up for a while, and his friends are looking for a blond named Madonna."

Penny grinned. "I can't picture you with blond hair."

"Don't," I said. "It really looked bad."

"Whatever happened to the gun?"

"I have it stashed. Got four bullets left." I shrugged. "Like, it makes me feel somewhat safe for the first time in my life."

I folded the linen tablecloth and put it in my backpack.

Penny noticed. "If you ran out the door, how'd you get that back?"

"When I heard he got snatched, I broke into his house. At first I couldn't find it, but it was in the trash out back." I ran my hand over the fabric. "It's the only connection I have to the day I was born. Or at least to the hotel maid who found me."

Placing the last of my personal items in the backpack, I turned to leave.

"Wait," Penny said. "You moving out for good?"

"Yeah. Got a great job today and it includes a room."

She looked down her nose at me. "What kind of job includes a room?"

"It's in a candy store. The owners are positively ancient. Jay, the old woman, said they do most of their baking at oh-dark-thirty. I think she wants to make sure I can get to work every day. They seem nice."

She relaxed a little. "How much are you getting paid?"

"I was too excited to ask."

"Well, I hope you aren't letting anyone take advantage of you. You act pretty tough, but you're young and some folks prey on the innocent."

"I can handle it. I've been through seven sets of foster parents. And Paisano."

Penny stood up and gave me a hug. "Take care of yourself," she said, "and come visit me once in a while."

"Sure," I said. At the time I didn't know how hard it would be to keep that simple promise.

CHAPTER 2

The last week of October and then November flew past in a flurry of learning and baking. As it turned out, both of the storeowners were cool. Henry (he insisted I call him by his first name) was funny and charming, not at all the pervert I thought he would be. Although sometimes I would catch him looking at me like I was some kind of alien. I would stick out my tongue or make a silly face at him and he'd laugh. Working with him was fun, and he seemed to like working with me, too. It was probably the novelty of working with someone who preferred David Bowie to Benny Goodman, but it could have been the funny faces I liked to make at him.

Jay was tough on me. I've never been good about following rules, and the store had plenty. If I overslept or forgot to change into my white shoes, Jay would grumble about how she expected me to be more responsible. She insisted my friends and family would depend on me one day, and if I didn't learn now, they would be disappointed. Henry usually said something like, "Jay, lighten up. The girl is only sixteen, give her another fifty years."

"Thank you for coming to my defense, handsome," I'd said, "but maybe Jay's right. I shouldn't be so lax. I understand the need for rules; I just don't like them."

Henry laughed. "Don't let that old woman fool you," he said to me, "she's been known to break a few rules herself."

Jay shook her head but a grin tickled the corners of her mouth. "It's been such a long time since I was sixteen, sometimes it's hard to remember."

It was so unlike me, but I found myself wanting to please them, getting up before Jay had to call me a second or third time and, for the first time in my memory, keeping my room neat and washing the dishes without being asked. The big epiphany came when I realized I didn't have an exit plan. I ALWAYS had an exit plan, and I always used it.

Thanksgiving was a quiet day for me. I rolled out of bed at seven-thirty, hours after I would normally be up. It was chilly in the house, so a thick red cotton sweater and blue jeans fit the bill. After washing my face, I pulled my curly dark hair up in a banana clip and backcombed it into place. The Watsons planned to visit a friend early in the day and left me at home alone to roast the turkey; something I was looking forward to doing.

I met Jay and Henry downstairs as they were leaving. Picking up a potluck dish of scalloped potatoes, Henry said, "We would have invited you but I'm afraid you'd be bored to death with all us oldsters talking about things that happened long before you were born."

Jay kissed me on the cheek. "We should be home by four and we'll have a nice dinner here. The bird is in the oven. Would you baste it every thirty minutes for me? You're sure you'll be okay here alone?"

"Seriously, it's okay. Thanksgiving's never meant anything to me. It's, like, a family thing and I never really had a family."

"All the same, don't forget to baste that bird and put the pumpkin pie in about two."

After they left, I boiled water for tea and fried an egg. The quiet house left me feeling strange. I usually enjoyed being alone but found the stillness empty rather than calming.

I wandered around the house. TV Thanksgiving Day specials were sappy, so I decided to take a long bath and trim away some of the hair I'd fried trying to bleach it blond. It had good natural curl when it was healthy but that was going to take a couple of years.

After the bath, I settled in to watch the Macy's Thanksgiving Day Parade. I was startled when I heard the car pull up in the alley. I rubbed the sleep from my eyes; apparently, I'd napped on the sofa most of the afternoon. *Crap, I forgot to bake the pies.* Racing to the kitchen, I pulled out the bird. *Not too dry.* And put the pies in the oven just as Henry came in the back door with a big box in his arms.

"I like your new haircut," he said as I helped him unload the box.

"It needed a good trim; it was, like, getting so gnarly. I'll set the table and put the potatoes on now that you're home."

"Thank you," Jay said. A big smile beamed from her wrinkled face. Obviously, her visit with friends had raised her spirits, or she had had a couple of cocktails. Setting another box on the table, she said, "We brought home some of Tara's best jelly. She makes it from her very own strawberry patch. You know strawberries are awfully hard to grow in the mountains. I've got some watermelon pickles, too."

After I helped them put away all their treasures, we sat down to the nicest holiday meal I'd ever had. There was great food served on beautiful crystal dishes, tall candles, cloth napkins decorated with autumn leaves, but mostly, there was truly great company. Throughout the dinner we planned the store's holiday specials. Henry talked about the traditions he grew up with while Jay shared her favorite holiday candy recipes.

In early December, I was coming down the stairs when I heard Henry talking to someone. It didn't take a rocket scientist to know who it was.

"…a girl of about sixteen or seventeen. She has blonde hair and is about five foot three. Her name is Madonna J. Monroe. She is wanted for questioning."

"Well, mister, mister?…" Henry said.

"Detective Snow, District 2."

"Well, sir, I can't say I've ever met anyone who goes by the name Madonna. I'll keep your card and call you if the young lady turns up around here."

"I'd appreciate it," the detective said. "The last we knew, the girl was on the streets and that's not a good place for a teen."

"No, it isn't. Hopefully she's found someplace safe."

The tinkling of the bell told me the detective had opened and closed the door. I waited to see if Henry was going to say anything more.

"Jay," he called, "we need to talk."

Hearing footsteps, I pressed my back against the wall as he walked by the bottom of the stairs on his way to the kitchen. *Holy crap. What am I going to do now?*

I raced up the stairs and started to pack. I didn't have much, but it was long enough for Henry to climb the stairs. He was standing in the doorway when I turned around. His green wool sweater hung loosely, reminding me of an older Mr. Rogers.

"Is there something you want to tell me?" he asked.

I took a deep breath. "I didn't do anything bad. I was just, like, in the wrong place at the wrong time."

He nodded toward my backpack. "Are you going somewhere?"

"I didn't think you would want me here." My throat was tightening as I stood there. I felt like hanging my head down, but I didn't. He wouldn't see me cry.

"Can I trust you?"

I was taken back by the question. "Yes, of course."

"That's all that matters. We welcomed you into our home and we need to know we can trust you. Part of trust is being honest about what's going on here." He took my backpack and set it back on the dresser. "Now, is there something you want to tell me?"

I sat down on the bed. "It really is nothing. For a couple of weeks I, like, lived with this guy who was a dealer. I never did any of the stuff myself. The guy is in jail, but I think that detective is looking for his friends."

Henry sat down beside me. "We all have a past, yours is just more interesting than most."

"I understand if you don't, like, want to be involved."

He put an arm around my shoulder and gave me a squeeze. "You're safe here. We could never turn you away. You don't have to be afraid to tell us anything. If you don't want to talk to the detective, I won't make you."

I didn't know what to say to that. I laid my head against his shoulder and whispered, "Thank you."

I took to wearing my aviator sunglasses whenever I left the house. The detective wasn't the only one looking for me. That drug dealer ran with a group of bikers, tough bikers. They wouldn't be happy that I got their connection popped.

Jay decorated the entire house for the holidays. There were twinkling lights in every window and green garland with big red bows around every doorway. On the walnut television console in the family room, Jay placed dozens of beautiful holiday cards from friends and family. Charlie and Maxine; Tara and Bob; Caitlin and George, the names meant nothing to me, but when I asked Jay who they were, she was unusually silent. "Just old friends and family," she'd said. "Maybe you'll meet them someday."

It was unnerving how on some days I felt so much a part of the Watson family and could so suddenly be reminded I was not.

The holidays were crazy, and I could only imagine how busy it would get come Valentine's Day. I didn't have much time to think about getting my GED, but I was learning tons about running a candy store. We were up every morning by four and elbow deep in pastry dough by five. The store opened at six to a line of customers looking for cinnamon rolls and croissants. Jay worked beside me while Henry worked the sales floor. When things slowed down in the afternoon, I would watch the register and Henry and Jay would retire to the kitchen to plot the next day's buying frenzy.

By Christmas week, we were all exhausted. The Watsons were special, and for the first time in my life, I wanted to celebrate Christmas. I didn't have a lot of money to spend on gifts. My wages were small and tuition was going to be expensive. Not only that, but Henry and Jay seemed to have everything they wanted. I walked the Villa Italia mall looking for the perfect present, anything that would tell them how I felt. Buying the right gift was particularly hard. Many foster parents made me work for them, but they never gave me the love and respect I received from Jay and Henry. It was like buying gifts for parents you had only now discovered. While walking through the Denver Dry Goods store, I stumbled on a three-tiered crystal display tray. It was the most elegant serving piece I'd ever seen. It was also several hundred dollars. Styled after the Federal Glass Company's

Madrid pattern Depression glass, it matched several pieces Jay already owned. It wiped out my entire savings. I wish it could have been more.

Christmas Eve dinner was another elegant roasted turkey with all the trimmings. A light snow began to fall and I felt like I was living in a Christmas card. A white Christmas was a rare treat in Denver, and it made my first Christmas with the Watsons genuinely special. I set the table using Jay's crystal, hoping to present my gift as the dessert plate. I placed a false-bottom cardboard box wrapped with red floral paper and silver ribbon over the crystal tray loaded with bonbons, fudge, peanut brittle, and caramels.

As Henry carved the turkey, the subject of my GED came up.

"I'll be completing it right after the holidays. It's just been so busy."

"That's good," Jay said. "You'll have more time in January. I feel a little guilty, we did keep you rather busy these last two months."

Henry placed a thick slice of meat on my plate. "How many hours of study do you think it will take?"

"I don't know," I replied, passing the mashed potatoes to Jay. "It's a general education test. You know, like, basic math, science, history, and English. I should do fine."

Jay passed the gravy to me. "Your math skills seem pretty strong, you have no problem with multiplying or dividing recipes."

"History can be way harsh. I read a lot, so English shouldn't trip me up."

"Maybe I can help you with history," Henry said. "After all, I was here for a lot of it."

I had to smile. "Ancient history, handsome. You're not *that* old."

He ruffled my hair. "Only on some days."

We finished the main course and it was time for dessert. Bringing the wrapped box from the pantry, I placed it in the center of the table.

"Jay, would you do the honors. Just lift the top off."

Her eyes lit up as the gift was revealed. "It's perfect," she said with tears in her eyes. "I don't know what to say. Thank you so much."

Henry inspected it a little closer. "It's the same pattern as our wedding crystal. Where did you ever find it?"

"It's a reproduction. I'm so glad you like it."

Jay took me in her arms and hugged me. "Like it? I love it!"

Now tears came to my eyes. No one had ever hugged me like that. I was at once terrified and thrilled. Of all the gifts I could have received, the love these two people showed me was by far the most precious.

My other gifts included the usual: sweaters, pants, socks, a handbag, and a recipe book. Then Henry announced my promotion and raise. The added responsibilities would help me learn how to run the business end of candy making.

The next morning we arose to two feet of snow. The entire city was shut down as the snow continued to pile up.

"I was six years old when we had the big blizzard of '13," Henry said, sipping his morning coffee. "They hauled snow by the wagon loads and piled it up in the new civic center park. The snow was still there in May."

"I've never seen so much snow," I said, joining him at the table. "Like, how will people get to work?"

"These days, we have four-wheel-drive trucks and snowmobiles. Those that can will help the hospitals, and the rest of us will take a brief vacation."

It was weeks before the streets were back to normal, just in time for the stock show crowd. It seemed ridiculous to me that people, who would normally be wearing suits or dresses, would dress up like cowhands for two weeks every January. I realized it was an economic boon to the city, but cowboy hats were more common than baseball caps when the stockmen came to Denver.

Throughout the month, Henry had me balance the sales receipts each night. Sales were steady but simple and the bank deposits straightforward: checks and cash. Sending the occasional credit card charge to the bank required a telephone transaction, but it wasn't too gnarly. The inventory of the kitchen was a whole other world.

"In order to know what you need to charge for a cake," he began one Monday morning, "you have to know how much you paid for the ingredients. Flour is seventeen cents a pound, butter is a dollar eighty-nine a pound, and sugar is twenty-eight cents a pound."

He pulled out a scale and set a cup of flour on it. "A cup of flour weighs four and a quarter ounces. If we make two dozen cookies, we need three cups of flour."

I pulled out a recipe. "One cup of sugar at eighteen cents, one cup of butter at a dollar eighty-nine, one egg for sixteen cents." I jotted down the cost of the half-and-half and the vanilla. The salt cost less than a penny, but Henry insisted on adding a penny for the salt and baking powder. "I came up with four dollars and forty-five cents."

"Now divide that by twenty-four cookies."

"Eighteen cents a cookie," I said, checking my figures again. "We charge forty cents a cookie."

"It's not just the ingredients. There are other costs incurred, like heat for the oven, new pans every ten years, mortgage on the store, taxes, and of course your wages." He pulled out a tax form. "We pay you two dollars an hour, but we also pay the government half of your Social Security tax as well as workman's compensation insurance and Medicare."

"I see." I looked at my numbers. "Oh, wow. We don't make much on cookies, do we?"

Henry smiled at me and ruffled my hair. "We're doing okay. This store has been in my family for more than eighty years, so the mortgage is just the tax bill each year and some regular repairs."

"So, like, how could you afford to pay me?"

"Stocks." He motioned for me to follow him to his desk. "We invested well. Jay has a real talent for picking the right companies to invest in." He pulled out a ledger with several dozen companies listed. There was a curious abbreviation next to the names. "That's the stock name," he said, pointing out his latest acquisition. "It's important that you pay attention to what companies are growing at a steady rate."

He frowned and narrowed his eyes. "This is important, Jett."

I rolled my eyes. "But finances are soooo boring."

He put a large hand over his eyes and massaged his temples. "Financial stability is the difference of living paycheck to paycheck and having a little nest egg to get you through the hard times." Henry dropped his hand and blew out a sigh. "I want you to meet with my broker next week."

I had come to the candy store to learn the art of creating beautiful objects out of sugar, but Henry never let up. Each week was another lesson, and after a while it started to make sense.

Meanwhile, Jay was the artist. Both of them made the majority of candies, but it was Jay's delicate flowers and butterflies that stopped people in the street to look in the window. From a simple gum paste, she created elegant cake toppers of ribbon and roses, sprays of lilies and pansies, forget-me-nots and bleeding hearts. The delicate wings of her butterflies were nearly sheer and bursting with bright colors.

As the months passed, I found myself worrying less and less about Social Services. There was a good chance my foster parents never reported me missing. After all, if Social Services thought everything was okay, the checks would continue to come in. The detective still worried me some. He had the wrong name, but if anyone from the west side happened into the store, they would surely recognize me, even with dark hair. For that reason, I tried to make sure Jay or Henry were always working the showroom with me in the event I needed a fast retreat.

Valentine's Day was insane. Jay taught me how to make gum paste flowers and her special creamy chocolates. The secret was using hazelnut oil. Many of the candies didn't freeze well and had to be made fresh. The sales receipts reflected the extra hours we put in, more than tripling the sales for the month of January.

March was a bit slower at the store and by the middle of April I had my GED in hand. As was usual, when I got home from school, the kitchen was warm, and dinner had been laid on the pastry worktable. Jay and Henry waited for me by the table. Henry was dressed in his usual white pants and white shirt, his longish gray hair combed back from his narrow face. Jay sported a modest dress with a tiny flower print, her huge white apron, and of course her crystal necklace. It was like her signature. I'd never seen her without it. From the kitchen radio, tuned to KBPI, Cheap Trick wailed, *I want you to want me*. The fact that Jay actually liked rock and roll was a total bonus.

Hanging my jacket on a hook by the back door, I slipped off my street shoes. Jay insisted we wear only our white work shoes in the kitchen, even if we were just sitting down for dinner. The aroma of Cornish game hens and twice-baked squash filled my nose with mouthwatering scents, making my stomach growl. In the center of the table was a three-tiered spice cake with cream cheese frosting and sugar graduation cap.

"It's beautiful," I said, feeling my cheeks warm from a blush. It was highly unusual to be the center of attention, unless, of course, I had been caught doing something wrong.

Behind her small square glasses, Jay's green eyes sparkled. "Henry and I have a little graduation present for you. We are ever so proud."

Henry handed me an envelope. It was a simple card congratulating me on receiving my GED. Inside was a check, made out to the Denver Institute of Art for a thousand dollars. My hands shook and I nearly dropped the check. Tears sprang to my eyes. No one had ever given me anything like this.

"Thank you! Thank you! Thank you! I don't know what I've done to deserve you two. I'll make you so proud. I promise!" I cried and hugged them both.

Even though my employers took care of most of my basic needs, it would have taken two years to earn enough money to pay for culinary school. Now I would be able to start with the June semester.

After dinner we went upstairs to a little family room where the three of us usually gathered to watch television. The burnt sienna shag carpet had seen better days, and an intricate afghan in fall colors was draped over the back of a brown pleather couch. White sheer curtains muted the view but not the sound of cars on the busy street below.

Sitting in a recently reupholstered wingback chair that must have been in the family for fifty years or more, I watched Tom Selleck artfully escape from Higgins's Dobermans, Zeus and Apollo, by jumping into a sporty red Ferrari 308. Like *Taxi*, *Magnum PI* was a show we rarely missed on Thursday nights. As Rick and TC helped Tom run down another outlaw, I marveled how comfortable the little room was, so unlike the mansion on the TV set. I'd spent my share of time in more lavish homes but rarely had I felt more secure.

As we watched, Jay and Henry sat on the couch next to each other holding hands. Sometimes, Henry would whisper to her, and she'd giggle like a schoolgirl. At times like this, I liked to imagine they were my parents (or grandparents by their age). For a time I fantasized she was my long-lost grandmother. When I mentioned this to her, she laughed and assured me that she wasn't.

"You would be a wonderful granddaughter all the same," she said. "Someday I'm sure you'll meet my children."

Henry and Jay's love for each other and for me filled the candy store and made it a home, the first real home I'd ever known, and I couldn't have been happier.

As the cooler days slid by to a warmer spring, Jay had me doing more and more of the baking. She taught me how to make creamy white divinity, candied fruit, and peanut brittle: all of it excellent training for culinary school.

One day while I was working the sales counter, a local baker stopped in. Mr. Gulbranson regularly purchased Jay's fripperies for his wedding cakes. Holding a delicate spray of lavender columbines, he marveled at her talent. "I can make a dozen different frosting flowers," he said, "but Jay's sugar creations are astonishing."

"She's so amazing. I love her butterflies."

He walked over to a display of sugar strawberries. "How delightful these are. My, but they do look almost real. I've never known Jay to make fruits. I'll have to have these, too."

I was so proud. Those were my strawberries. "For sure? All of them?" I asked.

"Yes, I think I'll use them for my daughter's graduation party. They should keep for a couple of weeks."

"If you keep them dry, they should last a year or more." While carefully placing the strawberries in a waxed-paper-lined box, I added, "I'm so glad you like them. I made them myself."

"Well, young lady. It looks like you have a promising career ahead of you."

"Jay is an awesome teacher." I showed him a bouquet of daffodils. "We made these together."

"Very nice. I could use an extra hand during the summer months. I usually make three or four wedding cakes a week."

"Well, like, I'm in school right now, but I'd love to help you next summer." I walked him to the door. "Thanks so much for coming in today," I said. "We'll see you next week."

"My pleasure. Keep working on your art."

I danced back to the kitchen to apprise Jay of Mr. Gulbranson's comments. Her big white apron with its myriad of pockets, as well as the table in front of her, was covered in dark powdery cocoa. "Looks like you're ready to be popped in the oven," I said teasingly.

She swept a pile of cocoa from the counter into a bowl. "The lid was stuck, and when it finally came off, cocoa went everywhere."

"Way harsh."

We were cleaning up the mess when the back door opened and Henry came through, laden with groceries.

"Here, let me help," I said, taking a sack from his arms. "Mr. Gulbranson bought all my sugar strawberries today," I said proudly. "He even ask me if I would help him next summer during wedding season."

"That's excellent," Henry said as he unpacked a paper sack filled with dry goods. "Your first sale. How exciting!"

"Oh, crap." I said, suddenly realizing I'd forgot to charge him. "I'm such a total airhead. I didn't ring them up."

"Well, you'll have to go to his shop in the morning and get the money," Henry said.

"It was only a couple strawberries."

Jay looked up. "You said he bought them all."

"One or fifty," Henry said, "she needs to get the money for them. I like Mr. Gulbranson well enough, but this is a business."

I felt my cheeks warm. I hated the thought of asking for the money. I was just happy knowing he liked my work. "I have some money," I said. "I'll take care of it."

Henry shook his head. "No. You'll get the money from him. You don't want him to think he can get candies for free just because you made them and not Jay."

He was right. I knew this, but in my heart it was hard to ask for money for something I truly loved doing.

Henry wrote up the invoice. "Never give your work away for free, Jett," he said. "If you don't value your work, you can't expect anyone else to value it."

Most of those late days of spring were spent with Jay, but as time went on she became a little more distant. Something was making her anxious. While watching Henry reading his evening paper, she would fondle her necklace, a nervous act she did without thinking. I was worried she might be sick, but whenever I asked about it, she would smile wanly, pat my hand, and say, "Someday you'll understand. Don't fret about it."

Someday you'll understand seems to be the fallback answer all old people use when they don't want to answer you straight. When I asked the orphanage director where my parents were, he said, "Someday you'll understand." Well, I still don't understand. When is someday? I wanted to know what was bothering Jay today, not wait until I was in my seventies to figure it out. Some days I would see her staring at the calendar or looking through old pictures. Maybe it was something old people did: a way of reliving their youth. She never offered to share her pictures with me, and I never asked to see them.

Henry didn't seem to notice the change in Jay's mood. He remained full of energy and quick with a joke. Not only was he giving me history lessons, he insisted I learn how to run the store, meaning we were spending more and more time together every day. The two of us had become first-rate friends, often laughing at the silliest of things. Sometimes I felt a little guilty, but I enjoyed being with him. He was easy to talk to and he seemed to know me better that I knew myself.

One day, while making sugar paste roses with Jay, I suggested I might be getting too close to Henry, taking him away from spending time with her.

She laughed. "Oh, I think there's enough Henry for both of us."

I rolled fondant on the foam mat while Jay pulled round-bottom bowls from a wire rack. "I'm not interested in stocks," I said, "but I think Henry wants me to be able to run the store. Are you two planning on going somewhere?"

"You have a good head on your shoulders. Someday you might want a business of your own. The things Henry is teaching will last a lifetime." Jay dusted the bowls with powdered sugar. "But it wouldn't hurt to go out with someone your own age on occasion."

Placing cut circles of fondant in the bowls, I said, "The boys from school are so lame."

Jay laughed. "Yes, I'm sure they are."

"I'd like to find someone like Henry, only younger."

"I'll bet he wishes he were younger, too."

"You don't think . . . "

"No, no, my dear," she said as she mixed sugar and cornstarch in a saucepan. "We all wish we were younger. The joints start to ache, and you realize there isn't a lot of time left. You're going to find the right man one day."

"You're not that old," I said curling the edges of the rose petals I'd cut from the fondant.

"Sometimes I feel like I'm centuries old, and sometimes I feel like a kid again. At seventy-two, I've had an incredible life."

"Did you, like, always know what you wanted to do with your life?"

Jay looked off at some distant memory. A smile tickled the corner of her mouth. "Pretty much. I always enjoyed making cakes and candy. I've had other opportunities, but once I fell in love with Henry . . . " She touched the necklace she wore. "This store is Henry, and Henry is my rock. Lots of things change in this world, but never Henry, and never this store."

Jay and Henry were so much in love it made my heart ache to find my own rock. "It would be so cool to have a store of my own one day. And a partner like Henry."

"You're ambitious, that's good," she said, letting go of the necklace. "Running a store is a lot of work. You'll have good times and bad times, but don't let life throw you." With a wooden spoon she stirred in corn syrup, glycerin, water, butter, and salt. "Remember, you're a lot stronger than you think. Everything you've been through in your brief past is preparing you for the future."

My brief past consisted of half a dozen foster homes. I had no idea who I was, or where I came from. Placing the last of the rose petals in the holding bowls, I said, "Thanks, Jay. You and Henry have been so good to me. I never had a mother or father, but this feels like home."

"It is your home, Jett, for as long as you want it." She began to brush the sides of the saucepan with water to keep the taffy sugar from recrystallizing. "We have some time before the taffy is ready to pull. Why don't you put those bowls on the rack to dry and see if Henry needs help with the Mother's Day display?"

I went to the storefront where Henry was arranging sugar butterflies around a basket of chocolates. He was having trouble reaching the deepest part of the display case.

Most of my life, I'd been shuffled from home to home. Some were horrible, while others were merely bad. Realizing how much these people had come to mean to me, I was angered that I hadn't found Jay and Henry sooner and afraid they would disappear from my life as quickly as they had entered it. In a moment of nostalgia, I hugged Henry and asked him to let me finish the window dressing.

CHAPTER 3

I started culinary school on the sixth of June 1982. As summer blossomed, so did my skills as a chef and as a candy maker. Once I'd learned the fundamentals, cooking took on an air of creativity I'd never explored before. Wednesdays and Saturdays were my homework days, and I practiced my skills on Jay and Henry.

On Tuesday night I brought home a leg of lamb. I'd made beef and pork roast before. They were simple. I'd never even tasted lamb and this was homework for class: a major grade. I could tell Jay was anxious to help me and I loved sharing projects with her, but I made her sit at the table and decorate truffles while I worked.

"I met a boy at school," I said, combining honey, mustard, rosemary, ground black pepper, lemon zest, and garlic in a small bowl. "He and his lab partner share the workstation across from Bambi and me." I covered the lamb, and put it in the refrigerator to marinate overnight. "He's kind of cute and his name is Bobby. He isn't much of a chef, but he usually partners with Mike, who is. Bambi isn't any better than Bobby, but she makes up for it in fun." I went to the sink to fill the teakettle. "The four of us trade pranks and recipes. I've learned to look closely at my baking powder and baking soda. Turns out they really aren't interchangeable."

Jay laughed. "It's good for you to spend time with friends your own age."

"Bambi wants to go Rollerblading after school tomorrow."

"What time will you be home?"

"Early. I have to finish the lamb."

Once my homework was out of the way, Jay and I made Fettuccine Alfredo and pork tenderloin with plum chutney: an excellent dinner for three.

The next day, Mike told us they couldn't join us for skating but would find the time soon. Coming home early, a bit disappointed, I preheated the oven to four hundred fifty degrees.

Jay came out of the pantry, eyes wide. "That was quick."

"Bobby couldn't make it. I hope he isn't blowing us off. Bambi is adorable." Bobby was really cute. I hadn't been attracted to anyone since my disastrous relationship with the drug dealer. Taking the lamb from the refrigerator, I asked, "What time will Henry be home?" Cutting several one-inch slits in the roast about four inches apart, I stuffed it with slivers of garlic.

"He should be here within the hour. He just went to the doctor about the pain in his arm," Jay said from the pantry where she was doing the monthly inventory.

"I'm glad he finally went to see someone." Henry had been complaining for two months but had refused to see a doctor.

"Henry can be frugal to the point of nausea," she said.

I laughed. Jay could be as bad as Henry. "Better late than never."

I placed the lamb on a rack in a roasting pan and sprinkled it with salt. Placing potatoes coated in olive oil under the roast to catch the juices, I said, "This should be done by six. I'm going upstairs to brush up for my test on Friday."

"Would you like me to start the mint sauce?"

"No. I need to take a plate to school and I have to make everything myself."

Forty-five minutes later I was back in the kitchen. The scent of roasted lamb filled the store. Henry was setting plates on the table. "Gold is down again," he said. "Commodities are usually pretty safe bets."

"You told me the best time to buy is when the markets have fallen," I said, mixing chopped mint, sugar, salt, hot water, and white wine in a small bowl.

"Yes. My broker has moved some real estate. Interest rates are ridiculously high right now." Henry peeked in the oven. "Looks good. I think the government's fiscal policies are going to come back and bite us in the butt."

Jay laughed. "I could handle that. It's my pocketbook I don't want them biting into. The rates will come back down, they always do."

"Adopting artificially low interest rates as an economic policy can be risky," Henry said. "People snatch up real estate and stocks at the lower rates, creating an economic bubble."

My mind drifted to more interesting topics. Jay and Henry often discussed economics and history for hours at a time. They could spend the entire evening talking about the Depression or World War II. Taking the roast out of the oven, I covered it with tin foil to let it rest for about ten minutes before carving. I steamed the asparagus and slow-cooked the carrots with butter, cinnamon, and ginger.

"So, like, what did the doctor say?" I asked.

"He said I'm old and to get used to it."

"Like, seriously?" I said, unbelieving.

"Like, for sure," he quipped.

"Way harsh, man." Rolling my eyes, I set the roast on the table. "So, didn't he give you anything for the pain?"

"It's annoying, but not bad enough I need pain pills."

Jay helped me scoop the vegetables into serving dishes. "He has arthritis. The doctor gave him a prescription for ibuprofen."

"Well, I'm glad that's all it is," I said.

"You wound me. I'll be on drugs for the rest of my life." He sliced the roast and served each of us. "But there is a quality of life to consider, and it does help with the stiffness."

I had been worried about Henry, but Jay was the one who seemed to be in the most pain. She never complained, but there were days when she was unusually quiet. She and Henry began to spend more and more time together, leaving me to take care of the store. A nagging fear someone would recognize me tickled the back of my mind, but Jay and Henry needed time alone. Their youngest daughter had left home nearly thirty years ago, and now, having a teenager in the house must have been stressful.

One day while organizing supplies in the pantry, I heard them come into the kitchen. It sounded as if they were in the middle of an argument. Henry said he was afraid. Though I never heard what he was afraid of, Jay seemed to share his fears.

"There's no way for us to know how this will turn out," Jay said. "I can't see into the future."

"I can't suffer the thought of living without you, Jay. You are my world."

"Hopefully that will never happen."

My stomach knotted and I stepped out of the pantry. "Are you dying?" I asked Jay.

"No, no, my dear," she said. "Everything is as it should be."

"So, what does that mean?" They were totally freaking me out.

"It means don't worry. I'm healthy as an ox."

I looked at Henry.

"And so is he," she said.

I tried to put it all out of my mind and concentrate on my studies, but I felt more anxious with each passing day.

I came home from school one day in August to find Jay holding Paisano's gun in her lap.

"This was in your drawer upstairs. Do you want to talk about it?"

I did and I didn't. It wasn't my proudest moment. "I got that last summer. It belonged to a guy named Paisano." Sitting at the table next to her, I explained how the gun ended up in my drawer. She was understanding. I was embarrassed for not having told her about the gun sooner, though I was sure Henry told her about the detective.

"You know it doesn't do any good setting in your drawer unless you're attacked in your bedroom."

"I didn't know what to do with it. I didn't want to throw it away."

She studied the piece for several heartbeats, turning it over in her hands. "I'll put it in the safe. If you ever feel like you need it, you know the combination."

 "I don't think I need it anymore. You and Henry make me feel safe. Paisano's in jail, and I only met a handful of his friends."

Jay opened the cylinder and expertly removed the bullets. "It never hurts to have protection. Before you carry around a weapon like this you should have a few lessons." She set the gun aside. "There are so many ways you can be hurt. I wish this gun could protect you from everything, but the bottom line is, you're just going to have to rise above it." She spun a bullet around in a circle on the table. "Don't worry about Paisano. He has his own path to follow. You just keep your eye on your dream and don't let anyone tell you that you're crazy for having it."

"I don't know what I want yet."

She chuckled. "When there are so many things to choose from, it's hard to pick just one."

Before meeting the Watsons, I'd never had much interest in the greater world, but it was a scary place these days. Most of the nightly news had no effect on my daily life. In those days, my greatest fear was Paisano or one of his friends would recognize me on the street. Although the more time that past, the less I worried about Social Services. Surely, if they were looking, they'd be looking for a girl living on the streets.

Maybe the world had always been violent, but I reached a point where I didn't want to see the news anymore, only listening with half an ear. In July, Tamil guerrillas ambushed and killed thirteen government soldiers in Sri Lanka, causing Sinhala mobs to riot and kill thousands of Tamils. On the day of the riots in Sri Lanka, Jay and I were in the kitchen making fondant.

I was beginning to wonder if we actually were going to hell in a handbasket, I asked, "Do you think we're headed for World War III?"

I think she was startled by my question. "I hope not," she answered softly. "I have children and grandchildren. War is a terrible thing. No one escapes its terror." She sprinkled gelatin in a small bowl of cold water to soften it.

"So, you were around for the Second World War but, like, I've never heard you talk about the first."

"World War II. I was too young to know much about the Great War."

"What was it like for you and Henry?"

"Generally, things were hard for all of Colorado after the First World War," Jay said, sifting confectioner's sugar into a large bowl. "Most folks were dependent on mining and when the war ended, the need for munitions dried up. Toward the end of the twenties, the weather turned dry and the few farmers who survived the loss of the European market after the war lost whole fields to drought. Henry and I were blessed. Many good folks went hungry. Henry's father was a smart man. He managed to hold on to most of his life savings and even provided for many people who lost everything."

I took the gelatin mixture to the stove and began heating it. "Did you and Henry, like, have this store during the Depression?"

"You really should stop saying that word. It makes you sound uneducated."

"What word?"

" 'Like.' You use it at the most inappropriate times. One day you'll want to break that habit, and it won't get easier with age. As I was saying, Henry's father owned the store. It's always been Watson's Candies. We both worked here, and eventually Henry inherited the store."

When the mixture was clear I added almond extract, corn syrup, and glycerin, stirring it slowly until it was clear. "Did Henry fight in the Second World War?"

"No, he has a heart murmur." She made a hole in the powdered sugar she'd sifted and poured the liquid mixture into it. "Henry and I stayed occupied making pastries and desserts. Union Station was exploding with new people coming to Colorado. Hundreds of prestigious dignitaries and military officials stayed at the Oxford Hotel. The Federal Center was the government hub in those years."

I stirred the sticky fondant with a wooden spoon as Jay sifted more sugar into the bowl. "I thought military people, like, … oh, sorry. I thought military people stayed on military bases, not in fancy hotels."

"Only the top officials stayed at the hotel. Queen Marie of Romania visited once. Presidents Taft, Truman, Theodore Roosevelt, and FDR were some of the more famous people who came to Denver in those years."

"Cool! So why did all those presidents come to Denver?"

She looked at me, and I shrugged. There was no way I was going to give up *all* my slang. "Colorado," she said, "being in the middle of the country, was safer from attack than Washington, D.C., so the government moved many of its federal facilities here."

"Like NORAD, the Air Force Academy, and Rocky Mountain Arsenal?"

Jay sifted more sugar onto the marble pastry counter. "Yes. We have several military installations. By the late 1950s Colorado was second only to Washington, D.C., in number of federal government offices. This helped Denver recover from the Depression faster than other states."

"It doesn't make me feel safer. Henry says Denver will be target number one in a nuclear attack."

Jay looked sad for a moment. "War may be good for the economy, but it's never good for people on the whole."

We both kneaded the fondant, adding more sugar here and there until it was smooth and pliable.

"I guess Denver wasn't big when you were my age," I said.

Jay laughed. "It wasn't a truly large city until the seventies."

"Seriously?" We each kneaded a pinch of oil into the fondant and then wrapped it tightly in plastic wrap.

"It's had a few growth spurts. The war was big, but so was the oil boom of the seventies."

"I guess I was too young to remember."

"It's hard to see changes when you're truly close to them. Time will give you a different perspective."

But I didn't want things to change. I was happy. In the candy store, I felt safe and warm no matter what was happening in the outside world. By summer, even my fear of Paisano had begun to wane only to be reawakened after a summer concert.

Bobby invited me to see the Grateful Dead at Red Rocks Amphitheatre. When we reached the park the sun was just setting. It's a long climb to the base of the theater from the lower parking lot, and then you add one hundred ninety-two stairs to reach the top row of seats. The outdoor theater held more than nine thousand people and every seat was filled. Although we were up near the top, the music was clear and vibrant. The sky was cloudless and the city lights twinkled behind the stage like a field of diamonds. I loved music, but this concert was more about hanging out than it was about the band.

Bobby was older than me, old enough to buy a bottle of Goldschläger. I didn't have much experience with alcohol, but it tasted like cinnamon candy. As we passed the bottle back and forth we sang along to every tune the band played. I was surprised by how many songs I knew and the more we drank, the louder we sang. Desert air can get chilly after the sun drops behind the mountains and, although

I was feeling warmth from the Goldschläger, Bobby loaned me his leather bomber jacket.

When the concert ended, he held me by the arm to guide me to the truck. I'm guessing he didn't drink as much as I had because he seemed to be on top of things while I was dizzy and quite giggly.

In the parking lot, a guy in thick biker leathers called out to me. "Madonna," he shouted.

"Let's go," I said to Bobby. "Hurry."

"That dude know you?"

"No, he thinks I'm someone else."

"So tell him you're not her."

"Let's just get out of here." Paisano's friend was striding toward me, and when I opened the truck door, he began to run.

"Madonna, I know that's you. Wait. I need to talk to you!"

"Go, Bobby! GO!" I slid into the seat and jammed the lock in place.

"Where are we going to go? Traffic's backed up to Morrison Road."

I was starting to panic. "Whatever you do, DON'T open the door." A moment later the guy was pounding on my window.

Bobby reached over and opened the glove box. He pulled out a small handgun and pointed it past me at the guy in the window. Bobby thumbed the window control, and the window slid down silently. "You might want to back off, dude," he said in a deep voice.

The guy at the window backed away with his hands up. "I know that's you. Your hair is different, but I know you. There's a price on your head, little lady."

The truck lurched forward, and I began to relax a little.

"What was all that about?" Bobby asked between clenched teeth. "That dude was wearing the Sons of Silence colors. How do you know him, and why did he call you Madonna?"

"It's a misunderstanding. I've never seen him before."

"Clearly, he thinks he knows you."

"It's nothing. Really." My hands were sweating and my heart was pounding. Bobby had a gun. What kind of guy carries a gun in his truck? Not that I wasn't grateful, but why did I always fall for bad boys and thugs?

It took forever to clear the parking lot, but by the time we were heading east down Sixth Avenue, Bobby had shelved the subject of the biker dude, and I had remembered how cute my champion was. Feeling frisky, I tried to distract him by playing with his leg and talking about recent movies.

"Come on, Bobby," I said. "Harrison Ford is way badder than Richard Gere."

"You have to admit Gere is better looking," he replied.

"But *Officer and a Gentleman* is a total crybaby movie."

"Like *Blade Runner* isn't. How can you not cry when Roy dies in Deckard's arms?"

"Rachael is no Cinderella."

The conversation went on like this until Bobby pulled the truck into the alley behind the store and shifted into park. He reached over and pulled me into his arms.

"Would you like to be my Rachael?" he asked, kissing me on the forehead.

"Mmmm."

He kissed me on my ear. "I would be a bad-ass Deckard." When his lips reached mine I was feeling dreamy and warm. He was an awesome kisser, and his mouth tasted of cinnamon. I slipped off his jacket. He unbuttoned my shirt slowly. His lips made a trail of fire down my neck. Soon he had his hand and his lips inside my bra.

"I can't see you as Paula," he said between kisses. "You're not cut out for factory work."

"Mmmm," was all I could manage to say.

As I leaned back against the window, the door flew open and someone grabbed me from behind and pulled me from the truck. He was strong. I screamed, clutching at my open shirt. Bobby jammed the truck into gear. It wasn't until then that I realized Henry was standing over me, shouting at Bobby as he squealed away.

I was so embarrassed. I found myself thinking having a father could be a total pain in the butt sometimes.

When Henry turned toward me his eyes were dark and his face was red. I thought he was going to blow a gasket. "What were you thinking?" he shouted. "How old is that boy?" He stepped closer to me. "You're drunk, aren't you? I can smell it."

"No," I mumbled, but the lie was pretty obvious by the way I was listing to the left.

He took me by the arm and marched me inside, slamming the screen door against the wall. Jay was sitting at the marble cooling counter, sorting recipes. She looked unconcerned and maybe a little sympathetic. She took off her reading glasses and shook her head.

Impossibly, Henry sounded even angrier. "You know what they were doing out there, don't you?"

Jay stood slowly wiping her hands on her paisley dress. "Henry, she's sixteen. She's bound to be interested in boys."

"She's drunk," he stammered. "And that boy . . ."

"If I remember right, you weren't much older than her when you got drunk the first time."

"Things were different then. Kids were older. More grown up."

Jay went to the stove where a teakettle simmered. "Sit down, Jett. Drink some tea before you go to bed. Maybe the hangover won't be so bad."

I can't imagine how bad the hangover would have been if she hadn't fed me tea for an hour, because the next day, my head pounded and I couldn't tolerate the smell of frying bacon. I skipped breakfast and headed to school. I was so exhausted I nearly fell asleep in class.

Evidently, my run-in with the biker dude scared Bobby enough that he took up with a new girl the next week. It was probably for the best, as Henry really didn't like him. I'd never had an overly protective father before and at times it was maddening.

A few weeks later, when Mike asked me to go to Elitch Gardens, I jumped at the chance. I'd only been there once when I was about eight, and I adored crazy rides and fun music. When Mike came to pick me up, Henry grilled him for an hour concerning his intentions toward me. I was totally mortified, but Mike said it was okay. We had a great time, even if the park was getting run down. The carousel was spectacular with its beautifully painted horses and sleighs. We must have ridden on it for hours, just talking about candy and pastries.

Unfortunately, we never went out again after that. Mike's father had a stroke and he had to go back to Grand Junction to take care of his mother. He was a nice guy, not the kind of guy that makes your heart skip a beat, but nice. Like so many other friends I'd known, I missed him when he moved away. Luckily, I still had Bambi to hang with.

One day after school, Bambi and I walked over to the newly completed Cherry Creek trail to go Rollerblading. The concrete was wide and smooth, and the bums usually stayed away during the day. When we reached the intersection of Sixth Avenue and Speer Boulevard, I saw Penny, my ex-roommate from the Rescue Mission. She was sitting on the lawn by the creek eating a sandwich from a brown paper bag.

"Hey, Penny," I said. "How are you? You look great."

"Jett?"

"Yeah." I introduced her to Bambi, and then asked, "What are you doing here?"

"Eating lunch," she replied. "I'm on break."

"Oh? So, like, where are you working?" I mentally scolded myself for saying *like* again.

"I took a job at DGH. I work in the janitorial department. Nothing fancy, but I'm gettin' by. I'm still at the Mission until I can save enough money for first and last months' rent on an apartment. You're looking good; you seem happy.

"I am. Jay and Henry are great. A couple more months and I'll graduate."

"Graduate?" Her eyebrows lifted.

"Yes. The Watsons paid my tuition for culinary school. How did you get the job at DGH?"

"I'm not sure. One day pastor Jim came in and said I had a job at the hospital if I wanted it."

"Way cool. I'm happy for you!" And I was happy, though I felt bad that I hadn't been over to visit her. She had been the closest thing to a real friend I'd ever had.

"I'm happy for you, too," she said. "That ex-boyfriend ever catch up to you?"

"No. Still watching my back. I think the police gave up though. Anyway, Jay and Henry have been great. I'm sorry I've been so busy. Between work and school I just don't have much free time."

"I understand. You'll always be able to find me at the hospital if you need me."

"I'll remember," I said, giving her a big hug. "I'll see you around."

"Yeah. Don't be a stranger."

"I won't," I promised and gave her another hug.

As the weather turned cooler Bambi and I spent less time together. A new man had come into her life and she was crazy about him. He was older and well educated. I could tell she was in love. It was good to see her happy and so much calmer.

Bambi's new beau was back in Kansas City for the week, so we got together one weekend to hit a few yard sales.

"So, like, do you ever hear from Mike?"

"Not since he moved. We weren't that close. Look at that great dress!"

We moved over to a rack holding several prom dresses.

"Love the shoulder pads in this," I said.

"Oh, oh, look at this hat! It's nineteen twenties to the max." She put the felt cloche over her fully permed, bleach-blonde hair. "I love this. It's so retro."

"It's you."

"Crap. I'm totally broke. I spent my last dollar on those parfait dishes at the last place."

"I'll get it for you, you must have it." I paid the lady five dollars for the hat. Walking back to the rack where I'd left Bambi looking at dresses, I saw a large round mirror with beveled edges. Something about it made me stop. It was heavy, about two and a half feet in diameter, and very heavy. "Look at this," I called to Bambi. "Isn't it interesting? It looks old but the silvering on the back is totally intact."

Bambi walked over, sporting her new hat. "That's a nice mirror."

"It's only twenty dollars. I wish we had a car."

"Since you bought me this wicked cool hat, I'll help you carry the mirror."

"Thanks. I really love this." Looking at her reflection in the mirror gave me an idea. I ran over to the rack where I'd seen a twenties-style beaded shift.

"Here," I said, handing the dress to Bambi. "Put this on."

She slipped the dress over her spandex tube top and shorts. "All I need is a cigarette holder and a feather fan."

"You look like you just walked out of a speakeasy."

Bambi twisted her fingers in her perm to make finger waves. "We should get this for Halloween. We could go as flappers."

"That would be totally awesome. Help me find an outfit."

We spent the rest of the day carrying the mirror from one garage sale to the next. We finally found a dress for me at the Goodwill store. Tired and hungry, we made our way back to the candy store. Bambi stayed for dinner that evening and helped me hang my new mirror.

Once I had the mirror on the wall in my bedroom I was struck by the thought that it was the first piece of furniture I'd ever owned. What did that say about me? I'd never owned more than I could carry in a backpack. Tears streamed down my cheeks. I was so happy at that moment, and yet so scared. Jay and Henry were dreadfully old. One day they would leave me, too. It was usually me who ran away, but leaving Jay and Henry was beyond imagining. They made me laugh and feel safe, and loved me like a granddaughter.

They taught me how to be responsible and how to relax. With their love, I believed I could take on the world, be anything I wanted to be. And what I wanted most was for my time with them to never end. Besides, I was a chocoholic to the max, and the sweet smell of melting chocolate and baked sugar greeted me each morning while lemon bars or toasted coconut sang me to sleep each night. Life was beautiful.

October was a busy month. Taffies and lollipops were popular treats, but it was Henry's caramel candied apples that kept the bell on the door ringing all day. Henry said his secret was using fresh whipping cream and extra dark molasses. Whatever it was, we must have made a thousand caramel apples and nearly as many chocolate-covered cherries.

On Saturday, the twenty-third, I would celebrate my seventeenth birthday and I was truly feeling like a kid in a candy store believing Jay and Henry had an awesome surprise for me. They'd been particularly secretive over the last few weeks, and I was dying to know what they were up to. They had given me a home, a family, and paid for my education. There was nothing they could give me that could compare to what I had, except, maybe, to know who my real parents were, but even that lost most of its appeal. I had Jay and Henry now; I needed nothing more.

It was just about closing time and I was adding up the day's sales receipts when I heard the *whumph* of an explosion. The glass windows rattled, followed by the sound of crashing in the back of the store.

I raced into the kitchen where I found Jay lying on the floor, a heavy beam across her chest. There was a hole in the ceiling above the stove and the back wall was on fire. I tried to move the beam that had once supported the upper floor, but it was too big. "Henry!" I screamed. "HELP!"

"Don't try to move it," Jay groaned. "Get Henry, please."

I ran to the stairway and screamed for him again. I dialed the fire department as he came down the stairs.

"I'm here," he cried.

"In the kitchen!" I yelled. "I have the fire department on the line. See if you can help Jay!"

When I returned to the kitchen Henry was trying to lift the beam, but it wouldn't move. Fire was sprouting up everywhere.

"No!" Henry cried. He started beating at the flames with a linen tablecloth as they came closer. "God, please no. Don't take her." With the closest flames held in check for a moment, he bent down to take her hand. "Where is that damned fire department?" He was coughing, choking on the heavy, dark smoke saturating the room.

Jay looked up at him with teary eyes. "Our time together has been everything I thought it would be," she said. "I wouldn't change a minute of it. Do you hear me? Not a minute of it."

Tears were streaming down his cheeks. "Jay, I can't lose you."

With a bloodied hand, Jay reached up and wiped the wetness away from his cheek. "Not a minute of it, Henry. Not one minute."

Turning to me, she said, "Take good care of Henry. He's the love of my life."

"It's going to be okay," I said. "The fire department is on the way."

"Jett, promise me, no matter what happens, promise me you'll take care of Henry."

"I will. I promise."

A rumble filled the room. Something slammed into the back of my head and everything went black.

CHAPTER 4

I felt like I'd been drugged. I couldn't move, my arms were too heavy and my legs were too weak. Over the fireworks going off in my brain I could hear Henry telling me I would be alright, that help was coming. A man picked me up in his arms and I drifted in darkness again.

Sometime later I opened my eyes to a white ceiling. It was plaster and very high. My mouth felt as if I'd been eating sand. I knew I wasn't dead because death couldn't hurt this badly. Snapping my eyelids closed blocked the painful light burning my eyes, but it did nothing to ease the hammering between my ears. I could hear the concerned voices of strangers, muffled and quiet. Someone was holding my hand. I felt a cool cloth laid on my forehead followed by a bee sting in my arm.

I woke up in a strange room on a narrow metal-frame bed feeling like an elephant was stomping around in my brain. Everything in the room was painted white. Although the wall sconces were dim, even that low light seemed to make my head feel worse. I closed my eyes again. Reaching up, I felt thick bandages wrapped around my skull. *They're too tight. That's why my head hurts so badly.*

The bindings needed to come off. I tried to sit up and immediately regretted it as a wave of nausea overwhelmed me. I retched over the side of the bed, each surge of dry heaves making my head hurt worse. I felt weak but couldn't stop vomiting.

A cool hand touched my arm, and I slowly turned my aching head to see a long-faced woman dressed in white.

"Take this and put it in your mouth," she said. She gave me a cool washcloth, wetted with something minty, and helped me lay back on the bed. My stomach began to settle down as she put another cool compress over my eyes.

There was something archaic about the way she was dressed. When I heard her move away from the bed I lifted the compress to take another look. Her white dress buttoned down the front and was fitted at the waist. It came well below her knees, almost to her ankles. She was definitely a nurse, but not like any I'd seen. She wore a funny little white cap across the back of her head. It looked perfectly ridiculous there. Then I remembered. It was October. This must be her Halloween costume. I relaxed a little and fell back to sleep.

The next day was much like the day before, vomiting up bile and an aching in my head. The nurse was still wearing her long white dress and the room reminded me of an old movie set. For a moment, I thought I might be in one of the rooms at the newly renovated Oxford. The papers claimed it was going to be turn-of-the-century and authentic, but the windows were a different shape than I remembered. These were tall and narrow, with minimal light coming in.

The smell of the place carried the tang of alcohol and something else that I couldn't place, like the wood smoke of a campfire mixed with motor oil. There was a humid smell, like mold or a wet animal. Maybe there was a dog close by. The unfamiliar smell was second only to the foreign sounds. An old-fashioned horn beeped and was answered by the *ugga, ugga* of another hand-held horn. It was more than disconcerting, the very air felt *wrong*.

"Are you in pain?" the nurse asked as she held up a small glass vial and studied the label. "This will ease the discomfort and help you sleep." She drew a liquid from the vial into a syringe. Sitting on the chair next to my bed, she wrapped a cord around my arm. I'd been to the doctor enough times to know she was planning to give me an injection.

"No," I slurred. "What is that?"

She had an honest face and kind eyes. "It's for the pain."

I *was* in real pain but I was more afraid of the medication. The few times I'd had the opportunity to "experiment" with drugs I hadn't liked the effects. I don't like things that cloud my mind.

"No, please. No more," I said, straining to be heard. My breath was shallow as if there were a vice around my chest making it hard to talk.

I didn't know what I was afraid of, but I could feel my heart start to race. My brain felt as if it were exploding from my skull. She must have seen the panic in my eyes because she held my hand and stroked my cheek. "You have been through much. I'll be right here if you change your mind."

As I turned my head to watch her get up, I felt another wave of blinding pain. "Well, maybe just a little."

On the next day a doctor came to see me. He was dressed in a dark gray, slim-cut suit. The pants were baggy tweed and the single-button jacket was long. I don't know what struck me as more unusual, the pocket watch on a gold chain or his felt fedora. Maybe they celebrated Halloween all week? That would make sense if I were being treated at Children's Hospital.

"My name is Doctor Mortenson. How are you feeling today?"

"Like I've been run over by a Mack truck."

He tilted his head, blinked a few times, and then jotted notes on a metal clipboard. "Do you know where you are now?"

"I was about to ask you the same thing."

He made another notation. "Can you tell me your name?"

"Jett. Jett Oxford."

"Very good," he said smiling for the first time.

"And what is your father's name?"

"I don't know."

"Your mother?" he asked with a frown.

"I don't know."

He looked sympathetic. "It isn't uncommon for a person to become disoriented with a head injury like you've received." He felt my cheek. "Your fever seems to have broken. That is a positive sign. Now explain to me how you came to be hit by Mac's truck?"

It was my turn to blink at him. "Noooo," I said slowly. "I said—that's what I felt like. That was just an expression. I don't know what hit me."

"I see." He scribbled again. "What do you recall from that day—the day you were hit by the truck?"

"Seriously, I wasn't hit by a truck." I had to think for a while. Everything was fuzzy. "There was a fire in the kitchen."

The doctor jotted more notes. "You were trapped in a fire? The kitchen, was it in Mac's home?"

"Hello? I don't know anyone named Mac."

"I see. Do you recall if your parents were in the kitchen at the time?"

Memories struck like lightning. I shuddered. "Oh my God. Is Jay okay? She was trapped under a beam. What about Henry? Where are they? Did they get out of the fire?"

"The fire in the kitchen?" he asked.

"Yes, at the candy store. I think there might have been a gas leak." My head was pounding again, and I was seeing sparkling lights in front of my eyes. I closed them to stop the room from spinning. The doctor didn't know who I was. The firemen must have brought me in. That means—I couldn't even think the words. Suddenly, I was furious. It wasn't fair. How could Jay and Henry be taken like this? This couldn't' be happening. It had to be a nightmare.

"I can see this has greatly upset you," he said softly. "I am dreadfully sorry."

The nurse placed a cool compress on my head. "It is nice to have you wake after all this time. Your mind has been entirely muddled up with flights of fancy. We were quite worried."

Standing, the doctor lit a cigarette. "You must rest now. I'll return on the morrow."

"Wait," I said. "How long have I been here?"

"Seven days."

"I've been asleep for seven days!" Vomit rose in my throat.

"You did wake briefly now and again. Miss Winston fed you some broth. As she has said, your mind has been rather muddled. I'm afraid you took a powerful knock to the head, young lady." He patted my hand. "Rest now. Miss Winston, get her some oatmeal. She has a need to get her strength back."

The two of them stepped away from my bed, retreating just far enough so that I could hear only bits of their whispered conversation. The first puzzle seemed to have something to do with my tan lines. I had worked hard to get a nice bronze color last summer, and it hadn't been easy with classes and working full time. The doctor said my coloring was in stark incongruity with my soft hands.

"I'm quite certain those hands have never touched a laundry tub," he said shaking his head. "Only in the islands would so much skin be bared to the sun."

"She must come from a family of great means," the nurse said. "Though I can't imagine any family that would allow a young woman to expose so much skin in any country." She pursed her lips. "The whole of the abdomen has been exposed."

"I'll check with the circus. Performers and gypsies can be quite unconventional." The doctor glanced back at me, but I pretended not to be listening. "Be sure to write down everything she says. Maybe we shall find a clue to her origin. The accent is unfamiliar."

As the doctor left the room, a shiver ran down my back. I had been on my own in strange places before, but none as weird as this. Fear tickled the edges of my mind, but it was the anguish of losing Jay and Henry that was making my head hurt.

Slowly, the gravity of my situation became apparent. Over the past year, I'd grown so accustomed to the familiarity and security of the candy store I'd become lax about my surroundings. Now, I was thoroughly scared, maybe for the first time in my life. This was more than a new location, a new building, new people; this was different in a way I couldn't explain. What would I do if the store had burned down? Maybe I should try to find my friend Penny.

The nurse set a light metal tray on my lap and poured a cup of milk from a glass bottle. I ate a little oatmeal and felt better. My head still ached, but the food helped calm my stomach. "Where am I?" I asked between bites.

"This is the south wing."

"South wing of what?"

"The Denver General Hospital. You needn't worry. You'll have the best care."

I felt better, and at the same time I felt worse. The name was familiar, but the last time I was at DGH having my appendix taken out, the place looked a lot different.

"Thank you, Miss Winston," I said. "That's good to know."

"Call me Marjorie," she replied kindly as she folded a linen sheet.

"Marjorie, then. Do you think you could check on someone for me? I have a friend who works in the janitorial department. Her name is Penny, Penny Anderson. Could you let her know I'm here?"

"Of course, my dear." She smiled at me, looking a bit like Penny for a moment.

"I think I'll sleep now."

Marjorie nodded and took the metal tray away.

I lay there for hours, trying to make sense of what I was seeing and hearing. It was more than some Halloween prank. Both the nurse and doctor spoke with an unfamiliar accent, as though English wasn't their first language. They seemed overly polite and more than a little stiff.

The room was too hot as well. A radiator against the wall rattled and hissed; one more oddity in a room full of weirdness. The dresser in the corner looked to be fifty years old or more, though it was in excellent condition. I never cared for antiques, but as antiques went, it was a nice piece.

I threw off the sheet. My hospital gown was white cotton and much longer than I'd remembered other hospital gowns being. I had no underwear on. I assumed my clothes were in the dresser. I tried to recall what I'd been wearing the day of the fire. I was surely wearing jeans. I wore almost nothing else. It had been a chilly day so I had probably been wearing my favorite red turtleneck sweater.

I looked up at the high ceiling. Plaster. Water pipes painted white crowded into a corner and were wrapped with what was likely asbestos. The floor was covered with tiny white tiles, and the curtains were made of thick baize. I wanted to look out the window but I didn't have the strength to get out of bed. Weak and a little freaked out, I tossed and turned for what seemed like hours. Eventually, I fell asleep and dreamed of caramel candied apples burning in the window of the candy store. Jay and Henry stood behind the glass unaware of the walls folding in over them.

When I opened my eyes again, my sheets were soaked with sweat. Last night's dream was gripping my heart, crushing it like grapes in a wine press, making it bleed, red and warm. I wanted to see Jay and Henry again. I wanted to tell them that I loved them. I couldn't remember saying it. Tears streamed down the sides of my face and settled into my ears. I laid there quietly crying for several minutes before I forced myself to take stock of my situation.

Sunlight was streaming through a crack in the heavy drapes covering the tall windows. Same room. My head still hurt, but the beating was a mild pounding, more like a bass drum than a freight train. My stomach growled at me—demanding to be fed. I sat up slowly, and a wave of dizziness crashed over me, though, thankfully, it passed quickly. I fluffed my feather pillows against the metal headboard, and sat back against them. Save for me, the room was empty. The astringent smell of disinfectant mixed with wood smoke permeated the room. The damp smell of animals and the tinny traffic horns reminded me of a circus. One must be quite close to the hospital. That would explain why the doctor mentioned it, though I'd never been accused of being a circus performer before.

The sound of a key turning in a lock brought my attention to the door. Old fear rebounded as I realized they had locked me in my room. This had to be the psychiatric ward: they don't lock up regular patients.

Marjorie smiled brightly as she saw me sitting up. "Well, well. Bless my soul! You must be in better spirits today. Doctor Mortenson will be pleased." She set a tray of food on my lap: oatmeal, lightly browned toast, and apple juice. "He shall be here momentarily to see how you are faring this morning."

"Thank you," I said. "I am hungry."

"Splendid. That means you're recovering." Her crisp white uniform complimented her slender figure, although her shoes looked clunky and uncomfortable. "I was unsuccessful in finding your friend. Are you quite certain she works at this hospital?"

"Yes, I'm sure."

"I shall inquire further."

As I sipped the juice, Marjorie opened the heavy drapes, letting sunlight fill the room. There was chicken wire imbedded in the glass. Definitely the psych ward. But why? What could I have said or done to make them think I needed to be locked up? And what was with the crazy costumes? Even if it was Halloween, they should have known better than to dress so weird if they were taking care of people who had trouble dealing with reality already.

From the dark walnut dresser, she retrieved a clean set of sheets. "Do you think you can sit in that chair?" She pointed to the antique-looking wingback chair by the window. Its fabric was a deep forest green adorned with bouquets of pink peonies and yellow roses.

"Sure," I said. "This apple juice is good. It tastes fresh pressed."

Her eyes widened a fraction and then saddened. "Of course it is, dear."

I finished my breakfast and set the tray aside. "I'm ready to move now, but I think I might get dizzy if I try to stand."

Setting the sheets on the foot of the bed, she came over to help me. I was right; standing made my head swim. The hospital gown twisted around my legs and bared my bottom to the world. Marjorie slipped a cotton house jacket over my shoulders and took me by the arm.

My destination was about six feet away. Morning sunlight danced over the armchair, making it inviting. I'd been in the dark too long. Marjorie walked slowly toward the chair, holding my elbow firmly in her cool hands. As I passed the window I looked out. The dusty street below was lined with Model Ts. A horse-drawn wagon rumbled past a brick tenement where litter and milk bottles sat on the steps, looking like a Charlie Chaplin movie set. I looked at Marjorie's tightly braided hair with its silly nurse's cap, and then everything went black.

When I woke, I was back in bed, and Marjorie was taking my blood pressure. The doctor was pacing back and forth near the foot of the bed. The moment he saw that my eyes were open he came to my side.

"You mustn't tax yourself so," he said. "It was sheer luck that Marjorie was within reach to catch you. Heaven knows what would have happened had you hit your head again."

Marjorie looked worried. "I saw your face go white. I should never have moved you from the bed. I'm so sorry."

"Don't be," I said. "I wanted to see outside." I was feeling dizzy and more than a little scared that I actually was mental. My head wound had me seeing things. I was calling up images from *Bugsy Malone,* but I couldn't understand why. I'd had crazy dreams before, but this was a nightmare, and I couldn't seem to wake up.

Marjorie handed me a glass of cool water. My hands were trembling. I studied the glass. It was real and not unusual in any way, other than the fact that hospitals usually used plastic or paper cups.

"We shall keep you under observation for a tad longer," the doctor said. "At least until you recollect the names of your parents."

"I'm an orphan," I said softly. "I never knew my parents." After all this time, I still felt shame when telling people I'd been abandoned.

"I see," said the doctor. Understanding flashed in his eyes. "Do you recall where you had taken room before the accident?"

"I live at the candy store."

The doctor looked distressed. "You live in a candy store?"

"Yes. I make candy at Watson's Candy Store. I live upstairs."

I saw a flicker of plausibility cross his face.

"You can call and ask them," I said. "The number is 555-6047."

He blinked at me, and just that fast, I knew I'd said something wrong.

"Maybe we should call the Watsons," Marjorie offered.

The doctor shook his head. "She was delivered to us by the Watson boy. He claims he doesn't know who she is."

"The Watson boy?" I had never met their son. Could he have stopped in that day? "Call Jay or Henry. They'll know who I am. I swear to it."

"Henry is the boy who brought you in. I don't know of this Jay."

My heart started pounding. Henry wasn't a boy. He was old enough to be my grandfather. Maybe they had a grandson called Henry? They never spoke much of their family.

The clothes, the old cars, the peculiar cadence of their speech; my skin danced with goose pimples and I shivered. I ignored the fear creeping up my back. "What is today's date?"

"October the twenty-ninth," Marjorie said.

"And the year? What's the year?" I was starting to hyperventilate. I was being swept away by emotional forces so strong I couldn't stem the tide. Tears flooded my eyes, blurring the scene before me. I was so afraid of what they were going to say.

"Why, it's 1927, my dear."

CHAPTER 5

I stared at the doctor and suddenly realized why I had been placed in the psych ward. "No. No. No, it can't be. It can't be. It can't be. What is happening to me?" I covered my eyes with my hands and willed the nightmare to end.

Marjorie's cool fingers pulled my hands away from my face. "You're just a bit confused. You'll be better in a few days."

No, I won't. I won't be better until I get back to 1982. I wanted to run, but I had nowhere to go. If it really was 1927, most of the people I knew hadn't been born yet. Could my mind being playing some cruel trick? Could I be imagining this?

The next few days were the hardest days of my life. One moment I thought I truly was insane and the next moment I was trying to convince the doctor that I wasn't. Every answer had to be self-screened for unusual words or references. Not knowing anything about 1927 made it more difficult. I couldn't even remember when Prohibition had ended or who was president. *Oh-My-God! The Great Depression. Was it in 1928 or 1929? The Dirty Thirties were all about the drought. Maybe I still had time. Please don't let me be here when the Depression hits.*

Fear threatened to overwhelm me only to be replaced by rage. *How could fate do this to me?* I'd lost many families in my life. Most of them I was better off without. But not Jay and Henry. They loved me.

Then, I was back to thinking I was totally mental. It's not like I fell through some hole in the timeline. That really is crazy. I'm just hallucinating. There's no such thing as time travel. It's 1982. I know it's 1982. Unfortunately, this wouldn't be the last time this particular conversation played over in my head.

The next morning I was sitting in the chair by the window watching cars drive by with their wide running boards and spoked wheels. The majority of them were Model As or Model Ts, mostly black with the occasional one painted bright red, yellow, or blue. Oddly, I remembered reading the autobiography of Henry Ford in the fifth grade, wherein he said, *"In 1909 I announced one morning, without any previous warning, that in the future we were going to build only one model, that the model was going to be 'Model T,' and that the chassis would be exactly the same for all cars, and I remarked: Any customer can have a car painted any color that he wants so long as it is black."*

I was frustrated that worthless pieces of trivia would crowd my thinking when information that could help me acclimate seemed to vanish into thin air.

Over the next few days, my head wound healed and my strength returned. I was keeping it real and doing my best to cover the anxiety I felt. As long as everyone thought I was bonkers, this would be my home.

Marjorie was the key. Her speech pattern, her way of moving and attending the doctor all spoke of a time when women knew their place in the world…and it wasn't running multinational corporations.

"Tell me about yourself," I said as she made up my bed.

"Goodness me, but I'm not one half as interesting as you are."

"I like to hear you talk, it's soothing."

Marjorie's eyes softened. "I'll do my best to keep the stories interesting."

"Maybe you can start with what you do on your day off."

Marjorie was delightfully entertaining when she explained the process of washing her uniforms. It was good to know there were no automatic washers and dryers, not because I looked forward to the hassle of wringing clothes out by hand, but now I could add one more machine to the list of things that hadn't been invented yet.

It felt like I was waking up in a foreign country without a visa and was constantly worrying about being arrested as an illegal alien. Information about using streetcars, storing perishables in an icebox, and loading wood into the stove helped me center myself when the doctor came round asking his questions about my past. Certainly, he believed I was hiding something.

As long as Marjorie was with me, I was allowed to go outside and get fresh air. We walked up and down Sixth Avenue in front of the hospital. It hadn't changed that much over the past - no, the next - fifty-some years. In 1982 there would be a driver's license bureau across the street. Now it was a warehouse. Who knew if they even had driver's licenses in 1927?

Until I had a place to go, the doctor wasn't going to let me leave the hospital. If this was, in fact, 1927, I had no home. Even with my experience living on the streets and learning how to work the system. The problem was, I didn't even know where to find the system in 1927. I had no money, and my job wouldn't exist for another fifty years. Even the dress I was wearing had once belonged to Marjorie; the kindly nurse had brought me a pair of shoes and a coat, as well. I needed a solid plan, and Marjorie was my only friend. She was my Penny in this new world, finding me when my life was in ruins, lost and hurting. How strange they should both be working at Denver General Hospital.

"Thank you for the coat," I said. "It's pretty cold out here."

"I have discovered the November wind cuts through most any garment. Would you like to go back to your room now?"

"No," I said pulling my coat tighter. "I like the air. How long do you think I'll have to stay at the hospital? I really want to get out of here."

"Don't you see how highly improbable it is that he should let you go before you recover your memory? We don't even know where you lived before coming to us."

"Is that important? Can't I just live someplace new? Start all over?"

"But, my dear child, what will you do?" Marjorie looked distressed.

"If I had a job," I said to Marjorie, "and a place to stay, Doctor Mortenson would let me leave the hospital, wouldn't he? Problem is, I can't get a job or find a place to live if I can't leave here."

"Certainly I would like to help, but once he gets a notion in his blessed old head, there's not much for me to do about it. And he believes that you should regain your memory before releasing you."

"What if my memory never comes back? I can't stay here forever. There must be someplace where a homeless girl can crash for a while."

"I'm sorry, what did you say? Gracious me, but sometimes your words get all out of place."

"Someplace to stay," I corrected.

"My, but this is a quandary. You need a place to live until you fully recover, but it must undoubtedly be a place where the doctor can still care for you."

We walked a few more paces, before she added, "I might know a place."

"I'm all ears," I said, and Marjorie looked at me like she'd swallowed a bug.

"The Denver Orphans Home. It's on Albion Street, near the City Park."

Now I felt like I'd swallowed a bug. My memories of Denver Children's Home hadn't faded at all. I knew the place well. It was a two-story, red-brick, Revival-style building that took up most of a city block. How uncanny it was that I'd be sent back there again. Suddenly, I felt like laughing but refrained. Marjorie would surely think I was in hysterics.

"Do you think Doctor Mortenson would let me live there?"

"He might consider it. He visits the orphanage frequently. I don't know why he couldn't continue to care for you there. You don't seem to be a danger to yourself, but he's mystified by how you came to be hurt."

I had dropped the story about the fire when Marjorie assured me there had never been a fire at the candy store. "Oh, thank you," I said kissing her on the cheek. "I know I'll get better if I can find work."

"You're an odd duck." She had that distressed look on her narrow face again. "You need never hope for it, even I'm not such a pessimist as that. A pretty girl like you should be looking for a husband, not employment."

Marjorie wasn't particularly pretty. She had a pointy nose and too many teeth for her mouth, but she was one of the nicest people I'd ever met. "Are you married?" I asked.

"I lost my husband in the war ten years ago. I joined the Red Cross to help care for the returning soldiers. When Joe died, nursing was all I had to sustain me."

"Why didn't you remarry?"

"I'm rather aged to begin a family now. I'm twenty and nine."

I thought that sounded like the perfect age to start a family but didn't say it.

We returned to my room, and Marjorie helped me into bed. I didn't need the help but it was comforting. Feeling so incredibly alone in my whitewashed room, totally missing Jay, I dozed. Cruel foster parents and bad boyfriends filled my dreams. It was a blessing to be awakened later that afternoon when the doctor came to see me.

He mopped sweat from my brow. "You're pale."

"Just a bad dream."

"Please tell me about it."

I couldn't. He would have no reference to understand my world and would surely think I was crazy. The dreams oddly felt more real than the hospital room. "I don't remember. I was being chased by a bad man."

"Can you describe him to me?" He took out his little writing pad.

I described Paisano. It wasn't as if they were going to find him.

"Italian, you say. Might you have lived in the Highlands?"

"I don't think so."

"This man in your dream. Have you seen him before?"

"I don't think so."

"In your dream, where were you?"

"A big house."

"What did this house look like?"

I described a seventies apartment complex, two small bedrooms and no view.

He studied my face. "You said it was a big house."

"It felt big, or maybe I just felt small."

He nodded. "That would be a natural reaction to fear. In your dream, did you recognize the man, did he seem familiar?"

Crap. Now the doctor would be chasing this for another week. "No. I'm sure it was no one I've ever met."

"Ah, a stranger. At least you are showing signs of recovering your memories. Dreams may seem disjointed and confusing but they are often memories from your waking world. The house you described might be a place you once lived. From this day forward, I want you to write down everything you can remember from your dreams."

As if! For sure you would lock me away and toss the key. "Sure," I said. "Anything else?"

"I want to try a rather unusual treatment. Hypnotism can often break through the mental block our minds put in place to protect us."

"No way!" I could never let someone in my head. The first time television or airplanes came up, I'd be sent to Fort Logan, or wherever they sent the terminally insane.

"I want you to think about this. It could help us find your family.

"I have no family."

Marjorie must have mentioned the home, because he was grilling me extra hard this morning. It was hard not to say anything that would make me sound mental. "I'm healthy now. My head doesn't hurt and I can work. Maybe this bed would serve someone else better. Marjorie is wonderful, but other patients need her, too." I gave him a minute to think about that. "Marjorie mentioned the Denver Orphans Home."

He nodded. "Very well," he said solemnly. "I'll check with the administrators this afternoon." He put his stethoscope in a brown leather bag. "I did inquire as to whether they knew of you, but they didn't. It's unusual to have girls over the age of sixteen at the orphanage."

"I may have come from another home. Did you check them all?"

He smiled at that. "No. I did not, and you may be right. I'll keep watch over you until we have figured out where you belong. Surely someone is missing you."

Yes, but they'd never think to look for me here.

He stood to leave. "There is much mystery about you. You may be hearing from a Detective Matthews. I suggest you try to remember anything that could help him find your assailant."

Great. Detectives were never a good thing. In this time or any other.

The next day, Marjorie and I sat on a wooden bench in front of the hospital. A red and white car with a black roof and whitewall tires on thin wheels with metal spokes rolled to a stop. "Nice Model T," I said.

"Don't let Doctor Mortenson hear you name it a T. That's a Chrysler, Series E."

"Oh." They all looked like Model Ts to me. "Are you coming with us?" I asked.

"Yes. The doctor expressed concern that you may not acclimate to your new surroundings without mishap."

"Without mishap. He thinks I'm going to freak out and start babbling nonsense?"

Marjorie cocked her head, and I realized I'd done it again. She smiled slowly. "Yes, he thinks you might cast a kitten on him."

I laughed. "I promise to be good," and remember that line.

Rolling down the car window, the doctor waved to us. "We've a one o'clock appointment. I thought we might drive through uptown to see if anything stirs your memory."

"That's very nice of you," I said, not knowing where uptown was.

Marjorie opened the front passenger door for me to get in, but I chose to sit in the back where I could hide my reactions if necessary.

Without a word, she climbed in next to the doctor and the car jerked into motion.

We were only one block off Speer Boulevard. This I knew by the angle of the street and its relation to the hospital. If there hadn't been mountains to the west, I'd have been completely lost. As we drove, the buildings looked unfamiliar. They were small and mostly made from red clay brick. There were few trees and most of them were young. As the street turned east, I could see several beautiful, large homes, mansions to be exact. We were passing the Denver Country Club. There were trees in front of the expansive building, but the tall hedge that secluded most of the property in the eighties hadn't filled in yet. It was astounding how uncomfortable it was to see my world so drastically changed in a mere breath. I wanted to wake up and find things normal again, big trees and old, old houses. Closing my eyes and holding back tears, I wished with all my being to go home again.

We turned north on University, crossing over Sixth Avenue once more. Marjorie asked me if anything was familiar. I recognized some of the homes, but telling her would have stirred a conversation I didn't want to have. When we turned east on Colfax, my heart caught in my throat. East High School was unforgettable.

Marjorie must have sensed my reaction because she asked, "Did you attend high school?"

"Yes, but only through the tenth grade."

"That's not unusual," she said. "Only the fortunate or wealthy attend high school."

Dr. Mortenson nodded briefly. "I thought you might come from good family stock. Good teeth and uncalloused hands, you understand.

You have said many times that you were orphaned. How is it you attended high school?"

The question died in the air. What could I tell him? Say that I attended East High School while living with my last foster parents? And if there were no foster parents in 1927, would he turn the car around and head back to the hospital? I could feel Marjorie's eyes boring into me as I remained silent, staring out the car window at the passing city.

When we turned on to Albion Street, the sight of the two-storied, red-brick building chilled me to the bone. Its arched windows and big front steps looked so much like I remembered yet somehow larger and colder. Over the door, the number 1501 stood out like a cold sore on a supermodel.

The sprawling fifty-room home was clean and looked nearly new. That was more than unsettling - it was truly frightening. How could something so old look so new? Something so familiar look so unfamiliar? My stomach turned and sweat drenched my body.

I told myself to be strong, and we climbed the steps. Behind the doctor, Marjorie walked by my side. The smell of wood smoke drifted heavily in the air. Stepping through those doors again gave me shivers, making my heart hunger for the world I had known only weeks before.

The tour was blissfully short: classrooms, workshop, and kitchen. The handmade lace curtains of the dining hall added softness to an otherwise stark room. Wooden floors reflected afternoon sunlight in a room capable of seating one hundred twenty children. The room was more than half-filled with young boys. It saddened me that there were so many orphaned children. During my last stay, the place had been much less used.

When we reached the dormitory, I was given a bed and left to unpack my belongings while the doctor made the arrangements for my admission. The boldly-striped galatea twill dress I was wearing had once belonged to Marjorie, as did the gingham dress in my bag. Hanging the garment in the wardrobe, I wondered once more what had become of my own clothes.

"I'll have to return with the doctor," Marjorie said softly. "You will be well here, won't you?"

"Of course," I lied. "I'm no stranger to making new friends."

She hugged me briefly before meeting the doctor at the top of the stairs.

"We shall both return on the morrow," he said. "Get plenty of rest and please keep a record of your dreams for me."

They walked away, and I had to keep myself from chasing after them. Returning to my dorm room, I reminded myself that if I were to ever find a way home, I had to leave the hospital. I left the candy store in October of 1982. Surely the store was the key to going home. I could check it out in a day or two, but first I had to survive the orphanage.

Sitting on the bed, I stared out the window, missing Marjorie's comforting chatter. I reassured myself that I would meet other girls here, not much unlike going to a new foster home. The real difference was not the place, but the language. Half the time I didn't understand what people were saying. Strange phrases, like *dimbox jaunt* and *go chase yourself*, made me constantly stop and think.

Keeping mostly to myself over the next few days, I fell into a steady rhythm of sewing and cooking. Hiding my lack of experience when it came to using a treadle sewing machine was easier than having to be shown around the kitchen. Culinary school hadn't prepared me for the industrial-sized scullery of the orphanage. The large wood-burning stove was especially daunting, but to my surprise, the easy, rhythmic pumping of the sewing machine's foot pedal was relaxing.

Wash day was a whole new experience, and I think some of the girls resented having to teach me everything. One of the girls nicknamed me Princess, and I don't think she meant it affectionately.

A small girl of fourteen or fifteen offered to help me. Dull brown rag curls surrounded a square face with buckteeth. "Set six dining chairs face to face," Alice said. "Then put those three large washtubs, each between two chairs."

I nodded and did as I was instructed.

"Toss those sheets in the first tub and then add a pan of boiling water from the stove. Ruth tells me you can't remember where you used to live."

"I lived in Colorado Springs," I said.

"Wait. Add some cold water, and a cup of Fels-Naphtha soap before you start scrubbing."

"Good thinking. That would have been way hot."

She looked at me with her head cocked to one side. "Yes, it would be quite hot. The water was boiling," she explained slowly as if I was dimwitted.

From the doorway, a brawny redhead named Ruth said, "I don't believe our princess has washed clothes before today." She carried a basket of towels and dumped them at my feet. "Have you?"

"Not often, I guess."

"Well you will have the opportunity to do laundry often here." She left to retrieve more items to be washed.

"Don't let Ruth frighten you," Alice said with a smile. "She's more bark than bite."

For what felt to my burning hands like hours, we scrubbed on a washboard, wringing the clothes out by hand and then placing them in a rinse tub set on two other chairs. I was obviously out of my element, but Alice was nice, teaching me how to do the job as painlessly as possible.

When the rinse tub was full, we poured more boiling water over the clothes and stirred them, once more wringing them out by hand, while other girls came to take away the wet linens. Because it was cold outside, they hung the majority of laundry in the basement and the remainder in the kitchen.

"Ruth said you were in the hospital before coming here to stay."

"I was. I was hurt. Got hit in the head."

"Is that why you don't remember who you are?"

I was beginning to wonder how much Ruth knew about my situation. "I suppose."

"You poor dear. That must be awfully frightening."

"I have my days."

After two days of laundry came a full day of ironing. I thought I'd died and gone to hell. My saving grace was the knowledge that Sunday was reserved for church and rest. By Saturday, I was sore from head to toe. My hands were blistered and my feet throbbed.

On Sunday, I nodded off at church only to be nudged awake by Alice every couple of minutes. She was shy but followed me almost everywhere.

"We would like to thank the Ladies Circle," the minister said in a deep baritone voice, "for donating several large turkeys to the Denver Orphans Home."

His words reminded me Thanksgiving was less than a week away and I hadn't had the chance to go to the candy store yet. Would it make a difference if I went this week or next? When dealing with time travel, did days or weeks matter?

"It's wonderful, isn't it?" Alice whispered to me.

"What?" I said jerking back from my thoughts.

"You were crying. I thought you were crying because all the children will have a wonderful turkey dinner for Thanksgiving."

Patting her hand, I said, "You're a real gem. Of course I'm happy everyone will have a traditional meal this year."

I spent the day before Thanksgiving in the big kitchen with eleven other girls. The wood-fired oven was new to me and after putting too much wood in the stove for the third time, I was put on pastry duty.

"I'm a better chopper or taster," I said.

Ruth handed me a rolling pin. "The bread has risen. You'll find it in the panty but don't 'taste' it or there'll never be enough."

I understood the reason for her comment. I was healthier than most of the girls, not fat, but bigger and stronger than most of them. I smiled and then slipped into the pantry.

Kneading bread gave me a keen sense of serenity I hadn't felt since waking up in the hospital. Just when I thought I could get used to being here, someone would call me out for saying "cool," "totally," or "lame." Most of the girls thought I was totally whacked. When I surprised them with my skill with spices and a few cookie recipes, even Ruth softened. She still called me Princess, but the nickname didn't push my buttons anymore.

The next day was a swirl of excitement. I never realized how noisy that many children could be. The servings weren't large, but they were delicious. Alice and I ate in the kitchen with a couple of the older girls. As the girls chattered about boys and Christmas wishes, I warmed my feet by the oven.

Sitting next to me on a wooden stool, Alice handed me a box wrapped with newspaper. "I know it's a little early, but I wanted you to have these."

I opened the box to find a pair of woolen stockings. I'd seen her mending them the day before and I was touched. She didn't have any more than the rest of the girls, but she noticed I didn't have any stockings.

"Thank you so much, Alice. That was so sweet of you." I gave her a hug. "I have nothing to give you."

"I know," she said. "I don't need anything. I thought your feet must be cold."

Ruth said, "And Alice doesn't want the bread smelling like your feet anymore."

I pulled my feet away from the oven, and the rest of the girls laughed.

It was a wonderful feeling, and for a brief moment, I forgot to think about going home.

Being one of the oldest children at the orphanage, I was tasked with teaching math to the younger ones. The classrooms had wooden and metal desks mounted to wooden strips resembling a long toboggan. Chains of colored paper hung from the center of the room to the tall windows in celebration of Christmas. Paper stockings with the names of a hundred children lined the windowsills like so many fireplaces. It was a pleasure to get out of laundry duty, although I felt a little guilty. When I could, I'd ask for Alice to assist me.

"Don't think I haven't noticed you've asked for my help on laundry day," she said as we gathered textbooks. "It's ducky of you."

"It's all I can offer to repay you for your thoughtfulness."

"Bunk. You're a darb gal. You needn't repay me for doing as I would for anyone else."

I turned away to hide my confusion, thankful the housemother hadn't asked me to teach English. Math never changes. As far as I knew, one plus one would always equal two. Then, again, I always believed 1983 would follow 1982.

CHAPTER 6

I was folding clothes in the laundry room when Alice came in looking restless. She pulled me to the side and whispered. "A dick in the parlor asking around about you."

"A what?"

"A policeman," she clarified.

I shook my head and gave her a wan smile. It seemed as if falling through time hadn't changed my life all that much. There was a doctor trying to lock me up, and now a detective here to dog me for answers I didn't want to give. Would I soon be hiding bikers and drug dealers, too? All I needed now was to find some old couple to take me in. I hung up the last sheet and headed for the stairs.

I slowly made my way to the parlor, trying to remember everything I had told the doctor. Could they have found someone fitting my description of Paisano?

The housemother stood beside a short, round man with a mustache like the banker from the *Monopoly* game. He smiled kindly as I entered the room.

I nodded and waved a hand, inviting him to take a seat on the small couch as I sat in a wooden rocking chair near the door. The housemother handed me a delicate teacup.

The policeman wasted no time. "My name is Detective Matthews, Miss Oxford. Doctor Mortenson cautioned that my questions could introduce new trauma. You must let me know if you are overly uncomfortable. Can you tell me what happened on the twenty-third of October?"

All I could remember before waking in the hospital was struggling to free Jay from a fallen beam. I looked down at my hands to avoid his eyes. "I needed to find employment and a place to live." Was that so unreasonable?

His voice softened. "You were unescorted, were you not?"

I nodded.

"Do you remember where you had intended to present yourself?"

"No." I looked up to see if he believed me. "I was looking for a teaching position."

By the optimism in his voice, I knew I'd given him a fresh clue.

"As a scholarly woman, there should be some record of your education in Colorado Springs. Where did you go to school?"

Panic forced me to look down at my hands again as I scrambled for a new lie. "I don't remember."

Suspicion crept into his reply. "You know you came to Denver alone with the intention of working as a teacher, though you can't tell me who you were proposed to meet. I should admit, your memory seems to be quite selective, Miss Oxford. There are not so many schools in Colorado Springs. It shan't be difficult to find where you were educated." He licked the tip of his pencil and made a note on his pad of paper. "We shall discover who you were intended to meet with that day."

What would he do when he found no record of me? I pressed one more lie. "I remember living in Hawaii when I was younger."

I had expected more questions about how I might have come to the mainland, but the officer merely jotted down a few notes in silence.

Before he could frame the next question that I surely couldn't answer, I stood. "I'm kind of tired," I said.

He jumped up and took my hand, looking admonished. "I regret these questions, but if we are ever to find your assailant, we must learn what happened that day. May I reserve the right to return?"

"I'm not going anywhere."

After Detective Matthews left, I realized my mistake. Hawaii wasn't a state yet. What were the chances the man might not even know about the islands? If I planned to stay out of the loony bin, I needed to get some hardcore information about where I was living. It wasn't like a set of *Encyclopaedia Britannica* would be of any help. I would have to depend on copies of newspapers. Lots and lots of newspapers.

Finding time to go to the library was trickier than finding the library. Although I went to Fourteenth and Broadway where the Denver Public Library had always been, I was redirected to a Greek building located in Civic Center Park. There were wide steps leading to oversized doors set under a deep portico with fourteen thick columns across its front. I was reminded of the Lincoln Memorial. It was two stories high with the window on the first floor being at least a story and a half tall. From the side you could see large windows that let light into a garden-level basement. As impressive as the building was, it was much smaller than the library of my day.

I wandered through the various rooms, trying to decide where to start. I paused at the adult fiction. I'd always been an avid reader, and a modern book might help me sound less foreign. I picked up a book called *Miss Billy Married* that looked interesting.

I strolled casually through the Nonfiction and Reference areas unsure of what to read first. Although I would enjoy looking through the Art sections, I needed to focus on a world that had been gone forty years before I was born. A sign over several thick bound hardbacks read *Law & Business.* Knowing the laws of the day was important but was too overwhelming to think about. The next section was Local Studies. That wasn't going to help. Neither would History be of much use at this point. I stopped under the sign that read "Science & Technology" wondering if there were any reference books on time travel. I needed to find a way home, but to do that, I needed to stay out of the loony bin. The trip through the science department would have to come on my next visit, as I chose to spend my time with newspapers.

Scanning the shelves, I found a book that would be the most helpful. The *Montgomery Ward* catalog would have the latest devices and the proper names for everything. I sat down at a table and began thumbing through the pages. The catalog's pictures and descriptions were absolutely fascinating; from the Coleman gas-powered steam irons to the flat panel brassieres.

I was happy to be there, away from a world I didn't understand. The library was warm and overly stuffed with books, making it the perfect hiding place from questioning police and doctors.

It was a cold and snowy Saturday in early December, and the brick and plaster walls radiated frigid air. Thoroughly engrossed in *The Age of Innocence* by Edith Wharton, I sat on my bed with a wool blanket wrapped around my feet. Reading current novels was helping me to assimilate. The language of the era was much more formal than I was accustomed to hearing, though the average person wasn't nearly as proper as the written works; not so different from the common tongue of my own era. I found women of the late twenties were quite similar to those of the 1980s. It would seem we were all trying to find our place in the world. Young people were discarding old rigid ideas about their roles. In 1927, women were embracing consumerism and personal choice. Like their later descendants, the women of this time were caught in a "culture war" of old versus new. It seemed to me that every generation of women tried to gain more freedom than the last. With the invention of the Pill, women of the sixties had their sexual revolution. In the seventies the challenge was breaking through the glass ceiling of the executive office, but the young women of the eighties seemed to have more in common with the twenties than any other time in history. In the twenties, women were only now allowed to vote, the Great War had just ended, and everyone seemed to have more money than they needed. Even with alcohol prohibition, young people flouted the laws, drove fast cars, and partied all night.

In the eighties, it was the eighteen-year-olds who were newly allowed to vote, the Vietnam War had ended, and the stock market was booming. Everyone knew drugs were illegal, but they seemed to be everywhere. Disco had died and Punk Rock music was vogue. Maybe I wasn't as out of time as I had thought.

The housemother knocked on the door frame. "Miss Oxford, you have a gentleman caller."

"Who is it?" Who would call on me? Dr. Mortenson had just seen me yesterday.

"He says his name is Mr. Watson."

I jumped off the bed. "Watson? Henry Watson? Is Jay with him?"

"He's quite alone."

"I can't believe he found me."

"Young lady! Your shoes!" But I was racing down the stairs and through the hall toward the front parlor. I nearly knocked over two boys playing marbles. "Hey!" they shouted after me, too late.

In the waiting room, I pulled up short as a young man of about twenty, holding his hat in his hand, rose from the chair, bowing slightly. "How do you do?" he said.

The room began to spin. I grabbed the door frame for support as my breath caught in my throat and my heart seemed to stop. He dropped his hat and grabbed me around the waist to keep me from falling.

Lowering me to the closest chair, he said, "I didn't mean to frighten you."

"You didn't. It's just . . . " I knew those Paul Newman blue eyes. This was Henry. He was also fifty-five years younger than the last time I'd seen him. Dark wavy hair and a finely chiseled face, he was so— well, so cute!

Taking a seat in the chair across from me, he said, "Forgive me, miss; my name is Henry Watson. I was possessed by a passion, I must confess. I've been wanting just awfully to see you again. I called on the hospital and they told me you were here." He leaned forward in the seat across the little tea table from me. "The nurse told me your name is Miss Oxford, like the hotel. My father's candy store is across the street."

I could have told him that. I could have told him many things about his life, but that would only land me back in the psych ward. "Yes, like the hotel. My first name is Jett."

He dipped his head. "I'm glad to meet you, Miss Oxford."

"Please. Call me Jett. 'Miss Oxford' sounds so formal."

He smiled kindly, his right brow arched in a perfect Commander Spock imitation. "How are you? How is your head?"

"I'm much better, Henry." I was still trembling but regaining my composure. If I'd learned anything over the last two months, it was to hide my shock whenever possible.

"Is this where you live?" he asked timidly.

"Yes."

"Pardon. I meant to ask, is this where you lived before the accident?"

"Oh." That wasn't something I could explain. "The accident seems to have knocked my memory loose. I can't tell you where I lived before. Somewhere in Colorado Springs, I think."

"That is most tragic. I live with my family above the candy store where . . . "

I must have looked ill because he took my hand in his. "Forgive me for reminding you. Do you have any family? Someone I could call on?"

"No, no I don't. That much I do remember."

He looked over at the small Christmas tree in the corner by the plate glass window. Popcorn and cranberries decorated the branches beside blue and white papier-mâché ornaments.

My eyes followed his. Someone passed by in the hallway.

I lightly squeezed his hand. "Are you the Watson boy who took me to the hospital?"

He looked uncomfortable. "Yes. I found you unconscious. Whoever did this to you at least had the courtesy to place you in our kitchen. Had they left you outside, you surely would have caught your death of cold."

In a world that made no sense, finding me on the kitchen floor of the candy store somehow seemed right. "Thank you for taking care of me."

"You—you looked—would you like to go for a walk?" He stood suddenly nervous.

"Let me get my coat."

"And shoes," he said, looking down at my stockinged feet.

I left him in the waiting room. Thoughts of the last year swirled in my head, melting together like marshmallows in hot cocoa. His voice was the same. His eyes were the same, but he wasn't at all the same. His back was straight and his hands were strong. What would Jay be like? Would she still like me? Could we be friends? Would she understand?

Returning to the waiting room, I greeted Henry warmly. "I'm ready. We can't go far though. I don't have any boots."

He looked at my worn-out shoes and blushed. "Where are your overshoes?"

"It's fine," I said. "We just won't go far."

"Why, it's snowing."

"Yes, it is," I said as I walked out the door.

As we walked toward the end of the block, Henry said, "In a sense, it is my responsibility as it was I who discovered you that day. It was all so hurried, but I'm thoroughly and unalterably convinced you were placed there for a reason."

I had the same feeling, although I had no idea how I landed in 1927 or what it had to do with him. "I'll tell you," he said. "Just now, I want to help you find your home."

"That might be harder than you know."

"It will be my quest."

What I needed was to find a way back to the eighties. The candy store and Henry were the only connection to my world. "I'd like to see the store again."

"Wouldn't it be . . . ?"

"I can handle it. I have experience as a candy maker. Could you use an extra hand for the holidays?" I'd grown accustomed to that look of surprise whenever I mentioned working.

"You wish to work there?"

"I could really use the money."

"Why ever do you need money? Are you in trouble?"

Yes, but not the kind of trouble you're thinking of. "I could use a new place to stay, maybe an apartment somewhere. I don't belong here." I waved my hand, pink from cold, indicating the sprawling mansion that was the orphanage.

"It's possible I have underestimated you. I know few flappers."

 "Seriously? You think I'm a flapper?"

He looked chided.

"I thought flappers were girls who danced to Jazz music and did the Charleston in speakeasies."

He laughed. "Yes, I suppose they do. Josephine, my fiancée, loves to dance. I was just thinking you were rather independent and a little unconventional with your wanting professional employment. I had judged you to be from a family of means."

"I'm sorry," I said. "That was ridiculously forward of me, wasn't it?" Hearing his voice, it was hard not to think of him as my old friend. Then I looked at him and everything went all fuzzy. "I have no family, Henry. I need to work."

"Of course. I didn't mean to offend you. A girl as pretty as you should have no difficulty finding a husband."

"I don't need a husband. I need a job. I thought of the store because I've attended culinary school."

He regarded me with wonder for some time before he spoke. "Well, we do often need help through the holidays, but I shan't make a promise."

"Oh, that would be just awesome." When I saw his left eyebrow rise, I quickly said, "Wonderful. It would be wonderful."

He handed me his gray woolen scarf because I was shivering. "Maybe you should meet my family first. I'll speak with Father."

"Thank you, Henry, for everything."

He smiled that familiar, but unfamiliar smile and my stomach flipped. Confusion over what I was feeling in that moment must have shown on my face because he reached for my hand.

"Whatever you might need, I'll be here to help."

While walking back to the door, all I could think of was going home. Well, kind of going home; as close as I was likely to get. Not knowing how I got here left me with no clues as to how to get back, but the candy store was the only connection I had.

As we walked he seemed to be lost in his own thoughts, looking slightly uncomfortable, and I was afraid I'd been too forceful. He was being such a gentleman.

He bid me good day on the steps and returned to his car. Grabbing the banister to keep from chasing after him, I watched as the only person I knew from both worlds drove away. I felt my heart sink as my link to 1982 evaporated in the cold winter air. Tightness in my throat made me place my hand on my neck only to realize I'd forgotten to return his scarf. I prayed he would come back for it soon.

I'd learned that Dr. Mortenson made regular rounds every other Wednesday morning if he wasn't too busy at the hospital. I was feeling more comfortable in my new surroundings. Once the doctor took my vitals, he began the usual questions about the things I remembered.

"I've scoured the north side of the city without locating the house you described in your dream. I can only ascertain that the memory is a mixture of images." He put away his stethoscope and thermometer. "If you should notice any unusual bewilderment, you must tell me. You had many interesting flights of fancy when you first woke up in the hospital." He slipped his woolen jacket on.

"I'll let you know. I think I'm doing okay, now," I said as I walked him to the door. "I'm just a little fuzzy about my past."

"Head injuries can cause a person to think things are real when in fact they are not. Visions, you might say. The mind has a way of covering up the pain of great tragedy by inventing a new reality." He patted my hand. "You mustn't be afraid to tell me if you're ever confused about what is real."

Panic flooded my mind. Was I truly crazy? Did I invent a whole world to cover some tragedy I didn't remember? I watched him walk to his car, the Chrysler Series E. Across the street, a woman in an ankle-length wool coat and close-fitting bell-shaped hat was towing a little girl sporting rag curls. I didn't belong here. I knew it in my heart.

That night my dreams were filled with images of my life with Jay and Henry. I woke to find my pillow soaked with tears and a crippling ache in my heart.

As the next two days passed, I grew less and less confident about Henry's return. Alice assured me he would come back, but she had no way of knowing that.

"I saw the way he eyed you, Miss Jett," she said. "He'll be back."

"I hardly know him." And I didn't. The man I knew was in his seventies, not the young, attractive man I'd met on Saturday afternoon.

Alice turned over the dress she was sewing and began to hem the sleeve. "Was he the daring cake-eater that rescued you?"

"Were you listening to us?"

"I overheard only a pinch of the conversation whilst I was sweeping the hall." She looked chided. "He's airtight, the Real McCoy. Don't you let him get away."

I didn't know for certain what she was saying but "don't let him get away" was clear enough. "He has a fiancée."

"Rhatz!"

"Yeah, what you said." I smiled and went back to sewing my blouse.

CHAPTER 7

Later that afternoon Henry did stop by to ask me if I'd like to see the Christmas lights on Sixteenth Street. "My fiancée and her brother will be joining us. Afterwards, we can dine with my parents, if that pleases you."

"Seriously? That sounds awe—great." I've always loved walking past the Denver Civic Center at Christmastime with its beautiful lights. This year, it would probably look like something out of a TV rerun of *The Waltons*. It didn't matter. I was grateful to have Henry in my life again. His fiancée surely must be Jay. It would be like her to have shortened the name Josephine to Jay.

After explaining to the housemother where I was going and when I expected to return, I was allowed to leave with Henry. Alice, the dear, had loaned me her overshoes to keep my feet dry. I do believe the precious girl worried more about my toes than I did.

Henry's dark blue sedan looked like a Model T, but I wasn't about to make that mistake again. "So," I said, "this is an excellent car. Is it new?"

"No. It's Father's automobile. It's a '23 Maxwell Club. It has a good heater and windscreen cleaners, though."

Check. Windscreen, not windshield. "A good heater's important this time of year," I said as he opened the car door for me. I caught myself looking for the safety belt that hadn't been invented yet. I don't think Henry noticed or, if he did, he was too kind to say anything.

We headed west on Colfax and I gazed out at the buildings. Many of them were smaller than the buildings that would replace them in fifty-five years. Nice hotels, motels, and small apartments lined the road, making it look more like a California tourist strip than the Colfax I remembered. To my surprise, a streetcar passed us on the right. In fifty years there would be mostly rundown motels, XXX theaters, and seedy topless bars along this stretch of the street.

As we drew closer to the city center, the houses were grander and businesses lent themselves to a wealthier clientele. As we drove past the Ogden Theater, I saw a line of smartly dressed people waiting to see the live show, a play by the look of it. Passing this place in 1982, I would have seen spray paint on windows and homeless people gathered around trash barrels.

"Are you comfortable? Shall I put on more heat?" Henry asked.

"No, I'm fine," I said, as comfortable as I could be seeing as I was fifty-five years from home. "Just looking at the homes. They're so beautiful."

"It is a fond dream I have, to live on the hill one day. I should like a fine house with a view of the mountains. Pennsylvania, Clarkson, or Washington Streets would do well."

"There are so many lovely places there. You and Josephine would be very happy."

An unexpected shadow passed over his eyes. "If I'm to live in this dream, our stocks will have to do better than they've done this last year. Father expects me to manage Watson's Candies one day."

"Isn't that what you want, to make candies?"

"If I could choose, it's music that gives me the greatest joy. As of this moment, however, I'm not truly sure what I want for my life."

"Do any of us ever know what we want in life?" Turning away, I gazed out the window once more. "Even when you get what you want, it can be taken away in a flash."

"I'm sorry. That was insensitive of me. You've been through a ghastly ordeal and I natter about buying a big house on the hill."

A slow smile crept over my face at the sound of his use of the word "natter." We turned right on Broadway, driving past the Brown Palace. The brickwork was so much more ornate than I remembered. It was still an astonishing building.

"I sincerely hope you won't mind that my friends will be accompanying us on our motor tour. We are to pick them up at Holy Ghost Church where Rory is rehearsing."

"Of course it's okay. I want to meet them, especially Jay."

He cocked his head, one brow raised.

"Josephine, I mean. Didn't you say her name was Josephine?"

We parked on Nineteenth Street. The church looked much the same now as in the early eighties. In my time, so many buildings were being torn down to make way for skyscrapers. It was delightful to see what had originally stood in their place. Hopefully, this church would survive the massive urban renewal projects of the future.

Inside the church a choir was finishing the last refrain of *Oh Holy Night*. It was lovely. When the music died, the choir began to break up. Several young people passed us, greeting Henry with gusto. Apparently he was well known.

"Is this your church?" I asked.

"Only recently. My parents are Lutheran, but Josie is Catholic. To be married, I was obliged to convert to Catholicism. Here they come now."

A cheery girl with curly auburn hair pulled a tall man of about twenty down the aisle toward us. Built lean with the same red hair, the man had to be her older brother.

"Hen-ry!" she shouted as they drew closer. This would be Jay-Josie, I mentally corrected myself. Henry's fiancée. I smiled.

"Wait until you hear the chin music," she rattled on, "about that face stretcher, Dorothy Williams and that baby grand, Mort. So obvious the way she carries a torch for him. Why, you would never believe it, but Mort walked into Eddie's joint with a dolled-up hoofer from Artie's gin mill. And there she was, wearing his handcuff, a genuine orchid! Dorothy had been on a toot. She was in a big lather, and it didn't take long for the row to get lively. So the big six tells Dorothy to pipe down. Poor Eddie had to give Mort and his Sheba the bum's rush."

Henry kissed her on the cheek. "It isn't polite to gossip, Buttercup." Shaking the other man's hand, he said, "Rory, you should keep Josie out of those places."

"Oh, she wasn't at Eddie's. She heard the story from Jackson." He looked at me curiously. "Well, who's the blind date?"

Blind date? My heart was pounding. Was I supposed to be this man's date?

"Not a date, Rory," Henry said. "Just a friend. Don't get fancy ideas."

"Pretty," he replied to Henry, although he was looking at me. "Airtight. I'd say."

Twisting a ginger curl around her finger, the girl smiled at me. "You're the gal Henry found in the kitchen of the store."

Henry placed a hand lightly on my shoulder. "Jett Oxford, I'd like you to meet my fiancée, Josephine Elizabeth, and her brother, Rordan William Doyle."

Rordan took my hand and brushed his lips across my fingers. "The name isn't familiar, but by the green eyes and smattering of freckles across your nose I would guess you have a bit of Ireland in your blood."

I felt my cheeks warm.

"Henry, you're always so formal. Call him Rory, and you can call me Josie."

She was about my age, with gray-green eyes and a smile almost too large for her slender face. Rory, on the other hand, had a serious face that reminded me of David Bowie without all the flash.

"What was all that about Dorothy and Mort?" I'd been lost from the moment she'd said "chin music".

"Oh, just a bunch of hooey," she cooed. "Dorothy sings at a local joint where we like to hoof it on weekends. You're far more interesting. Jett is a great name. I have a string of jet beads my aunt Sophia gave me last year. They're all the rage you know. Henry tells me your last name is Oxford. Are you related to the owners of the hotel?"

"No, I think the hotel is named after Oxford, England."

"Ooh. And she knows about England!" she said, tossing a look at Henry. "You didn't tell me that." She turned once more in my direction. "Have you ever been there? To England, I mean?"

"No, though I'd like to visit someday."

Coats were strewn over the back row of pews. Rory pulled out a long black wool coat for himself and a fox fur coat for his sister. I surmised the family had some money.

She wrapped her arm in mine and turned me toward the door. "Let's get a wiggle on. I can't wait to see the lights. I read in the daily they are going to ignite more than three thousand electric lights this year. Isn't it pos-i-lute-ly jake!"

From her exuberance, I gathered she was sincerely excited about the lights, although she could be naturally spastic.

When I looked back at the sanctuary, waves of *deja vu* swept over me, like seeing buildings or streets that looked familiar but were somehow unfamiliar, like the twenties and the eighties were crashing together in my mind.

I had to make a conscious effort to think of Henry's fiancée as Josephine. I didn't dare slip and call her Jay, unless, of course, I was the one who gave her the nickname. *No, I don't belong here. If I change something here, I may never get home again. Unless that was why I was here, to give her the name.* I was driving myself mad with the possibilities.

The brisk air slapped me in the face as Henry held the door for us. The setting sun, slanting through the four- and five- storied buildings, gave everything a surreal glow. The jingling sound of cars and the clopping hooves of horses reminded me how far I was from home. My heart yearned for the days when the tang of smog would replace the smell of wood smoke and horse manure.

Josie and I crawled into the back seat of Henry's car. Before we even sat down, she was telling me all about Christmas Mass. "You'll have to come see Rory play the organ. My eldest brother is extraordinarily talented."

"What's the meaning of this?" Rory asked from the front seat.

"I'm just getting Jett square on your musical skill," she said. "You should hear him on the saxophone, too. Sometimes he performs at a local joint with Henry. He doesn't take me often. Apparently it's unbecoming for women to dance and sing in gin joints." She laughed with an infectious gaiety.

"Josie," Henry scolded. "You're going to give Miss Oxford the wrong impression. She'll think you're a wanton woman."

"I *am* wanton. I'm *wonton* for you to take me out dancing tonight."

"Not tonight, Buttercup. I promised to introduce Miss Oxford to my parents."

My heart fluttered. We were going to the candy store. Somewhere in my mind, I knew that had to be my ticket home.

Josie didn't sulk. Instead, she began pointing out the lights shining from various windows. A sleigh jingled past us on the right and she began to sing:

"Dashing through the snow,

In a one-horse open sleigh,

O'er the fields we go,

Laughing all the way."

She was a wonderful singer, and I was compelled to join in. Soon Rory and Henry were singing along. We followed *Jingle Bells* with *We Wish You a Merry Christmas* and *Deck the Halls*. In all of my life, I'd never sung Christmas carols with friends while oohing and ahhing over lights and holiday decorations. I was having the time of my life.

The car was terribly drafty and the small heater wasn't keeping up. Luckily, there was a heavy quilt in the back, so Josie and I snuggled underneath. We had only met an hour before, but I was smitten. If the older Josie I had known was my long-lost grandmother, this girl was the sister I'd never had. She laughed at everything and made the most outlandish comments. Although I didn't know what she was saying most of the time, her brother and Henry seemed amused.

"I want to stop at the Palace for cocoa," Josie said as we traveled up Seventeenth Street.

"We'll have to save it for another night, Buttercup." Henry said. "We have cocoa and cookies at the store. If we stop now, we shall be late to dinner, and Mother loathes anybody who's late to her meals."

Josie rolled her eyes. "It wouldn't be the same, you understand," she said conspiratorially. "It's the holidays at the Palace and I want to show Jett off to my friends. They're sure to be impressed."

"Next time, Josie." Rory piped in. "Don't get in a lather. You don't know who is going to be there tonight."

"Might be nobody—might be everybody." She turned back to me. "Have you ever had cocoa at the Palace?"

"No. I've never had the chance." I was assuming she meant the Brown Palace, but I couldn't be sure.

Turning onto Sixteenth Street, we rolled the windows down. The sight was breathtaking. Evergreen garland, suspended from electrical lines, draped from the faces of buildings to the center of the avenue where a single large silver bell hung above the passing cars. Giant red velvet bows topped the doorways of many storefronts while stacks of toys and holiday treats decorated the windows. A light snow was drifting down, covering the muddy lane in brilliant white. Shoppers, arms full of packages, darted in and out of shops. Down the road, I could see the Daniels and Fisher Tower. In my time it had been dwarfed by skyscrapers, but today it was the tallest building in the city.

We passed the D & F Tower and turned on Blake Street. As the car drew closer to the store, my heart started beating faster. I wasn't sure what to expect. Would the store look the same? Would I even know it at all? I would be meeting Henry's parents, long dead by 1982. What if I magically reappeared in 1982? What happened to the original Josie and Henry? What would happen to this Josie and Henry? Of course, they were the originals, but would they still be there when I returned? Then again, what if nothing happened at all?

CHAPTER 8

When we turned back on Seventeenth Street, the first thing I noticed was Union Station. It looked much larger and more ornate that I remembered, but much of that had to do with the size of the surrounding buildings. More than that, it was the huge grillwork of metal resembling the Parisian Arc de Triomphe, boasting the word *Mizpah* in lights over the arch, that caused me to gasp.

The car stopped in front of the store.

"Here we are," Henry announced.

"Come on, Jett," Josie said as she stepped out of the car door Henry had opened for her. "Mother Watson is a wonderful cook. She has promised to teach me. One day, I'll know everything about baking."

When I walked around the car, I faced the store. The plate glass window of the store looked so much like it had looked in my time. The displays were festive and beautiful. Tiny packages wrapped in brightly colored paper accented the chocolates and peanut brittle. A tree of candy-covered popcorn held the place of honor in the center of the window, tiny cinnamon candies were its ornaments, and a white taffy star graced its top. A garland of spun sugar wound around the boughs of the tree, making the most beautiful presentation.

As Henry led me through the door, I was assailed by the smell of baked goods, and tears streamed over my cheeks. He grasped my shoulders to steady me. "Oh, my dear. Forgive me," he said. "This was so thoughtless. Of course it would be difficult for you to return to this place after what happened to you. I am so awfully sorry."

"It's okay, Henry. I'm fine."

"Clearly, you are not."

"I just need a moment to catch my breath."

He led me to a straight-back chair by the register. "I should have realized this would be difficult. And here I thought to entertain you."

"I wanted to come. Remember: this was my idea."

Josie knelt beside me and took my hand in hers. "I can't imagine what you must have suffered that day."

She was right about that. No one could have imagined what I'd been through. I had a hard enough time believing it myself. Her gentle touch spun me back to the days before this nightmare had started, to the days when Jay would comfort me over a fallen cake or a jerk of a boyfriend. I missed the older woman but found myself clinging to young Josie.

"What kind of piker would do such a thing?" she said, stroking my hair.

I was trying hard not to cry. Rory brought me a cup of hot tea. Behind him, two people, probably Henry's parents, hovered near the doorway to the kitchen. Henry paced by the front window, obviously at a loss for what to do next. The next few moments passed like a dream. I kept closing my eyes, wishing myself back to 1982, but each time I opened them, the more permanent 1927 felt.

Taking a deep breath, I stood and put out my hand. "I'm Jett Oxford. Thank you for inviting me to dinner."

The older woman smiled. "This is Thomas Henry Watson, Sr. and I'm Lillian Elsa Mae. You may call me Lillian, and my husband goes by Thomas."

"It's very nice to meet you. I didn't mean to freak out on everyone."

The two elder Watsons exchanged uncomfortable glances.

"Really, I'm better now. It's very nice to meet you," I repeated nervously.

"Why, yes," Mrs. Watson said. "It's lovely to meet you, as well. My Henry insisted on bringing you home for dinner." Her smile was brighter now. "I told him I thought that was a jolly nice thing to do. Are you sure you're well?" She held out her hand to me.

"Yes, ma'am."

"My Henry tells me, also, that you have some knowledge of candy making."

So much was riding on making a good impression, the mention of my skills made me absurdly nervous. "Yes," I said with a calmness I didn't feel. "I've made taffy, bon-bons, fudge, toffee, truffles, and assorted chocolates."

"A chocolatier? Henry didn't mention that you were a chocolatier." She led me through the kitchen and into the large dining room to the east of the baking room. In fifty years, that room would hold two wall ovens, a three-compartment sink, and a side-by-side freezer.

Henry's father ushered in the rest of the group.

Indicating that I should take a dining chair near the fire, Mrs. Watson said cheerfully, "Miss Doyle, will you be so kind as to take the chair to Miss Oxford's left? You girls look a little pale. The fire will do your constitution good. Rory, if you please, sit here next to Henry."

An elegant dinner was spread across a dining table large enough to feed ten but set for eight. Each place setting featured more dishes than I usually used for a dinner for four. A large gold, flat plate was at the center of each setting. On the charger sat a white china dinner plate with delicate pink roses and gold trim. In the middle of each of these were placed a salad plate and a soup bowl. Above the main setting, to the right, a bread plate held a roll and bread knife. Centered above the dinner plates were a dessert plate and a small saucer I assumed was for fruit or ice cream. To the left of this, above an array of three forks, a wine glass, a water glass, and a teacup on its own saucer took up the remaining space. That there was still enough room for a full roasted goose and half a dozen side dishes was the absurdity that surprised me most.

As Thomas Henry Sr. came in, Lillian Watson handed him the carving tools. "Connor and Brigid should be ringing any moment."

Josie leaned toward me. "My parents," she said. "I believe they like to be relieved of the little ones for a time."

"Little ones?" I asked

Rory nodded his head as he took his seat. "Me brothers and sisters. We're Catholic."

I must have looked confused because he explained, "There are thirteen of us."

"No way," I said. "Your parents had eleven kids?"

"Fourteen," he said with a grin. "We lost a sister a few years past, and I wasn't counting me—my," he corrected, "parents."

I didn't know what to say to that. Luckily, the bell rang at the door, and Lillian Watson jumped up to let the Doyles into dinner.

A rather tall, round-faced man in a long black dinner jacket escorted a plump woman sporting streaks of gray in bright red hair into the room. Rory, Henry, and Thomas stood, so I did as well. Beside me, Josie looked slightly bewildered and slowly rose to her feet.

Lillian introduced the new couple. Connor took my hand and raised it to his lips just short of a kiss.

"It's a pleasure to meet you, Miss Oxford," Brigid said, extending her hand.

"Nice to meet you," I replied, returning the gentle squeeze of her fingers. Her pale skin was dotted with freckles. As she sat in the chair her husband held for her, I noticed the necklace she wore. A clear-cut crystal held by delicate silver filigree. I'd seen it many times before. I looked to my left. Of course, Jay-Josie would have inherited the necklace from her mother.

I said little throughout the meal, preferring to absorb the atmosphere and learn what I could from them. Everyone was kind enough not to ask me too many questions. Rory and Henry had attended music classes together and that was how Henry came to know Josie. The Doyles came to Colorado because Philadelphia's upper crust didn't like the Irish. Although Connor Doyle was a civil engineer experienced in designing railroad bridges, work was difficult to come by. Fortunately, the family had money through a trust fund from a construction company established by an uncle back in Philadelphia. The conversation clarified that being Irish had negative implications where Denver's elite was concerned, even worse than those in Philadelphia. The bigotry surprised me. There were always people who didn't like Blacks or Hispanics, but the Irish?

"Has your family had such issues in Colorado Springs, Miss Oxford?"

"Please, call me Jett." The familiar embarrassment over not having a family crept up my cheeks. "I haven't had much trouble, I guess."

"Must be the black hair," Connor said.

It was good to know the Watsons were tolerant people. Thomas Watson and Connor Doyle talked about several candidates they were hoping would replace well-known Klan members throughout the city. I didn't remember much about the civil rights movement but did remember enough to know the Ku Klux Klan was known for lynching Afro-Americans.

While eating my apple pie, I learned that until two years previous, Klan members controlled the Colorado State House and Senate, the office of Secretary of State, as well as city councils in many Colorado towns. Even Mayor Ben Stapleton of Denver and Governor Clarence Morley were known Klansmen. I couldn't wrap my mind around the idea of the KKK in control of my city. Even more appalling was that none of this history was taught in the schools of my day.

"How can that be?" I asked. "Why would people elect men to office who so openly hate black people?"

Thomas Watson looked surprised. I didn't know if it was my question or the vehemence with which I asked it. He glanced at his son, his right eyebrow rising, and then explained, "It wasn't so much about hating our negro brothers. The Klan's propaganda focuses on Italian and Irish Catholics, as well as Jews. They insist that these people," he said, pointing to his dinner companions, "pose a threat to the nation's Protestant values. Since Colorado is predominantly Protestant, the message played well here."

"But it's still prejudice, even if it isn't about the color of skin." I felt queasy and ashamed, even though all of this happened long before I was born.

Thomas Watson continued, "Stapleton and Morley stood for law and order against bootlegging, gangsters, and rampant crime, something Denver has had more than its share of. There are a few well-known Italian families whose bootlegging has created ongoing territory wars on the northern side of the city. These Klan men sought to tighten the morals loosened by Jazz music, new dances, and the influence of Hollywood."

"As if we'd believe that," Brigid Doyle piped in. "Those men frequent the dance halls as much as anyone. It's power they seek." Her husband gave her a stern look.

"So what happened?" I asked. "Why did they all leave office?"

"By heaven, I assure you, they haven't, young lady," Connor said with grim candor. "But it must be confessed, they are much less vocal now that the Colorado Grand Dragon is being investigated for tax evasion and corruption. We can thank C. C. Hamlin, the publisher of the *Colorado Springs Gazette* and the *Evening Telegraph*. His scathing editorials opened the eyes of many of those who had been seduced by the protection of anonymity. Hamlin asserted secrecy was the refuge of moral cowardice."

Thomas smiled as he sipped his water. "Hamlin went so far as to infiltrate the local klavern and publish a list of its leaders. Colorado Springs did well keeping the Klansmen at bay, owing much to a staunch police chief who wanted no help from the secretive society."

"Our own should have been less willing," Brigid said.

"Yes," Connor agreed. "Colorado Springs showed great restraint, while Salida formed its own fraternal order, the Sons of Italy, and drove the Klan out by shotgun."

As dinner came to an end Henry's father suggested the men retreat to the storefront for a cigar. Henry and Rory followed the men, leaving me with Josie, Brigid Doyle, and Lillian Watson. We sipped on tea and the older women talked about an upcoming holiday party, a masquerade, the Doyles were hosting. Apparently, the Doyle home was enormous. It had to be, to hold thirteen children.

Josie began to clear the table, and I jumped up to help her. "Do your parents always host such big parties?" I asked her as she began filling a large tub to wash the fine china.

"We do when we can." She handed me a drying towel. "Mother loves to show off her family. She's quite immodest, if the truth be told."

"Your house must be massive."

"Not so terribly large as some, but adequate."

I would later learn that a twelve-thousand-square-foot house was "quite adequate".

"I hope you'll be there. We'll have such fun."

"I don't know," I said, stacking the dinner plates in the hutch. "I don't have a costume and I don't have a job to afford one."

"A job!" Josie put her hands on her hips. "We might as well understand each other at once. There's a good many nifty fellows in this town. You shan't be needing a job!"

"I don't intend to marry. Not any time soon, anyway."

"Hooey! That's all very well to say now. Of course you'll marry. Leave it to me."

"No, really. I want a job."

Head tilted to the right, she looked at me as if trying to figure out if I was jerking her leg. "Swell. Let's get you a job then, by golly."

"Henry is asking his parents if I can work here."

"They're contemplating it," Henry said as he stepped through the doorway carrying two ceramic mugs. "We had quite a talk this past evening."

"Come then, is it a go?" Josie asked as she filled his coffee cups.

"Father has to adjust himself to it, and Mother worries that you might not acclimate well."

"Acclimate?" I said.

Henry looked abashed. "To working in a place where you endured such tragedy. I'm ashamed to own it, but I should have thought of it myself."

The best days of my life had been in this place, but I couldn't tell him as much. "No way," I said. "You're very thoughtful, Henry. Remember, I begged you to bring me here. I'm okay with this. I was just a little ... " My voice trailed off. What was I? Angry? Scared? Confused? Hurt?

Josie slipped her arm around my shoulder. "Of course you were. I think it's jolly brave of you to come back here."

Henry cupped Josie's chin in his broad hand. "Don't think I don't see what's going on here." Turning toward me, he said, "Josie has a proclivity for collecting strays, much like her mother. Promise me you won't allow my dearest to make a project of you."

"Henry! I do no such thing. I only seek to help when I can. Speaking of which, you must inspire your parents to take on extra help."

"I'm sure they'll let us know soon. Miss Oxford, would you like join us for Mass on Sunday morning?"

"Mass?"

"Josie would love to see you there, wouldn't you, Buttercup?" he said, winking at his fiancée. "She's been quite amiable this evening. She's usually much more reticent unless, of course, you are her latest endeavor."

Josie snapped him on the butt with a towel as he scooted out the door.

Alone again, she said, "Don't listen to him. But I would like to see you at Mass. Are you Catholic as well?"

I didn't have a religious preference. I always thought there must be a higher power out there, call it God or Fate, but right now, I wasn't too happy with the cards it had dealt me. "No, but I once went to a Church of Scientology with a friend."

She gave me that half smile that told me she was waiting for the punch line.

"Kidding," I said, "though I went to a Baptist church."

"Nertz!" she said, eyes bugging out. "Are you on the level? Were there negroes there?"

Crap. I did it again. "It was only once. I was with my friend Rosa."

"Is she a negro?"

"Yes, but I haven't seen her in years." Rosa and I had been foster sisters when I was eleven. We got caught smoking in the bathroom of her church. Two weeks later, we were both back in the system. I lost track of her after that. Integration had come a long way by the eighties, but there were still places I didn't go without an invitation.

"I have a negro friend," Josie whispered. "Her name is Julianne Florence Rosa Parker. Isn't her name po-so-lute-ly the ritzy! She's a jazz singer at Murphy's. She goes in for Bohemianism, and all that rot. Her boyfriend, Lincoln, plays the piano. He's got the confounded temperament that goes with his talent, I suppose—though why a man can't play a song and keep his temper and a level head I don't see!"

"Does he hurt her?" I asked.

"Oh, no. It's himself that's always finding a fist to the jaw. Six or seven months ago, to be sure, he got in with a set of fellows at

Murphy's—Clayton Brown and his clique—that were no good. Those two are real bimbos."

"Not too bright, huh?"

"Not bright? What's not bright?"

"The guys Lincoln is hanging with. You said they were bimbos."

"Yes," she said slowly. "They're hard-boiled tough guys."

Okay, that threw me completely. I thought a bimbo was an airhead. I tried to cover my confusion. "Rough crowd, then?"

"Well, I'm not such a fool to go into Murphy's by myself."

Rory was standing in the doorway with Josie's coat. "Let's call it now. Father's outside waiting in the car."

"Can we give Jett a lift home?"

"I'll see her home," Henry said from behind Rory, holding out my shabby coat with its patches glaring under the kitchen light. I looked down at my faded dress and mended stockings, but before I had a chance to get comfortable in my embarrassment, Josie was hugging me and telling me again how wonderful it was to meet me.

Nearly prying her off of me, Henry assured her, "I'll bring Miss Oxford to church on Sunday. You shall continue to share the town gossip then, my dearest." The smile on his face said he was teasing.

"Oh, come, don't be such a gimlet." She laughed and kissed Henry on the cheek. "You think I'm butting into what doesn't concern me; but I'm not. What concerns my friends, concerns me. I can't abide to see her hurt."

"I know that, Buttercup. We have established you would take in every stray cat in the city if your father would stand for it."

She stuck out her tongue as Rory helped her into her fur coat. Giving me another quick kiss on the cheek, she said, "It was so nice to meet you. I just know we are going to be the greatest of friends," and with that, she scurried to the door. Henry and I followed.

"I should return in three-quarters of an hour," Henry said to his parents as we walked past them. He held the shop door open for Josie and me as we stepped out into the cold December night where the Doyles were already in the car waiting. Rory took a gentlemanly pace walking me to the passenger side of Henry's car. He wished me a good night as he helped me into the front seat. He kissed my hand and it caught me totally by surprise. "Thank you, Rory," I mumbled. "It was nice to meet you as well."

As Henry started the car, I said, "Rory is quite the gentleman."

Henry stole a glance at me before returning his eyes to the road. His mouth had lost its customary smile. "Yes, he is."

"The whole family seems very nice."

Henry reached over and turned on the heater. "Are you warm enough?"

"I'm fine." The words died in the air.

When we turned onto Colfax, I said, "Josie's a great girl. You're a lucky man."

His smile returned. "Yes, she's a wonderful girl. So full of life."

"She comes from a good family."

Henry looked over at me. I wasn't sure, but I thought I said something wrong. I replayed my statements. No slang.

A prolonged minute later Henry said, "Normally, a family of her stature wouldn't consider an offer from a man like me, but the Doyles are different. They're Irish."

"Oh," I said, but I really didn't understand what that had to do with the price of tea in China. "You told me that you became Catholic in order to marry her. Is there more you should have done?"

A hurt look crossed his face. "I'm a working man."

"Well, yeah. I wouldn't marry a man who didn't have a job."

He grinned this time. "Her family has money. Coal mines in Pennsylvania. Connor Doyle works as an engineer, but he doesn't need to work. When he first came to Denver he worked on the Cathedral Basilica of the Immaculate Conception."

"Which one is that?"

His brow jumped up slightly. "That one," he said, pointing out the window at one of Denver's most iconic churches.

"Oh," I said, feeling stupid for not knowing the name of the church. "It's a beautiful church. I've never gone inside."

"It is beautiful. He was lucky to get the project. Lately, it's hard for him to find engineering positions, but they do have wealth in their own right."

"They dress very nice."

"There's a rather large circle of relatives still living in Philadelphia. Even with all their money, they've found society in the west to be ever more intolerant, if that can be believed." Henry slowed down for a couple pedestrians crossing the road in the falling snow. I was glad to be in the warm car with the heater on full.

"The daily press was brutal," he continued. "The harder the Doyles tried to be accepted, the more outrageous the defamation. The breaking point came when Josie's sister, Bridey, succumbed to scarlet fever. The Doyles were refused advertising in the daily press."

"They weren't allowed to place an obituary notice?"

"Only a couple of lines and none of that about the family. Brigid Doyle had written a beautiful tribute to their child, but the press wouldn't have it. To make matters worse, on that same day there was placed an editorial decrying the savage and criminal nature of the Irish race."

"That must have hurt."

"Mother Doyle was beside herself with anger but too much of a gentlewoman to lash out. She often came to the store to buy special items for her parties. Although she spoke with my mother many times, she would never admit her insult."

"Too proud?"

Henry nodded. "Mother, by the by, has fixed ideas of right and wrong. She said to Mother Doyle on that occasion, 'Do you think I shall let you sell yourself for such a thing as that? No, my good woman, I will not abide this.' In a rage, Mother and Father refused service to a few of society's most prominent women that day."

Henry turned the car onto Albion Street. "We attended the funeral, and later, at the Doyles' family home, Mother marshaled the forces of women friends, who under her direction made sandwiches, cut cakes, and brewed coffee. Mother and Brigid Doyle have been jolly friends unto this very day."

"I'm glad your family has an open mind about these things."

"I have been thus trained," he said with a slight smile.

"So Mr. and Mrs. Doyle are overlooking the working status of your family and trusting their heart."

He blushed. "We are what we are, I fancy. I promise our children should have every advantage that college, special training, and travel could give them."

"I'm sure you will provide them every opportunity."

"I shall, and Josie never does anything by halves."

When we reached the orphanage, I was beaming with happiness. Although sad that the night had come to an end, I would be seeing all of them again on Sunday. I reached for the latch on the door and opened it as Henry raced around the car.

"Miss Oxford, you confound me." He took my hand, helping me out of the car. "I cannot be expected to open the door if you are so quick to do it for yourself."

"I'm sorry. I didn't expect you to open my door."

"I *am* a gentleman."

"Of course you are. I just never . . . "

In silence, he walked me to the door. I'd hurt his feelings and I didn't know how to explain myself.

"Good night, then," I said with as much charm as I could muster.

"Good night," he said, kissing my gloved hand.

Watching him drive away, I wondered how he could be so like the Henry of my day, and yet so different. Josie was different as well, less private than in the future. Maybe it was something she would learn in time; call it growing up. Still, I was glad to know this younger and more vibrant version of her.

CHAPTER 9

On Sunday, Henry came for me at nine o'clock in the morning. "Good morning, Miss Oxford. I hope we haven't arrived too early. I was keen to get started. Mass begins at ten, but I would like to have time to speak with Rory before we go in."

That was good news as I was looking forward to seeing Josie. Her companionship didn't feel like charity, it felt real, and having spent years in foster care, I knew the difference. Still, I was a little embarrassed to be wearing the same dress, though it couldn't be helped, it was the nicest dress I had. Maybe Henry would have good news about a job and I would be able to afford better.

I slid into the back seat next to him, as his parents were seated in the front.

"Good morning, Miss Oxford," Mr. and Mrs. Watson said in unison.

"Good morning," I replied. "Thank you for coming to get me."

"It is our pleasure," Henry's mother said lightly. "You made an impression on my husband." She gave his hair a gentle tug. "You're not a stranger to speaking your mind. How refreshing! You have much in common with Miss Doyle. I believe my son will have his hands quite full."

"She's a great girl," I said.

"Yes, but do be careful not to follow her into everything." She looked at Henry.

"She is spirited, but not foolish," he said in her defense.

"You will know it in the years to come." Her smile told me she approved of Josie but worried her son might not keep up.

Thomas Watson harrumphed. "You wouldn't know it, but my Lillian was a honeycomb full of bees at that age."

"Of a certain, I was not."

"You led forty-seven women in a demonstration against the income tax in 1912."

"I was merely with them. I was not their leader."

That started another conversation about taxation and politics that lasted the rest of the drive. Mr. Watson stopped the car to let the three of us out at the front door of Holy Ghost Church where Mr. and Mrs. Doyle, standing on the steps, greeted us warmly. I didn't see Josie or Rory, but Henry waved me toward a side door where several young people were talking.

"You're looking fit as a penny from the mint," Josie said, kissing me on the cheek as I joined the group. "Everyone, let me introduce Miss Jett Oxford. She's new to Denver."

I had to think fast when someone asked me about my hometown. "I lived in Colorado Springs," I said, hoping no one in the group was from the 'Springs.

"That's got to be a seventy-mile motor ride," one of the young men said.

"Yes," I said. "It was a rather long trip."

I was making the rounds, introducing myself and shaking hands, when I met another young lady, about fourteen or fifteen. Only then did I realize I probably should have given each of my new acquaintances a small curtsy instead of a handshake. If Josie or the other girl noticed my screw up they chose to ignore it. As a cover, I mentioned Colorado Springs was quite small and I didn't meet people from the big city often.

Among the group, I met two of Josie's sisters and five of her brothers: Sean, fourteen; Liam, thirteen; Caleb and his twin, Caitlin, twelve; Roark, nine; Finigan and his twin, Fiona, eight. "I don't expect you'll remember all their names," Josie said, smiling. "I have trouble on occasion myself. The other four little ones are in the nursery. Mother will be picking them up before Mass."

Rory slipped away as the rest of the crowd chatted about holiday plans. Everyone was excited about the Doyles' annual New Year's Eve party. Apparently, the musicians hired for the dance were friends of Rory and Josie and better known for their jazz performances.

The rich sound of an organ playing *Oh Come to Me* signaled it was time for us to take our seats. I dutifully followed the crowd as we all filed in to the high-backed wooden benches. As we settled in the back pews of the church, I suppressed a giggle. Most of my brief experiences attending church led me to believe the most popular seats were always in back. Some things remained the same from one generation to another. Holy Ghost Church wasn't terribly large and it appeared the Doyle family was most of the congregation.

Satin robes and lighted candles shimmered like a dream and colored light from the stained glass windows danced across the faces of the assembly. Behind the priest, Rory played the organ for a small choir of men who sang opulent hymns. I hadn't smelled so much incense since the late seventies. The priest applauded Christ's bravery. Though he would be crucified, he never turned from his mission. Though his life may not have been what he would have chosen for himself, he rose to the challenge that God had given him. "Go forth," he proclaimed, "and do good works with the life our Lord God has given you."

After the most elaborate and ritual-filled service I'd ever witnessed was over, we followed Rory and Josie to their home: a large Victorian with fat, white Christmas candles lighting up the deep bay windows. A wreath of holly swayed to and fro when an elderly man in a tall black hat opened the door. The man called out, "Come now. Your aunt Laoise has been waiting for hours. She's near drunk you out of eggnog."

Mrs. Doyle kissed the man on the cheek. "Uncle Paddy. It's so nice to see you. When did you arrive?"

"We must have just missed you this morning. I let myself in through a side door. When did you and Connor take to locking your house?"

Mrs. Doyle led a trail of children into the house while Mr. Doyle carried the littlest one, Tara, asleep in his arms. "Paddy, good of you to come."

"It's been several years now since your last letter. One would think a body never moved before. We would never want that you should go alone through all the ages. You might have sent us a note on occasion."

"We're doing fine here."

"We worried," Paddy said as he followed Connor Doyle into the house.

"We didn't wish to burden the family."

"Nonsense. It just so happens we stumbled upon a boarding house not far from here. The previous tenant having been called away suddenly, the landlord found herself with a month's advance rent and two vacant 'parlors' on her hands. We snapped them up, quick as you please."

"We have plenty of room here. You needn't go elsewhere." Connor waved a proud hand, indicating the large home.

"We like to be on our own, son. It's very near."

"I must warn you, Denver hasn't been as welcoming as we had once hoped. You will have to bear it as I have had to bear it."

"There are a good many Cathedrals here."

"That is the Mexican influence. Colorado has only been a proper state for fifty years. Much of this land was once Mexico."

Paddy looked concerned. "Are you getting work, old chap?"

"On occasion; mostly manual work. The design positions customarily go to local engineers, or those of the right affiliation."

"Well, if that isn't the limit! I suppose manual labor is better than none. I know you don't need to work, but one is always happier, I think, to be busy."

I followed Henry into the drawing room. In the corner was a Christmas tree that must have stood eleven feet high. Its glittering star grazed the copper-colored tin ceiling tiles. Hand-blown glass ornaments were painted in brilliant colors and beads of silver and gold draped every branch. Beneath the tree was set an electric train and village, including little cardboard houses and a skating rink. The laughter of children playing rang through the room and the smell of cookies drifted in from the kitchen.

"Play a song for us, Rory," shouted a little girl, tugging on Rory's suit pants.

"Yes! Please! Please!" cried a chorus of small voices. While the tiniest of them besieged Rory, other children played with packages wrapped in pretty paper, trying to guess what marvelous surprise was inside.

As Rory pulled out his guitar, Caitlin sat down at the piano. By the third note I recognized the melody. Josie began to sing *Oh Danny Boy*, and I was swept away to the rolling green hills of Ireland. She had the clearest voice I'd ever heard.

After a beautiful rendition of *Johnny I Hardly Knew Ye* and *The Hat My Father Wore*, Josie tugged on my arm. "I loathe asking, but it's my day for domesticity. Would you join me while I make tea and help mother with dinner."

"Sure, I'd love to help." We left the rest of the family singing *I'll Tell Me Ma*, a delightful children's song.

My brief time at the orphanage taught me to be less awkward in a 1920s kitchen, but not any less astounded by the sheer number of dishes. I filled a copper kettle with water from a pump faucet as Josie retrieved several glass jars of dried leaves. I watched her carefully fill the tea strainer and was reminded of the ingenuity of the Lipton flow-through tea bag.

Inside the dining room, two sideboards laden with food flanked a long oak table set for sixteen. The elegantly set table rivaled the dinner at the Watsons', though this table was nearly twice the size. The white bone china had ruffled edges trimmed in gold. Stacked as they were at each place setting, they resembled a fine white rose. In the center was a teacup followed by a soup bowl, then the salad plate, the bread plate, the dinner plate, and lastly, an emerald green charger. Matching condiment dishes and a delicate teapot sat in the center of the table flanked by tall crystal candleholders. Surprisingly, even the youngest children had lavish place settings.

Like having men open doors and kiss my hand, I was struck by the formality of every meal. In my experience, many families ate standing at a breakfast bar or in the car on the way to work. There was a fast-food joint on every corner and the latest in TV dinners had overtaken the frozen food shelves of the grocery stores. Lunch rarely consisted of more than a sandwich and a piece of fruit.

The beautiful table spread might have been due to their status in society, or it was possible the elaborate spread was laid because I was a guest. But whatever the reason, they served their meals in this elegant setting and never appeared pompous or pretentious.

Once everyone was seated, Connor Doyle carved a fat roast beef while a woman named Guadalupe served the remainder of the meal: potatoes with gravy, green beans, boiled tomatoes, and assorted pastries. It was the second best meal I'd had since arriving in 1927.

After eating, Fiona took the smaller children up to the nursery while Caitlin, Josie, and I cleared the table. Guadalupe was there to help, but Brigid expected her older girls to do much of the kitchen work.

"There might come a time," she said, handing Josie the teapot, "that you won't have a domestic. Then where would you be, not knowing how to heat water and clean plates?"

"Yes, Mum." Josie smiled and gave her mother a little curtsy.

"Now don't be brash." Brigid's grin suggested this was a common banter. "A good wife knows how to run a household, and what better way to learn than to get your apron dirty."

Caitlin carried a platter of meat to the kitchen and I followed her with other side dishes balanced on my arm as I'd learned from my brief stint as a waitress at the White Spot.

"You must teach me that trick," Josie said. "I've not even seen Guadalupe carry so many at once. Look, Cait, see how she does that."

I felt conspicuous. "It's nothing."

"Ho, but it's wonderful. Much like the waiters at the Denver Dry Good's Tea Room."

Caitlin gathered more plates. "Have you served in a tea room?" she asked me.

"No. It just made sense to carry as many as I could balance."

"Mummy," Josie called into the parlor where Brigid was entertaining Laoise and Paddy. "Can we visit the Tea Room soon? It's been a long time, and Jett would love to take tea there, wouldn't you?" She turned to me, all smiles.

"Sure," I answered. I'd heard of the Tea Room but never had had the money to dine there.

"Laoise would love it, too," Josie said. "We could go tomorrow."

"Oh, I have to work tomorrow. My day for kitchen duty." I surprised myself by how much I wanted to attend tea with these ladies. "Maybe we can go on Wednesday. I'll see if I can get out of my class if Alice covers for me."

"Rhatz! I was hoping to purchase shoes for the holidays."

Caitlin handed me a drying towel. "My sister loves to shop. She has more shoes than she needs," she grinned, "but I always get them once the shiny has worn off."

I looked down at my own shoes: very unshiny.

"I'm so wretched. I didn't mean to offend you." Her cheeks bloomed scarlet and I thought she was going to cry. "That was ever so uncivil of me. Mother would put me over her knee for such a thing as this."

"It's okay," I said quickly. "It really doesn't bother me to wear hand-me-downs." She still looked stricken. I shook my head. "Hand-me-downs are gifts and I'm never ashamed of a gift."

Henry came to see me the next day to tell me the candy store would be taking me on throughout the remainder of the holidays. I was glad to hear the news because I had yet to find the key to my return to the eighties. Although I firmly believed it had to be at the store, my research in *The Principle of Relativity* by A. N. Whitehead and *Side Lights on Relativity* by Albert Einstein only served to confuse me. That time was relative made sense when you understood the concept of "time flies when you're having fun and drags when you're bored," but how time could be made to run backward was beyond my comprehension.

Henry and I sat in the little parlor where I'd first seen him. Alice came in to offer us black tea.

"Thank you, Alice," I said, taking the tea service from her. "This is very thoughtful."

She curtsied quickly, her eyes never leaving Henry's face.

"It's nice to meet you, Miss Alice," Henry said with a disarming smile. "Miss Oxford has mentioned you in the past."

"She is a fine gal, sir."

"Yes, she is."

Flattered by his remark, I felt my cheeks warm as I bent down to serve the tea. Alice left a moment later and we were alone again.

Henry sipped his tea. "We begin baking at four in the morning. I will come here each morning at three-thirty to bring you in, but you may have to take the trolley home. Late-day travel should be safe. Father is willing to pay two dollars a week if you work Monday through Saturday."

I nearly spit out my tea. The minimum wage in the eighties was more than three dollars per hour. Henry was asking me to work for less than five cents an hour.

"Well," I said, staring into my cup. "If you think that's a fair wage."

When I glanced up again, the look on his face told me I'd said something unexpected. I would have told him to take a hike if it wasn't so important to find a way home, and the candy store seemed to be the most reasonable place to start searching. "I'd love to find a place of my own, though I'll be staying here at the orphanage a while longer. My housing costs here can still be supplemented by teaching and domestic duties if I get home at a decent hour."

"It may be possible for you to return in time to make the evening meal. I understand that to be one of your main domestic duties."

"I also teach math for three hours each day, but maybe I can get out of some of the cooking." I didn't have high hopes on that account. Cooking was much harder than teaching.

Before leaving, Henry asked me if I'd like to go to Mass again on Sunday.

"That would be lovely."

He turned as if to leave but stopped and looked back at me. "Have you ever . . . ?" He shook his head. "Forgive me. I don't quite know what I was going to ask. There is something—something unusual about you."

What could I say? The silence grew uncomfortable. He looked away and said, "Well, I'll see you on Sunday, then."

After he left, Alice came into the parlor. "He's a looker," she said with a grin.

"He's spoken for."

"There's a fire between you two a blind man could see."

"Don't be a bonehead. He's just being nice to me. I think he worries."

"Well," she said, sitting down and pouring a cup of tea for herself. "If that's your story."

"Seriously. He's in love with Josephine. If you saw them together, you would know that."

"The news is you will be working early in the morning."

Sipping my tea, I sighed. "Yes. Dreadfully early in the morning."

"You will be working with Henry."

"Oh, I'm sure it's his mother I'll be working with. Henry makes deliveries in the mornings."

Alice looked up at me and smiled. "Well, that's your story."

"Alice!" Heat rose to my cheeks and I turned away to the sound of her laughter. The truth was I didn't know how I felt about Henry. Only a few months ago he was my grandfather and the husband of my grandmother. Well, not actually, but that's how I thought of them, until now. Trying to understand any of this was exhausting.

That night I dreamed about firing bullets into a glass table covered in cocaine, but it was Henry I was running from this time. I didn't believe Henry would ever hurt me. I was running because I was afraid of hurting him. How could I stay away? After all, the candy store had to be my ticket home. Unfortunately, that meant spending time with Henry.

CHAPTER 10

As luck would have it, Lillian had to run to the market one day, leaving me to monitor the store. Henry and his father would be gone for several hours as they had driven to the mountains to find a Christmas tree. I jumped at the chance to search the store.

I didn't know what I was looking for exactly. I had no instruments to test the air or the magnetic polarity. I had to settle for a divining rod made from a broken branch I found on the way to work. I'd read about pioneers using divining rods. Forked tree branches were often used to find water, but I thought it might be possible to find a magnetic anomaly or a supernatural disturbance with one, as well.

I had no understanding of what time was. Was it a measuring device like a ruler, a device that measured change? Could a person move from six inches to three inches along the ruler? Maybe the ruler moved and the person was still. If that was the case, could I do something to cause the ruler to place me back where I was last October? If three inches was always three inches and six inches was always six inches: that would mean everything was preordained and nothing I could do would have any effect on the future.

Maybe the past was set but the future was fluid. The past must be fluid. My being here was proof of that, or was it?

According to some of the Eastern religions, time was circular or nonexistent, merely something humans created to mark their experiences. Unfortunately, most of my religious teaching came from reading about the Beatles and their Indian Guru, Ravi Shankar, which was to say, I knew nothing. Was it possible to achieve oneness with the universe through meditation and, in the moment, find my way home? It was worth a shot.

I started in the kitchen because that was the last place I remembered standing in 1983. The kitchen was where the fire took place and where I "came through" on this side in 1927. After a few attempts, I could feel the subtle pulling downward as I walked across the kitchen floor. I noted the place in my head and went to the basement. There were three pipes that intersected there. Well that solved one question. Divining rods really could locate water. I checked the store showroom and the pantry. I tried the bedrooms upstairs and the tiny root cellar, but nowhere had my divining rod showed any more reaction than the kitchen.

I pointed the rod at the corners of the room and then the floor and then the ceiling. The strongest point was near the back door about halfway between the pantry and the icebox. I sat down on the floor in a lotus position and closed my eyes, concentrating on every memory of my other life. "Oomm, oomm, oomm," I chanted. "Oomm, oomm, oomm."

I could hear the steady tick-tock of the pendulum from the grandfather clock in the dining room. I tried to remember what the original store sounded like. There was a similar clock in my world, but the pitch was higher. We had made rolls that morning and the scent of fresh baked bread hung in the air, exactly like it used to smell. "Oomm, oomm, oomm."

I could taste moisture in the air. It was going to snow anytime now. During my first Christmas with the Watsons, we were buried in a blizzard for days. I concentrated on that memory, trying to make it real. I was feeling exhilarated, joyful, blessed. "Oomm, oomm, oomm." The familiar sound of the back door creaking open and footsteps coming closer told me it was working. I could feel the chill of December air kiss my cheeks. I could hear Henry's voice call out, "We're home."

"Oomm, oomm, oomm."

"Jett?" he said. I opened my eyes, and a handsome man of twenty stood staring at me. He knelt down by my side. "Are you hurt? Dad, come quick. Something's happened to Jett."

I scrambled to my feet. "I'm okay. I was just . . . " What could I tell him? "I was exercising. I like to stretch my legs and yoga is good for the posture."

"Yoga?"

"I'll explain later," I said. "You're home early. Did you get a tree?"

"We did. There was a lot on Colfax selling trees. Dad felt the time we'd save would be worth the money."

Thomas was standing in the doorway. "Everything alright?"

"Yes," I said. "I didn't mean to frighten anyone."

"Well, then. Son, can you give me a hand with this tree?"

We spent the rest of the day decorating for the holiday and drinking eggnog. Thankfully, Henry never mentioned my "yoga" exercises to anyone. I hadn't returned to my own time but the hour I'd given over to meditation had left me feeling much more serene in the present.

The first few days, we saw little of each other after he dropped me off at the store. I was persistent in asking about Josie every chance we were together. After a few days he promised to invite her to visit with me. "She is a darling," he said. "I, myself, get sullen if I don't see her for a span of time. She will be delighted to know you've been asking after her."

The next day, Josie came into the store while I was setting out a display of chocolate truffles. As bubbly as ever, she asked me to go skating with her.

"I have a class this afternoon. Maybe we can go tomorrow."

"Oh! That would just be the ant's ear! Rory's friend from college will be joining us." She jumped up on the counter and began fondling the stack of receipts on a spindle. "He's airtight." She winked at me conspiratorially.

I would come to learn most every man of marrying age was "airtight" in Josie's book. That is, except for Henry. He was more than airtight, he was a real hotsy-totsy. "Is Rory's friend here for the holidays?" I asked.

"He likes to ski. He's from Vermont, but he says the skiing is better here."

"I'm sure it is."

"We've had our share of snow this year. The Nordic National Ski Association Championships are to be held at Genesee in February. I don't believe he competes, but it would be jake for him to see the tournaments."

"What does he do?"

Her head cocked to one side. "Do? He skis."

"No. What does he do for a living? What's his employment?"

"Ahh, yes. I think he plans to be a musician like my brother."

That wasn't a surprise. It seemed all Rory ever talked about was playing music. Henry and Rory played jazz in the small clubs on Blake Street when they could. Josie invited me to tag along a time or two. On one rare occasion, they allowed her to sing. She had a beautiful voice.

"His name is Paul Bachmeier. I've not met him, but I saw a picture of him in a school photo of the track team." She smiled a most mischievous smile. "You know he's fast, then."

"I'm sure he is, but I'm not looking for anyone too fast."

Henry came in, dusting snow off his coat. "Good day, ladies."

Josie jumped off the counter and gave him a peck on the cheek. "Good day to you, my handsome sheik."

Henry blushed a shade but wasn't unhappy with the endearment.

"Paul is coming in on the one o'clock train. Rory is to meet him at the station. I was just asking Jett to go skating with us after Paul arrives. Would you like to come with us?" She winked at me. "We would likely need an alarm clock."

"Alarm clock?" I asked. "Are we going to be late?"

She cocked her head. "No, a chaperone, you silly bunny."

I did feel silly. I also didn't know why we needed a chaperone to go ice-skating.

"I have the use of a car," Henry said to me with a grin. "That's what Josie needs. Rory can be your alarm clock."

She batted her lashes seductively. "Yes, I suppose a car would come in handy." Turning back to me, she asked, "Do you have ice skates?"

I had two dresses, one old coat, one pair of socks, and a pair of shoes. "No," I said. "I don't have long pants or mittens, and I've never been ice-skating."

"Well, that does it. I'll have to bring you home with me. I have an outfit you can wear. I should have remembered how Henry found you."

"How Henry found me?"

Henry gave her a stern look, but she ignored it. "Yes. He found you naked there on the floor. He covered you with the closest thing he could find, a white linen tablecloth. He's such a darb."

I felt the blood drain from my face. I had been wrapped in a white linen tablecloth upon entry to both my original world and now this one. My skin crawled up my back as the irony of it set in.

Josie was at my side in a flash. "Oh. I am so sorry. I should never have said word one. I thought you knew. That must have been so awfully traumatic to be found naked like that."

She could never understand how traumatic, how confusing. I had never been ashamed of my body, but the thought of Henry finding me passed out on the floor without a stitch of clothing was more than awkward.

"Now, I've gone and upset you," she said. "I certainly didn't mean to. Sometimes, I'm so thoughtless."

"It's okay. I'm all right. And I don't need your charity."

"Charity! Why, you would be doing me a great favor."

Henry put a finger to her lips. "Jett isn't a beloved project. Mind her pride."

"Oh, I never meant to offend. My aunts are always sending me dresses suited for a deb, but I'll never have need of them. And I have several coats I'll never wear."

Henry nodded and lightly touched my shoulder. "What she says is true. She gives away more clothes than most women will ever own."

I felt she was making up for having embarrassed me, but I nodded, agreeing to accept her gifts. She brightened visibly.

Taking the streetcar to Logan the next morning, I walked the next few blocks to the Doyle home. The air was crisp and cold but showed no sign of snow. The bright sunshine would make for excellent skating later in the day.

A mob of children greeted me at the door. In a way, it reminded me of the orphanage but with happier and better-dressed children.

After approving a few drawings and toys, Josie took me up to the bedroom she shared with her sisters, Caitlin and Fiona.

"You simply must have a dress for the party," Josie said as she opened a wardrobe stuffed with clothing.

"Party? What party?"

"Why, you silly bunny, the masquerade party!"

"Oh." After church that first Sunday there had been much discussion about the event, but I hadn't considered the thought of actually attending.

"Mother loves to sew," she continued, unaware of my confusion. "She was the finest dressmaker in all of Philadelphia."

Josie laid several dresses across the bed. Of the four girls, only Josie and Caitlin would be wearing gowns at the masquerade party. "Here is my dress." She held up a sleeveless red satin shift with white velvet trim accenting the low square neckline. The skirt was layered with red chiffon lace ending in a twenty-inch train.

"Isn't it jake?" Josie crooned.

"It's really nice," I said. "What is Caitlin wearing?"

"This one is hers." It was blue taffeta with a dropped waist and a high neckline. The sleeves were loose-flowing squares of white silk and the kerchief hemline was bare inches from the floor.

"And this is for you!" It was an emerald green velvet gown cut with the same dropped waist that draped into thick folds at the kerchief hem. The sleeves were sheer silk with tiny beadwork vines encircling the loose cuff.

"I couldn't," I gasped. "It's too beautiful."

"Of course you can." Josie put the first two dresses away. "I wore it last year, so mother will have to remove the sleeves and maybe alter the hem. I wouldn't want anyone to recognize it." She threw the frock over her arm and started for the door.

"No. It's fine. Really, I don't want your mother to change anything."

"You can't wear the exact same dress. All the same fellows will be there."

"From my experience, fellows don't look too closely at dresses."

Josie laughed. "You're likely to be right about that."

"It's wonderful of you to loan me a dress for the masquerade. Please don't ask your mother to do any work on my behalf, though."

"It's not a loan. You can keep the dress."

"No way! It's much too expensive."

"It's not. It belonged to my aunt and my mother before her."

Caitlin leaned against a bedpost. "Josie wore it twice, with some alteration to be sure. Please take it so I won't be obliged to wear it."

Josie shook her head. "You would not. We were going to donate it this year."

"Donate it?" I asked.

"Yes," she said, stroking the velvet. Now I could see the wear. Some of the nap had been crushed and worn thin. "Mother always hosts a bazaar in the spring to raise money for the Denver orphanage as well as some of the other homes for girls."

A chill ran down my back. Even if I'd never met Josie, this dress may well have come to me in the end. "Okay," I said. "But I don't want you to change a thing on it."

"You have me, then. I'll not have Mother touch the dress. It's good fortune that my aunt is a woman of taste. We shall now find a scarf or jewelry for your hair. Oh! And a mask, of course."

She was right about having tons of clothes. In the eighties, most girls had a dozen dresses, a few nice pantsuits, half a dozen pairs of jeans, shorts, blouses, and several casual tops. But for this period, Josie had a wardrobe to be envied.

As we combed through her wardrobe, Brigid Doyle came in with cookies and hot tea. "Caitlin," she said, "be a dear and gather up Tara, Kevin, and Roisin. Please take them to the nursery. They've been under my feet all day."

"Mother," Caitlin wailed, "I want to help Josie find clothes for Jett."

"Miss Oxford doesn't need your help, but I do," Brigid said as she ushered her out of the room.

After the others left, Josie pulled out a large steamer trunk and, with each piece she offered, assured me that if I didn't take it, it would be sent to the various girls' homes around the city. As she tossed one article after another at me, I was overwhelmed by her generosity. Suddenly, I saw a pink cotton dress with big, puffy sleeves. It was far too small for me, but I thought it would look darling on Alice.

"I know this girl who would just love this dress. May I?"

"Oh, but of course. Any friend of yours is welcome to whatever we have."

"You're a doll! Thank you."

"Would you like to take anything else to the other girls at the home? It would please me to give them clothing they actually want."

I picked out a couple more items, trying to control myself. I'd never had much need for a large wardrobe myself, but I loved the thought of giving these beautiful clothes to the girls at the orphanage. I felt a joy and intimacy I'd never known before. As an orphan, all I had ever dreamed of was to have a family of my own. It was so strange how life seemed to satisfy my prayers, but not actually answer them.

Josie and I tried on clothes, ate cookies, and drank tea until noon. Now I had four more dresses, a pair of silk stockings, a woolen coat, and a new cloche. I could have had at least a dozen more items, but I had to restrain my new friend.

"We have to hurry. We are to meet Paul in an hour. Henry should be here soon."

I settled on a pink sweater and gray woolen pants. Josie insisted I leave the pants.

"Those are my brother's pants, you silly bunny," she said. "I shall not let you go out of this house like that. What would the neighbors think?"

After much discussion, I opted for a heavy gray skirt and itchy wool stockings. My new black coat and a gray muff completed my attire. I may not have known how to skate, but I was going to look good falling down.

Henry gave a soft whistle of approval when he saw us come down the stairs.

"That coat, it is especially becoming," Henry said as he opened the car door for me.

"You know how Mother is," Josie said, sliding in next to me. "She insisted Jett take it, and it wouldn't be politic of her to offend Mother."

"I'm certain your mother was quite insistent," he said, winking at me. He held the door open for a moment as Josie slid in. "Your own red coat will surely be seen from Pikes Peak."

"My brightly colored coat is my declaration of independence. There are days I should like to wear it to church. I'm in the fashion, sir."

"Sometimes, I believe you set the fashion, Buttercup."

His words made her beam.

The train station was incredibly busy. A constant flow of announcements told passengers where to pick up their luggage or meet their train. Hundreds of people darted from the ticket windows to the tracks and from the tracks to waiting taxis. I swore there were more passengers here than at Stapleton Airport the day before Thanksgiving. As we waited for Paul's train to arrive, Josie told me more about him, which certainly wasn't much. He was taller than Rordan and played the violin. He was in his mid-to-late twenties. His family was in the tire business and doing quite well for themselves.

She had missed one thing. He had the worst breath and teeth I'd ever encountered. For all his money, he should have seen a dentist more often. I was glad to have him take the front seat of the car. With his long legs, he would have been uncomfortable in the back with Rory, Josie, and me. When he took off his fedora, he reminded me of the square-faced Elton John, before the singer began to lose his hair, right down to his wire-rimmed glasses. Somehow the baggy pants, bow tie, and long, striped suit coat looked perfectly natural on him.

The skating rink was swarming with life: laughing children, spellbound lovers, and the occasional older couple. Rory helped me into my skates. Being nervous, I wanted to watch for a while. Paul and Rory finally coaxed me off the bench. To my astonishment, ice-skating was enough like Rollerblading that I took to it instantly. I didn't skate perfectly but did manage to stay on my feet.

"Never been on skates," Josie snorted.

"I guess I'm a natural," I said, grinning from ear to ear.

Josie grabbed Henry's hand and they drifted gracefully away. I stayed close to the rail for the better part of an hour before venturing into the throng of skaters near the center. There was a small and dark lump in the center of the rink. Thinking someone might trip over it and get hurt, I skated over and picked it up. It was a child's mitten. Scanning the dozens of children playing chase and other games, my eyes stopped on a little girl who looked to be frantically searching her pockets. I was nearly run down by a couple boys as I made my way over to the girl. "Is this yours?" I asked.

She looked up at me and then at the mitten. "Oh, yes. Thank you. Mother told me just this morning that should I lose one more set of mittens I wouldn't be allowed to have another set, and my fingers get so awfully cold."

Handing her the lost mitten, I realized my own fingers were cold. A stand offering hot cider and cocoa caught my eye. "Would you like something to warm your hands? Hot cider sounds good to me right now."

She smiled. "Mother gave me a nickel to buy cocoa."

"My treat. You save your nickel—in case you lose another mitten."

She smiled wider. "You're a nice lady."

We sat on a bench watching the skaters glide by. The sound of loud voices drew my attention. Near the edge of the rink two large men in heavy dark coats had Rory and Josie backed up against the wall.

"This ain't no place for a Mick," the biggest of the two said in a surly voice.

"Excuse me," I said to the girl as I got up to see why they were harassing my friends.

"Who let you Harps in? We don't need any dewdroppers here," said the other man, shaking his fist.

I was standing next to Rory now.

"Scum," said the first, waving a hand in the direction of the exit. "You Harps got no business in a classy place like this. You smell of panther sweat. I suggest you take your rummy skirt and get out of here before someone takes the two of you for a ride."

"Listen, dipstick," I said. "This dude has more class in his little finger than the both of you put together."

"Yeah?" the first thug said. "Tell it to Sweeny."

"This is totally bogus," I said, turning toward Rory. "Who are these jerks to tell you to leave?" In my anger I slipped, and my right foot went out in front of me, bumping the biggest guy's left foot, the one he happened to be resting all his weight on. As his foot went out from under him, he reached for his friend, bringing both of them down in a pile at my feet. I stared at them in surprise. Rory placed his arm in front of me as if to protect me from their certain anger. By now, Henry and Paul had come to see what the commotion was all about.

"What's this?" Henry asked.

"Jett knocked down these two crashers for razzing Rory and me," Josie said.

By now the two men had regained their feet, but being out numbered five against two, they shot us a dirty look and skated away.

"I didn't mean to . . . " I began, but Rory interrupted me, kissing my hand.

"You're exceptional. My thanks to you," he said.

"It was an accident. My foot slipped."

"So did your mouth," Josie said laughing. "That'll teach those Ethels."

Rory looked sharply at Josie. "You shouldn't say things like that."

"Like what?"

"Don't call people names. It's unbecoming, and frankly, beneath you."

She looked admonished.

"Seriously," I said. "I didn't mean to knock them down." Not that I was sorry it happened.

"You're too modest," Rory said.

The whole incident brought up memories of the day Bambi, Mike, Bobby, and I were on the Cherry Creek trail and Bambi had been harassed by a couple of 'roid boys. I couldn't get over how similar the incidents seemed. The time and place had changed, but that gut-wrenching feeling I had when I realized I'd placed myself in danger was *exactly* the same.

It was last July and the heat was scorching. Bambi had her boombox cranked. Bambi and I were skate-dancing on our Rollerblades to Aerosmith's *Rock and a Hard Place.*

"Ohmygod," she had said as the boys lagged behind us. "Like, we *totally* don't got all day."

I was reminded of what Jay had said about using poor language. Like Josie and her use of slang, Bambi was a smart girl, but at that moment she had sounded ignorant. The similarities were astounding.

I was waiting for Mike and Bobby under a bridge and Bambi had kept going. A few minutes later, two bulky guys in spandex shorts and muscle shirts had cornered her. I was pretty fast on my skates and as I got closer I heard the guy with a patchy beard say she had wicked big ta-tas, and the other creep wanted to pencil her in for a good boinking.

"Hey, penis-breath," I shouted at them. "Leave her alone. She ain't your type."

The beard turned toward me. "Well, maybe you are," he said, grinning.

"You know what happens when you use steroids? Big muscles, little dick. You ain't worth my time."

"Are those two scrawny dudes with you?" he'd asked. Next to these 'roid boys, Mike and Bobby looked small but not out of shape as they hustled toward us.

"Yeah, they are," I said. "Time for you to boogie on." To my amazement, the two men shrugged and walked away. Sometimes I opened my mouth and the most ridiculous things fell out.

Bobby had leaned close to my ear. "Next time, warn me if you're going to throw me under the bus. I'm a lover, not a fighter."

"'Roid boys are notoriously uncoordinated," I'd replied, feeling horribly guilty for putting the guys on the spot like that.

Mike gave me a friendly punch in the arm. "Remind me not to make a pass at you."

That day last summer, Bambi had looked at me just the way Josie was looking at me today. I never thought of myself as a tough girl, but I was protective of people I cared about, sometimes to the point of stupidity.

That the two incidents were so similar made my head hurt. It was as if I was reliving the last year of my life in a confusing jumble of random actions with the same results. The job at the store, the friendship with Jay–Josie; even the nurse who cared for me was astonishingly like my friend Penny, the woman who found me under the bridge the day I escaped Paisano. My brain wanted to explode with all of the absurdities. Everything was the same, but yet, everything was completely different.

"You should have seen her, Henry," Josie said. "She's a real bearcat."

"I suspected as much." Henry answered, placing a protective arm around his fiancée. "What was all the trouble?"

"The same," Rory said. "They didn't like the color of our hair."

Henry ruffled Josie's hair. "I think it's a splendid color."

That simple gesture knotted my stomach. My Henry used to ruffle my hair just like that.

The parallels continued in a bizarre way. My feelings for Bobby were not so unlike the feelings I now had for Henry. While I always considered Bobby to be out of my league, Henry was what? Out of my destiny? Out of my world?

The most confusing aspect of my feelings for Henry came from remembering him as my friend and caretaker of nearly eighty years old and then seeing a man of twenty. When I heard him speak, without looking at his face, he appeared in my mind's eye as the old Henry. Then I would look at him and my brain would tell me one thing while my heart would turn to mush. Although I was happy for Josie, some days I was incredibly jealous of her, and it was totally driving me whacky.

The remainder of the day was splendid. I skated with Rory and Paul several times and occasionally with Henry, although most of his time was taken up with Josie. As the day waned several children had become enamored with Josie and me while we led them in *A Tisket a Tasket,* a game I'd only just learned to play.

When the sun dropped below the range of mountains to the west, a chill wind told us it was time to call it a day. As tired as I was from skating for hours, I jumped at the offer to have dinner with the Doyle family once again. The housemother had given me permission to be out until eleven, and I wasn't about to waste it.

When we arrived at the Doyles', the domestic help was already preparing dinner. Connor and Brigid invited us to join them in the drawing room where we spent the next hour singing songs. It was an incredibly musical family. Even the littlest ones could sing and several played simple instruments as well.

Over dinner Paul regaled us with stories of Vermont and New York. It was all so exotic. Even though I'd seen many movies and photos of the places he described, it was all so new to me. The New York of this day was as renowned as the New York of my time.

When the conversation turned to politics I found myself totally engrossed. I needed to learn what was happening or chance another blundering encounter with the doctor or detective.

"I understand," shared Paul, "that President Coolidge opened the Holland Tunnel from his yacht using the same key that had been used for *opening* the Panama Canal in 1915."

"I am bewildered at the thought," Lillian said. "Imagine, a vehicular tunnel under the Hudson River."

"It is quite the engineering feat," said Connor. "It is a shame the engineer died before seeing it completed."

"The engineer?" I asked.

"Yes, Clifford Milburn Holland," Paul said. "He died in 1924. I believe it was his heart. The man worked on several tunnel projects. The tunnel was known as the Hudson River Tunnel, but it was renamed in his honor after he died."

"Oh," I said. "Like the Boulder Dam being changed to Hoover Dam."

Several sets of eyes turned on me. *Crap, crap, crap. I've done it again.*

"I've not heard of this dam," Henry said.

Connor leaned back on the legs of his chair. "You have some odd notions, young lady. One can only assume you're referring to the Secretary of Commerce, Herbert Hoover."

I didn't know. The name J. Edgar Hoover popped into my brain and then I was totally rattled. I realized the dam must not have been built yet. My education was sorely limited. I had always thought Hoover Dam was built in the twenties. Roosevelt was the Depression president. If it was a Depression project, shouldn't it be the Roosevelt Dam? Thankfully, I was saved from explaining myself by Thomas.

"I've heard rumblings," Thomas said, "about a possible dam slated for the boulder canyon on the Colorado River. It could be the Secretary of Commerce is somehow involved. It would be like him to try to name the project for himself to gain publicity for his presidential campaign."

"I've heard," Paul said, "that the dam will supply California with much needed electricity. Like New York, and Wall Street in particular, California is a boon."

"The wealth of Wall Street is a popular topic of the daily editorials," Thomas said, "but I fear the instability of the German economy. I'll not soon forget how easily the States were drawn into the conflicts of Europe."

Connor nodded. "The *New York Times* has posted on the economic status of many European countries as of the close of the Great War. According to the writings of Larisa Reisner, Germany lost much."

Thomas said, "Weimar's economy is doomed by high labor costs. The system of state arbitration will drive labor costs up, rendering German goods uncompetitive on world markets. The export surpluses that should finance reparations will never be materialized."

Paul shook his head. "I respectfully disagree. I would argue that the stock market crash in Berlin this past May is the primary factor for the subsequent fall in investment spending."

Connor buttered a fat roll. "They owe much of their economic recovery to the stimulus of American dollars in the form of loans."

"I have family in Berlin," Paul said as he passed the bowl of fruit salad to his left. "Stresemann has had great influence, and the workers in Germany are able to afford much these days. The German Republic is a most fertile ground for the modern arts and sciences. Berlin, in particular, is a thriving center of many new art movements such as expressionism."

"But their economy is inflating at a drastic rate," Thomas said. "It can't go on. There must be a balance between labor and value."

Paul said, "According to the Volkischer Beobachter, the hyperinflation that Germany suffered a few years ago was caused by Jewish bankers and financiers dictating policy to the world and holding it to ransom." He took the bowl of potatoes from Josie and spooned a few onto his plate. "The new leader of the NSDAP is a stout proponent of the workingman and warns us of the dangers of religious fundamentalist and Stalin's Marxist ideologies. I understand he is an excellent orator." Paul cut his beef into small bites. "His name is Hitler, Adolf Hitler."

I almost spit out my peas.

My discomfort unnoticed, Paul continued, "Everyone should read his memoir, *Mein Kampf.* It means *My Struggle.* My father sent a copy to me. The man is gaining popular support by attacking the Treaty of Versailles and promoting anti-communism."

I could barely keep my mouth closed. Gentle, soft-spoken Paul was a Nazi. *How can I tell these people what a monster Hitler would become?* I settled for saying, "Charismatic people are capable of swaying good men to do evil things. I don't trust him."

"What do you know of him?" Paul asked.

"Not much." What I did know was too far in the future to suggest. "If he is all you say he is, he would be terribly powerful, and powerful people can be extremely dangerous. Absolute power corrupts absolutely." Now Henry was staring at me. I couldn't remember where I'd first heard the phase, but hoped it had been said before 1927.

"Please don't mistake my meaning, Miss Oxford," Thomas said with concern. "Whilst sometimes when you speak I feel you haven't the luxury of a formal education, at other times you go and say something quite brilliant. I had no notion your studies included the writings of Lord Acton."

It was a curious compliment.

Paul seemed to regard me with interest now. I wanted to quote all the great thinkers in hope of swaying support in this dangerous situation but "yaba daba doo" was all that came to mind. I liked Paul. I was having a hard time seeing him in this new light though. I felt helpless to change the course of history, but maybe I could get to this one man.

I would have to go back to the library to learn what I could of present-day politics. I'd seen articles about the Bolsheviks and I recognized the names of Stalin, Trotsky, and Lenin, but without more Russian history, I didn't know how to frame the argument. I knew Stalin would help the United States win the next war, but he, too, would murder millions of innocent people before the end of the century. Feeling frustrated, I ate the remainder of my dinner in silence. What good did it do to know the future if you had no way of changing the bad parts. World War II was going to be bad and the Depression was right around the corner. The crash of Wall Street might destroy the lives of everyone at this table. Suddenly, the beautiful dresses Josie had given me weighed heavy on my mind. *Oh, why hadn't I paid more attention to my Henry when he tried to teach me about history and finances?*

CHAPTER 11

Josie had insisted we get together at her house on the thirtieth so we would have all night and day to prepare for the masquerade party. While helping me curl my hair in rags and pins so it could be swept into an elaborate coiffure, she listed all the young men who would be attending the party.

"Those who would partake in our hospitality are not what one would call 'society,' but good fellows all the same."

"I told you. I'm not looking for a man."

"Nonsense. All women need a decent fellow to care for and to take care of them. You won't be able to stay at the orphanage forever. What will you do when they put you out?"

I hadn't thought about it. As long as I was teaching a class or two, I thought I would be safe from eviction. But Josie was right; the housemother was always asking about my propositions.

"I'll deal with it soon enough, I guess. In the meantime, don't try to hook me up."

Josie giggled. "*For sure*," she teased. "I won't *hook* you up."

Breakfast was served much like dinner: formal with several courses. My dress was going to be tight enough without eating everything the Doyles offered, so I tried to go easy on the chow. I did have a slice of ham, an egg, toast, and tea. Josie and I talked about the party as Rory and Paul scarfed down bacon, ham, sausage, biscuits, eggs, fried potatoes, oatmeal, and what looked like canned pears.

Josie poured heavy cream on her oatmeal. "The party is going to be berries, just berries!"

As usual, I had to wait for context to understand what Josie was saying. Though I guessed "berries" meant a good thing.

"I posted the invitations last week," Rory said. "All of the art community is ablaze with excitement. Paul, you must meet my fellow musicians. Mum has invited everyone."

"Of course, she should never have done it," Josie insisted as she sipped her apple juice.

Rory helped himself to more ham. "Done what?"

"Mum invited Mrs. Crawford Hill."

"Who?" I asked.

"Only the most famous socialite in all of the city, Mrs. Crawford Hill. She is most likely to be hosting her own gala this evening."

Rory rolled his eyes. "Then I guess you won't have to worry about her coming tonight."

"Mum gets ever so depressed when those high hats snub her."

"So why does she do it?" he asked, stuffing another biscuit in his mouth.

"Because I can," answered Mother Doyle from the door. "Rordan, you needn't eat everything on the table. It will keep well enough."

She took a seat near us opposite Paul and Rory. "I will always invite everyone in my social class and let them be the ones to lack manners by declining to answer. I will not be accused of having poor etiquette. The tables, one day, may be turned."

"But they never acknowledge you, Mother."

"And for that, we can be thankful, as I wouldn't want them to come, what with their bigotry and such. But it is what a civilized family does, to invite the lot of them. How they would titter and gossip about our party if they knew we would be entertained by jazz musicians." Brigid smiled brightly.

Josie shook her head. "Well, they're going to miss a wonderful party, Mother."

Brigid beamed. "I promise you, they will."

"I'm going to have a bath now. Is Maria busy?" Josie stood.

"It's her day out. Guadalupe is helping with the little ones. She should be down soon. Shall I send her to your room?"

"That would be wonderful, Mother. Can someone bring up the black steamer trunk from the basement?"

Mrs. Doyle looked over at the two young men just finishing their breakfast. "Rordan and Paul shall retrieve it for you."

From the looks on their faces, I gathered the trunk was rather heavy.

On the way to the bedrooms, Josie said, "Let's check the decorations in the ballroom. Maria and Guadalupe have been working on them all week."

The ballroom took up the entire third floor above the master suite of rooms and the nursery. I counted eight dormers where the evening sunlight trickled in to compete with an array of Japanese lanterns. A huge, arched Palladian window on the gable end of the room overlooked the gardens on the west side of the house. The musicians' gallery was on a raised landing overlooking the ballroom. Because there were no columns or partitions, the room was perfect for dancing and the vaulted ceilings would amplify the music of the band or orchestra. I marveled at the beautifully polished parquet floor.

As promised, the room was draped with a chiffon-like fabric and the cocktail tables decorated in gold and silver lamé. Red and gold Christmas decorations added to the sense of festivity. I wondered how well the little ones would sleep with a couple dozen partiers dancing until all hours of the morning.

After a hot bath, Josie helped me into a Flat-O-Form bra, effectively binding my breasts so that my gown would hang gracefully from the shoulder. The gown itself was made of satin and batiste, with light boning to flatten the diaphragm as well as the bust. Several hooks ran down the high back. It wasn't comfortable, but it is what one did in the day. Guadalupe helped each of us into our gowns. Even bound, the dress was snug across my chest.

Josie found a beautiful headdress of jet beads and peacock feathers for me to wear while her cap was a net of fine crystal beads with oval marquise-cut rubies set in silver filigree. A ruby necklace accented the low cut of her dress. With a wide smile she thanked Guadalupe for her help and sat gracefully down on the bed.

"Let's review the list once more," she said in all seriousness.

"As you wish," I said, sitting in a Morris chair across from the bed.

"First we have Paul. Paul is incredibly nice, but he'll be leaving for the east soon. My brother Rory would be a good catch. Be sure to dance with him often."

"As you wish."

"Now Samuel Highgarden comes from a good family, but he's promised to Mimi Johnson." The list went on and it soon became clear that Josie's choice for me was, first and foremost, Rory. Although the playful redhead and I had bonded as friends, there was a mystery about Rory; he was holding back. But I wouldn't pry; I had secrets, too.

Josie had suggested we skip lunch so we could pig-out at the buffet all evening. Because we were hungry, we were the first to enter the ballroom. The band was seated on a small riser in the corner of the room. I shouldn't have been surprised to see an elegant female vocalist greet us as we crossed the floor, but I was. Josie had given me the impression that black jazz singers only performed in the Five Points speakeasies. I turned to see Paul's reaction but he was engrossed in conversation with Connor. The singer was dressed in a red and white sequin and lace shift dripping with black beaded fringe that accented her trim figure whenever she moved. A wide black sequin band sporting soft feathers encircled her tightly braided hair.

"Julianne, you look so beautiful tonight," Josie said as we reached the stage.

"You're such a dear to welcome me. You have a lovely home."

"I'd be a beast if I didn't. When did you arrive?"

"We're only now tuning up."

"Julianne, I'd like you to meet my friend, Jett Oxford." Josie turned back to me. "Jett, this is the lovely and talented Julianne Florence Rosa Parker."

"Very nice to meet you," I said, slipping off my glove and holding out my hand.

Julianne's dark eyes met mine warily, but after a moment she smiled and shook my hand. From the corner of my eye, I saw Josie flinch. I'd done it again. Maybe I should have curtsied. Later that evening I understood that was not my mistake. No one took Julianne's hand unless it was gloved, and even then, only Mrs. Doyle and Mrs. Watson. It was then that I realized how progressive these two ladies were.

In costly evening gowns and correct swallowtail coats, guests rubbed elbows with names famous and infamous in Denver's art and music world. If it had ever crossed my mind that this would be a stuffy shindig, I was dead wrong. Many guests were as much a part of the entertainment as the eclectic jazz band in the corner, who, by request, also played an Irish jig and what might have been a German polka. In another corner, someone was reciting lines from a recent play he had written, and by the lavish buffet table, two women were fawning over some hand-painted stationery.

As new guests arrived, Josie introduced me to painters, sculptors, actors, and, of course, many musicians. The room was filling up fast now and she led me over to a friendly-looking man.

"This is Samuel Highgarden," she said. "Samuel, this is Miss Jett Oxford." He was stocky, resting his weight on one leg like a western cowboy.

"A pleasure, Miss Oxford," he said, brushing his lips across my gloved hand.

"Nice to meet you."

"Well, bless my soul! If it isn't Miss Mimi Johnson," Josie said as a rail thin woman came into the room. Before the woman had a chance to get her bearings, Josie tucked her arm through Samuel's and dragged him to Mimi.

"Oh, it's so good of you to come." Josie beamed at the new arrival.

"I wouldn't have missed it," Mimi said, smiling through scarlet lipstick. "This is the social engagement of the year." She allowed Samuel to take her hand.

"You look ravishing tonight, Miss Johnson." He bent to kiss her gloved fingers.

"Why, thank you, good sir." Mimi blushed prettily in pink lace and white satin; her dark hair, in a swirl of braids, framed her face.

"Would you like something to drink?" he asked. "Father will be here after nine o'clock with my cousins, Ida and Leona. I'm afraid I must entertain them a good part of the evening."

"Until then, I'm going to have you all I like," she said, nestling into the curve of his arm and allowing him to lead her toward the punch table.

"What was that all about?" I asked Josie as soon as the couple was out of sight.

"She thinks he's perfectly wonderful in every way, I should judge. In fact, she simply raved over him."

"I gathered that much, but why did you push him on her the moment she arrived?"

"Did I truly do such a dreadful thing as that?"

"Duh."

Josie burst out laughing. "For heaven's sake, what have you got hold of now? What is 'duh'?"

How could I explain? "Never mind," I said, somewhat exasperated. "Why did you force Samuel to greet Mimi?"

"He is good and kind, and means well, I suppose."

"But . . . "

"Well, did you see the way Abigail has been at his heels all night?"

"And he's promised to Mimi."

"Not yet, but I expect it any day now."

"And you don't want Abigail to interfere."

"I shouldn't say this, but Abigail has broken off three engagements. It's not my affair, but I do so love Mimi and Samuel."

I nodded my head. Abigail wasn't Christie Brinkley, but she was a definite headturner. As if she knew we were talking about her, the tall blond walked over.

"Good evening, Miss Josephine," she said, holding her head high and somehow making the simple words sound demeaning.

"Hello, Abigail. I'd like you to meet my friend, Jett Oxford. She's new to Denver."

"Hello, Miss Oxford. I couldn't help noticing your dress."

"Thank you," I said. "I think it's beautiful. Josie gave it to me."

"Why, yes, of course. That's where I've seen this garment before. Josie wore it last year, and I believe her aunt wore a gown dreadfully similar three years back."

"Truly," Josie said. "My dear Abigail. I hadn't realized you were so old as to be attending my mother's galas these many years." The silence stretched a shade too long before Josie said, "Forgive me. That was rude."

Abigail's perfect bow-shaped lips smiled thinly as she tugged at her elbow-length black gloves. "I saw Mimi come in. She isn't shy in her pursuit of Samuel. She has her arm locked in his as if she's afraid he might wander away."

In return, Josie batted her kohl-darkened lashes. "They are such a lovely couple."

"I suppose it never hurts to come from a wealthy family," Abigail said, ignoring Josie's taunt. "Cattle, isn't it?"

"He has plenty much money of his own." Josie cleared her throat with a shallow cough. "He's wasted little time in wooing her. I heard he took her to the theater only last week."

Abigail looked smug. "He asked me to the theater last week as well, but I had a prior engagement. He must have been forced to ask

Mimi when I couldn't attend. Well, it only goes to show you where his heart lies."

Josie adjusted her headpiece as if she'd lost interest in the conversation. "If the truth be told, Samuel was, at present, attending the play with Mimi. It was she who suggested Samuel call on you. It was for Mimi's brother, he asked you to join." Josie paused just long enough for her words to set. "Is it true as you say, you were dining with Daniel Crenshaw? I've heard he proposes marriage as regularly as he puts gasoline in his jalopy."

Abigail blanched, but before she could utter a sound, Josie grabbed my arm. "Look, there's Rory and Paul. I think they shall be playing for us tonight. Come. Let's see what they're devising."

She led me across the room in a rush. "I know," Josie said. "I was somewhat boorish to Abigail. I don't know why she has to give us the high hat, and at our own party."

"Some people have to put others down so they can feel better about themselves."

"I'm ever so glad you aren't like that. By George, but she was game over that dress."

"I don't mind. I'm proud to wear it."

When we arrived, Rory was introducing Paul to Julianne. If he felt anything other than respect, he didn't show it. Could I have misunderstood the conversation at dinner that night? Maybe Paul was only picking up bigoted ideas because of the German newspaper he was always reading. After all, he liked the Doyle family and they certainly weren't German. I felt the need to keep my eye on him all the same.

"Where have you been?" Josie asked her brother after Julianne went to join several other musicians at a table reserved for them.

Setting his saxophone on the table next to the small riser, Rory said, "Paul and I picked up some giggle water and have just this minute come in from an automobile ride." He grinned widely at Josie's look of shock.

"We wanted to have a go at the entertainment tonight and required a certain amount of liquid encouragement. Would you like a quilt?"

"No," Josie said.

I just stared with my mouth open. I had no clue why Rory was offering Josie a quilt.

"Swell, that means more hooch for the boys."

"Don't let Mother catch you with that."

"You didn't hear it from me," Rory whispered, "but it was mother who sent me out to get it. She put some in the punch."

Josie's jaw dropped to match mine. "Are you on the level?"

"Honest as the day is long. She says it helps people relax and be more social."

"Hey, Henry. Over here." Rory waved.

From across the dance floor, Henry's eyes searched the room.

"Paul, get us set up. I'm going to find Mother. Don't start without me."

Paul placed his stand-up bass next to the table and opened a case holding a guitar.

"Cool," I said. "Do you play both of these?"

He looked at me curiously. "I do. I also play a few reed instruments, but I didn't like to take from Rory's accomplishments."

Josie offered, "Rory plays the saxophone and clarinet."

"As well as the organ and piano." I recalled how beautifully he had played at church on Sunday.

"Since there is no piano in the ballroom, he'll play the saxophone tonight. Henry plays the trumpet and sometimes a guitar."

"All you need is a drummer," I said, thinking it would be nice to hear some rock and roll.

"Oh, Paul can play the drums, too."

"Seriously?"

Josie smiled. "Seriously. I can play the piano but that's all. My little sister Caitlin plays beautifully. She takes after Rory."

The only thing I could play with any success was the stereo, and that wasn't going to be invented for a few years yet.

Rory came back with Henry, carrying two delicate glasses of punch. He handed a glass to Josie.

"You doll up nice," Josie said, taking the glass and kissing Henry on the cheek.

I had to agree. All the men looked pretty good tonight, but the indigo satin jacket Henry wore made his eyes especially blue.

As we chatted, Abigail was making her way toward the stage. "Nice chassis," Paul said, looking her over.

"That's so not PC," I said, offended.

He turned to me. "Peace?"

"P. C. Politically correct."

"Politically correct?" he mused over the line. "That doesn't make sense. If something is political, it's political, and not necessarily correct. If it's correct, it isn't political, it's correct."

Now he had my head spinning. "It isn't nice to talk about a girl like that."

"Like what?"

"Calling her a chassis. Talking about her body like that."

Paul looked hurt. "I meant it as a compliment. She's pretty."

I was starting to feel stupid now. Even Josie was looking at me like I had boogers hanging from my nose.

Rory leaned toward me. "Then I guess I shouldn't say she has nice gams."

I rolled my eyes but didn't say a word. I was out of my element, for sure.

Abigail made the rounds, greeting Rory and Henry as if they were paupers and she a queen, but when she turned on Paul, the Ice Queen dripped with smarmy compliments. Paul was handsome, Paul was talented, and Paul was someone she wanted to know.

Abigail slipped her arm in Paul's and leaned over confidently. "It's such a travesty, don't you agree, that Josie couldn't have a debutante ball. How will the dear girl find a properly refined man?"

"That's way harsh," I said. "Are you brain-dead? Henry's a great guy."

Everyone was staring at me now, thinking I was about to go ballistic, I'm sure. "Come on, Josie," I said. "I'm hungry, and the guys should probably tune up." I could feel their eyes on me as I walked away.

Josie caught up to me in a heartbeat. "Did you see her face when you asked if she was brain-dead?" She giggled. "You're a real live wire. Where do you come up with those things?"

I shrugged. She wouldn't believe me if I told her, and I was dying to tell someone. My greatest fear wasn't screwing up common etiquette but letting slip the truth. Surely, I'd be locked away forever if I did.

As we walked passed the buffet table for the third time, Henry's mother joined us.

"I've been waiting to speak to you, my dear," she said to me. "Thomas and I have decided to keep you on through Saint Valentine's Day."

"That—that's great. Thank you so much."

"You're extraordinarily talented. We're glad to have you."

The rest of the evening we danced and flirted with all the young men. In between singing a few blues numbers, dancing to the latest jazz rift, and eating more than a girl of her slight build should be able to eat, Josie shared stories about other parties and some of the more notorious guests who had attended. I wanted to tell her about things I'd done, but couldn't. A part of me was sure she would understand and accept anything I told her; yet another voice in the back of my mind said, *You can't trust anyone. You don't even know what is true and what isn't. Maybe you* are *crazy.*

The longer I was here in 1927, now turning to 1928, the more real this life became and the more my old life faded away. Jet airliners, color televisions, the moon landing; these were the devices of science fiction.

CHAPTER 12

The political conversation over the holidays led me to the library once more. It was comforting to sit in the quiet hall, away from the constant activity of the orphanage. The hours at the library also gave me much-needed time to practice my penmanship. The housemother had been appalled when I gave her my first class outline. Although I had learned cursive in school, I printed more often than not.

I returned *Nature's Teachings* by Reverend J.G. Wood and *Radio Activity* by E. Rutherford. Skimming through the books, I knew they wouldn't tell me anything about time travel. Unfortunately, *Science and the Future* by Haldane was of no help either. Although his view of the future of man was strikingly familiar, he never discussed ways to transport a human in time. I was beginning to believe I would have to wait for whatever force of nature brought me here to decide to send me back. Try as I might, I couldn't find any books by Stephen Hawking or anything about black holes. I did read *The Time Machine* by H. G. Wells, hoping for insight. While it was a fascinating story, I couldn't find anything in the candy store that might be interpreted as a time machine. I was heartened by this, as I never wanted to wake up in a world run by Morlocks.

In a corner I thumbed through *An Inquiry into the Nature and Causes of Wealth of Nations* by Adam Smith. If I wanted to save the Watsons and Doyles from financial ruin, I would need at least a minimum understanding of economics. The problem lay in that no one seemed to agree on what made for a good and thriving economy.

I was inspired by *On Liberty* by John Stewart Mill and decided to give the book to Paul along with some articles written by Winston Churchill.

The National Western Stock Show had evolved over the years. In my day, the rodeo was a huge attraction. Thousands of participants flocked to the city to buy and sell cattle, horses, and all nature of livestock. Although the Stock Show of the twenties had little more than cattle and the 4-H Roundup event, it drew crowds from all over the country. Thomas and Henry went to purchase meat for the year and a local butcher stored it in a locker for them.

"It was a good show," Thomas said, "but the prices are higher than I remember."

"You say that every year," Henry said as he took off a pair of boots I'd never seen him wear before. I smiled to myself. They looked good on him.

Lillian came into the kitchen and kissed Thomas on the cheek. "You must be hungry. I'll heat up a plate of chicken."

"We are," Thomas said settling down by the stove and lighting his pipe. "Some of the vendors had samples, but the price they were asking was beyond reason." He glanced over the *Rocky Mountain News* as Lillian and I prepared a late lunch.

"Well, doesn't that beat all? Did you see this?" he asked.

"What is it, dear? I haven't read the dailies yet."

"The Supreme Court of Tennessee overturned the conviction of John Scopes on the technical ground that the fine was set by the judge rather than, as the state constitution required, by the jury."

"The man convicted in the Monkey Trial?" Henry said from the pantry.

"Don't call it that," Lillian scolded. "It wasn't about evolution, it was about the states' right to dictate school curriculums."

Thomas sighed, and I realized this had been a subject of great family discussion. "States shouldn't enact laws prohibiting the teaching of evolution."

Henry sat down at the table, munching on an apple. "Until one theory or the other can be proved, they should teach both."

"The problem," Lillian said, "is that when science proclaims a theory, they claim it is a proven fact."

Henry nodded. "And Fundamentalists claim the Bible is a history book and all its writings are literal and factual."

The discussion went unresolved for the evening.

January wasn't a big candy season, but with Valentine's Day just around the corner, Lillian was teaching me new skills every day. Although candy was the mainstay of the store, the Watsons had a few select items in high demand. Across the street, the Oxford Hotel had a bakery, but it was the "Watson's Cinnamon Roll" the hotel clientele most desired. The hotel ordered trays of rolls, so Lillian was up at four in the morning churning out her unique family recipe for potato-bread rolls.

When I came into work at five, Lillian left me in charge of rolling out the dough and slathering on her special mixture of butter, sugar, and cinnamon. The day was chilly and the oven's fire gave the kitchen that feeling of home that can't be created any way other than through fresh baking bread, cinnamon, and a wood fire.

While standing in the kitchen, rolling out the third batch of dough, I heard voices. In the showroom, as the family liked to call the front of the store, Thomas Watson was telling Henry about some stock he'd purchased the week before. His broker felt it should do well enough over the next two years to pay off the second mortgage on the store and still have the original investment. I realized Thomas Watson had mortgaged his store to invest in the stock market. "I also bought a few items on margin," he'd said with pride.

This was bad. When the market crashed, the Watsons would lose everything.

Turning in aimless circles I tried to remember everything my Henry had once said about the great stock market crash of the twenties. I knew it happened in October. October 29th, 1928; no, October 28th, 1929. Why couldn't I remember?

I still had a few months either way. But how was I going to convince Thomas Watson that he needed to sell all his stock and pay off the store? I knew so little about the stock market.

OH, HOLY CRAP!

It suddenly hit me why Henry of my time had spent endless days teaching me about economics. Of course, he and Josie recognized me when I showed up on their doorstep. They knew I would be here now. This was awesome! I could tell them I had come from the future. Maybe they would even know how to send me back.

I jerked the apron off, intending to tell them all about the crash and the imminent Depression when the second epiphany hit me. Of course they knew about me in the eighties … because all this had happened fifty-five years in *their* past.

Oh crap, oh crap, oh crap. I still can't tell them I'm from the future. But they remembered me, so I must have made an impression. Did I convince them to pay off the store? Think, girl. What did Henry tell you?

What stocks did they buy? Did they invest in bonds? They owned the store in the eighties. Henry said his father left it to him free and clear. When did his father die? He told me, but sadly, I didn't think it was important.

Okay, pull yourself together. You have to talk stocks and bonds like a man. No way. They'll never listen to me. I'm a homeless girl who likes to make candy.

I went back to making the rolls. My heart hurt. I needed to help them, but I didn't know how. One word about the future and I'd be back in the hospital with Dr. Mortenson and Marjorie.

It was hard to sleep at night as dreams of the eighties tangled up with the twenties. I woke each morning sure it was 1982 until the sounds of streetcars and smell of burning wood jerked me back to my nightmare of 1928. For days, I stewed over the problem of how to help my friends. As a part-time employee, I was not someone who had deep financial conversations with the storeowners. To make matters more difficult, the Doyles had invested heavily in the stock market as well.

Thankfully, Paul gave me the opening I needed, although I had to settle for speaking with Henry and hoping he would speak to Connor Doyle and his father himself.

It was a cool Saturday afternoon in February. As usual, a large group of us went to most social events together. Sometimes joined by Mimi and Sam, but usually just the five of us. This day, Rory had been asked to help his dad haul wood from Golden, so it was Jay, Henry, Paul, and me who had been to the picture show to see *The Jazz Singer*. I wasn't impressed with the quality of picture or sound and couldn't feign an excitement I didn't share. One day my friends would see epic movies in Technicolor on screens twenty feet high, movies like *Star Wars*, *The Godfather*, and *Jaws*. I blamed my lack of enthusiasm on a headache.

"I know what you need," Paul said as he opened the car door for me. "The drugstore at the corner on Second and Broadway has a wonderful cherry phosphate."

I didn't know what a phosphate was, but it probably wasn't aspirin. "Don't worry about me," I said. "I'll get over it."

"That would be swell," Josie said. "We'd love a phosphate, wouldn't we, Jett?"

"Sure." This would be another new experience, one that didn't sound too frightening.

Five minutes later, we were sitting in a quaint drugstore with shelves upon shelves laden with little glass bottles. The bottles varied little save the tiny print touting a profusion of remedies for everything from the common cold to gout. It was fascinating. The counter was wooden, as was the floor. I looked for chrome and vinyl stools and then realized it wouldn't be until the forties or fifties that malt shops would replace the corner drug store. On the back wall was a sign professing "For Headache and Exhaustion Drink Coca-Cola. 5 Cents a Glass. Delicious and Refreshing."

I was pretty exhausted, so I ordered a Coke.

Josie cocked her head. "Coke?"

"I'll have a Coca-Cola," I quickly revised.

The man behind the counter gave us each a drink. Josie had a cherry phosphate, while Paul and Henry had a drink called a Black Cow. Even though it was cold outside, I was used to drinking my Coke over ice. Since the drink was cool, I didn't make a fuss about the ice. It tasted good, but different.

As we nursed our sodas, Paul was telling Henry about investing in the newest telephone technology. That sounded like a smart thing to do. Telephones were going to be around forever. Ma Bell might lose value during the crash, but she would recover eventually. The phone service to London from New York had only been established the past January. Once more, that uncomfortable shade visited me, reminding me how many things that I had previously taken for granted hadn't been invented yet. One day, everyone would have his own private phone number. One day, blue jeans would be in vogue, and one day electric rollers would replace rags and hairpins.

Josie was excited about being able to call London from New York. "Do you realize now we can telephone New York and they can connect us straight away to London."

"Do you know anyone in London?" Paul asked. A grin tickled the edge of his lips.

"No, but don't you think it's just jake that you can make the call?"

"Yes, I suppose it is. I should like to speak with my family in Berlin."

Josie beamed. "Talking movies, conversations with someone half the world away, and electric lights in every home—don't you love living in the modern world?"

I giggled. There would be many new inventions in the next few years. It would be fascinating to see the world change the way it would. Not so fascinating that I wouldn't go home given the chance, but to see it through the eyes of those who don't know what's coming would be fun. Knowing what inventions would make it and what things would only be a passing fad could help me select the right stocks. I had to choose wisely so as not to sound insane. "I think you should buy Coca-Cola stock," I said, knowing it would be around at least as long as telephones. "Isn't it wonderful? The ads even say it's good for headaches. Everyone gets headaches." Okay, this was pushing it, but if that's how Coke stayed on top of the game, who was I to tell them their marketing was a joke?

Henry gave me that look again; the look that said I said something outside of his expectations. "What do you know about investing in stocks?" he asked.

"I know that you can give money to a broker and he'll buy small parts of a company. If the company does well, so will the investor."

"It isn't that simple," Paul said. "There are lots of companies that buy and sell other companies. There are commodities, precious metals, and bonds."

"And there are blue chip stocks," I said, "which are stocks from well-established and financially sound companies. They're usually leaders in their industries and household names, like Coca-Cola."

"All stocks are doing quite well now," Paul replied. "There is much money available. Banks are ever more willing to lend money, so everyone is investing in new businesses."

"So, what happens," I asked, "if the banks decided to collect on all of their loans?"

"Why would they do that? They're making money on interest."

"If the bank foreclosed on a loan, the bank would take the business, right?

Paul's brows knitted. "Why would they foreclose if the payments are being made? The banks don't cause businesses to fail."

"The banks already own most of those businesses because they're bought on credit, right? What if the bank suddenly sold all their stocks in the auto industry at these extremely high prices and bought, say, a movie company?"

It was Henry who answered. "If the bankers suddenly started selling off their stocks, the stock prices would drop."

I nodded. "Now the person who invested in the auto industry can't pay his home loan because the bank foreclosed on his stock margin and he can't sell the automobile stock for what it cost him last week."

Henry wasn't about to give in. "The automobile industry is doing great. They're making cars faster than we can buy them."

"Well, if that's true," I said, "who is buying all of the extra cars? If there are too many cars on the market, the price of the cars will drop, meaning the auto company you bought yesterday might not be worth as much today, but you would still have to pay back the loan you used to buy it. If you can't pay back the loan, you have to close or sell. Now another person can buy back the loan for half of what it cost you. And if you close, everyone working at the auto plant is out of a job, so they can't pay their home loans either."

"Well," Paul said with interest. "I suppose you would have to sell other stocks to pay off the automobile company loan."

"And by selling off that stock, those prices would drop, too, wouldn't they? Then more and more people would sell, and then everyone would want to cash out their stocks and get their money from the banks, but the banks wouldn't have any money because they loaned it all out. Now the smaller banks fail because they were investing in the borrowers." I was starting to scare myself.

Henry looked over at Paul as if to judge his reaction to my extreme prognosis.

Paul shook his head and said, "If the banks fail, and I'm not saying that's possible, who would get all the property bought on credit?"

Henry got it. He understood the point I'd been trying to make. "The bankers," he said, "who were ahead of the game. The ones who held real property and promissory notes."

Paul brushed off my dire prediction. "Things are going so well, why would the banks do something that could potentially, and I mean, potentially, cause such devastation?"

Henry rubbed his chin in deep thought. "I suppose in doing so, it would potentially make those investors very, very wealthy."

Paul looked at me closely. "What if the government took over the banks to protect us?"

"If the government ran the banks, they would control the economy." I thought for a moment. "If they controlled the economy, wouldn't that be like communism?"

"That's when the government owns all the raw materials and land. There is no private property." Paul sipped on his drink.

"What is socialism?" I asked.

"When the government owns all the major industries as well," he replied.

Henry shook his head. "It not that simple, but doesn't sound like there's much difference. Socialism refers to a range of collectivist political and economic ideas that may or may not promote high levels of state intervention."

"The state has to interfere, Henry," I said. "Someone has to divide the spoils. Someone has to hand out the food and shelter. Who would do that if not the government? If everything you have is bought on credit and the government or some wealthy banker owns all the money and your mortgages . . . " I let them think about it for a while. "Isn't it better to own your own company, house, and car?"

I don't know what caused the crash, but my Henry told me some people made out splendidly while others lost everything. "If stock prices drop, you could buy companies back for pennies on the dollar. That's what I would do."

"Where would I get the money?" Paul asked. "According to you, I just lost everything in the stock market when the prices fell."

"If I had any money now, I would buy land, but only if I could pay it off and afford the taxes. I wouldn't take on any debt."

Henry stared at me. "You're quite ambitious."

Josie was getting antsy by now and, being the gentleman that he was, Henry offered to take us to a new dance place.

"I need to get home," I said. "I have domestic duties calling my name."

Josie chuckled as she tugged on her bell-shaped cloche. "You're so funny. It's unfortunate you can't come. Rory and Henry are playing in the band."

"I'm sorry. I love listening to you guys play. I'll be there next time, you can count on it."

As much as I wanted to go, being around Henry made me uneasy, always on my guard not to share a joke or memory that hadn't taken place yet. I was too comfortable with him and he was very relaxed around me. The familiarity was to be expected, we were good friends in the eighties. Seeing him as a young man, knowing how loving and generous he could be, I was envious of Josie and it was taxing to hide my feelings. The days Henry was called away from the store were almost a blessing. I could enjoy my time with Lillian, much like I had once enjoyed my time with Jay. If hiding was what I had to do, I would. Not only was I sure getting involved with Henry would ruin any chance of my going home, I could never do anything to hurt Josie, the younger or the elder.

I was more comfortable at the orphanage now. Visiting the library to read old newspapers helped immensely. Having a job kept me away and helped me dodge questions from Alice and the other girls, although I always looked forward to the days Marjorie would visit. She wasn't one to pry into my past, preferring to focus on my current friends.

She sipped tea in the parlor, watching the snow fall. "I've not seen any reports of the Doyles' party in the daily gossip columns. Perchance I missed it."

"Denver society tends not to report on certain people, no matter how rich they are." I nibbled on a cookie. "But it was magnificent."

"Their home must be lovely."

"It's about the nicest place I've seen. Imagine having a ballroom in your house. Will the doctor be coming by today?" I asked.

"No, but he'll see you tomorrow. Is everything alright with you?"

"Yes, I'm fine. I was just wondering." I liked to mentally prepare myself for his visits. During December and January, I had seen Dr. Mortenson on occasion. He seemed less concerned about my memory now that I seemed to have adjusted well to my new surroundings, but a new suspicion was rising.

I sipped my tea and changed the subject, hoping to learn anything new. "That detective, Matthews, came by last week to see if I could tell him anything else," I said nonchalantly. "Of course, I couldn't. He just won't let up."

Marjorie looked unsurprised by the news. "I have found detectives love a mystery."

I sighed. "It really isn't important that I remember these things. I'm doing just fine."

The next day, as promised, the good doctor sought me out. "I'm to understand you have grown rather close to the Doyle family."

"Yes, Henry Watson introduced me to the family in December. I told you this. Josephine is a great girl. She's Henry's fiancée."

"I understand they are a family of means."

I considered him for a while. He had once accused me of being from a wealthy family. Could he suspect they might not be new friends? "They have been especially nice to me. I lost everything last October, and they've been enormously generous."

He wrote something in his notebook. "How many hours are you employed?"

"Counting my duties here, about fifty to sixty hours a week."

"You're dressing in fine apparel these days."

"Miss Doyle gave me some clothes. She said they were planning to give them away to a girls' home anyway, and I'm close to her in size."

Something about his remarks had me on edge. Ever afraid of being sent back to the psych ward, I was careful with my answers.

"I've come to understand you often engage in financial conversations."

What that had to do with clothing was beyond me. "We have discussed the stock market among other things."

"And do you advise them on purchases?"

This was tricky. I did, to a small extent, but the way he was asking told me my answer should be no. "I don't know one stock from another," I said.

Again, he made his notes. It was to be several months before he again brought up my seemingly uncharacteristic relationship with the Doyle family.

The following day I worked on a new recipe for gingerbread. Ginger was a luxury we had been saving for Henry and Josie's engagement party to be held on Saturday, the twenty-fifth of February. It wouldn't be a debutante ball, but it was sure to be a spectacular event.

Josie was bouncing off the walls with excitement. She'd come to the store to tell me about the guest list. "Paul has decided to stay on until after the party. Isn't that the ant's ear?"

"I think he's taken with more than the skiing here," I said, spooning dough onto the rolling mat. "He hasn't taken his eyes off you since before Christmas." I wasn't sure what was keeping Paul in town, but I had my suspicions.

"Oh, applesauce! Such a thing is preposterous. Paul and I are just good friends. He knows I'm promised to Henry."

"Until you're wearing Henry's ring, you're still shark bait."

Josie giggled. "How perfectly funny!" she said. "Shark bait?"

"You know what I mean."

"He has been awfully nice. Now that he's had out his sour teeth, he's quite pleasant to be around." She smiled in a gentle manner. "I felt ever so sorry for him when he got here. He was in dire pain."

"Oh, for sure, but he had a good supply of tooth powder to help ease the worst of it." The powder was pure cocaine, and it surprised me how frugal he was with his medicine. Many people from my time could have polished off an eight-ball in one evening.

"Where is everyone?" she asked, stirring the cookie dough.

"Thomas and Henry are shopping, and Lillian is upstairs sewing."

"I was hoping to see Henry. Mother wants to make sure my dress won't clash with his suit."

"Won't he be wearing black?"

She shrugged and stuck her finger in the dough to taste it.

"Don't do that. Other people will be eating this."

Chided, she went on to say, "Mother is inviting the entire city to my party. She refused to plan a ball for my sixteenth birthday because of the awful piece in the *Denver Post* newspaper about Irish interlopers."

"We've only made our home in Denver for little more than five years. Mum doesn't know a terrible number of people. When she tried to join the local flower club they nearly ran us out of town. Dada attempted to join the country club, but that, too, was a disaster."

Flashbacks of that first dinner with the Watsons and my introduction to the Colorado KKK jerked at my heartstrings. The Doyle family was the most generous family I'd known. Not just to me. Several times a year they took food and clothing to the poorhouses.

"What changed her mind about this party?" I asked.

"We have made some new friends, and Henry's family is inviting everyone they know." In a hushed tone, she added, "Mother Watson still has several connections through the suffragists she knows. Once you've gone to jail for a friend, they don't soon forget."

"*Oh—My—Gawd!* Lillian Watson went to jail?"

"JETT! You say the dandiest things." She giggled conspiratorially. "*Oh—My—Gawd.* I feel so decadent saying that. *Oh my gawd…*"

"I'm so sorry. It's a bad habit."

"*Oh—My—Gawd!* You slay me."

Damn. Damn. Damn. Have I just created the first valley girl? "Don't let your Mum hear you say that. She'll eighty-six me, uh, ban me from your house. But Lillian?"

"Doesn't that take the cake? She went to jail for protesting the treatment of women when she was eighteen. Though they let her out on account of being in the family way. I believe she would go to jail for anything she felt strongly about. Lillian would never ban you from her home, no matter what you said."

"All the same, I think we should watch the language around the parents."

Josie did her best to never swear in front of her parents, but in our favorite drugstore, you could hear her high-pitched *Oh my gawd*'s and *fur sure*'s from across the room.

CHAPTER 13

On the night of Jay's engagement party, the Doyle house was bright and cheery. Henry's mother and I had spent the previous week making cakes and special desserts for the many guests who would be attending. The younger children made beautiful paper flowers and colored paper chains to decorate the ballroom. In the corner, the bandstand was readied for the musicians.

While I helped Maria and Guadalupe set the round dining tables, Josie was in her room preparing for her dramatic entrance. We had stayed up until midnight, scheming and giggling over the perfect arrival. The blue velvet gown she would be wearing had arrived only two days earlier, four days after the promised delivery date. The girl had been fit to be tied. She was anxious about having to appear in the same gown she'd worn on New Year's. Although rumor had it Abigail wouldn't be attending tonight's event, Josie was sure someone would tell the Ice Queen and that she would die of embarrassment. I couldn't relate, having only had one ball gown in my life and that, a hand-me-down. Her distress was actually charming. It was all about her parents' reputation.

The small band began to play as guests drifted in from the drawing room. Much like the New Year's masquerade, the attendees were formally dressed. Elegant gowns, top hats, and tails flooded the room in a sea of color swirling about islands of small tables draped in bright white linen. Opposite the bandstand, a long table was set to seat the guest of honor, her fiancé, and each of their parents. Greenhouse roses of white and bachelor buttons of blue adorned the head table, which had been overlaid in blue and silver lace. Smaller flower arrangements of blue and white decorated the nine guest tables, each set for six.

The music stopped and all the guests turned to face the door. Thomas and Lillian Watson, in formal black and white, crossed the room and took their seats on the left side of the table as the bandleader announced their names. A moment later, Henry arrived wearing the same blue silk jacket he'd worn for New Year's. It would match Jay's dress perfectly. He walked over and stood behind his parents as the bandleader announced the hosts of the party. Connor Doyle was dashing in a white brocade tuxedo complete with black lapels. The lovely Brigid, in a sapphire silk kimono with peacock feathers in her hair, laced her arm though his and chattered gaily as they circled the room.

Once Brigid and Connor were seated the room grew quiet as the guests awaited the arrival of Josephine. They were not to be disappointed. The empire waist of her blue velvet gown was embroidered with crystal beads in an aspen leaf design. Above the waistband the bodice was dark blue satin. Pale blue chiffon draped from a square neckline trimmed with three rows of beads. The cuffs of her full-length white gloves were adorned with sapphire glass beads. Her luxurious tresses had been curled, shaped, and waxed until they couldn't move. Dark eyeliner encircled her green eyes and her cheeks had been rouged, making her appear slightly older than seventeen. She looked absolutely fabulous.

Nearby, I sat at a table with Rory, my escort for the evening. We shared our table with Paul and his date, Clarabelle, a cousin to Josie, and Samuel and Mimi.

"Josie is lovely tonight," Paul said. "That gown must have broken the bank."

"Totally," I said. "It's a beautiful gown. She was so nervous about the fit, she drove everyone crazy."

"It just couldn't be nicer," Clara said, taking a plate of hors d'oeuvres offered by a serving girl. "They must have invested well. If I'm not entirely mistaken, that is a French design by Coco Chanel, right down to the glass beads."

"Chanel?" I was surprised that the designer was known in 1928. Her designs were still among the most sought after during the eighties.

"I adore Chanel," Clara whispered to me. "They are ever so much more comfortable. I should be happy to never lace another corset."

Mimi agreed. "Chanel is all the rage in Hollywood. I've read Catherine Moylan wears nothing else."

Clara said, "Lillian Gish and Dorothy Revier have both been photographed in Chanel designs."

Mimi nodded. "Edith Head has created some of the handsomest Hollywood gowns."

The conversation left me in the dust. I'd heard the names Coco Chanel and Lillian Gish, but the other names were from a history I'd never been a part of.

As everyone settled in to eat, Connor Doyle rose and clinked his fork on his water glass. All heads turned. "Friends and family," he said. "Thank you for joining us on this joyous occasion."

Applause greeted him as he continued. "I fear this must come as an unwelcome shock to many a good young man here tonight, but our little girl is to be married soon." Laughter and more applause. "Henry, now is not the time to be shy. Stand up, son."

Henry stood, a smile creasing his face from ear to ear. His happiness was infectious. "As most of you know, I came to build my romance around this delightful girl four years ago when my own good mother came to be fast friends with Mrs. Connor Doyle." Henry smiled at Josie. "I came to understand a feminine hand is needed for canning fruits and preparing meals."

From the back of the room someone shouted, "Does that include making candy?"

"Why, yes, sir, it most certainly does, but it is not on account of her baking skills I asked Miss Doyle to be my wedded wife. It is because of her generous nature and her love of life." Henry's eyes watered and I thought he was going to cry. That was when I realized that I was crying myself. As Henry took Josie's hand in his, for just a moment, all was right with the world. *If my mission was to bring these two people together, my mission is done.* Although I didn't believe anything in the world could have separated them.

The band began to play a beautiful waltz and Henry escorted Josie to the dance floor. I felt an unreasonable stab of jealousy. Was my desire to have a relationship like the newly engaged couple, or was it Henry I wanted? He was kind and handsome, but it was more than Josie who kept us apart, it was time itself that confused the issue. The Henry I had known was my friend and so easy to talk to, but this adorable man made me giddy and shy. *I don't belong here. Henry belongs with Josephine and I just have to get over it.*

Table talk was mostly about music, discussion I'd grown accustomed to whenever Paul and Rory were in the same room.

"I have my own announcement to fashion," Paul said when the talk had worn out the topic of rhythm guitar versus the piano.

"Hadn't we better wait until after dinner, or until tomorrow?" Rory asked.

Paul sipped from his teacup. "I think everyone should want to know."

"Yes," Rory said. "But we can tell my parents later. I don't want to disturb their evening, and Josie looks so happy."

"Yes, well I suppose it's every Jack for his Jill."

I was listening intently now. Something was up and it had to do with both of these men.

Paul looked over at the blissful couple. "She wants these things for you, she would be happy, you know."

Curiosity got the better of me. "What are you two talking about?"

"My home is in New York," Paul said.

"Duh, we all know that."

Rory folded and refolded his napkin. "Paul wishes for me to join him in New York."

"And you think Josie would be upset?" I asked.

Rory shook his head. "No, she would nearly push me out of the door. I fear leaving her without someone to watch over her. She has had some hijinks."

I burst out laughing. "You think?" I could only imagine how many. "Don't worry about her, that's Henry's job now."

"Please come," Paul begged. "The apartment they showed to me is furnished with a sumptuousness beyond my dreams."

"I want to drink of life but I don't see how I can do thus. What would I do for employment?"

"Leave that to me." Paul pointed across the room to an elderly man. "That is Jack Murphy. He runs a juice joint down on Welton."

I know," replied Rory. "I invited him."

"But were you aware that he's good friends with the Dean of Julliard?"

"No way!" I stammered. "Julliard? The musical college?"

Paul nodded. "He has requested of us to play a concert at the Colorado Theatre in April; a real performance for Denver's social elite."

"As if we'd believe that!" Rory spat. "I'm Irish."

"Don't be squeamish. True talent knows no racial boundaries."

Rory looked stricken. "I can see the headlines now: *Upstart Irish Lad Fouls the Grand Dame of Denver.*"

"I am surprised, indeed, myself that I could have accepted in your name. Oh, come on. What do you say? I shall expire from suppressed emotion if you should say no."

A slow smile crossed Rory's face. "We shall see how the public favors us."

He had accepted the offer to play the concert, if not the bid to move to New York.

"They ought not to try to do it," Clara said quietly.

"Why?" I asked.

"The dailies can be ever so unkind when it comes to reviews." She nibbled at her cake. "My father was destroyed over his painting of the Garden of the Gods. It's a public park near Colorado Springs," she explained needlessly.

"Have you heard Paul and Rory play?" I asked.

"I've heard Rory play the organ at church. He is excellent."

"Weren't you here for the New Year's party? They're awesome." At the look on her face, I recanted. "They were really great."

"I regret to have missed the gala. I was traveling for the holidays."

"By golly," Paul said. "You must attend our next performance at Murphy's Place tomorrow night."

"On Sunday?" Clara stammered. "Murphy's is a gin mill, not in the least a proper place for a lady."

Paul popped a fritter into his mouth. "Come early in the day. We'll be rehearsing for the concert we're to play in April. Though, if you would care to wait until then, I'm quite sure the performance will be to your liking."

Clara shook her head. "Jazz, is it? I know I'm hopeless, but I like my music with a tune you can find without hunting for it."

"Rory and I can play anything," Paul insisted. "Julliard will be glad to have us."

"Rap on wood—do!" Clara said. "How can you boast like that?"

Paul and Rory smiled. "Because we're that good!" they said in unison.

Clara frowned. "Why, I do believe Josephine looks rather pale."

"It's all the face powder," I said. "We spent more than an hour on her makeup."

Clara laughed. "I must confess, it took me two hours to apply my own."

"Josie may have caught a cold. She was coughing this morning." I'd just gotten over a bad cold myself. "I think she picked it up from me."

"Well you take care of yourself. Don't let Henry keep Josephine from needed rest."

"I won't," I promised.

The rest of the night was a mixture of joy and sadness. I had no doubt that Rory and Paul would do fabulously at their recital, but I would miss them both. Josie was as excited as a kitten with a new ribbon. The wedding date hadn't been set, but the list of attendees was growing by the hour. I was surprised and thrilled when she asked me to be her maid of honor; after all, I had only come into her life three months ago. But that wasn't the last surprise of the night.

In the large wood-paneled foyer, I slipped on my wool coat. As I reached for the door, Mrs. Doyle took me by the arm.

"A moment, if you please," she said. "You mean so much to our dear Josephine and a lady of her stature needs a companion."

"I am her friend."

Mrs. Doyle looked at me with knitted brows. "Yes. You are a dear friend, but a girl of Josephine's distinction needs more. She needs an assistant. Connor and I have noticed what a calming effect you have on her. The girl is prone to excitation."

I couldn't imagine Josie being more animated. "She's sweet," I said.

"Yes, she has a whimsical nature, but that is not why I sought you out this evening. Come with me please."

She led me into the darkened parlor and turned up the lamp.

Taking the chair closest to the door, I asked what this was all about.

"Lillian Watson is my dearest friend, but there are things you might know about her."

"Shouldn't she be telling me these things?"

"She would in time, I'm certain. She is an exceedingly amenable person. Did you know that she had been imprisoned for vandalism as a Suffragist? It was a minor sentence and she went on to write for *The Queen Bee*."

Of course Josie had told me, but I tried to act surprised by the news while racking my brain to remember anything about the women's suffrage movement. I didn't know what it could have to do with me.

Mrs. Doyle continued, "When Lillian was eighteen, she worked on Clara Cressingham's legislative campaign. Though successful, there were many who felt women should stay out of politics. There was a small demonstration and she was arrested."

"Who was Clara Cressingham?"

"Why, she was a Coloradan woman elected to the legislature in 1894, the first woman in the country to do so. Of course, that was before you were born. Young women today are unaware of the trails of their mothers. I'm certain it was because of Cressingham that Nellie Tayloe Ross was elected governor of Wyoming only two years ago." Brigid smiled. "It was rather scandalous, I should admit. Many say it just isn't seemly for a woman to look ambitious, but I digress. Clara served as secretary of the Republican Caucus and introduced bills supporting the sugar-beet industry."

Okay, I could see the connection of sugar to the candy store, but I was still lost as to why it was important to tell me this. "You must be proud of your friend," I said.

"Very much so. She is a force of nature. Much like you, Lillian lost her family at a young age. She was lucky to find Thomas. He's a calming influence. As I said, Lillian is my dearest friend, and not afraid to stand up for what she believes is morally right, including the actions of society's most elite. To that end, she has come to my aid many times. Henry is a dear boy, much more like his father in temperament, but he is still his mother's son."

"Henry is not afraid to stand up for what he believes and this makes you uncomfortable because you think it puts your daughter in danger."

Brigid sighed. "Josephine thinks she has us fooled, but we know Rory has taken her to these jazz clubs where he and Henry play their music. I would demand that she stay away from these places, but as you know, our little girl doesn't take well to demands. I've spoken to Rory in the past about this very topic, but he seems to be of little help. He insists that it is she who suggests these rendezvous."

I didn't want to rat on my friend, but it was Josie's idea more often than not. What really threw me was that Brigid Doyle didn't feel she could control her. Maybe it was a sign of the times, but I had always believed parents had tremendous influence over their children in the past. But then an image of a young and wild Bonnie and Clyde crossed through my mind.

"What about Mr. Doyle? Surely . . . "

She smiled and patted my hand. "Connor has a temper and is inclined to shout on occasion, but never in these many years has he raised a hand to his children and they know it. Josephine has always been her father's favorite."

"What can I do to help?"

"You are a clever woman. I've heard you speak of politics and finance on many occasions. You also appear reluctant to place yourself in harm's way. My eldest daughter admires you greatly and would do anything you ask of her. Don't misunderstand my meaning. We're agreeable to some outings, but it wouldn't hurt for her to have a female chaperone when she's out with Henry. Although I'm sure she's innocent, public opinion can be exceptionally harsh. Connor and I would be grateful if you would spend more time here, at home with her. My daughter doesn't have the strongest constitution. I worry that she isn't taking care of her health."

"I can come over after I make dinner at the orphanage."

"We were thinking it might be suitable if you helped us with dinner here."

"I don't think they'll let me keep my room there if I don't do my chores."

"Why, yes, of course, as Josephine's companion, you would have a room here with us. Josephine tells me you're a teacher as well. The littlest ones would greatly benefit from the additional schooling."

She was offering me a job as a nanny to the littlest ones in the guise of keeping Josie home more often. "I have to think about it. I like my room at the orphanage." I could tell by the way her eyes widened; she didn't believe me.

"Well, no need to decide tonight. Good night, Miss Oxford."

"It's a very generous offer. I will consider it." It *was* generous, and I hated to disappoint her, but I needed a place where I could be alone with my thoughts. I still had days when the eighties felt so real I thought I would go insane.

CHAPTER 14

Even with all I knew about making candy, it was difficult to translate some ideas to the wood stove. The basics were the same. Taffy was taffy, but melting chocolate was a true art form on a stove that gave inconsistent heat. It wasn't until I made my first bouquet of sugar flowers for a wedding cake that I'd secured my place as a permanent candy maker at Watson's Candies.

Along with the offer of a permanent position, I received a pay raise. It wasn't enough to finance a room of my own, but it was enough to get me out of doing many of the domestic duties at the orphanage, leaving me time to study at the library. I still loved to cook, and they were pleased to let me help with most of the evening meals.

Knowing about Lillian Watson's political activism shed a new light on her quick acceptance of me. Both Henry and Thomas Watson were used to independent women, so my wanting to work and support myself was viewed in a positive light, a light they wanted to nurture. With each passing day, the impression of job stability increased and a sense of family began to grow, much as it had grown in my future time with Jay and Henry. I also managed to dodge the doctor once and the detective twice that month. Eventually, the detective caught me as I was leaving the library on Sunday afternoon.

"Miss Oxford," he called, "a word please."

I stopped short. This was the last place I'd expected to see Detective Matthews.

"Let's go back inside where it's warm," he said with a warm smile. I turned back to the large door as he opened it for me. Inside there was a small lobby with a couple of chairs and a table. He motioned me to sit.

"What's this about, sir?" I asked in my most innocent voice.

"I've questioned every school I know of and yet have been unable to turn up a single person who claims to know of you." He sat across from me.

"I'm sorry I can't be of more help."

He reached for my stack of reading and picked up a copy of *Nature and Science*. Thumbing through the journal, he stopped on an article I had flagged. "'Properties and Testing of Magnetic Material'?" He flipped a few pages. "'Extension of the Irregular Doublet Law'? This is unusual reading for a young woman." He looked at another journal. "'The Quantum and Its Interpretation'." Sizing me up as if he intended to arrest me should I try to run, he read another title, "'I Believe in Personal Immortality'? What was your teaching position again?"

"English," I muttered.

He lifted up the last magazine. *Everyday Science and Mechanics.* "Tell me again, Miss Oxford, what is your area of study?"

"English. Reading science journals helps expand my vocabulary." He gave me a quirky smile and I knew he bought the lie.

"Well, then. As I was telling you, I couldn't find any schools to corroborate your story. Is it possible you were selected for private employment?"

"If none of the schools know about me, I must have been coming to Denver to work as a private tutor." I hid my hands in my lap so the detective would not see me fidget. I never had trouble lying to authorities in my own time, but here the lies had to be vague lest they catch me in a truly impossible story, like living in Hawaii. That wasn't impossible, but it was highly implausible. "I teach math as well, and a little science. Surely a prominent family might have wanted a diverse nanny."

"That will be much harder to trace. I'll place a notice in the dailies inquiring if anyone has recently been unable to fill a teaching position. Mayhap, someone will come forward. Good day, Miss Oxford. Sorry to have disturbed you."

The walk home was long as I tried to think of a way to shake this detective. So far all I seemed to have done was make him more interested. Trying to learn everything about theoretical science was impossible. Without knowing anything about what caused me to slip through time I had no idea of what direction to look. Hindu meditation and trying to become one with the universe didn't work, but maybe there was something to quantum mechanics.

The next day, a light snow was falling, and the kitchen of the candy store was warm, smelling of chocolate. Henry and I were making fudge. A sense of melancholy crept into my heart. Once Josie and Henry had announced their plans to marry, I was sure I'd be transported back to my own time, a time when a little snow wasn't such a dreadful hassle, a time when cars actually had heaters that worked.

Adding sugar to the hot chocolate mixture, Henry said, "You seem despondent today. Is something troubling you?"

"It's nothing," I said, rolling out parchment paper.

"I thought you should be pleased with the additional employment. I know it gladdens my heart to have you here."

"I'm grateful, really I am. I love working here."

He poured the hot fudge onto the parchment. "Perhaps you need some sunshine. We can go to the skating rink later if you would like."

"No, that's not it."

"Then what? You're so beautiful when you smile."

Turning away, I felt the heat rise to my face and heard him laugh. I felt him ruffle my hair and my heart skipped a beat.

"Henry, you shouldn't . . . " I turned to face him and he was holding a piece of fudge near my face. "Eat this," he said, grinning. "Chocolate is the best medicine."

"I thought it was laughter."

He cocked an eyebrow, and I laughed. "So it is," he said, popping the chocolate in my mouth. "You look better already." He took a piece for himself. "We should still go to the skating rink after we finish this batch of fudge."

"I can't. I promised Josie I would help her with the wedding plans."

He pouted, and I shoved another piece of chocolate into his mouth. Grabbing my hand, he licked my fingers, making me laugh again.

"That tickles," I said.

"And tastes good, as well. See?" He unexpectedly slipped his chocolate-covered fingers in my mouth. The sweet, warm chocolate melted on my tongue and it wasn't funny, it was erotic. Looking in his blue eyes I realized how much I liked it.

I was mortified by my feelings. This was eighty-year-old Henry, husband to Jay. He was the man who would one day try to teach me about stocks and running a store. He was also twenty, young, and handsome. And he was promised to my best friend. I pulled away. "I have to use the bathroom," I said, darting from the room. Hiding in the john, I was hoping he would leave, though I had no idea where he would go. This was his house after all.

"Are you in distress?" he asked through the door.

"I'm okay. Maybe you should make that last delivery."

"Not until I know you're fine."

I washed my face with cold water and dried it with a hand towel. "I'll only be a minute. You can start cutting the fudge, it should be cool by now."

Retreating footsteps told me I was alone again. Checking my face in the mirror, I calmed my beating heart and opened the door. He was leaning on the doorjamb. "Oh, my. I thought you were in the kitchen."

"I wanted to be certain you weren't hurt. Mother's cutting the fudge."

"We should go help her."

He put his hand under my chin and lifted my eyes to his. "You are extraordinary. There are times I feel exceptionally comfortable with you. Perchance I understand why you ran away."

"If you do, then you won't do that again."

He stared at me. "I didn't devise it. I just . . . "

"Let's go help your mother." With that, he followed me to the kitchen.

We never spoke of the incident, but I was careful not to let Henry feed me chocolate again.

It was later in March that I stood by a sofa table in the drawing room of the Doyle home. Josie was showing me the pink silk fabric she'd chosen for the wedding. My new position at the store allowed me to decline the offer proposed by Brigid. It was hard to say no to such a gracious woman, but it was even harder to explain to Josie why I didn't feel right moving into her home. I needed days when I could be alone with my thoughts. My feelings for both Josie and Henry were complicated. I'd become so relaxed with them it was hard to keep up the pretense. I hadn't exhausted all my ideas for getting home, and Josie would ask too many question about why I wanted to learn about black holes. I somehow left from the store and arrived at the store—it had to be the key to going home.

"You cannot be resolute," she said. "Who, if not you, would help me with all these arrangements?"

"I'm so sorry, Josie, but I actually want to stay where I am." I didn't have a room of my own, but the girls at the home tended to be disinterested in my business, which suited me just fine.

"I had been overjoyed when I heard she'd done it." She pouted like a seven-year-old.

"You know I wouldn't make a good nanny."

"Fiddlededee! You would truly." She sat down on the sofa as a coughing fit took her.

"Your mother worries. You have to kick this cold. She wouldn't even ask me to do this if you didn't go to the clubs."

"Mother would believe me a trollop. Why, we haven't been to Murphy's but once since the Christmas season."

"I know that, but you do spend a lot of time away from home."

"Only to hear Henry prepare for his concert. He loves to play the trumpet and when we marry he will give it up to become a full-time candy maker. This is his hour to be the artist. I shan't miss this time with him or Rory. Father's work is plebeian. This is Rory's opportunity to rise above the likes of us. I would be a troll not to support them."

"Your father doesn't have to work."

"But Rory should be free to make a name for himself."

I folded the lace gently. "I know how important this is to you, but honestly, the concert isn't until April thirteenth. I insist you take care of yourself now or you'll be too sick to see their show. You've been coughing for a while now."

"As you wish," she said sourly. "It's only a few more weeks before the concert, I can be still if I must."

"Thank you. That's a weight off my shoulders."

With the evening's trip to Murphy's postponed, we settled in to sort through a collection of elaborately lithographed papers, trying to choose the perfect wedding invitation.

My library studies had left me confused and frightened. After weeks of reading economic books, I had no more insight into what caused the stock market to take a crap than I had when I'd first arrived. As for finding a way home, the few science journals that were written in English were beyond my simple high school education, although W.H. Rosser's *The Law of Storms Considered Practically* and Thomas Hunt Morgan's *Regeneration* looked promising. After two hours of reading I knew I was going down another useless rabbit hole.

I replaced the two books and went back to the social science department. It was hard to give up the fight to find a wormhole or magic doorway to the future, but my brain was better suited to economics than physics. I picked up a journal of papers by F. Y. Edgeworthy titled *Political Economy*. I learned that the United States was a democratic republic designed much like the ancient Roman Empire. Many countries were monarchies or socialist. There was also something called Marxism, although the finer points of the political philosophies were often lost on me. I liked many of the arguments Thomas Jefferson made in *The Federalist* and decided to show them to Paul and Henry. Paul had once mentioned how the bankers had been responsible for the recent crash of the German economy, and Jefferson seemed to share his distrust of central banking.

It was near the first of April when Marjorie and I met for a stroll through the city park. Ducks and geese scattered about the lake, looking for handouts from the usual walkers enjoying the beautiful spring weather. She reminded me of my friend Penny. Both women were stable, thoughtful, and kind. It was freaky that they both were employed by Denver General Hospital. I could tell Marjorie had something important to tell me in the way she was fidgeting and blindly walking down the park pathway.

"Marjorie, whatever has you so wound up?"

"It's my father," she said with some deliberation. "He isn't well. I was planning to place him in a home."

"And?" I said after a drawn-out silence.

"Nursing isn't what one would consider adequate employment for sustaining a household. My father needs more care than I can give him, especially when I'm at the hospital ten to twelve hours each day."

"Twelve hours a day? Oh my God. You must make good overtime wages."

"Overtime wages?"

I had to remind myself, the candy store wasn't an exception; most women didn't make a living wage before the seventies. "What I meant to say is, with all the time you put in, your supervisor must value you enough to pay you more."

"I spoke with him. I told him of my plight. He was not in the least interested. He lent unwilling ears to my remarks. I gave up in despair."

"What are you going to do?"

"I shall seek employment in one of the sanatoriums. I believe they will take my father."

"Does he have Alzheimer's?"

"No," she said slowly, and I knew I'd blundered again. "I was considering, a position at the Bethesda Tuberculosis Sanatorium. They have offered outstanding care for more than twenty years. Swedish Sanatorium has an excellent program as well."

I had to center myself once more. Tuberculosis was the number one killer in Colorado at the turn of the century. In the daily papers, I'd read several accounts about how it seemed to be slowing down, but the numbers of people dying each year was still distressing.

The editorials argued whether more people flocked to Colorado seeking a cure, thus raising the number of deaths, or if, indeed, the climate helped many to live who would have otherwise died.

"I'm sure they'll hire you. You're a fantastic nurse."

"Thank you. If they accept me at either of the hospitals, I shall be too far to visit you with regularity."

There it was, the thing that had her most upset. We had grown close over the past months. I think she knew how much I depended on her friendship. Without a car, we would lose track of one another. I couldn't let that happen.

"Perhaps there's a hospital closer?"

"Well there is the Jewish Consumptives' Relief Society. I've heard they take all patients regardless of religious affiliation. Their sanatorium is on Colfax, just outside of Denver."

"Perfect. You should try them first."

She smiled. "You are ever so optimistic."

I put on a braver face than she knew. I felt a knot in my stomach tighten. TB was deadly; that much I knew, and I didn't like the idea of

Marjorie being exposed on a daily basis. Although it crossed my mind that Josie could have TB, I knew she and Henry would live well into their seventies. "In the meantime," I said. "I'm going to a jazz club with some friends on Friday night. Would you like to come?"

"My day of work isn't finished until ten."

"Awesome! We'll pick you up at the end of your shift."

"I'm dead for sleep by then."

"A little bit of Rory's sax will wake you right up. And Henry plays a mean trumpet."

Henry and Josie picked me up at nine that evening. Josie looked tired, but bubbly as ever. I squeezed into the back seat between Paul and Rory.

"Welcome, Jett," Paul said as the car bounced forward.

"Hi, everyone. I hope you don't mind, but I asked my friend Marjorie to join us."

"That's wonderful," Josie said from the front seat. "Does she like jazz?"

"I don't know. I guess we'll find out."

"Is she a live wire?" Paul asked.

"I've never been out with her before. She's a little older, responsible."

Rory whistled through his teeth. "I hope she isn't a flat tire."

"Or a Mrs. Grundy," Paul added with a grin.

"You fellas, be nice," Josie said. "I'm sure Jett's friend is delightful."

"How old is she?" Rory asked.

"Twenty something. Look, I just want to show her a good time. All she does is work. She's a nurse at Denver General Hospital."

"How divine," Josie said as we pulled up to the door of Murphy's. "It's a rare treat to meet a working gal. I applied to work at Neusteter's department store once, but I didn't get the position."

"I didn't know that," I said. "You gave me such a ration about wanting to work when we first met."

"A what?"

"You gave me a bad time."

"I did not. I only insisted you would change your notions about marriage."

"You have me there." It was Marjorie who couldn't understand why I wanted to work. "So why didn't you get the job?" She didn't have to answer. As I said the words, I realized it would be her ginger hair that kept her from representing the large department store chain. "I'm sorry. You would have made an awesome salesgirl."

"Yes, I would. It's their folly."

"By the way, I offered to pick up Marjorie from work." I batted my lashes at Henry. "Do you think we could do that? About ten-fifteen, at Sixth and Bannock?"

"We can," Henry said as he opened the car door. "Let's get a table first. It's sure to be crowded."

Paul stepped in beside us. "We have a table reserved. It makes up for the lousy pay."

"Must be a sincerely nice table," Rory added.

The front door and windows of the building looked dark. If I hadn't known better, I would have thought it to be an office building, closed for the night. We slipped around to the east where a man in a newsboy cap leaned against a side door. As we approached, he stood and looked us over.

"Ho, Billy," Paul said. "Good to see you. Isn't it hot tonight?"

"Yes, and the wind is out of the north," he replied.

"Good then that summer is nigh."

It was a simple conversation to most, but an elaborate ritual password for those in the know. I'd heard similar exchanges on other nights. Billy stepped aside and opened the door. Once inside, we traveled down a long hallway until we came to a set of stairs leading down. Another long hallway and another set of stairs brought us to the basement of an entirely new building. Here another doorman asked about the traffic on Colfax.

I could hear music coming from behind the solid wood door. After a moment the doorman rapped on the door and the lock clicked.

The third doorman led us to a table near the band. I was pleased to see Miss Julianne at the microphone. Her soft, melodic voice had the entire audience enraptured. The band consisted of a stand-up bass, a small piano, and a snare drum. I didn't recognize the tune: a ballad, sad and sweet.

Rory held out my chair as I sat down. It was one of the things that most threw me in those early days, the way men always opened the door and held out my chair. I wasn't complaining; it just took a bit of getting used to.

Rory took the chair between Josie and me while Paul and Henry went to see about our refreshments. We girls rarely had anything stronger than lemonade. The few times I tasted what they called gin, my head hurt for a week. I couldn't say the same for the men in our group, though rarely did they get as intoxicated as men I'd known back home.

We barely finished our first drink before it was time to pick up Marjorie. Back through the gauntlet and we were just in time to see Marjorie step from the hospital door.

"Over here," I shouted, waving my arm. "This is Henry. Henry this is Marjorie."

Henry looked uncomfortable. "Very nice to meet you, Miss . . ."

"Winston, Miss Marjorie Winston. The pleasure is mine, Mr. Watson. You were the gentleman that brought Miss Oxford to us, were you not?"

"Yes. I'm grateful to you, Miss Winston. You have taken such good care of her."

"Her injuries were minimal. Miss Oxford could not have better care. Doctor Mortenson is an excellent psychologist. He studied under Mr. Edwin Guthrie at Johns Hopkins Hospital."

I was over all the mistering and missussing, not to mention I really didn't want Marjorie telling Henry about my crazy days in the hospital. "Shall we get back?" I asked pointedly. "I don't know when you're expected to play tonight, but you can't do it from here."

Henry laughed. "I certainly cannot."

As we made our way back to our table, Julianne was there, speaking with Rory.

"Dear Rory," she said. "It's silly of course, but I simply had to go to someone. I feel so nervous and unsettled."

"Why, what's the matter?" Rory stood and pulled out a chair, but she declined to sit. The other men at the table also stood. I followed Josie's and Marjorie's lead and kept my seat.

"It's Link," Julianne said. "He had acted not at all like himself tonight." Her dark eyes flashed. "I believe he's gone and done something stupid. There is to be a gathering on the river, and I'll warrant it will be a devil's carnival, too. I've heard rumor they're to meet with members of the Roma family."

"Joe Roma?" Rory said with disgust. "I sometimes wish Lincoln had not come into your life. Thugs, the lot of them are. Nothing but trouble. A man was shot over five pints of whiskey only last week."

"If he were like that I should die."

"Forgive me. I'm sure he's only being swayed by a desire to earn a good life for you."

"He left about an hour ago." She blinked back tears. "I wanted to keep him here, demand he stay and finish the show." Letting out a deep sigh, she leaned her beaded hip against the table. "I had to put pride in my pocket. I had to let him walk out on me."

Rory frowned. "He's not one to take kindly to demands from his gal."

"Would you please talk to him? He listens to you."

"He listens to me when I speak of rhythm and timing, but yes, I will try."

Julianne looked to be mulatto and I found myself identifying with her plight. Coming from an interracial family was hard enough in the eighties. I couldn't imagine how difficult it would be in the twenties.

Like me, she was caught between worlds. I would have liked to know her better.

Rory, Henry, and Paul played a set about eleven o'clock: Rory on the saxophone, Henry on the trumpet, and Paul on the stand-up bass, while the drummer and the piano player from Julianne's band sat in on several songs. Josie sang two numbers and the crowd went wild. It wasn't rock and roll, but it made my foot tap. The audience gave them a standing ovation at the end of the set, demanding, "One more song," and the band blew the roof off. Julianne joined them for the final number, *Bye Bye Black Bird*. It was nothing like the Beatles' version, but it was wonderful. Josie grabbed Marjorie and me by the hand, leading us to a table of four men.

"We'd like to dance," she announced, and the three quickest men joined us on the dance floor.

I was having so much fun, I didn't notice when Josie left the floor. Apparently, she had succumbed to another coughing fit. When I got back to the table, one of our new acquaintances was offering her a glass of water.

"Are you okay?" I mopped her head with a kerchief.

"I am fine now. I was a bit winded. Maybe we should get out and dance more."

I shook my head. "Not until I know you're over this cold." I knew she'd been sick too long for a standard cold but was furiously hoping it wasn't bronchitis or pneumonia.

"How long have you had this cough?" Marjorie asked.

"It's nothing. Truly, I'm quite well enough."

"She's had it for about five weeks," I said.

Marjorie shook her head. "You shouldn't be out dancing. You need rest. It may be nothing, but don't take chances you needn't take."

My eyes met Marjorie's and I could see her concern.

Shortly after the boys returned from the bandstand, Jack Murphy came over to our table.

"You boys sounded mighty fine tonight," he said. "See that man over there, the one in the tan fedora? He's my wife's eldest brother, and the man with him is Frank Damrosch, the dean of Julliard."

Rory went white, but Paul beamed. "Did he like the performance? I didn't expect him to be in Denver this soon."

"He just got in this morning from Chicago. Evidently, the artist he hoped to acquire there hadn't lived up to his reputation."

Paul looked a bit more subdued. "Did he say anything about our performance? This isn't the Colorado Theater. We planned to play classical numbers that evening."

"He only mentioned he was looking forward to the thirteenth. Good luck to you boys."

After Mr. Murphy walked away, Paul became animated once more.

"You must understand what this means. We can all have a place at Julliard, the leading music school in America."

Rory sipped on his drink. "We've still two weeks before the concert. We should spend every day preparing. Henry, you should spend more time on the guitar."

"I hate to be a flat tire," Henry said, "but I have employment waiting for me." He leaned over and kissed Josie's cheek. "And a beautiful wife to be. Surely you can't expect me to leave such good fortune behind." He smiled, but in his eyes you could see the desire to share this adventure with his friends.

Josie pulled her wrap over her shoulder. "I could never live with myself if I kept you from your dreams, my dearest. If this man should offer, you must go."

"No, Buttercup. I won't leave you to the likes of Samuel and his crew."

"Baloney!" she said. "I would only be glad to keep my man at home as long as it was something he also wanted. This is a choice opportunity. I shan't hold you back."

"You are such a gem," Henry said, kissing her hand. "If we must go, we shall see if there is room for all of us in Paul's apartments."

I felt a stabbing pain in my gut. I didn't want any of them to go to New York. I needed these friends in a way I'd never needed anyone before. Josie and Henry were like life preservers tossed to me in a swirling vortex of time. If I was here to make something right, it must center on these people and the store. To have them running the candy store was essential to my future. In all my days of working at the store, I had been unable to find anything unusual; certainly nothing that might cause a person to fall through time. Surely Josie and Henry must be the key to my returning home. I didn't belong in this time.

My mind was whirling. If Josie and Henry moved to New York they wouldn't be running the store in the eighties, and if they weren't running the store, I couldn't fall through time the day of the fire. I would never meet them. My heart ached. To have never met them would be to lose the most wonderful year of my life. Was that the answer? Did I need to give up the love I had known to return? Return to what though? The days spent sitting on the bench at the train station? Did I truly want to go back to that—to a world without Jay and Henry?

"All right, let's call it now," Rory said, standing up and downing his drink. "Let's go home."

Josie's lower lip protruded ever so slightly. "Why go to bed when the day is just beginning?"

"It's after midnight, Buttercup." Henry pulled her to her feet. "I should never have had you out this late. You're looking a bit peaked."

"I wish you all would stop mothering me so. I'm fine. Fit as a fiddle!"

CHAPTER 15

"But just now I've got a restless fit on me," Paul said as he loaded his bass into the car.

Rory nodded. "No matter how the performance goes tonight, I know you will be leaving for New York a week from Sunday."

"I will stay for your birthday, good fellow. But then I truly must be on my way. I've stayed months too long as it is."

Henry opened the door for Josie. "It's going to be magnificent, Rory," he said. "Must you buy trouble?"

"But if . . . "

"You're going to be great!" Josie said as she smoothed the chiffon of the blue gown she had chosen to wear. "You know you're the best musician in Denver."

"Buttercup. I'm hurt to the quick."

She fought back a grin. "Except for my Henry, you understand."

Holding up the hem of the only gown I owned, I slid into the back seat next to Paul. "I'm so stoked. This is going to be an awesome concert."

From the front seat, Josie grinned at me. *"Fur sure,"* she purred. "A totally jake concert."

"Did you telephone to see if you could get seats for everyone?" Paul asked Henry.

"Our parents will be seated in the fifth row, balcony. That was the best I could do."

Rory frowned as he shut the car door. "You would think they would allow our parents some concession."

"It was my understanding," Henry said, turning the ignition, "that the main floor is sold to season ticket holders. At least we should be assured of a crowd."

Rory didn't look pleased. "I hope they're true music lovers and not just high hats."

The concert hall was larger and more elegant than I'd imagined. According to Josie, Horace Tabor, a silver miner, had built the elegant theater in 1881.

"The name rings a bell," I said. "I heard about a girl named Baby Doe but I don't know the story."

"It was once called the Tabor Theatre," Rory said, "but the name was changed to the Colorado Theater in 1921. Now it also features moving picture shows."

"Baby Doe was Tabor's second wife," Josie said. "He was divorced and so was she. It was quite the scandal."

Henry nodded. "It is rather sad. Because of the Sherman Silver Purchase Act he lost all of his great wealth in the panic of 1893."

"Oh, Henry," Josie pleaded. "Jett doesn't want to hear about laws and mining."

I smiled. I needed to know about laws and the economy if I was going to help my friends, but this wasn't the time or the place for that conversation.

Three entrances to the grand hall converged into a rotunda, enclosed with beautiful stained glass. The elegant lobby was decorated with immense framed mirrors lighted by a large chandelier hanging from a ceiling painted with frescoes of a Spanish Renaissance flavor.

Paul retrieved our tickets from the will-call box and told us to wait in the lobby for the rest of our party. After a brief farewell and abundant good-luck wishes, the boys headed backstage. A short while later, Henry's and Josie's parents arrived, the men in coats and tails, and the women in their best gowns. Brigid Doyle wore a red velvet shift while Lillian wore an empire-cut gown in green and purple satin, her signature colors. Later, I was to learn the colors represented the suffragette movement, a symbol she wore quite often. By appearing with the Doyle family wearing her colors, she let others know she would suffer no disparagement regarding her choice of friends.

As we made our way to the first balcony, a swath of thick Wilton carpet in ruby red with an emerald green border lay before us, covering the hallways and stairways. The theater's interior boasted lavish mahogany and cherry wood for the seating and boxes. The auditorium sat fifteen hundred guests, with plush seats and curved balconies that faced the large stage. On the walls were paintings and murals in rich colors, while the ceiling was painted to represent a sky with clouds. Like the velvet cut carpeting, all of the seats were covered with plush crimson mohair. Heavy globes of crystal covered the gaslights. In my hand-me-down gown I felt shabby next to the elegant gowns and furs surrounding me as we took our seats.

When the lights dimmed and the curtain rose, the audience applauded graciously. I was surprised to see so many empty seats. I understood that Henry's small group was unknown, but the program listed several musicians who would be playing this evening.

The concert itself consisted of each musician playing a solo piece and in combination with the others. The choice of instrument was as important as the choice of song.

They played several beautiful classical pieces, including Mozart's *Dissonance* and Beethoven's *Archduke* which were Josie's favorites. She could name them all, Brahms, Borodin, Haydn, and Ravel. I didn't know any of the pieces, having spent my life listening to the sounds of the Beatles, Led Zeppelin, and Queen. Even without any classical knowledge, the concert was magnificent music.

Henry was the first of our friends to perform solo on the trumpet. Although I'd never heard the song *Potato Head Blues* I knew immediately it was a great choice. The crowd applauded madly when he reached the last refrain. I was so proud of him. I looked over at Josie, expecting to see her jubilant, but she was crying. And I don't think it was for joy. There was sadness in her eyes. I reached for her hand, and her smile bounced back, all trace of grief banished by my touch.

Rory was the next soloist. Josie informed me he would be playing *Singin' the Blues* on his C-Melody saxophone. I didn't know anything about musical instruments, but the song was great. Once again, I was reminded of a subdued David Bowie. He had excellent stage presence. "I'd have thought," I whispered to her, "that they'd have chosen a classical piece for their solo."

Josie shook her head. "The songs show their talent but also entertain. Their classical skill is showcased in the ensembles. You'll notice parts of each song feature one musician or another."

When it was Paul's turn to perform solo he chose the piano. I was not only surprised to recognize *Old Man River*—I had a music box as a child that played the song—but I was stunned by the sheer magnitude of the music produced by a solitary piano. I gasped when he began to sing. His voice was rich and deep, like a mixture of dark chocolate and creamy caramel. Paul's composition continued to build, filling the room and taking the audience for a ride *'long the ol' Mississippi*. When the song was over, the room was silent. I was afraid the listeners didn't like what they'd heard when suddenly the room erupted in jubilant applause.

Later that evening while returning home, I heard Henry tell Josie once more he could never leave Denver. "The candy store is my life. With it I can provide us a much more secure future than any working musician could hope to have." The knot in my stomach began to loosen. I realized then how worried I had been. Josie and Henry had to stay with the candy store so I could meet them in the future. If they weren't at the store in the eighties, I couldn't be here now. Then I realized: *if Henry went to New York, this would all be over.* The thought of this hurt more than expected. I would never know such love and friendship. This past six months had been such a happy time for me. Confusing on many days, but overall, very happy. *Was I guilty of trying to re-create the situation that landed me here? Should I try to convince Henry to attend Julliard?*

Josie smiled at Henry. "You know I could never leave Jett."

"She will always have employment with us, Buttercup." He kissed her on the forehead. "Now, if she could only teach you how to make candy."

Unexpected vertigo made my head spin. Josie had taught me how to make candy, and now was I supposed to teach her? For me to meet her in the future, I would have to help this young woman become the Jay I knew in the future. She currently cooked at home twice a week on Guadalupe's day off and she was pretty good. It wouldn't take much to teach her how to pull taffy and make sugar flowers.

The weather began to turn warmer as May approached, bringing back the red-breasted robins and a lovely pair of blue jays, who hung out by the carriage house. Henry named them Sal and Bess, never missing a chance to bring the birds day-old bread. He was truly the sweetest man I'd ever met.

"They prefer peanuts or sunflower seeds," Henry said. "See how he holds the seed in his feet and pecks it open?"

Sitting under the arbor, we watched the bird and its mate until Josie joined us.

"Here it is," she said. "The official telegram from Julliard."

"I was quite certain Paul and Rory would be accepted," Henry said, glancing at the proof as he handed the telegram to me. "A secretary from the school rang me last night."

Josie cocked her head. "You must be straight with me, Henry. Did they offer you a position?"

"It was a courtesy call. The telegram is official proof of admission."

"They rang up Rory as well," she said, unsatisfied with Henry's answer.

"My place is here. I'll have many opportunities to play my horn. Murphy's is merely one of a dozen juice joints."

"What about the Rossonian?" I asked. "I heard that Duke Ellington plays there."

"Where is this Rossonian?" Henry asked. "I should like to see Duke Ellington. I understand he's exclusive to the Cotton Club in Harlem."

"The hotel is on Welton, Twenty-Fifth and Welton, I think." I described the building to them.

Henry stared at me for a moment. "You must mean the Baxter Hotel. While it has an impressive lineup of musicians, Julianne has never invited me to play there."

"Have you been there?" Josie asked, eyes wide.

"No. I just heard that from someone. They must have been pulling my leg."

The two of them exchanged glances and I knew I'd said the wrong thing.

"Paul has his vouchers for New York ready," Henry said. "He bought tickets the day after the audition concert."

"He would have returned to New York regardless of the outcome of the audition," Josie said. "He misses his home. Mum is planning a congratulatory event to coincide with Rory's twenty-first birthday."

Two days later, Henry and I were making a huge cake in the shape of a piano. His cake-decorating skills rivaled his mother's. I still had much to learn.

"The recipe says this will make three layers," I said, thumbing through Lillian's recipe.

"Is that the Lady Baltimore? It's very popular."

"Yes. Is three layers too much?"

"If we use an especially light filling, it will do fine."

Crossing the room to the icebox, I had to step around a covered pile of bricks. It would be nice to have the kitchen remodeling done. The week before, the Watsons had invested in a new Sharp-brand gas stove, and I was in heaven. No more fighting to keep an even temperature when baking cakes. Though I still struggled with the other ancient appliances, the icebox was almost as bad as the old wood stove had been. It was nothing more than a wooden box, lined with tin. Cork was used to hold blocks of ice to chill the food, and a drip pan to collect the meltwater had to be emptied daily. In the summer, when you most wanted ice in your tea, the ice had to be preserved.

"Hi, Rory," I said. "Did you come to check out your birthday cake?"

He nodded from the doorway. "This is to be my moment of glory. Best I see to it that all the productions are acceptable."

Henry threw a walnut at him. "Just be pleased there *will* be a production."

I gathered the butter, sugar, eggs, and milk and took them back to the counter where Henry was showing Rory the design for the piano cake. "Did you preheat the oven?" he asked me.

"Yes. I'm so glad I don't have to stack wood. That gas stove has to be the greatest invention since sliced bread."

"Pardon me?" Henry said, his eyebrow accusing me of some new stupidity.

Rory stared. "Why would you want bread sliced? It would dry out before you could eat it."

Crap, sliced bread hasn't been invented yet. "I was just being silly. Forget I said anything."

The two men shook their heads and went back to the drawing.

In a large bowl, I creamed the butter and sugar together until the mixture was light. After beating the egg yolks, I added them to the butter mixture.

Across the counter, Henry sifted the dry ingredients together three times. "My dear friend, you will be most certainly missed. I hope you will find the opportunity to come back to Denver often."

"I shall do my best. Presently, I am here to see your father. I have a list of stocks he might investigate."

"He's away to the icehouse. You can leave the list on his desk."

"I'd like to see the list," I said, folding the dry ingredients into the butter mixture alternately with the milk.

"Why would you have a care for this?" Rory asked as he nibbled on a cookie.

"Curious."

Henry beat the egg whites until they were stiff. "Have you finances I'm unaware of? Perhaps a hidden estate? If you wish to invest, I can give you the name of a dandy broker."

"You know I'm broke."

His eyebrow danced. "I should like to fix you."

I felt my cheeks warm as I folded the egg whites into the batter.

Rory unfolded a piece of paper and handed it to me. It was a list of initials: AA, CL, JNJ, and PG. "What are these?"

"AA is Alcoa Inc., CP is Colgate-Palmolive Co., JNJ is Johnson and Johnson, and PG is Procter and Gamble Co."

"Those all sound like solid companies. People will always need soap and Band-Aids. I can't swear to Alcoa, but I like aluminum foil." I had no idea how much, if any, these companies would lose in the crash, although they would recover. They seemed like safe bets.

Rory laughed. "Is that how you would choose to invest? By buying the companies you use?"

Spooning the batter into the cake pans, I smiled. "Sure. At least I'll know they have one loyal customer."

Henry rolled his eyes. "This should be done in about twenty-five minutes." He checked his pocket watch. "Once done, we'll take them out of the oven and let them rest ten minutes before removing the cake from the pans to cool on the wire rack."

I nodded. "I'll start the fillings. So, Rory, do you have investments of your own?"

"It's all family money. Once I marry, a trust will be opened in my name."

I put sugar, walnuts, and water in a small saucepan over medium heat. "You have to marry to get any money?"

He looked uncomfortable. "My family will always take care of my needs. I should return home. Mother asked me to procure flowers. I'll place this on your father's desk. See you on the morrow, then?"

Henry stopped chopping nuts long enough to walk his friend to the store's office.

"Bye, Rory. Thanks for the stock tips," I said.

Henry came back to help finish icing the cake. "Rory tells me Warner Brothers opened the Warner Brothers Hollywood Theater at 6433 Hollywood Boulevard. The opening picture was *Glorious Betsy,* starring Conrad Nagel and Delores Costello."

"I love Hollywood movies. Tough business to get into. You have to look like Miss America to even get an audition."

"I should rather be Miss America," he said. "I've heard she earns more money than Babe Ruth or the president of the United States."

"Seriously?"

"There will always be a place for a pretty girl. In between screenings of the feature was the *Ceballos Revue* with Daphne Pollard, Harry Kelly, and the girls, so the patrons got their money's worth."

An old Elton John song came to mind. Hollywood created the superstar, taking pretty young girls and molding them into something almost obscene. I was glad to know that in my time the industry would employ more average-looking people. But men will be men and, in less than fifty years, Farah Fawcett would take the country by storm.

"You could be a movie star," he said seriously.

"Don't be ridiculous. I have zero talent for acting."

Something in the way he studied my face told me I'd struck a chord. "I think you have a great talent."

I let the conversation stall. I'd been doing the best acting job of my life over the past seven months. *Was he beginning to see through my snow job?*

The next day I sat on the bed in Josie's bedroom as she dressed for Rory's party. Caitlin had changed her dress for the third time and left us alone to discuss our surprises.

"Not here," Josie pouted. "When I've brought him the most beautiful instrument he has ever seen, and all the way under my wrap so I could give it to him the very first thing."

I lifted the brand new saxophone and examined it. "How do you want to give it to him? Doesn't he already have two saxophones?"

"I know enough for that; but this is finer than anything he's got. Won't he be pleased?"

"I'm sure he will be."

"I'll just run downstairs and put this in drawing room so it will be there when he comes in. We'll see how soon he discovers it."

I smiled at her back as I followed her down the stairs. Josie was just plain fun.

She set the gift next to the piano, but as the room filled with guests, it seem less and less likely that Rory would see her gift.

I recognized many of the faces. Abigail was with a new man. Her blond hair was swept up in an elaborate concoction of curls and braids. She looked as dangerous as ever, but when she greeted my friend, I think she meant the sweet words of congratulations.

She kissed Josie on the cheek. "You must be so proud of your brother."

"I am. He is a gift to all of us."

"I saw Henry's presentation. He played beautifully at the concert. Was he accepted to Julliard as well?"

"I don't know," Josie replied. "He never mentioned an invitation, but he had long decided to stay here in Denver."

Abigail looked across the room where Henry was in deep conversation with Paul and Rory. "A shame. He would have gone far, I'm certain. I was mad with the joy of it."

"He doesn't go in for that bohemian lifestyle," Josie said.

"Truly, but a shame nonetheless, isn't it? Such talent wasted on cookies."

"Henry will play here," I said. "Denver needs good musicians, too."

Rolling her eyes, Abigail smiled thinly. "We shall see. When do they leave for New York?"

"Three days hence. I shall miss them very much." Josie's eyes misted.

"Of course you will, dearest. You must tell me truly, does Paul have a woman in his life?"

I couldn't hide the shock in my voice. "You're not thinking of hitting on him are you?"

The tall blond turned to regard me, hand to her breast. "Hit him? Of course not, I was merely enquiring as to his status."

Jay shook her head. "He's never mentioned a girl. I had always assumed he was too concerned with his studies."

"He is surely a serious musician. Julliard only accepts the best. I can imagine the parties they will throw in his honor." Abigail glanced down her nose at the room of guests. "New York City is so glamorous."

"I don't think you're his type," I said.

Abigail studied my face. "Why ever not?"

I'd met men like Paul and Rory. They were careful to cover their feelings. I certainly wasn't going to tell someone like Abigail about my suspicions. She was staring at me, ice in her veins. I needed to say something. "I heard him tell Rory he likes tiny brunettes."

Abigail laughed uproariously. "My dear girl, you believe *you're* his *type*? How awfully sad you are, little moppet. A man never truly knows what he wants until he finds it." With those words, she glided away to speak with the current man of her interest.

"Are you truly game for Paul?" Josie asked. "I thought you would marry Rory."

"I told you, I don't want to get married."

"When Rory is famous, you'll change your mind."

"Come on, let's go see if we can lead Rory to his birthday present."

As we walked toward the piano where the men were gathered we heard Abigail exclaim, "Why this is a beautiful instrument." She held up the saxophone. "The tag says 'Happy Birthday,' so it must be yours."

When she handed the instrument to Rory everyone applauded loudly, and Josie sank into the closest chair. "That was to be my gift to Rory. Now everyone thinks Abigail gave it to him!"

"THAT BITCH!" I blurted.

"Jett!" Josie stood suddenly, hands on hips. "Keep your voice down! Someone will hear you." The corners of her mouth lifted slightly. "I know you're as angry as I am, but I don't believe her misdirection was intentional."

"Maybe not, but she's basking in the confusion, and I'm going to set everyone straight."

"It's fine, Jett." Cough, cough. She held a dainty handkerchief to her lips. "I don't want to make a fuss."

"Well, I do!"

I stomped over to the piano, my resolve firm. I wasn't much for making a scene for myself, but someone had to stand up for Josie. "Excuse me, everyone," I said. "This beautiful saxophone was a gift from Rordan's sister, Josephine." I stepped between Abigail and Rory. "She wanted to see how long it would take for you to find it among the other gifts. Abigail horned in, pretending it was her gift."

Abigail screeched, "I *never* said as much!"

"No, of course you didn't," I said to her. "You didn't have to say a word, just savor in the applause and let everyone believe what they will."

Her face turned bright red and she left the room without another word.

I felt bad then. I'd only meant to straighten out the misunderstanding, but I'd been cruel in my accusation, spot on as it was. I followed Abigail out the door. "Wait," I shouted. "I'm sorry that came off the way it did. I didn't mean to hurt you. I just wanted to set things right."

Abigail turned to face me. "Miss Oxford, I don't know who you think you are, but I know all about you. You seem to have neglected to make the connection. You will find that Abigail Mortenson is a well-respected woman in this town."

CHAPTER 16

My next visit from Dr. Mortenson was uncomfortable. I could never be sure what he and his daughter talked about. That Abigail didn't like me was apparent to me now, but I didn't think she'd lie to her father.

He took my blood pressure and temperature. I didn't know why he did this every time but suspected it was mostly out of habit.

"So, Miss Oxford. You seem to be looking quite well. No visions or dizziness?"

"No. I feel fine." I sat on a chair near the window. Sunlight streamed in and I wanted to be outside enjoying it, not in this dark parlor answering the same questions I'd already answered.

"Detective Matthews tells me you remember living among the Pacific Islands."

Wow. I'd forgotten I'd said that. When I hadn't heard from the detective for a couple months, I thought he'd given up on me.

"I must admit," the doctor continued. "We puzzled for some time over the suntanned skin you had when we first found you. What I don't understand is when you lived in Colorado Springs."

"I think I was only there for a few months."

He took my hands and turned them over in his. "You've been more physical in these last months, have you not?"

I had been. My hands were raw from the harsh detergents and from carrying wood. My cuticles were red and torn. "I try to do my share."

"You insist you have no parents, but you must have had a sponsor for your travels and education. Detective Matthews has found no record of your passage from the islands."

I was being backed in a corner and it was getting uncomfortable. It was funny how a little white lie always turned into a double feature in Technicolor. "I don't remember."

He paced the room several times. "Your friendship with Miss Josephine Doyle has grown. I understand you've attended both their annual masquerade and Miss Doyle's engagement party."

"Yes. As I said before, she's a nice girl and I work with Henry."

"You had never met Miss Doyle or Henry Watson before the twenty-third of October, yet they have practically taken you in as one of their own."

"I'm as surprised as you are." And I was. I couldn't understand how quickly I had been accepted. Thinking back to my first meeting with an older Jay and Henry, I'd had the same remarkable experience.

They had accepted me even with all my problems. "Jay—Josephine and Henry are incredible people. I think they would be willing to take care of anyone in need."

"I believe they are." He looked at me warily. "Some people are easily influenced."

I felt my skin crawl. What was he accusing me of doing? Apparently, he didn't think I was that fragile anymore. "I need to get back to my class now. May I be excused?"

He nodded. "I'll return in a couple weeks." As he walked to the door, he waved an arm, indicating the orphanage. "I'm glad you were able to find refuge here. If you are to be believed, you may have wandered the streets for some time before finding a place to live. It was fortunate you had wandered into the candy store that day."

If I were to be believed! What had Abigail said to him?

My next class wasn't due to start for another fifteen minutes so I went up to my room to lie down. My head was pounding. Henry and Jay—*no, Josie*—were loving people. I landed in the store because I left from the store, didn't I? Was the doctor accusing me of purposely going to the store that day to integrate myself in their lives? In my mind, I saw Henry's face smiling at me, his piercing blue eyes begging me to trust him. And just that fast, I saw him as an eighty-year-old man struggling with a sack of flour. My heart went out to him. I loved both of these men, but he wasn't mine and I didn't belong here. As easily as I had arrived, I could vanish again. I couldn't do that to Henry. I longed to find my own Henry, a special kind of person, someone to which I could tell the truth.

Seeing Rory and Paul off at Union Station was sad and happy at once. I would miss them both. They were rare male friends who treated me like a sister rather than as a conquest. Over the past month I began to recognize the signs of secrecy and shame. I hoped they would find the lifestyle that suited them when they reached New York. Rory was used to being harassed because he was Irish, and I knew he could handle most anything, but bigotry ran deep in the early twentieth century and it wasn't limited to race. Even Josie, kind as she was, had beliefs I didn't dare call into question.

Memorial Day fell on a Wednesday and the Watsons closed the store for the day. The Doyle family invited all of us to attend a picnic at Elitch Gardens. I was surprised to learn there was a zoo at the park. In my time, Elitch's was a theme park with major roller coasters and kiddie rides. There was a large picnic area with beautiful gardens, but the place had been showing its age. The park often gave away half-off coupons to Denver's schoolchildren in May to help augment its attendance. Unfortunately, I could rarely afford the half-price ticket.

"They have a lovely ballroom," Josie said as we bopped along Broadway heading northwest. "The Trocadero Ballroom has the most famous bands, coming all the way from New York. Someday, Rory and Paul will play there."

As we turned west on Thirty-Eighth Street, I saw the snow-capped mountains in the distance. They hadn't changed at all. If I blocked out the rumbling sound of the Nash Ajax we were riding in and the smell of burning wood and coal, I could almost find my way back home. The stately homes were familiar but several lacked the big shady trees I'd known.

Zap. It was gone as fast as that when I saw the ornate, Greek-Revival-styled stucco gate entrance. In the eighties the gate would be an art deco and aluminum monstrosity. Once inside, the gardens were as beautiful as I remembered, although the sound of birds and gentle conversation replaced the excited screams of riders and the *clickity-clack* of roller coasters roaring over their winding, undulating wooden tracks. A short distance from the gate, we came across the carousel. I gasped and staggered.

"Isn't it jake!" Josie squealed. "It's brand new from the Philadelphia Toboggan Company. I heard it took three years to carve by hand."

"It's—it's . . . " I trailed off. Only last August, I'd come here with my classmate Mike, my friend Bambi, and her latest boyfriend. Here was the exact same carousel Mike and I had ridden that day. The paint colors were brighter, as if it was more real now, or maybe it was my memory that faded the colors of my time.

The memories came flooding back. We had gone on every ride and, as the sun began to set, we found a place on the grass to listen to a rock-and-roll band. My mind was having real issues with what was real and what wasn't real. The moments when the twenties and eighties collided were the hardest to take. I was going to puke. Luckily, I knew where the ladies room should have been because it hadn't been that long since I'd last used it.

Racing away, I was quickly lost. Where there had once been a cinderblock building with large restrooms marked Men and Women now stood a shaved ice stand. I leaned over the bushes and lost my breakfast. Like a yo-yo bouncing back and forth, up and down, round and round, my head was spinning in circles. I began to cry. From my handbag, I pulled out the embroidered handkerchief Josie had given me. I wiped my eyes and blew my nose. It wouldn't be good for anyone to find me this way. A nickel bought a cherry snow cone and helped settle my queasy stomach. Finding a place under a shade tree, I tried to pull myself together. It wasn't easy.

I leaned back against the tree and looked up at the sky. For that moment I could have been anywhere at any time. What I wouldn't have given to have someone to confide in then. Always being afraid of saying or doing the wrong thing, I was alone in a way no one could understand. Slowly, I brought my mind back to 1928 and the friends I had abandoned without warning. As I walked back to the carousel, I prepared my story.

"I'm okay now," I said. "It must have been the breakfast I ate this morning."

Josie put her arm around my shoulder. "We'll just sit here until you regain your composure."

By midafternoon I was feeling much better, but Josie had taken a turn for the worse. Most days she did little more than read magazines and stare out the window, a major change from the girl who liked to dance and sing into the wee hours. This morning she had almost been her lively self, but as the sun slid toward the mountains she became more and more withdrawn.

"But, dearest, you're so tired," Mrs. Watson said, helping Josie unpack the picnic basket. "Please, go sit down. I'll take care of this."

"I'm fine, Mother Watson." With that, Josie pulled out a covered dish filled with fried chicken. "I made this myself."

"It smells wonderful," I said, taking the dish from her hands. She was pale and soon she began to cough.

"Maybe I'll sit for just a moment."

Josie's sisters helped Lillian, Brigid, and I set the table. The men sat in the next room, talking about politics and the state of the economy. The silver mining industry had taken a hit recently, but it was the eastern farmers who seemed to be in trouble now.

As I passed the doorway carrying plates of fine china for the dining table, I heard Thomas say, "Corn prices have dropped to ten cents a bushel. At those prices, the eastern farmers won't be able to sell enough corn to pay their mortgages."

Connor said, "I've heard stories about farmers choosing to shut down. They think life would be easier in the city."

"Might be that it is. Farming is hard work."

I'd never been on a farm in my time or this, but for me, city life was pretty good. I poured water from a silver pitcher into crystal glasses.

"The banks are free with lending these days," Thomas said. "Lillian and I are planning to buy a new car."

"Well, my good friend," Connor said, "could you wait until my purchase goes through? My broker is just now buying stock in Chrysler. I'm very optimistic."

"I think you should invest in U.S. Steel," I said with my typical forwardness.

I was standing in the doorway holding the pitcher, and Josie's father was looking at me as if I'd asked him to kill a baby. "Miss Oxford, I'm sure you mean well, but what could you possibly know about investing?"

I straightened my shoulders. "Cars are made with steel. There are dozens of carmakers but few steel suppliers. Steel is less risky."

Drawing on his pipe, Thomas couldn't hide his grin … so like Henry's. "Well, young lady, I plan to buy stock in Varney Airlines, what have you to say on the matter?"

"I think Pan American or Delta would be a better investment, but Hollywood has just come out with talking movies. That's what I'd purchase."

Josie was pulling at my arm. "It isn't politic to voice one's opinion on the matters of men."

I ignored her. "I'd buy Twentieth Century, Paramount, or Columbia Pictures." She tugged again and I let my friend lead me away.

"Why do you do that?" she asked.

"Do what?"

"Inflame them with your ideas about investments."

I wanted them to pull completely out of the market but that would never happen when things were going so well. I had to settle for giving them tips on the companies I knew would still be around in fifty years. "I don't mean to upset anyone. I'm sorry."

Josie gave me her most winning smile. "How do you know these things? That you even think about cars and steel astounds me, though it makes sense why it would be safer to invest in a steel company which wouldn't fail unless all the automobile companies failed."

The coming war would guarantee the success of U.S. Steel. "Everyone is flocking to the movies. I know they're going to be around forever. The first picture company to perfect the talking movie will leave the others in the dust." From the corner of my eye, I could see Henry listening to my explanations. "Instead of airlines, I'd invest in airplane manufacturers. Boeing sounds like a good company."

That was the way most days of the summer went. I would take every opportunity to tell Thomas and Connor which stocks to pick, and they would, in turn, roll their eyes and think me a foolish girl. I hoped some of the logic had swayed Henry but I couldn't be sure. Most days as we worked, Henry would tease me about my exasperation over the icebox and I would tease him about his penchant for eating all the broken cookies.

"Henry, I'm taking those to the Doyle's. I know you've only had five or six dozen cookies today, but these are for the Doyles."

"I wouldn't have to eat so many if you didn't break them taking them off the baking sheet."

"ME! It's been your job the last two days. I swear, I think you break them on purpose."

"You had best not be breaking cookies," Thomas said from the back door.

"I'm not, Father. It was only two cookies and it was quite by accident."

When Thomas went back outside to get another fresh block of ice from the truck, Henry said, "See, now. You've gotten me in trouble with my father. Truth be told, if you weren't fully grown, I'd turn you over my knee."

"You wish!" I said, snapping him with my towel.

He chased me around the table once before his father returned.

Detective Matthews came by the store the next day. "I understand you do some of the baking for the Watsons."

"Yes," I said, dusting flour off my hands. It was a stupid question, but I held my tongue. "I've been here since December."

"This is where you were found unconscious, isn't it?" He looked about the room as if seeing it for the first time, though I knew he'd been there on several other occasions. Henry said he checked the doors took measurements of the kitchen and the back stoop. He had even gone so far as to take pictures of tire tracks in the dirt alleyway.

"I don't know what you're looking for," I said. "I've told you everything I know."

"You were found inside on the floor, yet there were no signs of a struggle in here or in the alley. You must have been unconscious before you were dropped off. The part that rattles my brain is, why this candy store?"

I couldn't answer him. It was a question I'd tried to answer for months. At every opportunity, I would search the store for pentagrams or golden spirals. One day when I was on my own for an hour, I sat in the middle of the kitchen floor in the lotus position and hummed a mantra. Nothing happened.

The detective sighed. "I'm due for retirement soon and I hate to leave an open case. There is no record of you arriving by train, so I'm led to believe you came by motorcar. Do you drive, Miss Oxford?"

"No. I've never learned how," I lied.

"Nothing to be ashamed of. Most women never learn. Someone brought you to Denver, hit you on the head, and left you for dead on the floor of a candy store."

I nodded. "That about sums it up."

He looked at me through narrowed eyes. "Don't *you* want to know what happened?"

More than anything, but he was barking up the wrong tree and he'd have me committed if I steered him any other direction. "I'm safe now. No one has tried to hurt me again. The Watsons have been great."

He pulled on his chin. "They have taken you in. Perhaps there's a connection to the family I'm missing." Deep in thought, he strolled to the door. "Good day, Miss Oxford."

I was glad to hear the door close. My head ached and I realized I'd been clutching my fists so tight my fingernails had cut my palms.

In June, I agreed to be Josie's companion. She had taken a turn for the worse and needed daily care. As if she had no idea how sick she was, she and Henry tried to set the date for their marriage. Josie changed her mind several times. Currently, she was favoring Saturday, February 9th, 1929 but …

"I wanted so to be married at Christmastime, but all my wedding fabric is pink."

"Pink is just light red," I said.

"You're right! I should have a Christmas wedding." She flipped through the calendar for the hundredth time and settled on Saturday, December eighth. "Pink, red, and white! It will be lovely. I'll need a new coat, of course."

"Of course," I said. "Now are you sure this time?"

"Yes. Yes, I'm quite sure. December eighth."

She laughed, but it was clearly difficult for her, and I feared she would faint.

Laying aside the guest list we had been working on, I fluffed up the pillow behind her and helped her to recline on the couch. "You need to see a doctor," I said. "At this rate, you won't have the strength to walk down the aisle."

"I'm fine. I just overworked myself preparing breakfast for everyone."

"You're not fine. All you did this morning was cut fruit and now you can barely sit up on your own." I poured a cup of tea for her and placed it on the walnut end table beside the couch. "I'm taking you to see my friend Marjorie. You remember her, don't you?"

"Yes, she was the woman who came down to Murphy's last spring. Oh. I do miss Rory so." She sipped from the fragile porcelain cup. "She's a nurse. Tell me true. You believe this may be more than a simple chill."

I blew out a sigh. We'd had several similar conversations over the last couple of months. "Yes. Sniffles don't last for months. Marjorie works with people who have TB."

"Tee bee?"

"Consumption." Saying the word made my heart ache. It was a fitting name for a disease that was eating away the life of my friend. "We need to get you to a hospital where a real doctor can examine you."

"Silly bunny, I'm going to be fine. I just need a little more rest. Now that the boys have gone off to New York, I shall be bored to health."

"Josephine," I said sternly, "please don't fight me. You have to get better. You have a wedding to attend."

Maybe she'd finally grown tired of my badgering or she had come to realize she was getting worse each day, but she nodded.

"I'll not go to a hospital. I hate those places. If you truly think I should have a consult, I shan't stop you."

The doctor's visit was surprisingly brief, but the news was dire, and on July 10th Josie checked into the Agnes Memorial Sanatorium. Situated on high ground, seven miles east of the city of Denver, the complex of the sanatorium sat on forty acres of open prairie. To the south and east was a working ranch that would one day become the city of Aurora. The elevated ground provided an uninterrupted view of the mountain range to the west. It was beautiful, quiet, and yet scary in its implications. Agnes Memorial wasn't meant for people who were dying, but for those expecting to recover. As the papers recorded daily, these expectations were often unmet, and the dying were sent home or to a full hospital.

Connor Doyle drove the car up the tree-lined road and stopped in front of the administration building. There were five buildings in all, joined together by open walkways. The cloister connecting the pavilions ran directly in front of the main building. The stucco walls and red roof tiles gave one the feeling of being at a Spanish mission and the Southwestern style suited the landscape. I couldn't help feeling we were dropping Josie off at a convent.

"Do you see that building over there?" Connor asked as he helped his daughter from the car seat. "That's the power plant. All the rooms have electric lights and steam heat. Your mother and I acquainted ourselves with many possible sanatoriums. Agnes Memorial is the finest sanatorium in the area for those of our faith."

"It's lovely, Father." Josie coughed discreetly into her handkerchief. "I'm certain they will care well for me here."

Connor was an engineer by trade. The expanse and mechanics of the facility impressed him. He seemed compelled to tell us all about the power plant and the medical building. "The orientation of the sanatorium was carefully considered in regard to sun and wind, suiting the patients' needs for both winter and summer life. This arrangement gives each room direct sunlight every day of the year. The main building contains the offices, a library, parlors, and a dining room. There are also living apartments and private rooms for all of the employees, from the medical director down."

Connor was rambling. I realized then how frightened he was to be leaving his daughter here. He wasn't trying to tell us how great the place was, he was trying to convince himself.

I took Josie's hand. "You're going to be home in no time. It's like a vacation resort. Just look at that view." The entire Front Range and two hundred miles to the north, east, and south were entirely clear of anything more than a single tree.

A stout woman in an ankle-length black dress came out to meet us as Connor lifted Josie's bag from the backseat. "May I help you?" she asked. Her face was kind, no stranger to heartache.

"Connor Doyle. My wife and I met with the director last week. This is our Josephine."

"Hello, Josephine. I'm sure you are tired from your trip from the city. This won't take long." Looking at me with apprehension, she asked, "Mrs. Doyle, I presume?"

"Oh no. I'm Josie's companion. Mrs. Doyle wasn't feeling well today. She'll be here tomorrow to see that her daughter is settled. Can you tell me, is Marjorie Anderson here today?"

"I'm sorry, but it's her day out. I believe she went to town to do some shopping."

I was bummed. She had met Josie once in the early spring, and I'd hoped to reintroduce them. I trusted Marjorie to take good care of my friend.

Josie squeezed my hand. "You can come back tomorrow when Marjorie's here."

The look in her eyes told me she was as frightened as her father.

"Everything's going to be fine," I said. "You'll see. A week or two of relaxation and you'll be good as new."

The woman led us up several steps, through the arches of the open cloister and into the main building.

"You will note," the woman said, as she began the orientation tour, "the dining room is on the right. It has the full benefit of the morning sun on the east and south."

Pointing to the other side of the hall, she said, "These two reception rooms are where patients may meet their callers; we allow no visiting in the sleeping pavilions."

"Can there not be an allowance for my friends and family?" asked Jay.

"I'm afraid not. Our patients need rest, and visitors can be quite disruptive. I'm sure you will learn to appreciate the solitude."

I didn't think so. Josie was like wildfire and needed a constant source of fuel. For a moment I felt guilty. She was only here because I pushed for it. But she wasn't getting better at home, and I thought she needed professional care.

"Across the side hall from the reception rooms," the woman explained, "is the office for the clerk, where patients will transact their business and receive mail. Behind it you'll find the private office of the executive superintendent. Now, if you will follow me, I'll show you to the north end of the first floor where we will find the library."

It was spacious and well stocked. I'd never seen Josie read, but I hoped she would find reading a restful way to pass the days while she recovered.

Satisfied that we had fully appreciated the library, our guide led us back to the main hall. "The rear wing is reserved for the superintendent's family. The second floor is also occupied, on the north wing by the superintendent's and the house physicians' rooms, and on the south wing by quarters for the matron, housekeeper and nurses. There you will also find sleeping rooms for the servants."

Wide steps with shallow risers led to the upper floors. It was a beautiful and well-appointed sanatorium. I was starting to feel a little better about leaving Josie here alone.

"The third story," the guide continued, "is used for an assembly hall and will serve for occasional lectures and concerts."

"Concerts?" Mr. Doyle asked. "I thought the patients here needed their rest. How can you expect them to walk up three flights of stairs to attend a concert?"

"Any patient unable to go up to the hall ought not to be at any entertainment." Stepping once more to the front doors, she said, "You will notice, separated from the administration building by the cloister, two large sunrooms with removable glass for use in severe cold when a porch is too exposed."

Josie leaned against the doorjamb. "You don't think I'll still be here come winter, do you?"

Our guide smiled softly. "We have the very best doctors at Agnes Memorial. We shall plan to have you home for Thanksgiving."

"That long?" Josie said under her breath.

We were guided from the main building through a covered passage. The veranda had wide, open arches of seven feet and piers less than three feet wide and led to a spacious sunroom. Patients roamed the passageways from the main building to the sleeping quarters paying little or no attention to the newcomers. Most of them looked fairly healthy, and I found myself hoping that was true of the patients we couldn't see as well.

A nurse dressed all in white came up to our guide and handed her a sheet of paper. Turning to us, she said, "Your room is ready now. If you will walk this way."

Josie wrapped her arms around her father and he returned the embrace. "Be a big girl, precious. These people will do right by you."

"I know, Dada. I'll be brave." Josie gave her father another squeeze before turning to me. "Please say you'll come back tomorrow, please."

"Tomorrow and every day until you're well." I blinked back tears as I let the nurse lead her away. "She'll have a nice room, won't she?" I asked.

"The pavilions," said the woman in black, "are the essential working parts of the institution. Each one is two stories high, the upper story in all details like the lower. The bedrooms are all of the same size and arrangement."

Connor assured me the rooms were large and well laid out. "Brigid and I were allowed to visit the southern pavilion when we registered Josephine. She'll have every convenience."

Leading us back through the wide passage, the guide said, "We have gone to great length to see each room has adequate ventilation without causing draught. The sleeping rooms all open to the veranda, where a canvas partition is fastened to the wall between each two rooms. At night the drape is drawn out to the column between the arches, dividing the veranda into porches; one for each room. This gives privacy for the patients, whose beds can be rolled from the room through a wide door."

"That sounds nice," I said. "I love sleeping under the stars on a warm summer night."

She smiled at me. "Josephine is going to be fine here. She's young and strong. I promise we will take the utmost care to see she comes home soon."

We said our farewells, and I followed Connor to the car. The clouds had rolled in from the north. It looked like rain would hit Denver before we got home. I slid into the front seat, not knowing what to say.

A stoutly built redhead, Connor commanded respect. I'd never been alone with the man before and the silence was uncomfortable. Although Rory and Josie joked about his Irish temper, I'd never witnessed anything but gentleness from him.

Looking grim, he lit a cigar and pushed the start button. Several conversations went through my mind as he put the car in gear, and it chugged forward. Mostly, I wanted to tell him to stop buying stocks on credit, but I knew he wouldn't listen to a woman when it came to finance. That much had been made clear. Instead, I asked him what else they had showed him when he visited the hospital.

As we pulled onto Colfax, he said, "It's an impressive facility. You saw all the space and the openness of it. Back in Philadelphia, we didn't have indoor plumbing. I think I was most impressed by the water closets."

I had to think for a moment before I understood. "You mean the bathrooms."

"Each floor has a lavatory suite, tiled with white porcelain, with tubs, a shower, and three water-closet seats, each in a separate room. I've worked on many large constructions, but never have I seen one so well purposed as Agnes Memorial. I only hope the doctors are as good."

We rode in silence for a while before he said, "You will bring Brigid out to visit in the morning, won't you? She was quite upset to be left at home today. I would bring her myself, but I have an especially important meeting to attend."

"Of course I will. We can take the streetcar almost door to door."

"Thank you, Miss Oxford. You have been a Godsend to our little girl. She lacked direction before you entered her life."

I didn't know what I had done, or how I might have inspired her, but I knew she was a bit of a wild child. In my heart, I hoped it had been my influence, but in my mind I believed it was due to the illness that now had her locked away in a sanatorium.

CHAPTER 17

The next day, after finishing my shift at the candy store, I walked home to the Doyle house. The fresh air felt good and the walk gave me time to reflect. Not knowing how or why I was thrust into the past, I spent a lot of time reflecting. Searching for clues, all I had was some tenuous relationship to Henry and Josie, or, as she would become in December, Mrs. Henry Watson. She was so sick I wondered if I had failed somehow. Shouldn't I be protecting her so I could meet her one day in the distant future? Was it my friendship with Marjorie that would guarantee Josie's recovery? I couldn't remember when antibiotics were discovered, but the most devastating years for tuberculosis were in the late nineteenth century. That gave me hope as I walked up the steps to the Doyles' house.

Brigid gave Maria last-minute instructions as she slipped a lavender lace shawl over her shoulders. Adjusting her hat in the hall mirror, she asked me what I thought of the sanatorium.

"It's exceedingly well appointed. They've thought of everything. Lots of sun and fresh air, just what Josie needs."

"She had plenty of fresh air here. How are the doctors?"

"I only know my friend Marjorie. She took excellent care of me."

Brigid placed her hand on my cheek. "I'd almost forgotten, dear. That must have been so tragic for you."

"I'm fine now."

We chatted about the nice weather as we walked the couple of blocks to the streetcar station. The front yard gardens of the large mansions were ablaze with color. Brigid, a gardener at heart, shared the names and planting tips of several varieties of summer flowers. We didn't have to wait long for a streetcar heading east and I marveled at the simplicity of the design and at the stupidity of ripping them out one day in the not-so-distant future.

The doors folded open and we found a seat together near the front of the car. Two women who had been sitting in the row directly behind us got up and moved several seats away and I was once more reminded how intolerant people could be. Brigid must have sensed my anger because she put her hand over mine. "Do not judge, lest you be judged."

"That is so rude."

"They only know what they have been taught. Let's not give them a reason to believe they've been taught well."

I had to think about Brigid's words for a moment, but she was right. Being rude back to the women would only prove their point. Dropping the matter, we went on to talk about Josie's accommodations. I felt better knowing the medical building was used for scientific work and as a hospital for any acute cases. Surely, they would be using antibiotics.

Brigid clutched her handbag, studying the needlepoint design on its face. "The doctors assured us there are several treatments available."

"They're well staffed. I saw a dozen nurses when we dropped her off yesterday."

"That was one of the features that impressed me as well."

The seats were slowly emptied and the eastern plains opened in front of us as the streetcar stopped several times before reaching our destination. Once at the sanatorium, a nurse ran to tell Josie we were there. We watched groups of men and women playing chess and various board games. I couldn't remember the last time I played a board game. I hadn't touched checkers since I was ten.

We found an unoccupied table and waited. It wasn't long before that smiling face popped in through the door. I could see the smile in her eyes, but a cloth mask covered the lower half of her face.

"Ho! So good to see you today," Josie said, taking a seat at our table. "Any excuse to get out of bed."

"Are you doing well?" Brigid asked.

"Yes, Mummy. They treat me like a queen, waiting on me day and night. I shall get so used to this life, I shan't want to come home." Her giggle brought on a coughing fit.

I held her hand. "Henry would miss you if you never came home."

"Suppose they would let him stay here with me?" she teased.

"Maybe we should all move in," I said.

"Oh, that would be jake!"

"I have news from Rory," Brigid said. She pulled a letter from her handbag. "He misses us, though he is having a delightful time in the city."

"A letter. How wonderful. They must be attending the most fabulous parties."

The news was good. Paul and Rory had met several influential people in the New York music community and had achieved a small bit of notoriety of their own. The rest of the afternoon was spent talking about Josie's younger siblings and how they were already planning her homecoming party, sure to feature an elephant or a dancing bear at the least.

"This was my mother's," Brigid said, removing her crystal necklace. "Something to remind you of home."

"Oh, Mummy, I can't. That's your favorite."

"And you are my favorite little girl, just don't tell the others."

Josie laughed. "'Tis our secret."

Marjorie entered the reception room. She and Josie had reacquainted themselves over breakfast and Marjorie had requested supervision of Josie's case.

"How is your father?" I asked.

"He's doing better than expected. At his advanced age, recovery is uncertain."

We were all sympathetic as Marjorie told us of her father's struggle. "He's in the medical wing recovering from a collapsed lung."

"A collapsed lung!" I said. "How terrible."

"No, no. It's a common procedure. The doctors collapse the lung to rest it. That gives it time to recover from the infection."

It sounded barbaric to me, but I didn't know much about medicine.

"Now we must change the subject," Marjorie insisted. "We have strict rules about discussing any of our patients' conditions and that includes Miss Doyle's. A positive outlook is important to healing. Tuberculosis is contagious; therefore, visitation must be restricted."

"What do you mean—restricted?" I asked. "I know we can't go to her room."

"With rare exception, patients are not allowed to visit friends and family as to avoid the spread of infection."

"Even if we wear a mask?" I held Jay's hand, afraid to let go.

"Even so. Now I must get Miss Doyle back to bed. She is exhausting herself."

Brigid paled. "When can I see her again?"

"As long as she is free of fever, she may have two visitors once a week for one hour. Surely, you read the rules on the admittance form. We encourage letters to keep her spirits up. Now I really must get her back to her room."

Suddenly, Agnes Memorial no longer had the feel of a resort spa; it felt like a prison. Marjorie handed me a copy of the rules. The restrictions were plentiful from the strict bedrest to the mandatory hours in the sun.

```
7:15 - Rising Bell - Morning Toiletries
8:15 to 9:00 - Breakfast in the Dining Room
9:00 to 11:00 - Rest or Exercise, as Ordered
11:00 to 12:45 - Rest on Porch or in Sunroom
12:45 to 1:30 - Dinner in the Dining Room
1:30 to 4:00 - Bedrest. Reading. No Talking Allowed
4:00 to 6:00 - Rest or Exercise, as Ordered
6:00 to 7:00 - Supper in the Dining Room
7:00 to 8:00 - Extra Nourishment, if Ordered
8:00 - All Patients in Pavilions
9:30 - All Lights Out
```

This was terrible. To what kind of life had I condemned my friend? I prayed we'd done the right thing in choosing the Agnes Memorial Sanatorium.

On the long ride home Brigid assured me we had made the right decision to get treatment for Josie, but somehow I felt I'd betrayed her. She wasn't one for following rules.

Brigid got off at the Ogden stop and said goodbye. As I rode the streetcar west toward the candy store, I tried to figure out how to tell Henry he wouldn't be allowed to visit Josie unless her mother or father gave up their own visitation. And how was I going to see her? It might be possible to convince Marjorie to let me in, but I didn't think so.

What came to pass was a weekly meeting with Marjorie. Henry and I stopped by every Wednesday after work. Marjorie was guarded and I felt she was holding back. When I asked, she said Josie was holding on but hadn't truly improved.

In early August Marjorie told us the Doyles had approved the lung procedure. The thought of collapsing her lung made me panic.

"I want to see her. Please, Marjorie. I need to talk to her."

"Yes," Henry insisted. "I must see her as well."

Marjorie shook her head. "I'll see what I can do, but please don't get up your hope. The doctors are extraordinarily strict. If we broke the rules and something befell Miss Doyle, I could never forgive myself."

She had us there. We both wanted Josie to recover and neither of us was willing to jeopardize her health. Instead, we spent many afternoons in the lobby of the sanatorium discussing the future. Most days it was the wedding, but on other days it was the funeral.

"How can you plan a funeral when she's still very much alive?" A tear slipped from my right eye. "That's totally lame!"

Henry regarded me with a half-smile. "I'm not planning a funeral, I am only suggesting the day might come when we must."

"Well, it isn't here yet," I stammered.

"I've not told you about my sister."

"You have a sister?" I was surprised. He'd never mention her before.

"Yes. She was two years older than me. Maisey and I were quite close. She had been ill for several weeks and my mother insisted Maisey was going to be fine. I was away at my grandparents' farm the day she succumbed to scarlet fever. When I got home, her room was empty and her favorite doll was missing. I had convinced myself she wouldn't go anywhere without that doll, so she had to be alive." Henry's eyes watered and I reached over the table to hold his hand. He smiled. "I was only six. I didn't understand why my mother would lie to me. Why would she say Maisey died, when we knew she would get well? I was seven or eight before I understood."

"I see. You're preparing yourself for the possibility she won't come home."

"You sound so convinced of her recovery. I can't help myself but believe you. What if you're wrong?"

I couldn't say anything. If I told Henry I would meet them both some fifty years from now, he'd think I was totally off my rocker and call Dr. Mortenson. He was dedicated to Josie.

At that time my thoughts were bordering on indecent. I loved Josie and I loved Henry, though my feelings for Henry changed from moment to moment. On most days, he was a man of eighty dressed in a body of a gorgeous twenty-year-old, and I loved them both. In these moments the guilt would almost overwhelm me. I longed to find a man of my own like him. Bobby and Mike had been nice enough boys, but the truth was, I thought they were boys. Henry was a man, from the tilt of his tan fedora to the way he insisted on opening my car door.

The following week, as Henry and I drove to the sanatorium I brought up the wedding, hoping to put him in better spirits. He wasn't sad really, more like he was nervous. The usual cake ploy fell flat, so I opted for a random topic. "She still wants roses for the bridesmaids," I said as Henry opened the front door of Agnes Memorial. "In her last letter, she insisted."

"She can have any flowers she wishes. It's not for me to decide."

"I know that. What she wants is for you to be excited about it."

"Roses are lovely," he said, distracted.

"You should tell her that. You might even say they're the perfect choice."

"If that will bring her home to me, I'll tell her anything."

I could see I wasn't cheering him up, so I changed tack again. "Have you heard from Rory or Paul?"

"Yes, we received a post from Rory only two days past."

"Seriously? That's awesome. How are they?"

"They seem enormously happy. I was hoping to read the letter to Josie today."

"Didn't Connor or Brigid already come to see her?"

"They gave me the letter and said I should bring it to her myself."

The thought occurred to me that Henry might be just the ticket to raise her spirits. "Can I go in with you?"

"I had assumed you would. I rang the director this morning."

"Oh good. I miss her so."

"I do, as well."

I didn't want to intrude. "Are you sure it's okay? I mean, you haven't seen her in more than a month. Do you actually want to share this visitation with me?"

He looked at me, puzzled. "Josie misses you as much as she misses me. I shouldn't keep you from her." I was grateful. Henry was a generous man. I also wanted to hear what was in the letter, so I followed him into the reception room where Marjorie met with us.

"I'll be bringing her down for a few minutes, but I must warn you, she has little energy for conversation. If she looks like she's struggling, I must end the visit."

I turned to Henry. "That doesn't sound good."

"Mother Doyle said she was not improved."

"Not improved" was a total understatement. Josie was a ghost of the girl I'd met at Christmastime. Pale and weak, she looked like the slightest breeze would knock her over. I wanted to run to her, but touching wasn't allowed. I tried to hide my shock. But, of course, she would know how sick she was.

"Did you try collapsing her lung" I asked Marjorie.

"Yes. Please do not discuss treatment."

Josie sat at the table, resting her head on her palm. Her smile was wide, but it didn't reach her eyes. I kept telling myself that she couldn't die. What would happen to Henry? What would happen to me? Would I suddenly cease to exist because I would never meet the future Jay? And if I did, where would I go?

I was so wrapped up in my own life that I missed some of the conversation between Henry and Josie. He was saying, "The letter is dated August fifteenth. Your mother wished me to read it to you."

She sighed. "I'm so glad Rory had the chance to go to New York City. We should plan to visit as soon as I'm well."

Henry started to read:

Dearest Josie,

Time has been much to our favor here. The city is alive with prospects. Some are lucrative, while the most are more for the pleasure of playing my instrument. Mother has asked me to return home, but I have decided to weather the profitless intervals which punctuate my professional engagements.

Paul and I have been given the auspicious opportunity to go to London and Paris. We have booked passage on a steamer to Liverpool leaving the first day of September. From there, we take the train to London. We shall be

staying with friends in the great city for three weeks at
which time the London Pavilion has us booked for two
nights. We will be relieving the regular orchestra for a
showing of "This Year of Grace."

At once Josie's eyes brightened. "I'm so happy for them," she said. "I knew going to New York would be good for Rory. I would love to see London and Paris. "

"If there is any possible way," Henry said, "I'll take you there myself."

"How exciting for them. Steamship travel must be so elegant. I was just reading a copy from *Liberty* magazine how movie stars in Hollywood are booking passage on luxury steamers, where servants wait on them hand and foot. Ooh, or could you imagine? Flying in one of those zeppelins, or an aeroplane; landing in Paris like Lindbergh."

"Would you like to hear the rest of the letter?"

"Of course I would, you silly." Josie was looking better by the minute. I was convinced having company did more for her health than all that lying around.

Henry picked up where he'd left off:

We will be playing at a few smaller houses until
September twenty-fifth at which time we will sail to
Paris for eight weeks. We have been assured the music scene
in Paris is much more accepting of our Jazz than is
London. Paul has secured a five-day engagement for us at
Le Boeuf sur le Toit. The theatre has only recently
relocated to 6 rue de Penthièvre. It is one of Paris's most
celebrated theatres. While there are other, smaller
opportunities to be gained, we will have guaranteed work
at La Jave at 105 rue du Faubourg du Temple the fifth

through the twelfth of November. You may send a post to
either address while we are there.

"I so wish I could see him play Paris," Josie said wistfully. "If I can regain my strength, we could all go."

Henry nodded. "Rory will be home in November."

He continued to read: "We plan to be back in New York on November twentieth and to be home by November twenty-fourth for the holidays. Nothing can keep me from the wedding of my dearest little sister."

"Eight weeks in Paris. How glorious," Josie said as she laid her head on the table.

Marjorie was at her side in a flash. "You must not exhaust yourself, Miss Doyle." The look she gave Henry and me told us it was time to leave.

"Maybe," Henry said, more to Marjorie than Josie, "we should tell Rory to come home."

The fire was back in her eyes. "You can't tell him. He has this most wonderful chance to see Paris."

Ignoring Marjorie, Henry scooted over to Josie and took her in his arms. "I'm so afraid," he whispered. "I can't bear to be without you."

Marjorie desperately tried to pull them apart. "No touching! No touching!"

Josie briefly laid her head on his shoulder. "I'll be home when Rory returns and we shall all laugh about this." Backing away and turning her face toward me, she pleaded, "Don't tell Rory I'm sick. He must see Paris. If I can't go, I will feel better knowing he has been there. He's already on his steamship, so news of my illness will only serve to torment him." Her thin hands fussed with the hang of her gown. "I know your good heart, and I appreciate your kindness in everything," Josie said. "But I cannot burden my brother at the height of his career. I shall not."

"He will be angry if we lie to him," I said, knowing the words would have no impact on her decision.

"I should say so," Henry said. "He's my good friend as well as your brother."

"Please," she said, "when people try to make me change my mind, well, I never do. That's why I wanted Jett here—to take charge of it. You will see to the matter, won't you, Jett?"

Taking Josie by the arm, Marjorie said, "You both must leave, and I must go up and tend to this girl."

Before she could take Josie from the room, I had to ask Marjorie. "How much longer?"

She stopped and looked me in the eye. "I've seen others more sickly improve, though some, who seemed fully recovered, failed to wake in the morning. I wish I had better news."

Through September, Henry and I continued to visit with Marjorie every other day. We entertained ourselves in the reception room, often playing checkers or chess, while we waited for the nurse to take a break to chat with us. Over these long hours I began to know a different side of Henry. He could be playful one moment and serious the next. I blamed his moodiness on the uncertainty of Josie's fate. I, too, felt angry sometimes and lighthearted at others. One thing Henry and I shared above all else was our love for the girl we couldn't actually see.

I knew Josie was going to pull through, I'd seen the future. She would take me in again as she did last fall and care for me like a member of her own family. She would fondle her mother's crystal necklace when she was deep in thought and she would love Henry with a love so pure it was to be envied. What I didn't understand was why I was here.

"I need to be with her," Henry said. "She makes me want to be a better person."

"You are a good person, Henry."

He looked deep into my eyes, willing me to see something, but I was missing it. "I'm not," he said. "I have impure thoughts."

"I know. So do I, but we have to ignore them." *I don't belong here. I belong fifty years in your future, a future I don't want to destroy by being impulsive.* "We all have impure thoughts at times. It's only if you act on them that makes you a bad person."

He smiled and looked much more at ease. "You're an intelligent woman. I am blessed to call you friend." He moved his rook into the line of my knight. "You're my closest friend now," he said. "I feel I can share everything with you without judgment."

I studied the board. I wished I could tell him I knew what kind of man he would become one day. He was exactly the kind of man I was looking for, someone who would love me unconditionally. An explicit thought crossed my mind and I was overcome with fresh guilt. I looked up and saw it in his eyes as well.

"I have to go," I stammered. "I'll catch the trolley." Before he could stop me, I was out the door, running for the station. Head in my hands, as the streetcar rumbled along the track. *There's no denying it, I'm truly in love with him. How could I have let this happen? I'm going to mess up everything.*

CHAPTER 18

I went to visit Marjorie alone over the next several weeks and was grateful the sugar beet harvest kept Henry away from the store most days. Our conversations had become stilted and brief since that day at Agnes Memorial. Having done everything in my power to conceal my true feelings, I couldn't deny what I saw in his eyes that day. That still left several mornings that we had to work together.

While making fudge, he told me he'd received a letter from Rory detailing their time in London and asking about Josie.

"You can't tell him," I said. "It would break her heart."

"He should know. I'll tell him not to come home until we call for him."

"You know he'll be on the first boat. And if he wasn't, he'd be miserable knowing he's having fun in Paris while his sister might be dying. It's not like he can see her, even if he does come home." The words cut Henry to the core. I could read it in his eyes. "I'm sorry, Henry. I didn't mean to be so harsh."

"You're right, though. He would be just another tortured soul, helpless to do anything."

I reached for his hand. "We'll get through this, I promise."

"Thank you. I understand why I can't tell Rory, but he's always been my closest friend. I need to share this burden with someone. When you pull away, as you have so recently, well, I'm just lost without you."

"I'm sorry. I don't mean to be unsupportive, it's just ... " I couldn't tell him. The thought of wanting him made me shiver. I pulled my hand away.

"What is it, Jett?"

"Nothing, Henry. But please don't tell Rory."

"I won't. I promise. Let me motor you to the sanatorium today. I haven't been to visit this week."

"I know. We can leave after I get these cut and wrapped."

"I'll help you."

The next thing I knew we were laughing about the old dairy farmer who had such a sweet tooth he traded a month's supply of cream for five boxes of fudge.

All in all, Brigid seemed to understand Josie's wish to keep Rory unaware of her illness, knowing her son would come home immediately if he caught wind of it, and, like Henry, I wondered if her insistence on not telling Rory had more to do with her own fears. Having lost one child, Brigid exhibited great depth and understanding, but to lose a first daughter, and one of such good humor, was more than the strongest mother should have to bear. She and I had drawn closer as I shared what news I could from my visits with Marjorie and she hers with Josie. Although she couldn't say anything in front of the patients, Marjorie was free to tell me everything she knew about Josie's condition, and much more than she would tell Brigid. Most of it was uncertain, but I knew Josie had been moved to the medical building in mid-September.

Connor wasn't one to give up on his daughter, insisting that she was getting better each day. "Josephine knows herself. If she believes she'll be home before Rory, who am I to doubt her?"

"No one is doubting Josephine's optimism," Brigid replied. "The girl is afraid Rory will miss a unique opportunity in Paris. She forgets; he's so talented there will be other prospects. I'm certain Rory will be angry with us if death takes her before he returns."

I questioned Marjorie closely over the next few weeks. Her words were dire and my conviction that Josie had to live began to waver as October approached. My eighteenth birthday was less than a month away and a new fear replaced the old one. If my arriving here didn't have anything to do with the place, was the twenty-third of October the catalyst? Would my world once more be turned upside down in a heartbeat?

Sharing a room with Caitlin and tutoring the youngest children offered me a stable family life, not to mention the daily commute from Albion Street had been seriously cutting into my time and pocket money. The candy store was within walking distance, but not exactly next door, so Henry still came to get me on most mornings and brought me home most nights.

Because I had to be at the store before sunup most days I usually skipped breakfast, but on Sundays the whole family sat down to a eat together before church, after which we attended Mass and prayed for Josie's recovery. This Sunday morning Brigid was especially animated. Instead of going to church after breakfast, she led me upstairs to the linen closet.

"Josephine will be coming home again," she said, "but a soon-to-be wife needs her privacy." Picking out a bedspread from the closet, Brigid continued to outline her plans. "I'll move the small bed from the attic into the sewing room. She'll be happy there until December when she leaves us to live with the Watsons."

"Did you hear from Marjorie? Did she tell you she would be coming home?"

"She said I should prepare a room for her."

Excited, I helped her move a rocking chair and a small dresser into the crowded room. Bolts of fabric lined knotted pine shelves on the north wall and three mannequins aligned against the east wall as if waiting in turn to look out of the dormer window.

"The sewing machine can be moved into my room," she said as she stacked the linens on the dresser. "Go see if Sean or Liam can carry that for you. It's quite heavy."

By the end of the day, we had arranged a nice, if small, bedroom on the third floor.

"It's beautiful," I told her. "She'll love it."

"I don't think the poor girl has had a lick of privacy in her entire life. I hope she won't be lonely here."

"Caitlin and I will be just down the hall. She won't get the chance to be lonely."

Brigid hugged me, and I felt a love I'd only known from one other person.

My relationship with her was developing much like the relationship I'd had with the older Josie. If Jay was my long lost grandmother, Brigid was the mother I always wanted. It was confusing at times how Josie could be both my sister and my grandmother and Henry could be my grandfather and ... I had to stop *that* train of thought.

Making candy in October was uncomfortable, partially because the previous October had brought such turmoil into my life, what with landing fifty-five years in the past. The October before that, my sixteenth birthday, had brought Jay and Henry into my life. Although I missed my life with them, I had found a new and wonderful life here. Guilt had wormed its way into my restless nights. In my time, I'd been a lost child looking for a home of my own. They gave me all of that and so much more. Now, the Doyles had given me a home, including brothers and sisters. What would my eighteenth birthday bring? Much like my life with Jay in the eighties, I had grown comfortable with my life in the twenties. If there was to be another time shift, where would I end up? Would I find myself meeting Connor and Brigid when they were seventeen? I would certainly go insane if I was forced to leave another family I'd grown to love.

If I stayed here, would I witness the crash of Wall Street? I'd failed to affect any investments Thomas or Connor had made over the past year. I couldn't stop the crash if I didn't know how it started and all the books I'd read had conflicting ideas. As worried as I was about their financial future, it was thoughts of Josie that occupied my sleepless nights. That she would live was beyond question; I had met her in the future. The question that kept me awake was what that meant for me. Would I disappear once they were married? Would the older Jay and Henry be there when I returned? They had precious few years left, but I wanted to be with them in the end.

Evenings found me teaching numbers and letters to the youngest Doyles. I was still having trouble knowing when certain ideas and customs were realized. Halloween was one such idea. I tried to get the little ones excited about the holiday, but they didn't seem to know anything about it. Halloween was so big in the eighties, with costume parties and costume contests. There were ghosts and goblins, bonfires and bobbing for apples, and Henry Watson's famous caramel candied apples.

When I asked about prepping for the onslaught of candy sales, Lillian didn't seem to understand. After I told her about one of the parties I'd attended in costume, she understood the appeal, although she thought it sounded a bit unsupervised. I gave up trying to explain. Sadly, it appeared I was going to miss Halloween again.

After Mass the next Sunday, I asked Caitlin about her plans for celebrating Halloween. I slid into the car seat beside her. "Doesn't anyone know about trick-or-treating?"

"What's that?" she asked.

"You know, children going door to door asking for candy"

"I never heard of such a thing as that."

Brigid managed to decipher my question. "You must be speaking of All Hallows Eve," she said from the front seat of the car. "All Hallows Eve is the evening before Hallowmas, sometimes called All Saints Day. Though I don't know what this trick-or-treat for candy is, unless it comes from the custom of baking and sharing soul cakes."

"What's a soul cake?" I asked. "Is it a Catholic tradition? I've only recently been attending Mass. There's a lot I don't understand."

Brigid settled a fussy Kevin on her lap. "In some parts of Europe, groups of poor people, often children, would go door to door during Hallowmas, collecting soul cakes as a means of praying for those souls trapped in purgatory. The souls of the departed wander the earth until All Saints Day."

Connor slid into the car seat next to her, giving Kevin a stern look, and the boy grew quiet. "There are those who believe," he said, "All Hallows Eve provides one last chance for the dead to gain vengeance on their enemies before moving to the next world. In order to avoid being recognized by any soul seeking such vengeance people wear masks to disguise their identities."

It was starting to make some sense to me. I hadn't mentioned the idea of dressing in costume, only going door to door asking for candy. "Do you make or collect soul cakes?"

Brigid looked away. "The old Irish festival of Samhain, meaning End of Summer, is celebrated at the end of October where we would share food and have large bonfires. Most of these customs were left in the old country."

Behind us, in the rumble seat, four little faces stared at us in interest.

"I want to collect cakes," said little Erin.

"Oh, please. Can we get cakes?" Finigan asked, bobbing up and down.

From Caitlin's lap, two-year-old Tara said, "I like cake."

"Oh, no," I said to Brigid. "What have I started?"

"Don't fuss. We can share soul cakes with some of our friends at church, though I think the children are too young to need to disguise themselves from the departed."

"Do you have the recipe or would Mrs. Watson have it?"

"It's a simple spice cake made from nutmeg, ginger, cinnamon, and dried fruit, like raisins or currants. Each cake is marked with a cross before baking. Lillian will surely have several good recipes."

This was going to be fun. Josie's little sisters and brothers were in for a treat this year. I was sorry they wouldn't be allowed to dress up, but I planned to make lots of little soul cakes, like cookies, to hand out.

As the days grew colder, I became even more anxious about what might happen on the twenty-third. My temper was short and even the soft-spoken Henry avoided me when he could. After a particularly bad fit of anger over burning a batch of soul cakes, I apologized to Henry who had been in the wrong place at the right time.

"You're all to pieces," he said, "hugely dissatisfied, like everyone else."

"I'm not myself lately. I think it has to do with the time of year."

"You are referring to October of last year?"

"That must be it. Sometimes I'm scared or just confused. Dr. Mortenson seems to think I'm lying to him about what I remember."

He put a gentle arm around me, tucking an errant curl behind my ear. "It was traumatic for you as well as for me, changing my future in every way."

Could he know the future? Had I upset his life? I found myself wondering how things would have gone if he'd not found me on the floor that day. I stared at the kitchen floor.

With his right hand, he lifted my face to look in my eyes. "I'm glad I was there when you needed me. I've never felt so alive, so full of purpose."

It was hard to look back at him, but those Paul-Newman-blue eyes drew me in. "I'm sorry I got so angry about the cakes." *I'm sorry I've fallen in love with you. I could disappear tomorrow as easily as I arrived last fall.*

"Don't worry your pretty little head about it. I'll help you make another batch."

"No, but thank you. I think I need to get away for a while." I disengaged and headed toward the back door. "Would you be a doll, and put those burned cakes in the trash?"

He smiled kindly. "Of course, I shall."

"I'll see you tomorrow," I said, closing the door behind me. It was highly unusual for Henry to allow me to walk home unescorted, but he must have sensed my need to be alone.

Walking toward home, now the Doyle mansion, I prepared myself for the shock that would surely come the next day. Tuesday, October the twenty-third I would be eighteen years old. Almost an old maid by the standards of 1928, but just barely an adult by the standards I'd grown up with. Passing the Cathedral of the Immaculate Conception on Logan Street, I looked up at its twin granite spires. I wasn't a religious person by nature, but fear makes us reach for the intangible. I stepped through the heavy doors to find cool silence inside. The long aisle led to the statuary and the altar composed of pale marble. The prisms of sunlight played through the dozens of stained glass windows with the cathedral altar the golden prize at rainbow's end. I moved into one of the pews and bared my soul to any deity that might hear me. *If I can't go home, please, please let me stay here.*

The angle of light changed as the sun began to set. Brigid and Connor would worry if I wasn't home by dinnertime. Luckily, I wasn't far away. Walking south through the now familiar neighborhood, I looked for signs of change. Everything looked normal if normal was Denver's Pennsylvania Avenue in 1928. Normal people sat on their oversized porches or raked leaves from their well-trimmed lawns. The smell of burning leaves mixed with smoke from coal fires now seemed common and natural to me when once it assaulted my senses with its absurdity. *Is this real?* That was the question I could never truly answer. *Is this a dream I'll wake from come morning? Would I have any warning this time?*

Climbing up the steps to my most recent home, I could see all the lights were on. Something had happened. A stab of anxiety raked my stomach. Abruptly, I developed a raging headache.

CHAPTER 19

From inside, I could hear the sounds of angry voices. My hands shook as I opened the door. His back was to me, but I knew him. "Henry? What are you doing here?"

He spun around. "Where have you been?"

"I was at church. I needed to think." I looked at Brigid, who was sitting on the sofa wiping tears from her eyes. "Jay—Josie! Did something happen to Josie?" I raced to kneel before Brigid.

"Josie's the same," she said, placing her long-fingered hand on my shoulder. "It's Rory."

"Rory?"

"He's come home."

"But . . . " I looked at Henry.

"I kept my promise," he said, looking hurt. "Not that it did any good." He looked down at the floor. "I believed Mother Doyle had sent word. She denied it and flew into such an indignant rage that there wasn't a word of truth in the allegation, I had to sue for pardon before I got anything like peace."

From the doorway, Rory's voice boomed. "You aren't playing square. And I shan't stand for it. Where is Josie?"

Henry met Rory's eyes. "We didn't want you to cut short your tour. It was of a certain Josie's idea. You know how important your music is to her."

"Look here, Henry, you'll have to tell me, you know," Rory cut in decisively, "so you might as well do it now as ever."

I stood up and walked across the room to Rory. There was real fear in his face. "Josie is sick." I said. "She's being cared for at Agnes Memorial."

"Agnes Memorial! That's a sanatorium. How sick is she?"

I reached out and took his hand. "Very sick, but we have hope. Her nurse has asked us to prepare a room for her to come home."

Still angry, he turned away to leave.

"Wait," I said. "If no one told you she was sick, why are you home?"

When he looked back at me, I could see a pain that I didn't believe had anything to do with his sister. "Rory?" I said.

"It's nothing," he replied.

"Are you home for good?"

He ran a graceful hand through his ginger hair, longer now than it had been when he had left. "Maybe."

I let my questions go and helped Henry and Brigid sort through what had happened. The reason Rory had cut his trip short was unknown. That he was angry the family had kept Josie's condition from him was to be expected.

"I would never betray Josephine's trust," her mother said. "Though I'm not sorry he's come home."

Henry took a seat in a straight-back chair. "Could your husband have sent a post?"

Brigid shook her head. "He would never."

"He didn't come home because his sister is sick," I said. "Something else has happened." *Something has crushed his spirit.* "Did Paul return with him?"

Henry shook his head. "It seems they've had a quarrel."

My eyes traced the hallway where Rory had stood a moment ago. That was the pain I'd seen in Rory's eyes. He'd lost his closest friend. He still had Henry, but the relationship wasn't the same. "I'm going to talk to him."

"I'll go with you," Henry said.

"No, let me talk to him."

It was Henry's turn to look hurt.

"I'll only be a moment. He's had a lot to take in since he got off the train today."

"I suppose, then, I should be getting back to the store."

"I'll see you in the morning," I said. "Don't worry about Rory."

Brigid got up and was once more the strong matriarch I knew. "Supper won't make itself. Bring Rory when you've finished talking. He needs a good meal. He's thin as a willow branch."

"Will do," I said as I headed down the hall toward the back door.

I found Rory in the carriage house, sitting on the steps leading to the hayloft. They no longer stored horses and buggies in the building, though this looked like a recent change.

"Are you okay?" I asked. "I know the news about Josie is tough, but if I'm not mistaken, there's a lot you're not saying."

He looked at me strangely. "You're quite curious, Miss Oxford. I've met a lot of progressive people, but never anyone quite like yourself."

"I try not to judge," I said.

"Most people don't realize when they are because they know no better."

"I had to get used to the idea that other people didn't care for Irish immigrants." I sat on the step next to him. "People are far more tolerant where I come from."

"Where is it that you come from, Jett?"

I didn't answer.

"You once said you lived in Colorado Springs. It seems to me astounding that I should not then have grasped the fact that your imagination was already weaving a web of tales. I've known other people from there and you don't sound in the least like them."

I stared at the wall. "I lived on the streets most of my life. Some people have been considerate to me and others have been nothing but cruel. It doesn't matter what they look like, where they go to church, or who they love. Bad people are bad and good people are good."

"This is a universal truth." Holding my chin, Rory turned my head to face him and looked into my eyes. I could tell he wanted to tell me what happened, but he was afraid.

"Roooreee … " The voice cut through the dim evening light. "Where are you, Rory?"

Abigail! How could she have known Rory was home so soon?

He let out a sigh held too long and stood. Brushing the wrinkles out of his pants, he said, "I'll see what she wants."

"I'll come with you. Nothing in this garage for me to do."

He smiled. "Thanks, Jett. I can see why my sister thinks the world of you."

We walked out and met Abigail under a leafless birch tree.

"It's nice of you to call on me so soon." Rory lifted her hand and brushed his lips over her gloved fingers. "I've only now arrived home."

The statuesque blond looked me over and then her eyes slid to the carriage house door still standing open. "Were the two of you planning a motor car trip? I didn't mean to interrupt."

"No," I said. "We were just talking."

"A … lone?" The icy look in her eyes told me she wasn't nearly as shocked as she was pretending to be.

"What do you want?" I couldn't keep the anger out of my voice.

Rory patted my hand. "She's just come to see if I came home alone."

Really? Why would she care?

Rory slipped his arm in hers and began to walk her toward the street. "I saw your brother at the train station today. He didn't tell you Paul was not with me? That might have saved you a trip, and so late in the evening. I think Henry Watson is still here speaking with my mother. If you would like, I'll have him drive you home."

"So, where is dear Paul? His last post said he was starting a new role in a famous Parisian musical."

"He is. I don't suspect he'll be visiting our fair city again for quite some time."

"Wait." I couldn't hide my astonishment. "You've been writing to Paul?" Maybe I had things all wrong.

Abigail looked down her nose. "My brother introduced Rory to Paul." She tugged her gloves on tighter. "It sounds as if Paul is doing splendidly. Did I hear he might be moving to Hollywood?"

Rory's jaw tightened. "If all goes the way he plans."

"Oh, how wonderful it would be to live in California. I loathe these dreadfully cold Colorado winters."

"I suppose," Rory said, noncommittally.

"Tell me true, will he be visiting for the holidays once more?"

"I can't say if he will. Here's Henry now. Thank you for visiting."

Abigail laughed and gently pushed Rory's hand from her elbow. "Don't worry about me, dear boy. I have father's car. I can stay as long as you like."

"It's been an exceedingly long day and I've only just learned my sister is at Agnes Memorial. If you would be so kind as to cut short your visit, we can catch up another day."

Abigail looked as if she'd bitten into a sour apple, but she followed Henry down the steps to the street.

"Is she's really taken with Paul?" I asked.

"Abigail would appear to be a respectable California wife. The lifestyle would keep her happy enough if that's what Paul chooses."

Later that night, with the sounds of Caitlin's steady breathing coming from the bed next to mine, I tossed and turned. Brigid and I would be visiting Marjorie and the doctor in the morning. Then we would know if Josie was well enough to come home. That it was occurring on my eighteenth birthday wasn't lost on me. Anything could happen.

The smell of fried potatoes and toasted bread woke me. I looked over at the other bed, but Caitlin was already dressed and gone. Her cotton nightgown lay neatly over the back of her dressing table chair. The sounds of children laughing or complaining about getting dressed filled the air. Maria's gentle voice could be heard nudging the youngest into their Sunday clothes. Brigid was sure her eldest daughter would be coming home and wanted everyone looking their best. I wondered if it had been a good idea to get everyone's anticipation up. What if the doctor said no? The last meeting I had with Marjorie hadn't been that hopeful.

After breakfast, Connor and Brigid left for the sanatorium. I hadn't been invited to go with them, so instead, I went to the candy store to wait for the news with Henry. I found him wrapping taffies in the kitchen.

"Would you like some tea?" he asked.

"Sure. Don't get up. I'll get it." I poured hot water into two cups and filled the tea strainer. This tea was okay, but I had a serious craving for a cup of Celestial Seasonings's Red Zinger.

"Have you heard anything?" he asked.

"They should be meeting with the doctor just after noon. They're planning to stop and visit with Paddy and Laoise." I set a cup of tea on the table next to Henry. "Rory was fit to be tied this morning. He couldn't understand why he wasn't allowed to go."

"I'm not sure I understand the reasoning myself," Henry said as he sipped his tea and stared at the tray of unwrapped taffies. He was as worried as the rest of us.

"I think Brigid wanted to be alone if the news was bad," I said. "She tries hard to put on a brave face, but at times I can see how fragile she is."

"Connor is a good man. He supports her in everything."

I started wrapping taffies. "When you love someone, you can't help but be there for them. They become a part of you."

"Have you ever been in love?" he asked.

I thought about how I wanted to answer that. "Yes. I loved my grandmother and grandfather very much."

"I thought you were orphaned."

"They were a couple who took me in and taught me about life. I was a pretty wild thing back then. They were strict with me but in the most loving way."

Henry smiled. "You're still a pretty tempestuous one. I'm quite taken aback by some of the things you utter."

I grabbed more waxed paper. "I assure you, I've mellowed."

He shook his head. "There you go. I've never heard that phrase before this very moment, although I think I understand what you're trying to convey."

We passed the morning chatting about meaningless topics because the topic foremost on our minds was too painful. The store had a telephone and Brigid had promised to call as soon as she had news. Thomas was meeting with his broker and Lillian was tending the showroom floor. The sound of the phone ringing made my heart stop.

"It's Brigid," Lillian called to us. "She says the doctor is letting them bring Josephine home."

"Woo hoo!" I shouted. "We'd better get over there right now."

Henry was up with his coat and hat on before Lillian hung up the phone. "Are you coming, Mother?"

"No. I'll come over with your father when he gets home."

At the Doyle house, I paced nervously. "What's taking them so long?"

Rory relaxed on the sofa. "Mum likely took Josie to get a cherry phosphate. She loves them."

I opened the door to look down the street once more. Paddy and Laoise were coming up the walk. "Hi, I guess you heard the news, she's coming home."

Laoise looked impossibly sad. "We heard. That's why we're here."

It was only another minute before we heard the car pull into the carriage house. I was about to bolt for the door when Laoise held me back. "Josephine will be tired. We have to get her to bed, straightaway. Connor will be taking her up the back stairs. Wait here for Brigid."

"Taking her up the back stairs? But why?"

Rory was by my side in a flash. "What's wrong?"

Brigid stepped into the parlor where the family had gathered. Her eyes were red and swollen. "Josephine is dying. There is nothing more they could do for her, so they let us bring her home."

"But she *can't* die!" I said, knowing how ridiculous I sounded.

Brigid came over to me and held me in her arms. "We couldn't leave her there any longer, alone and scared. That's why the doctor let us bring her home." She was holding me but addressing the rest of the family. "We have to take precautions not to allow anyone else to be infected. Therefore, the littlest ones may only see her from the doorway and will not be allowed into the room. The rest of you must always wear a mask while visiting and wash your hands each time you leave her."

"I want to see her now," I said.

"When Connor allows."

Henry looked pale. It wasn't the news he'd been expecting. I wanted to comfort him, but there was nothing I could do or say to ease his pain with my own heart breaking to bits. Rory looked angry. I couldn't blame him. I was angry, too. It didn't seem fair that someone so full of life should be overcome like this. My need to see her had more to do with the date than anything else. I was sure fate was about to kick me in the teeth again and I needed to say goodbye.

It was about an hour later when Connor told Henry and me that we could go up to Josie's room. Rory had been to see her shortly before but left the house without saying a word to us. Henry and I climbed the narrow staircase, fearful of what we would find, but she was sitting up against her pillows, a smile on her face. Although deathly pale, her eyes were clear. My knees threatened to buckle, I was so glad to see her.

Henry pulled up a chair next to the bed and took her hand. "Oh, Buttercup. I've missed you so much."

"I've missed," *cough, cough,* "you as well. I wish you could have come to visit these last weeks."

He tucked her hair behind her ear. "We tried but were turned away."

"I know, love," she said softly. "They made it quite clear that to see you would be dangerous and that was a risk the sanatorium wasn't willing to take."

I sat on the side of her bed. "I'm not afraid. All you need is a good dose of penicillin." That was it. That was the key. I don't know why it took me so long to figure it out.

"Of what?" Henry asked.

"It's an antibiotic made from mold that grows on bread." I didn't know when it was discovered, but this was my friend. I had to do what I could to save her.

"What's an anti . . . anti?"

"Antibiotics. It's medicine that kills germs, stops infections."

Josie shook her head. "I had the best care doctors could give me. If they had this medicine, they would have used it."

"You can't die." I'm here to save you. I just have to get my hands on some penicillin.

"I love you, Jett, and you, too, Henry. Don't worry about me."

Henry brushed her hair back again. "You're my world, Buttercup."

"I'm not going anywhere for a while, so let's enjoy the time we have. Will you bring the chessboard with you tomorrow?"

"Of course I will, Buttercup."

"Bless you both," *cough, cough, cough*, "but it's been an arduous day."

"I'm right down the hall if you need me," I said, tucking her blanket beneath her. "All you have to do is call."

We left Josie to rest and returned to the parlor. Brigid was hemming a white dress, but I didn't think it was a wedding dress. I'd never felt such an aching pain in my heart. Through all my life, friends came and went repeatedly, some to new homes, some just disappeared, but never had I become so attached that their leaving caused such misery.

The family was quiet but not particularly melancholy. I'm not sure the youngest children understood what was happening. I put off the numbers lesson I had planned and went outside to catch my breath. It was cold, as October usually is, but fear was burning inside of me. I kicked around some dead leaves, trying to think of a way I could help. As much as I knew about antibiotics, it was impossible for me to make any. Somewhere, someone was experimenting with moldy bread. *I know penicillin was around after World War II. I know Madame Curie won a Nobel Prize and died from radiation poisoning, but did she discover penicillin? She was French or Polish. Fleming? Who was Fleming? Oh. Henry, why didn't you teach me this? Could it be that Josie didn't get sick in your past? If she did, she must have recovered because she was there to teach me how to cook and how to be a lady. She was there to love me when I'd given up.* I sat on the front step, staring at infinity. *Maybe the drug is available but hasn't come to the States yet.* Paul was in France. I was starting to feel hopeful again.

I raced up to my room and started a letter. I had no clue in what part of France the Curies would be, but it made sense that they would be at a major university in a big city.

Dear Paul,

I know this is going to sound crazy, but I really need your help …

An hour later I was hunting for Rory and found him sitting on the wooden bench under the grape arbor, carving a stick. I'd never known him to carve anything and I found it strange. I guess we all deal with grief in our own way.

"Hi, Rory. You got a minute?"

He looked up. I think it took a second for my question to register.

"What can I do for you, Miss Oxford?"

"For starters, call me Jett."

He nodded.

"I was wondering if you had an address for Paul? It's REALLY important."

He looked wary. "What could you perchance need to share with my friend?"

"I think there's a medicine in France that can save your sister." I could tell that wasn't the answer he was expecting.

"A medicine? How would you know such a thing as this?"

"I can't tell you, but please trust me. I want Paul to look up a couple of scientists."

"Look up?" His brows furrowed.

"Investigate, inquire about. I want Paul to search for these people and find out if they have this medicine."

"Dearest Jett, how would you know about this medicine if you don't know if these scientists have it or where they are?"

I sat still for a long time before I spoke. "We all have secrets, Rory. Secrets we don't dare share with others. Secrets that might cause us to be shunned, locked away, or worse. Please trust me when I say I only want what's best for Josie and I need your help."

"Paul is living with the director of his new musical. I have the address in my room."

He didn't get up. He sat staring at me for what seemed like hours. Finally, he said, "I know you never lived in Colorado Springs. I did some investigation into your story when the Watsons hired you. The family is close to ours. I have to acknowledge your loss of memory appeared considerably convenient. The element I find most distressing about you is, while your dialect is uneducated, you enjoy an unusual expanse of knowledge. Who are you?"

I sat down on the bench next to him. "Please trust me when I say I would never do anything to hurt you or your family. I do come from someplace very far away, a place where things are different, but I can't tell you about it. Please don't ask me, Rory."

He swung his foot back and forth. "I believe you know my secret though you have never uttered as much."

"I know when we fall in love, we fall. It isn't a conscious choice. When fate brings that special person into our lives, right or wrong, we have no control over the feelings they arouse in our heart." As I said the words, I realized I was trying to justify my own feelings for Henry. I didn't mean to love him, but that didn't stop my heart.

Rory stood and reached out his hand to help me up. "Let us post that letter. Maybe fate will smile on us both."

The long days while I waited for news from Paul were passed playing chess, Chinese checkers, and Parcheesi with Josie. She was in exceptionally good spirits considering the dire state of her health. Some days we even toyed with the idea she would still marry in December, though I think most of that was my own projection.

On her bad days I would hold her hand and place a cooling cloth on her forehead. It was on these days she would tell me how much my friendship meant to her, and these were the days I felt most guilty for loving Henry. I usually left the room when he arrived, claiming I didn't want to tire her, but I knew that was a lie. I was afraid Josie would see something in me, some stray thought that would break her heart.

The mail took so long in those days. I didn't receive an answer from Paul until the week of Thanksgiving. It was addressed to me with the stipulation I share his news with Rory. Unfortunately, he didn't have good news about the medicine. He had learned there was much research into *Penicillium glaucum* and *Penicillium notatum,* and that a Scottish biologist named Fleming isolated a substance he called penicillin from a blue-green mold that had contaminated his

Staphylococcus culture. The biologist would not, however, confirm the mold contained any antibacterial substance.

There was information about the musical being canceled and about a lying, deceitful Daniel leaving for Rome with one of the set designers. Paul was working at a local pub on weekends and he missed Rory desperately. He planned to return to Denver, hoping he would be forgiven for his arrogance.

Rory was jubilant, but I was crushed. I had convinced myself my whole reason for being here was to save Josie with a good dose of penicillin. I was wrong once again.

CHAPTER 20

"Cut my hair," Josie said one day unexpectedly. "I want it styled in a bob like the girls on the cover of *McClure's*. It would be ever so much easier to care for as well."

"What would Henry say? You know he loves your hair. I can tell by the way he's always ruffling his fingers in it."

She laughed. "It will still be red, just not a whole nest of it."

I obliged, and we had a wonderful day powdering our faces and painting our lips. Henry was surprised when he saw her. "You're looking of the fashion today," he'd said, but I'm not sure he approved. The powder made her look even more pale than usual. Caitlin, on the other hand, had loved the look and joined for our next makeup party.

It was on one of these days Caitlin showed me the dress Josie had chosen for me to wear at her wedding. While Caitlin's was pale pink chiffon, mine was deep red velvet with white fur trim. I had to admit, it looked like Christmas. Josie's dress was white lace with white fur trim and a long white fur cape. It was absolutely breathtaking. She wasn't strong enough to put it on for us to admire, so she asked Caitlin to model the dress. It was to become one of my fondest memories, yet one of the saddest. She told Caitlin to keep the dress for her own wedding one day and to let Fiona or Erin wear the pink gown. She stroked the red velvet of my dress and said to me, "You'll know when to wear this one."

"Don't be silly. I'm going to wear it at your wedding next month."

"Of course," she said. "My mind seems a blur sometimes."

As the weather turned icy, we were forced to wear coats in Josie's room. The doctors insisted the fresh air would help to heal her lungs, so the windows were left wide open. She was buried under blankets and quilts. We had tea together every day after I finished working at the candy store. Sometimes I'd tell her about this customer or that one. She loved gossip but was never malicious. She was more interested in who was engaged to whom and what the latest fashion was.

"You should buy new clothes. I've seen that same dress a hundred times now," she berated me.

"I like this one. It was the first dress you gave me."

"It was old even then."

"What do I need with pretty dresses? I'll only get flour all over them."

"A lovely girl like you shall attract a man."

I brushed her hair gently. "We've been down this road before. I don't want a man."

She sighed. "You will change your mind. Love will take you by the heart and you'll have no say in the matter. Best be ready with all your charms."

I had to laugh. I didn't think of myself as having any charms. "Well, if you insist, one dress." The reason I never bought clothes or trinkets for myself had a lot more to do with what the 1930s had in store for us than with my selflessness. When Henry couldn't give me a lift, I walked to work to save the trolley fare. I'd even cut back my visits with Marjorie except when Henry could take me.

Thanksgiving Day was unseasonably warm and it felt good to be outside. Rory and I were strolling down a wide sidewalk of beautiful red flagstone not yet buckled from time and shifting soil. We were on our way to Union Station to meet Paul, who must have booked his passage to Denver on the same day he posted his letter to be arriving so soon. The store was closed for the day, but the Watsons would be joining the Doyles for dinner later in the day.

"You are such a delightful mystery," Rory said. "I've been thinking about the financial advice you've been giving Henry."

"And?" I said, stepping over a rather large mud puddle in the street. When the stock market held through October I knew for certain it would happen the following year, in 1929. I had one more year to convince everyone to pull out of the market and pay off loans.

"I don't know how one could hope to become wealthy if he doesn't invest. I make so exceptionally little money playing at Murphy's, I can't afford to buy fuel for father's automobile, much less buy my own. Someday I'd like to have a house of my own as well, but without taking advantage of the rising stock profits I'm doomed to live with my parents forever."

"How can you buy stock if you can't buy gas?"

"Father has good credit with his broker. I met with him last week."

I shook my head. "I seriously wish you wouldn't buy on margin."

"I don't see any other way to secure the future."

A wagon loaded with barrels passed in front of us and I found myself wondering if what I'd been preaching for the last year was true. What if I'd imagined that future world? I was jolted back to reality when Rory asked, "How did you know about the penicillin research?"

"I heard about it from a friend."

Rory stopped walking and grabbed my arm, forcing me to look at him. "You don't remember any of your old friends, how is it possible you remember this tale?"

I gently disengaged my arm. "I can't tell you."

"Can't or won't?"

I blew out a long sigh. "You would think I was crazy. I can't go back to the hospital."

"Trust me."

"I can't, Rory. I can't trust anyone."

"You will one day. We all need someone in our life with whom we can be perfectly honest."

When I didn't disappear on my eighteenth birthday, I became convinced I needed to be here until Henry and Josie were wed. Whatever or whoever brought me here must have had a reason. Since

Josie and Henry were my only connection to the future, it made sense that my being here should put events in motion that would bring them to that exact place in time when I left them. Was it possible I was brought here to secure the financial stability of the store? Was I the key to making sure Thomas didn't lose everything in the market? Would I return once Josie was wed and the store was safe? I still didn't know what I would find when I stepped back into the eighties, but I intended to see if Rory was alive, and maybe Paul as well.

The train station was crowded with travelers trying to get home for the holiday. Rory spotted Paul first as he came through the wide doors from the platform.

"Paul!" he shouted over the din. "Over here!" He waved his arms above the masses. I could see it in his face. He was nervous but excited. Whatever happened between them was still unresolved. Paul glided through the crowd as graceful as any dancer and reached us by the exit door.

"Hi, Paul," I said. "You look good. Paris seems to agree with you."

Setting his suitcase on the floor, he lifted my hand and brushed his lips over my fingers. "You look enchanting as well, Miss Oxford." Turning to Rory, he gave the man a great big bear hug. "Good to see you, old friend. I've missed you."

Rory looked momentarily hurt but brushed it off quickly. Paul picked up his suitcase and we stepped out into the bright Colorado sunshine. "How I've missed this weather," Paul said. "It rains far too much in London and Paris."

After a few paces, Paul frowned. "You don't plan to walk the entirety of the distance to your house, do you?"

Rory looked chided. "Of course not, I'll hail a motor car." Leaving us, Rory went to the curb to employ a taxi.

Paul smiled at me. "Aren't you the surprise?"

"I don't know what you mean."

"I was so quickly over my head in the sciences, I was nearly arrested as a spy. I had to claim I was doing research for a university chum here in the States."

"Oh, my. I didn't mean to get you in trouble."

He studied my face for a long time. Long enough for Rory to return.

"We should go now," I said. "Everyone is excited to see you."

"How is Josie, by the by?"

"Not well," Rory said. "She's at home now, but the prognosis is doubtful."

"I'm sorry to hear that." Paul slid into the car. "I wish I could have found the medicine you sought."

Taking the seat beside him, I said, "I appreciate your effort. It was a real shot in the dark."

From the front seat, Rory looked back at us. "We haven't given up hope. Josie's a tough girl. If anyone can fight off this dreadful disease, it would be my little sister."

"You're so very right, good fella. Josie is nothing if she isn't resilient."

Over dinner that afternoon, Paul shared some wonderful stories about life in Paris. According to him, there had been many extravagant balls and well-attended community recitals. When asked why Rory hadn't shared these wonderful stories, Rory just smiled and said Paul was the better orator. I suspected Rory had been trying to forget much of his time in London, that is, until Paul came back to Denver.

It was no surprise that Abigail had managed to wheedle an invitation to dinner. It seems that her brother had received a message from Paul saying he would be visiting the Doyles on Thanksgiving Day and Abigail just happened to run into Brigid at the market. Poor Abigail was to spend the holiday unaccompanied, as her parents would be skiing for the week at Homewood Park, located in Deer Creek Canyon southwest of Denver. The charitable Brigid couldn't let the unfortunate girl dine all alone. Throughout the meal, Abigail hung on every word Paul said, most especially the stories about famous playwrights and musicians with whom he'd become acquainted. I tried not to judge her harshly, but it wasn't easy. Surprisingly, Rory seemed to encourage Abigail's affections.

Rory had changed. He looked at me with piercing eyes. "Because of you, I have furthered my political studies. While in Paris I happened upon the writings of Frédéric Bastiat."

"Who?" I asked, but by the blank looks on the other faces at the table I knew they wanted to know the answer as well. I spooned creamy potatoes onto my plate.

"He was a 19th-century pamphleteer." Paul said.

Rory interjected. "Paul doesn't care for his writings. Bastiat warns of a government so powerful as to pervert the law in the guise of protecting it. In his book, *The Law,* laws and lawmakers became the weapon of greed. Instead of impeding wrongdoing, it became guilty of the very evils it was designed to punish."

"Men need to be governed," Paul said. "This Bastiat would have you believe government is evil." He reached over and took my hand. "It is beyond my imagining. I confess, how it is that you know so much about a minor German political party. In reading his message I had felt true pride for my German heritage. It was only after encountering some of the party orthodoxy that I realized my mistake."

"I'm glad to know that," I said.

Paul refreshed his water glass. "The Soviet Union's Communist Party from gaining ground in political circles. Stalin has advanced ideas. The country is at peace."

What was Paul saying? Was he now a communist? Maybe, like Hitler, Stalin's true nature hadn't been revealed. Many a good politician had been corrupted by the system.

Henry nodded. "We cannot save all of the world, but we all must save what we can."

Thomas wielded a celery stick like a baton. "A man should have the right to own something. I can't say anything against the man who volunteers his labor and his body for the good of the country, but I'll ask him not to volunteer mine."

"I voted for Hoover," Brigid said. "He believes in the importance of volunteerism. He's a charitable man. He has refused to take salary for his presidency, offering to donate it to charity."

"He's a Quaker if I'm not mistaken," Paul replied.

"And I'm Irish Catholic," she said. "Half the country is Protestant. We should only be glad he's a good man."

Thomas mashed the potatoes on his plate. "His vice president, Charles Curtis, is of Native American ancestry from the Kaw tribe, I believe."

Brigid stiffened. "That doesn't make him an immoral person."

"Of course not," Thomas recanted. "I only mention it because it's rare."

Mollified, Brigid said, "He also founded the American Child Health Association. He's dedicated to raising public awareness of child health problems."

"Curtis?" Henry asked.

"No. Herbert Hoover," Brigid said, passing a bowl of brown gravy to me.

Connor leaned back in his chair. "I never liked Al Smith even if he is Roman Catholic, his stance on Prohibition notwithstanding. He is known for helping immigrants, most notably the Irish, rise up in American politics, but the corruption of the Tammany Society cannot be denied."

"You cannot deny he did great things for the Irish of New York," Paul said.

"It was as if the power made him a different person," Connor replied. "Or possibly, his choice of friends. The office of the president must be held by men of indisputable integrity."

As I sat listening to these men, I wondered if their feelings toward the newly elected president would change when the Depression was upon them. I left the table to take a light meal to Josie. She wouldn't eat much, but the idea of her sitting alone in her room was distressing. I knocked quietly.

Opening her sleepy eyes, she smiled at me. "I was having the most wonderful dream," she said.

I fluffed the pillows behind her to help her sit up.

"I dreamed you were with Mother and she was making your wedding dress."

I felt my lips curl politely. "Will you never give up on seeing me married? Who was it this time? Paul, maybe?"

She stared off into space. "I don't know. All I can remember is that Mother was happy and so were you."

"Well, when I find my prince, you and your mother will be the first to know."

She reached over and took my hand. "You're going to find the right man one day. He's there, waiting for you."

A much older Josie had said—would say—the same thing to me one day, only then, I'd want a man to love. I wouldn't have reason to fear losing him to a tragedy of providence. I'd envied Josie and Henry's relationship in the eighties. Though I still envied it today, I was afraid to let anyone know my secret. I grinned at her. "Of course he is. I'll find him any day now."

"Take good care of Henry," she said. "He's the love of my life."

"You're going to be okay. Look at how much stronger you are today."

"Jett, promise me, no matter what happens, promise me you'll take care of Henry."

"I will. I promise." I felt a chill. I'd heard her say those words before. I waited for the room to go black, but it didn't happen. I stared at my friend, pale and fragile, yet so full of life. Josie wasn't going anywhere soon, not on my watch.

Her mind was sharp and her tongue was as quick as ever. We spent the next few hours gossiping about Abigail and Paul. Josie was sure Paul was too smart to be taken in by a pretty face. "Paul tells us he may yet move to Hollywood. Abigail was all over that."

"A real Hollywood wife, I'm guessing."

Josie smiled. "She sees herself on the cover of *Photoplay* or *Motion Picture*. She does have the face for it though; this cannot be denied."

"Unless Paul has a fantastic job there, Abby's going to be let down hard."

Josie nibbled on her roll. "Abby," she said thoughtfully. "Well she's tough enough to take care of herself."

"Likely, she'll find a new mark as soon as she sees the ocean."

"Maybe she truly loves Paul."

I felt chided. "I guess I hadn't thought of that."

"She's not a bad person," *cough, cough*. "She's merely used to having everything she has ever fancied, I suspect."

"I had a friend like that once. Her name was Bambi."

"Bambi? What an odd name. Well, yours is quite unusual as well."

"Bambi told me it was just as easy to fall in love with a rich man as to fall for a poor man. I'm not entirely convinced."

The next week, Josie took a turn for the worse. The coughing increased and her fever returned with a vengeance. I'd been sitting with her most of the morning when Henry stopped by to visit. As usual, I got up to leave them alone.

"Jett, please stay," she said as Henry came into the room. "You are my truest friend and I must tell you how much your happiness means to me."

"I know," I said from the door.

"Please. Come play a game of Parcheesi with Henry and me. I want it to be like it used to be. Remember when we went everywhere together?"

I came in and sat on a chair by the bed. "I remember." The thought made my eyes sting. Henry pulled another chair over to the bed and began to set up the colorful board game. Looking at me, obvious anguish in his eyes, he said, "You're the only girl I've discovered who always forgave Josie's mischiefs. One might think you reveled in them."

I stared at him. "I love her," I said, point of fact.

"Yes, this I know well. One says lots of things, at times, you know."

"What are you trying to say?"

Henry took the other seat across from me. "Rory mentioned the letter to Paul. Actions are the heart of a body, not words."

Was he talking about the medicine? Did he know? Maybe it was getting Paul to return to Denver. That had pleased Rory.

Josie sighed. "Henry, be a saint and get us some tea. And I think a biscuit would be good, with jam?"

After Henry left the room, she said, "I had so much wanted you to marry my brother. Then you would always be my sister."

"I don't think I caught his eye."

"That's a true shame." She almost giggled, but that made her start coughing. I reached for her handkerchief to wipe the blood from her lip. My heart was breaking to see her like this. She was so weak and pale.

"What can I do to make you feel better?" I asked.

"Don't let your kind heart grieve too much over me. I'm no doe-eyed heroine in a melodrama, nor a wicked lover in a ten-penny novel, you know." She closed her eyes and rested a heartbeat before continuing. "I'm just an everyday girl in real life, flinging Henry into the very jaws of temptation."

"What are you talking about?" I stood, guilty and ready to run from the room.

Josie grabbed my hand with surprising strength. "I mean for you to be happy. You think I can't see it." Her hand fell away. "You love him."

"I didn't mean for this to happen." I felt my knees buckle.

"Nonsense, Jett." Her eyes closed and a tear rolled down the side of her face toward her ear. I brushed it away.

She coughed weakly. "You said it yourself; we don't get to choose who we love. I can see you love my brother, but as a sister loves him."

"Rory loves another."

A slight nod told me she understood. "He wasn't meant for you."

I sat down on the bed next to her thin body. "Don't talk like this. It scares me."

Her breathing was labored and I knew I should let her rest, but necessity held me tight to her side, as if every moment with her was a miraculous gift.

"You may as well know it," she whispered. "I'm going to die. I think you've convinced yourself this isn't true, but it is."

"No. You're going to be fine. You just need to regain your strength. I should go, now."

Her green eyes pleaded with me. "Please assure me Henry will be happy. He means the world to me. I wouldn't want another to stumble upon him while he's weak with grief."

"Hush now. You need to rest. I'll take care of Henry."

She began coughing again and I wiped her lips. Her fever was up.

"Promise." She barely whispered the request.

"I promise." I reached for her hand but she didn't have the strength to grasp mine in return. My heart started to pound and I couldn't breathe. I reached up to wipe her hair from her eyes but they were glassy and unseeing.

"Jay! You can't die!" I cried in horror. "You're going to be there when I come to the store. I'm going to work for you and Henry." I was shaking now, rocking her limp body in my arms. "You and Henry are going to teach me how to make candy, and count inventory, and close the daily books. You're going to teach me about history and stocks. I need you. I need you," sobbing to my core, "I need you, Josie. Jay, I need you." I held her close and petted her ginger hair. "You're my best friend. To hell with the future, I need you now."

Slowly, I laid her down on the soft pillows and placed my head on her unmoving chest. "I'm so sorry. I tried to find the medicine. I really tried. What good is knowing things if you can't use them to save the ones you love?"

I don't know how long Henry had been in the room. I felt his gentle hand on my shoulder. I heard the strain in his breathing. "She's gone," he said. *As if I didn't know.*

Anger swelled in my chest. It was wrong, all wrong. I jumped up and pounded on Henry. "No! She can't die."

He wrapped his arms around me to control my anger. "It's going to be okay," he whispered. "We'll get through this."

I was shaking. Angry that fate had taken her, angry that I couldn't save her, angry that I couldn't understand why. I moaned, "She can't die."

Henry sat me down on a chair. "We have to tell the family," he said with his customary control. I found it irritating then. I wanted the world to break into a million pieces like my heart was breaking.

I was glad to leave the room; I wanted to run away from the pain. I wanted to cut my heart out. Walking down the stairs, Henry at my heels, I didn't have to say anything. Chaos reigned throughout the house, as I found solace under the grape arbor. From the swing, I brushed away December's first snow and sat, wrapped in my despair.

CHAPTER 21

"The funeral mass is to be Tuesday at Holy Ghost Cathedral," Brigid stated bluntly to Aunt Laoise. "Following the mass, Josephine will be laid to rest at Fairmount Cemetery." Brigid was poised, her face clear of the puffiness of tears and restless nights. "Please see that the flowers are sent to the church. We can't possibly host more here."

Laoise nodded and carried a bouquet of white roses from the parlor.

I sat in a large oak rocking chair by the fireplace. *How could Brigid be so calm and practical?* I couldn't move. Once more, I felt my world was torn apart, my connection to the eighties shattered, and I was lost in time forever. As if mocking me, the family had stopped all of the clocks in the house at the moment Josie had died. It was an unusual custom, as was the idea of covering all the mirrors. Hiding the mirrors was actually a good idea. If I looked as haggard as the rest of the family, I certainly didn't want to see it.

As I stared out at the falling snow, cold as my broken heart, I felt a tug on my arm. Little Tara was clutching a worn rag doll. The yarn hair was matted and the red and white gingham dress was dirty from being dragged about. "Up?" she asked.

Her face was red and I knew she had been crying. "Of course." I picked her up and sat her in my lap. I brushed her copper hair away from her green eyes as she curled into a ball.

"Jate is sad?"

"Yes, little one. I miss Josie."

"Jo is in *hayvin* now?"

I nodded. I didn't know if there was a heaven, but if there were, Josie would surely be there. I rocked Tara in my arms until she fell asleep. At my feet, four-year-old Kevin pushed a train car back and forth.

The coroner had come to the house late on the afternoon of Josie's death to help with the arrangements. In my day, death was handled behind the closed doors of the mortuary. With cremation a popular choice, a mourner might never see the deceased at all. I felt strange watching the proceedings. Wearing gloves, the coroner gently closed her lifeless eyes and then proceeded to wash her entire body with a disinfecting fluid that smelled noxious. Although I understood the reason, I felt incensed that a stranger was touching her so intimately. He was thorough and thankfully quick. After putting away his chemicals, he pulled the sheet over her exposed body to her neck as if she were only sleeping.

Brigid came into the room carrying a white dress. "Is she ready for us to dress her?"

The coroner nodded and opened his briefcase. "I have a few questions if you please, necessary forms." He pulled out several papers. He began with asking her name and age and the time of death. The list of questions was long, and I just wanted him to go away. Once he was satisfied he'd done everything he needed to do, he left the family to make the final arrangements.

Brigid and I dressed her in the clean white gown, the same gown I'd seen Brigid hemming only days before. I had been fooling myself, believing Josie could not die, while her mother had been preparing for the inevitable.

It was a simple gown with long sleeves that hid Josie's thin and bruised arms. A delicate collar trimmed with crocheted lace brushed gently against her stylish new bobbed haircut. I pulled white stockings over her tiny feet while her mother placed Sunday gloves over the fragile hands, once so animated. I was wracked by a sob and Brigid put her arms around me.

"This is so hard to do," I said.

"It will get easier in time. The first day is always the hardest for me."

"It isn't fair."

"God has a plan for all of us. Whatever God had intended for my little girl to do, she must have completed it." She brushed my tears away with a gentle hand. "Now, be a darling and see if Rory is ready for Josephine. The coffin won't arrive until morning."

In the music room across the entry hall from the parlor, Rory laid white sheets over a wide board supported at each end by straight-back chairs. Other chairs were scattered about the room. "What are the extra chairs for?" I asked.

"For the wake." I must have looked dumbfounded, because he added. "We'll watch over my little sister until she's laid to rest. Some people believe the dead might wake and find themselves all alone. That would be quite sad, would it not be?"

I nodded, and then went to find Connor.

In the tiny sewing room, Connor picked up his frail daughter, thin from the long illness. He was a big man, strong from working with his hands. He easily carried her down two flights of stairs to the music room. Behind him, I followed with her pillow and a white sheet. As we passed the nursery, I saw Caitlin holding Tara in her arms. She didn't turn the little girl's eyes from the hall, but instead, she encouraged Tara to see her sister pass by. Rosin, Erin, and Kevin stood by Caitlin's side. I briefly wondered where Maria had gone. It was she who usually sat with the little ones.

In the music room, Connor laid Josie on the altar Rory had prepared. "This is where she would want to be," Connor said through a stream of tears. "She always loved music."

It was true. From the moment I met her, Josie's love of music propelled her through life like a warm breeze moves a sailboat across the water. She challenged her brother and her fiancé to be the best musicians possible. She loved to sing. Unfortunately, the church choirs were composed of men and singing in the clubs was frowned upon. Although there were times she was invited on stage with her brother, it was mostly in her own home that she could express herself to the fullest. Had she been born in a different decade, Josie would have taken the world by storm.

Propping Josie's head on the pillow, Brigid set to work arranging her hair and placing her arms over her chest as naturally as possible. The second sheet covered her from the waist down, draping to the floor. I placed a white ribbon in her hair and stood back. She looked like an angel, serene and waxen, but undeniably dead.

Uncle Paddy had been preparing the downstairs for guests before the coroner had completed his preparations. Busy in the kitchen, Aunt Laoise and Fiona made dinner while Maria and Guadalupe prepared the guest rooms for visiting family. Sean, Liam, and Caleb looked lost, so I sent them to the carriage house to get extra wood for the numerous fireplaces.

After dinner, I helped Caitlin get the littlest ones settled in bed. The clocks were stopped, but my body was telling me it was well past midnight. Caitlin looked dog-tired as well. Before retiring to our room we went to see if Aunt Laoise needed anything.

"I'm fine here with the menfolk," Laoise said, setting down her cup of coffee. "You two need to get some sleep. The house will be mighty swelled with visitors on the morn."

"Have you seen Mrs. Doyle?" I asked. "I want to make sure she doesn't need me."

"She retired to her room. Poor darlin' hasn't had a moment's peace today." Aunt Laoise sighed. "Shame to lose two daughters. Such a weary shame."

We passed the music room as we went up the main staircase. The low sounds of men's voices followed. Connor, Paddy, and Rory were watching over Josie through the night. It was nice to know she wasn't alone. Passing a flask seemed like a harsh way to grieve, but Rory had assured me they were celebrating the joy they shared with her, not celebrating her loss.

Fiona was in her bed when we came into the room. Caitlin and I quietly undressed and crawled under the covers of our own beds. The day had been so busy, the stillness of the room felt like a tomb. I stared at the ceiling, willing myself to sleep. From the bed closest to me, I could hear Caitlin sobbing into her pillow. Slipping out of bed, I crawled in next to her, my back against the headboard. "I know it hurts," I whispered.

She turned to me and laid her head on my shoulder. "Mum expects me to take Josie's place, but I'm not pretty and talented like her."

"Nonsense. Your mother only wants you to be you."

"Josie was the best at everything."

I turned to look at her in the dark. "Seriously?"

"She was the pretty one."

I shook my head. "I'll tell you about being thirteen. It's kind of like stepping onto a long bridge and not knowing what's on the other side. My foster mother used to tell me I was at the awkward stage, and, boy, was I. I used to trip over my own imagination."

Caitlin chewed her lip. "I don't trip, but my arms and legs are far too thin. I can't keep my hair in place, and I can't sing."

"You'll grow into your legs. As far as singing goes, why worry?"

"All good prospects should be able to entertain their husbands. I'll make a terrible wife."

Oh my God. She thinks her parents aren't proud of her. "That's a long way off. Let's just worry about today."

"But Josie was the eldest."

"Now you're the eldest and you have to put on a brave face for your little sisters and brothers. Help your Mum with the chores and try not to get into trouble."

"Josie used to get into trouble."

"Yes. Yes, she did."

A moment later, Fiona crawled into the bed with us. "I remember when Bridie died. I didn't understand. I thought she would come back one day."

Caitlin wrapped an arm around her sister. "Josie isn't coming back."

"I know. It won't be Christmas without her. She always made the best gifts."

"And sang the prettiest hymns," Caitlin said.

"And laughed the loudest," I added.

The unadorned oak coffin arrived just after dawn. Josie was laid out carefully. High-backed wooden chairs had been arranged in a large circle around the coffin where members of the family could watch over her. Because of her illness, the coroner insisted guests only go as far as the doorway to pay their respects, but immediate family could be invited into the room.

Only minutes after the room was set, a constant parade of visitors began ringing the bell, bringing cards and food. I wasn't a bit hungry, but I was grateful I didn't have to cook for those who might want to eat. Many of the guests were members of the church and some were local shop owners. The murmurings of heartfelt condolences and shared stories drifted around the edges of my perception. Throughout the morning, people of all ages strolled in and out, bringing a chilled wind with every opening of the door. Mimi and Sam arrived together, their eyes red with tears. I watched as the couple made the rounds, greeting the family. They looked comfortable with one another and it did my heart good to see them. Marjorie came in with her father. I was glad to see he'd recovered, yet part of me was angry that a man of sixty should live when a young girl of eighteen should be taken. She stopped to make introductions, and she left me with my thoughts shortly after.

Sitting there with the two youngest members of the family, one in my lap and one at my feet, I looked around for the other children. Connor and Rory manned the door, greeting guests, and directing them to the music room, parlor, or dining room as necessary, while Sean, Liam, and Caleb took coats and tried to look older than the young teens they were. On the sofa beside me, Finigan and Roark crouched, arguing over a toy horse. When the boys got too loud, Connor or Rory would scold them. At eight and nine, I'm sure the boys understood what was happening around them, but understanding and being able to sit still for hours are beyond most children's abilities. On the other side of the fireplace, Uncle Paddy lounged in an overstuffed chair with Erin and Rosin each on a plump knee. He entertained the young girls with coin tricks and stories. Every now and again, Connor would look over and thank Paddy with a nod of his head.

In the dining room, visible through the open pocket doors, I watched Fiona and Caitlin help their mother arrange the assorted hot dishes and cold cuts brought by visitors. Then I noticed Brigid rearrange the same five dishes a dozen times or more. She fidgeted over the placement of the forks and the stacks of napkins. She brushed an imaginary crumb off the tablecloth. Lillian tried to help, but Brigid kept going back to the long, food-laden table to move another dish.

I realized this was her way of grieving. By immersing herself in menial tasks, she was able to keep her emotions in check. I envied Brigid's strength. The two girls were as poised as their mother, although they had slept little the night before. It was only a guess, but I suspected Brigid had lain awake most of the night, too.

Henry arrived sometime after noon. He looked handsome in his black suit, carrying a bouquet of red roses. He made the rounds, greeting the guests and thanking them for coming. After a while, he went into the music room. From my vantage, I couldn't see his face, but from the set of his shoulders I was sure he was crying. He laid the roses beside Josie and slipped out the side door.

I laid a sleeping Tara on the couch and whispered to Kevin, "Stay here. I'll be right back."

It was cold outside. Yesterday's fresh snow was trampled by visitors, spoiling its pristine beauty. Henry was sitting on the bench under the arbor. I wasn't sure what to say to him.

"Hi."

He looked up, startled. "Hello."

"How are you holding up?"

He deciphered my meaning after a brief pause. "I'm doing well. Mother and Father asked me to run the store this morning, elsewise I would have come sooner."

"Your mother told me as much. She said time alone would be soothing. Was it?"

"I found myself torn. I wanted to be here. Although I have much more control of my emotions now." He motioned for me to take the seat on the bench next to him. "I wasn't *holding up* earlier."

I smiled. "I had a particularly bad day myself." I sat beside him, feeling the warmth radiate from his body. We both stared at the passing cars on the street without talking for a long time. I laid my head on his shoulder. In our own way, we shared much more than words could have expressed. The rest of the day was a blur, with people coming and going until the wee hours of morning.

Tuesday's mass wasn't what I'd expected. It was a service, but not one dedicated to Josie. At first I'd felt cheated, then I resigned myself to listen. The priest had requested we "do God's work." In my heart, I promised to do what I could, but in my mind, I had no idea what he wanted from me. I was more lost than ever. How could Josie die?

Henry was with me for most of the day. I believe he handled the loss far better than I. But he was more familiar with death. During the early twentieth century, many families lost children to fever and other common childhood diseases. Few vaccinations had been invented. The simple things I'd taken for granted while growing up were nearly magical in this era. How different Josie's life would have been if she'd been born only twenty years later.

As the day progressed I realized I was frightened. More frightened than I was in the first few weeks of being here, because, at that time, I thought it was all a dream. For the first time, since opening my eyes in the hospital a little more than a year ago, I realized I could never go back to Jay and Henry. Without Josie, that future didn't exist. If my duty was to save the candy store from financial ruin, where would I go when the crash came?

I stood by the open grave, Tara in my arms and Kevin hugging my leg. The priest was telling us about God's plan. Explaining how we are all a part of His plan with our own part to play. As they lowered the coffin into the ground, I was struck by an epiphany. Could I have been wrong about everything? If Josie died in1928, how did I meet her? If that future could be changed, did that mean the history I'd learned in school could be changed as well? Was there a way I could keep the stock market from crashing? Keep Hitler from killing over six million people? Maybe I was thinking too small. Could I use the Doyles' wealth to meet politicians or bankers who could change the future? *Don't be ridiculous. I hadn't succeeded in changing Paul's political views for the better, if I had really changed them at all. How could I affect Wall Street or international politics?* I watched Connor place a shovel full of dirt on the coffin. *Maybe, I'm just meant to save one family.*

CHAPTER 22

The Doyle family's annual New Year's Eve masquerade ball was to be held a mere two weeks after Josie was laid to rest. For several days, Connor had tried to convince Brigid to cancel, but she refused.

"We didn't cancel Christmas, and I shan't cancel the ball." Josie's mother folded a tea towel and placed it in the drawer of the buffet. "The dear girl was so full of life, she would frown on us if we buried our heads and shunned our friends."

Connor looked tired. "It's too much. You haven't rested in weeks. Our friends will understand."

She shook her head. "Connor, I want to do this. I need to be with my friends."

I set aside the book I'd been reading to Erin. "Be right back," I whispered to the little girl. I stepped into the dining room where the couple had been arguing. "I'll help her, Mr. Doyle," I said. "Rory, Caitlin, and I can do all of the decorating and all of the cleanup." I hoped the others wouldn't be mad at me for volunteering them, but I knew why Brigid needed to keep busy. Each day she came back to herself a little bit more, but a loss like this was going to take time. Another week of commotion would actually help rebuild her strength. "All the invitations have been sent. To cancel the party would be as much work as holding it."

"I doubt that," Connor said harshly before walking out of the room.

"Thank you, Jett, but I don't wish to burden you with this."

"It's not a burden. I want to help." I picked up another tea towel and began to fold it. "I need to stay busy to take my mind off Josie. Sometimes the thought of her almost overwhelms me."

Brigid hugged me. "You are such a darling. Thank you."

It did help. I felt much better after sorting through dishes and planning table arrangements. Even Caitlin cheered up at the thought of dressing up for the night. After engaging the younger children in making paper chains and paper doilies, we helped Rory and Paul interview a small band. So many guests had promised to come, Maria and Guadalupe prepared three large turkeys and a goose along with the usual side dishes of winter squash and potato casserole. While I had the week off from the store, Henry, Lillian, and Thomas made extra cakes and desserts for the guests.

Helping Henry carry in assorted sweets, Caitlin asked, "What are these?"

"Candied apples. I made them myself."

"They're kind of gooey."

Henry laughed. "I made a mistake in the caramel recipe, but they taste splendid."

"They look odd," she said.

Henry ruffled her hair. "I made them just for you." Opening a large box, he pulled out a beautiful white iced cake decorated with green holly leaves and red berries made of marzipan. "This is for your guests. Do you think they'll approve?"

"Oh, yes! It's going to be a grand affair," she said, sounding older than thirteen.

"It will indeed," Henry replied.

"You don't believe people will think us callous for throwing a gathering so soon, do you?"

I laid aside the ribbon I was curling into bows. "Caitlin, you worry too much about what others think. It's really none of your business what goes on in somebody else's head, now is it?"

"I don't want anyone to think badly of Mum."

"Your mother is the most generous person I've ever met. If people think badly, it's their loss."

Rory rubbed cleaner on the silver punch bowl. "Jett's right. Stop worrying and start polishing or people will think badly for having to eat off tarnished silver." He smiled and Caitlin relaxed.

The next day, Caitlin and I were in our room planning what to wear to the party. She opened the wardrobe and pulled out the pink chiffon dress that she had intended to wear at Josie's wedding. That's all it took to throw me back into the funk I'd been fighting so hard to get out of for the past week.

"I don't know if I should wear it," she said. "It's so pretty but . . ."

It was a beautiful gown: stylish and mature. "I think she would have wanted you to wear it. You certainly can't leave it in your closet forever."

"You're right, of course." She laid it on the bed. "I miss her."

"I miss her, too," I said, fighting back tears. "We can make a mask to match the lace. You're a young lady now. You'll be expected to dance with men."

She looked so frightened I almost laughed.

"I don't know how to dance," she said.

"Nonsense. Rory has been teaching you for years. Even Tara can dance."

"You're a lot like Josie. I'm glad you're here."

"So am I."

As we pulled out the red velvet dress Josie had given me, Caitlin's spirits lifted. "You will be the belle of the ball this year," she said.

I shook my head. "No, you will. Let's try a little color on your eyes."

We spent the rest of the afternoon playing with makeup much the way her sister and I had done in the past. Caitlin wasn't Josie, but she was like another sister, albeit, much younger.

Caitlin looked beautiful the night of the ball and Henry was the first to ask her to dance. All in all it was a pleasant night. The dress the family had given me to wear was beautiful and expensive. A guilty pleasure at times mixed with moments of missing Josie so much I nearly cried.

Marjorie, who had become quite close to the Doyles through Josie's long illness, shared my table along with Caitlin, Rory, Henry, and Paul.

Although her father had recovered from his bout with tuberculosis, Marjorie had decided to keep working at Agnes Memorial. I worried she would contract the horrific disease and fate would rob me of another friend, but she claimed the work was rewarding. Later that evening I was to learn that a doctor from the sanatorium had taken an interest in her and they were to be married in the spring. I was happy for her. She had once believed she was too old to find love. Laughing, she announced that the offer had renewed her faith in the male species.

While dinner was being served the band played a soft number, meant to inspire conversation. Across the table from me, Paul picked the meat from a turkey bone. "So why do you think Hoover is traveling all over Latin America if it isn't to meddle in their affairs?"

"The Monroe Doctrine," Henry said, "was directed against Europe, not Latin America."

"So you think we shouldn't interfere?" Paul set the stripped bone aside and stabbed a roasted carrot with his fork.

"It's different when the country is on your border," Henry replied sipping apple cider from an amber-colored glass.

My attention wandered away, and I found myself listening to Henry.

"I actually don't care who this Mohandas Gandhi is," he said, "or why he refuses to work with the British government. It's none of our affair."

"And Germany?" Rory asked. "What if Germany is unable to meet the reparations payments owed to the Allied governments? Germany is struggling. Will Russia help or take advantage? It may not be on our border, but it is the home of Paul's family."

They had my attention. I knew Gandhi would be giving the British hell for years without so much as throwing a stone. Germany, on the other hand, was about to throw more than stones. "You can't turn a blind eye to the world," I said. "If Germany rebuilds, Hitler will try to take over the world."

All three men turned and stared at me.

"This Hitler is no one," Paul said. "Few people have even read his work. Your fascination with the man is nonsensical. It is Stalin who is changing the political landscape of Europe. His five-year plan will save his country and show the world the way forward."

I had to marvel at the change in Paul. He went to Paris touting the works of Hitler and came home a fan of Stalin. Possibly, the bohemian lifestyle had made him chafe at the restrictions society imposed on people like him, causing him to reject Hitler's teachings. But I couldn't understand why he was promoting Stalin and one of the worst totalitarian regimes of the twentieth century.

"You believe Stalin will save Russia?" Henry asked. "Stalin is a communist and revolutions have a way of spilling over to other places. You have family in Germany and Germany *is* struggling."

"I think we should keep a close watch on Hitler and Stalin," I blurted. "Gandhi is peaceful enough. We can't let communist ideas take hold. Freedom is too important." My dinner was getting cold, but I couldn't eat.

Henry cocked his head. "How do you feel about Latin America?"

"They're poor," I said. "They need our help, but military involvement is never good."

Paul leaned back in his chair and studied me. "What, if anything, would make you imagine we desire to send our military to Latin America?"

The room was beginning to feel hot. "If there's civil unrest, the president won't want it spilling over to the United States, but if the government takes sides, they've essentially declared war on one faction or the other."

"What would you have us do about Germany?" Rory asked. "You sound as if you want to oust this Hitler without so much as a 'how do you do, sir.' "

"I don't want to let Hitler rise to power. It's too late to stop Stalin." There, I'd said it. I had no proof, but I had to say it. "Both men will kill millions of their own countrymen and crush anyone who believes in true freedom. They will control everything from the news programs to the literature allowed. His schools will indoctrinate all their people until their will has been stripped from them. The Bill of Rights we hold so dear in this country will be shredded throughout Europe."

Rory suddenly, to my delight, asked me to dance. Once on the dance floor he placed a hand under my chin, lifting it so he could look into my eyes. Ordinarily, this would have seemed a romantic gesture, but from the look in his eyes, he wasn't feeling romantic.

"How do you know these things you talk about with such authority? Mohandas Gandhi is no one. Why do you insist he's peaceful and that Adolf Hitler is not? How can you say with such certainty that these men, Hitler and Stalin, will ravish Europe?"

I tried to think of what might make sense to Rory. "Paul read Hitler's book," I said. "Surely he told you the man believes the Aryan Nation is the only nation worthy of life and that all other races should be eradicated."

Rory frowned. "Hitler believes the German race is superior and that the Jewish bankers are the cause of Germany's troubles. And, yes, he does have a peculiar hatred of certain races. Do you read German?"

"No. Someone told me what it said." I was being backed into a corner. "In *Mien Kampf*, Hitler lays out his plans to rule the world."

Rory was quiet for some time. "I don't believe you, you know," he said at long last. "Not that I think you're lying about what the book says. I think you're hiding something else. At first, I thought you might be from a foreign country, maybe even Germany."

"Rory, please don't ask me. I don't like to lie."

He stopped dancing. "So, you are lying?"

"Only about where I come from. Everything else I've told you is true to the best of my knowledge."

He led me back to the table. "Only because Josie trusted you I shall let it rest. She had an uncanny way of seeing the goodness in people."

Rory was clever, and I tried to steer clear of him for the first week of January 1929. Fortunately, Paul found them a gig playing jazz at a local club. For the foreseeable future they would be working while I tutored Rory's siblings. I was usually working at the candy store when he finally rolled out of bed each day. We saw each other in passing and I noticed Rory was reading John M. Keynes, *The Economic Consequences of the Peace*. I would rather he read *The State* by Franz Oppenheimer, and maybe then he would see the dangers of an overly powerful government. While I worried about Rory's political leanings, Brigid worried that her son had given up on Julliard and was traveling fast down a path of "turpitude and debauchery."

It had always been Rory's love for his little sister that brought them home at a decent hour, that kept him from indulging in too much whiskey, that made him want to do great things. Paul wasn't the best influence he could have right now. Paul had always craved the spotlight, even controversy, but something had happened in Paris that made him outright flamboyant. At times Rory would try to rein him in, but Paul would snap at him, and they wouldn't speak for days. They spent an inordinate amount of time in some pretty rough neighborhoods and, according to the daily editorials, it wasn't a good time in America to be different.

Dr. Mortenson came to visit again in late January. Setting a black leather satchel on the table, he pulled out a glass thermometer. "Miss Oxford," he began politely, "we have not had much time to talk over the past year." He took my blood pressure and my temperature. "Pardon me for not being more attentive. My daughter has spoken of you many times. I was confident you were quite recovered of your physical injuries. I understand you moved from the orphanage last summer after the Doyles' oldest daughter was admitted to Agnes Memorial."

I nodded. "It was shortly before. I was her companion."

"I understand she passed away in early December."

Again, I nodded.

"The oldest son, Rory, has been away since early last summer but has returned."

"Yes, he went to Julliard to study. He came home before Josephine died."

"Are you close to the young man?"

"He's my friend."

"He hasn't spoken to you of marriage?"

"Seriously? No way. He's my friend."

He wiped his brow with a kerchief. "What do you remember of the day you were found on the floor of the candy store?"

"I came to Denver looking for work. The next thing I knew, I was at the hospital."

"And you have no memory of your education? You are familiar with the writings of German politicians, yet you don't remember where you were educated or where you lived before coming to Denver seeking employment?"

So, Paul had relayed the conversation to Abigail. In the future, I would have to be extremely careful of what I said in front of him. "Rory's friend Paul had the book. I glanced through it."

"A book written in German?"

That was a slap in the face. Paul was a first-generation German immigrant; of course he would speak the language. "I overheard some men talking about it on the trolley," I lied.

He studied me for several minutes. "You were hired on as a companion to Josephine Doyle, but I see you are still living here, partaking in their considerable wealth."

"What are you accusing me of, Doctor?"

"Why have they kept you employed?"

"Maybe you should ask the Doyles."

He shook his head. "You still won't tell me what happened to you the day you were injured? I can't help you if I don't know how you came to be hurt."

"I don't remember."

"Young lady, I've had many years of experience working with all manner of children. I can tell when you're not being truthful."

He stood and put his hat on. "I shall ask them."

"I'd never do anything to hurt these people. They're like family to me."

"So you keep telling me." He opened the door to leave. "You don't seem to have any remaining physical complications that I can detect, but the inconsistency of your memory is quite troubling. Indeed, quite troubling. Expect another call from Denver's investigation division."

Oh, great. Just what I needed.

As the winter of Twenty-Nine passed, the entire Doyle household grew more quarrelsome. Brigid, usually having an even disposition, yelled at the boys almost daily. Connor came home late and said little to the family. The little ones, who didn't understand, threw tantrums at the slightest provocation. I could see all the signs of grief, although I had no idea what to do. I took the children to the park when I could, just to give Brigid some quiet time.

In those days, Henry was the one person I could always talk to. Many mornings we worked side by side at the store. While I still felt guilty about my feelings toward him, it helped to tell him about my concerns about the Doyles. Some days I would complain about the tension and other days I struggled to find ways to help. And there were the days I didn't talk at all. I most wanted to tell him the truth, that I loved him but that I didn't belong in his world. I was a child of the eighties, of a world of television sitcoms and MTV. How and why I was still here boggled my mind. There were days I was sure I'd changed the past in some way and I would be trapped here forever, yet my other life was so fresh in my memory I couldn't give up believing I would one day be returned. Henry seemed to understand my quiet moods and didn't push for conversation. When he did, it was usually about the latest candy recipe or the best way to display cakes and cookies.

One day, while I was particularly annoyed with Paul and Rory, Henry suggested we visit them at the club. "You understand this will pass?" he said.

"I know everyone hurts, but Rory and Paul are headed for serious trouble. I'm afraid we'll find them dead one day."

"They don't drink that much and neither of them are keen on fighting."

"There are people who don't need much of a reason to hurt someone."

He looked at me, one eyebrow raised. "Who would do them harm?"

I didn't want to tell him; after all, Henry might not be as accepting as I'd hoped. "Let's just see if we can give them a little direction."

He shook his head. "You confound me."

That night over a glass wine, I tried to find out what happened in Paris. I had a pretty good idea. Rory was deep in his cups by the time Henry and I arrived.

"Looks like you two are working on a real bender," I said as playfully as I could muster.

"I'm only starting," Paul said.

"Good. That means you can still play an instrument. Henry, why don't you and Paul jam while I spend some quality time with Rory?"

After the others left I turned to Rory. "Listen to me. You can't carry on like this. Someone's going to figure it out."

"I don't know what you're talking about, as usual. You speak another language most of the time."

"Paul left you for someone else while you were in Paris. That's why you came home. What I don't understand is why you didn't go back to Paris after the two of you made up."

"I'm afraid you're quite mistaken, Miss Oxford." He pointed to the small riser that served as a stage.

Abigail. I hadn't seen her come in. She was chatting away with Paul. A couple of her friends joined her at the stage, flirting and making small talk. Had I read the situation wrong? Was this all one-sided? I watched the performance for several minutes and realized, it was a performance. As I watched, Paul became more animated the more attention he received.

"Rory, have you considered going back to school?"

"Can't."

"Because you went to London?"

"No, because I can't leave my mother now."

"Oh my gawd. Are you crazy? You're mother's fine. It's you she's worried about. You're the one who's staying out all night long and likely to end up facedown in the Platte River. Your mother's upset that you haven't gone back to New York." I took his hand. "Go back to school. Take Paul with you and start again. If you go, he'll follow you."

"But Abigail …"

"Don't worry about her. Paul doesn't love her. He's protecting you."

There was real fear in Rory's eyes. "My feelings—they're that obvious?"

"No. When I was in high school, I had a friend who confided in me. Most people are so full of their own lives they can't see to the end of their own nose."

"You must not tell anyone. If my family should learn … " He looked down at his hands.

"You can trust me. I'd never do anything to hurt your family. As accepting as they are, taking in a stray cat like me, I don't think they're ready for this." *Or the secret I'm keeping.*

CHAPTER 23

Spring came slowly. My grief was less acute now, but the stress of Dr. Mortenson's hounding and fear of the impending Wall Street crash had taken its place. The promised detective was a younger man than I'd expected. He was actually quite charming, meaning I had to be extra careful with my story.

"Miss Oxford, I presume?"

"Yes," I said, holding the door open to the handsome man on the front step.

"Thank you for agreeing to see me. My name is Detective Bell. Lieutenant Matthews retired in December."

He couldn't have been more than twenty-five. "I was expecting someone—I don't know—older, I guess."

He smiled, showing a beautiful set of perfect teeth and darling dimples in his cheeks. "I assure you, I can handle the assignment."

I'll bet you can.

"May I come in?"

"Oh. Sure. I didn't mean to be rude." I led him into the parlor. "What can I do for you? Dr. Mortenson said you had some questions."

"I know this must be difficult for you. Forgive me if my questions seem callous, but we still have no leads regarding your attacker."

"It's okay. I'm fine now."

"My concern is for other women who might not fare as well should the scoundrel strike again."

Well, I felt foolish. Of course they would still be searching for my attacker. With all of Dr. Mortenson's insinuations that I was conning the Doyles in some way, I thought this man was here to investigate me. "Of course. Though I don't think I can tell you anything."

"We shall see. Would you like to take a walk? It's an exquisite day and I'm usually trapped in an office shuffling through papers. I relish the rare chance to get fresh air."

"Let me get my jacket." I turned to retrieve my coat from the hall and nearly stepped on Caitlin. "Oh. I didn't see you there."

"I only arrived a moment ago," she said, not taking her eyes off of the young detective.

"Nice, huh?"

"What?"

"The detective. He's cute."

Caitlin turned thirty shades of red. "I . . . "

"I'll introduce you. You can entertain him while I get my coat."

Caitlin looked as if I'd asked her to kill him.

"I'll only be a moment." I said, leading Caitlin by the hand into the parlor. "Detective Bell, this is Caitlin Doyle. She'll attend you while I put on a jacket. It might look sunny out there, but it's not exactly bikini weather."

Both sets of eyes looked in my direction. *Oh, crap.* I raced away before they could ask me what *bikini* meant.

Having only been gone less than three minutes, I didn't think Caitlin suffered too greatly. "Okay. I'm ready to go."

"A pleasure to meet you, Miss Doyle," the detective said as he lifted her hand to his lips.

Caitlin smiled but remained mute. I don't think she said a single word while I was gone.

As we walked, the detective asked the usual questions about what I remembered from the night of the attack. Unfortunately, I remembered too many things that wouldn't make a lick of sense to him.

"You came from Colorado Springs, correct?"

"Yes. I was looking for work."

"How did you travel? Is there a friend who may have shared the motorcar ride?"

"I took the train."

He looked puzzled and glanced through his notes. "And when you arrived at the train station, there was someone here to meet you?"

"No. I didn't know anyone here."

"You came to the city alone? A young girl such as yourself should have retained a companion, or at the very least, had someone here to meet you."

"I suppose I should have."

He regarded me for several heartbeats. "Why did you leave Colorado Springs?"

"I told you. I was looking for work."

"Is there someone in your past who might seek to hurt you?"

"No."

"If you traveled by train, you must have arrived on the one-forty on the afternoon of October the twenty-second. Lieutenant Matthews couldn't find a record of your ticket purchase. Could you have used another name?"

"I don't think so. Maybe."

He looked more confident. "Master Watson didn't find you unconscious until the evening of October the twenty-third. Where did you go when you left the train station?"

"Maybe I arrived on the twenty-third."

"Miss Oxford. The twenty-third was a Sunday. There were no commuter trains from Colorado Springs."

"Oh."

"Where did you go when you left the platform? The Watsons' store is only twenty yards from the train station. Did you go to the store, perhaps with someone you met on the train?"

"I don't remember leaving the station. I've told Dr. Mortenson all of this."

"Did you talk to someone at the station?"

"No. I usually keep to myself."

"Had you ever met Master Watson before the fateful evening?"

I couldn't meet his piercing dark eyes. *Yes, I've met Master Watson before but he had never met me. How crazy would that sound?* "No. I didn't meet him until he came to the orphanage to see how I was doing."

"Do you find it curious that he would search you out?"

"I never thought about it. He said he was worried."

"He had to search for you. The information wasn't readily available."

"He's a nice man."

"Is he?" The detective stopped for a moment. "Try to remember, Miss Oxford. Did you meet him at the station when you arrived?"

"No." I began to panic. Henry was a suspect. "Henry has been nothing but kind to me. I asked him if I could work at the store. I wanted to make candy. He was engaged to Josephine Doyle. He introduced me and they took me in. Henry's loyal and honest to the bone."

The detective began walking once more. "I see."

"What? What do you see?"

"There is a dangerous man out there. A man who savagely attacked you and it's my job to find him."

I had to come up with a story to throw him off the trail. I hated to think I was framing an innocent man, but Henry was innocent, too. *What was the name of the guy Julianne's boyfriend was mixed up with? What if I said I was supposed to meet him?* I shook my head. "I can't tell you. I do remember, but if I say anything . . ."

"This is a dangerous man and he needs to be jailed for what he did to you."

"Honestly, I don't know how I ended up at the store, but I was here to meet a man named Tony Roma." This was a total lie, but it would at least be a believable lie. According to Rory and Henry, the Roma family could use a little investigation. Bootleggers were serious criminals and maybe their investigation would lead to the thugs that killed that kid over a couple pints of whiskey last winter. I had no idea if the Roma family had a Tony, but it was the only name that came to me. I hoped the future restaurateur would forgive me for exploiting his name. "A short Italian guy met me at the train and took me to his house."

"Can you describe him to me?" He took out his little writing pad.

"I really don't remember much."

"What kind of car did he have?"

I looked up and down Ogden Street and settled on a black Model T. It looked like every other Model T and there were hundreds like it.

The detective wrote a few notes on his pad. "Thank you for finally telling us the truth. I understand why you were frightened to say anything. Even though the man is only a tad bit over five feet tall, Joe Roma is considered a giant among the city's underworld. You can be assured we will do everything in our power to protect you."

I had to make up a story on the spot and it had to be a story I could repeat. The truth is so much easier to remember, but that would land me back in the psych ward. It was an old story, but it might work.

What the hell. I described Paisano to the detective just as I had to the doctor.

"Italian, you say. Does the name Carlino mean anything to you?"

"No." I was shivering in spite of my woolen coat.

He looked sympathetic. "Where did they take you?"

"I don't know. It was a big place."

"What did this house look like?"

I described the apartment complex where Paisano had lived.

"Was it a rooming house?"

"Maybe. All I remember is there were these guys who came over to make a deal for some whiskey. I was supposed to be with one of them but I refused."

He nodded. "Did he seem familiar?"

"No. I've never seen him before. I was tired and drunk. Yeah. I was drunk. I didn't want to party with this guy, so Paisano got mad and started hitting me."

"Paisano?"

"That's what they called him."

"The man who came to make a deal for whiskey or the short man who picked you up from the station?"

"The short guy."

The sun was setting by now and I was sincerely cold. "I don't want them to find me," I said, shivering from more than the cold. "If they think I'm dead, they won't come looking."

"I understand."

"Seriously. Don't tell them about me."

"We will use the utmost discretion."

We walked in silence for another ten minutes. "I wish I could tell you more, but that's all I remember. I must have passed out when Paisano hit me."

"Why do you think they dropped you off at the Watsons' store?"

"I'm clueless."

"Well, thank you for helping us. I know it's been difficult." We had arrived back at the Doyles' house. He took my gloved hand and raised it to his lips. "We have a rather large amount of information on the Roma family. I shall begin this very night to discover the identity of your assailant."

"Thank you, and good night." I walked up the steps and then turned back to him. "I know I shouldn't be making a major deal out of this, but please don't tell the Romas you're investigating my assault."

He smiled gently. "Your secret is safe with me."

On the fireplace in the dining room sat a Roger's Receiver Model 130 radio. It was March the twenty-fifth, a Monday evening, and I was working late. Lillian and I were mixing cake batter and listening to *The Voice of Firestone* on the NBC network. The show featured classical, semi-classical, and operatic music.

The radio announcer made a comment about the falling stock market prices and my stomach clenched. I was sure the big crash would be this year because it didn't come last year. I was certain it was the late twenties and that Black Tuesday would happen in October. This fluctuation had to be a false alarm.

It started rather slow over the next few days. Prices began dropping and soon a panic struck across the country as margin calls were issued. Numerous people didn't have enough money to cover their margins, making the rest of the stockholders freak.

Later that week on the KOA Farm Report, banker Charles Mitchell made the announcement that his bank would keep lending despite the volatile stock prices.

"That should calm the market. If banks are investing, others will feel safer about their own investments," Henry said.

I wasn't as optimistic, but by the end of the week Mitchell's reassurance stopped the alarm.

As often as I could, I told Henry to sell his stocks and save his money, but it wasn't until that mini crash on March twenty-fifth that I finally got his attention. Thankfully, Thomas Watson took note as well.

Lillian and I had mixed several batches of cookie dough when Thomas and Henry got home. The Watsons' new Kelvinator had been delivered to the brand new eight-storied Montgomery Ward store on south Broadway. Thomas had borrowed a neighbor's truck to pick it up that morning. The two men came through the back door looking angry for men who had just brought home the latest in refrigerator technology.

Thomas took a glass out of the cabinet and filled it with water. "I had a margin call and had to take money from savings to cover the losses." He sat heavily on a stool by the pastry table.

"Oh, dear," Lillian said. "How much did we lose?"

"Enough to have paid the mortgage for a year," he answered solemnly.

Lillian, who had been wrapping cookie dough in waxed paper, sat on a stool beside him and wrapped an arm over his slumped shoulders.

"We'll make it back. We have five new orders for wedding cakes only this week."

He looked up and smiled at his wife. "You *are* precious. If I lost everything, I would be a wealthy man as long as I had you."

She kissed him on the cheek and went back to wrapping dough.

"Best we get that new refrigerator in the house, son." He got up and motioned for Henry to follow him. "I'll ring my broker in the morning."

Henry was saying something about plane travel as the screen door closed on them.

"Are you going to be okay?" I asked Lillian. "You won't lose the store, will you?"

"Of course not. Hand me that other bowl."

I gave her the dough I'd just finished mixing. "Stocks are so fickle."

"You have to unload the other ones," Henry said to Thomas while they moved the new Kelvinator into the recently remodeled kitchen. It was the Watsons' first electric refrigerator with a freezer with ice cube trays. "If you sell them now, you'll only lose a few hundred dollars."

"A few hundred!" Thomas grunted as he set the heavy appliance down. "There's no such thing as a few hundred."

"What about the other stocks, the ones that have already covered their margin?" Henry pulled a kerchief from his back pocket and wiped the sweat off his brow. "Maybe you should sell those now. Get out while the value is there."

"I've been working on those already. Harry isn't happy with me. He doesn't think I should pull out of the market."

"He's your broker. He makes money when he sells stock, of course he wants you to keep buying more."

"I don't want to pull out completely, but I don't know what to keep and what to sell."

I was in the corner, mixing bonbon dough. I wanted to tell them to sell everything, but I wasn't sure that was the right answer. I listened to the two men talk while they leveled the refrigerator. I was just glad Thomas saw the sense in not having a lot of money out on credit.

Rory and Paul left for New York in June. It was uncertain if Julliard would take them back, but Paul had a friend who was going to put in a good word. A death in the family could be easily overlooked for a truly talented musician.

Before they left, Rory asked me to go for a drive. He wanted to talk. I'd successfully avoided his direct questions for months, but I couldn't refuse to take a drive with him. The car rumbled up Highway 40 toward the mountains. There was no I-70 through the hills in 1929, and the roads were not even paved outside of the city.

"I wanted to thank you for pushing me to go back to New York," he said, dodging a particularly large rock on the road. "Paul was quite angry at first, but he saw the trueness of your warning."

I wanted to ask him what he meant. It seemed every time I opened my mouth, I was spouting *Danger-Danger-Will Robinson*. "Did you read those books I suggested, *An Inquiry into the Nature and Causes of Wealth of Nations* by Adam Smith and *On Liberty* by John Stewart Mill?" I asked.

"Enough of them. I'm unclear how you can know so much, please forgive me, while knowing so little."

Here it comes, the reason for the trip to the mountains. I said nothing.

Rory drummed his fingers on the steering wheel. "Last year you anticipated the power of the bankers over the economy. I must admit it. I was surprised by the flux in the stock market just this March. You suggested certain stocks might do better than others. U.S. Steel makes sense. All the car manufacturers will need steel. Can you tell me the logic of investing in movies?"

Whew, not at all where I thought this was going. "Sure," I said. "As manufacturing gets better, life will get easier. They invent new appliances every day. Less time spent getting to and from work, or spent taking care of the house, means more time to go to movies."

He laughed so hard he nearly ran off the road. "I can see why Josie loved you. You are adorable."

I tried to look indignant but that only made him laugh harder.

"I don't know where you get your ideas, but sometimes they make sense, so I've convinced Paul to invest most of his family fortune in U.S. Steel and Columbia Pictures."

"I think you'll be happy."

"That reminds me of another issue," he said. "I was glad I could be home for Josie's last days. We were close."

"I know. I would have told you she was sick, but she would have blamed herself for you giving up your dream. She would insist you follow your passion, never asking if it's realistic."

"She did blame herself for some time after I returned. I had to explain myself and beg forgiveness until I thought I would die from lack of breath. But we also spoke of other things, of other loves."

"I know she was afraid to leave Henry alone."

"She told you this, that she wished for you to marry Henry?"

"*What?* No! I can't marry Henry."

"Jett, calm yourself. Henry belongs to none now that Josie was taken from us, and I believe he's most fond of you."

I stared out the window, afraid to meet Rory's eyes. In truth, I was more than fond of Henry, but I couldn't be with him. Not only did it feel wrong because he'd belonged to Josie, but *I* didn't belong here. "She told me to take care of him. That's not the same thing at all."

"She loved you as much as she loved Henry."

I let the comment hang in the air. I remembered so many times the three of us shared. Even with others around, it was as if we three were inseparable. I think that's why it hurt so much to lose her.

"Henry's a good man," I said at last. "I'll see that he finds a good wife." *I can't be the one to marry him because whenever I complete my task here, I'll be gone.* "Don't worry about Henry. Just get your degree and land a spectacular gig in New York so I can come visit. I've always wanted to see New York City."

He looked over at me. "Gig? You sound like Josie. She loved to pick up slang. I couldn't understand what she was saying half the time."

As we drove back toward the city we passed several large ranches. Ahead, the city sat in a valley, its buildings small in the distance. It was at times like these that I felt most out of place. A few scattered farmsteads off Highway 40 would one day become the booming city of Lakewood. Where the flat land in front of the foothills met the edge of the Platte River valley someone had built a small subdivision. We drove passed Sloan's Lake where to the north I could see large mansions that would one day be chopped up into low-rent apartments.

"Be sure to write often," I said.

"I will. I enjoy penning my thoughts."

"I want to know about every party you attend."

He laughed. "Now you sound like Abigail." He sobered and said, "You were right about that as well. Paul doesn't love her, but she's become a good friend. Paul has asked her to come to New York."

"Seriously?"

Paul slowed down for another car to cross the road. "She will be an asset to us. Beautiful women get invited to the best places."

"That makes sense."

Paul stopped in front of the house. "I'm going to stop at the candy store. Is there anything you want me to tell Henry?"

"No." I let myself out of the car. "I'll see him in the morning."

"Yes, you see him most every morning." He smiled and then drove away.

Great. That's all I needed, Rory pushing me toward Henry. Maybe I should have told him why I can't marry anyone.

The next morning I was at the store at sunrise. Over the eastern plains the sky was turning pink and orange like a prairie fire. Henry met me at the door. "You're early. I would have come for you. I don't like you walking in the pre-morning light."

"I enjoy the walk. It gives me time to think."

"I hope you are well on such a beautiful day as this," he said, picking up the milk bottles from the stoop.

"It is beautiful. How are you this morning?"

"Well. It was good to see Rory last night. I do hope things go satisfactorily for them in the city. It will be difficult to start over again."

I put my apron on and began to gather the ingredients for cinnamon rolls. "They're tough boys. Don't worry about them." The dough was already raising; Lillian had been up for two hours already. She dumped dough out on the counter and began to kneed it. "Morning, Jett. You're early."

"I couldn't sleep."

"Is everything all right?" she asked

"Fine. I love summers. I like to see the sun come up."

Henry put the milk in the icebox. "We should take a motor car ride to the Rocky Mountain National Park. I've heard Estes Park is beautiful in the summer."

Lillian floured her rolling pin. "We shall likely have to fight through crowds. Just today, the *Denver Post* claimed the additional tourism has been the redeemer of the town."

Henry greased a baking sheet. "Colorado needs other economic interests besides cattle. Ever since the war ended, the farmers in the east have been in jeopardy. If it were not for the cooperatives, I don't believe any of them would survive."

"Well," Thomas said from the back door, "we can thank them for the price of sugar beets."

"Morning, Mr. Watson," I said as I slathered fresh butter, sugar, and cinnamon on the flattened dough. Turning back to Henry I said, "I thought everyone in the country was doing great and money was flying around for the last ten years."

Henry shook his head. "During the war, Colorado farmers did well because of European food demand, but everyone suffered after the war when wheat, sugar beets, corn, and cattle prices all collapsed. A good many farmers were bankrupt and their farms went on the auction block. To save themselves, some of the farmers began cooperatives."

"And the price of commodities will never be the same." Thomas put a box of dry goods in the pantry. "If I baked only cookies and folks wanted cake, I would go out of business."

Henry looked over the table at me. His half smile and raised eyebrow told me his father wasn't done speaking.

"After the silver crash, the Colorado mining industry collapsed."

"I didn't know there was another crash," I said. "I mean, a silver crash."

Thomas poured a cup a coffee and sat by the stove. I think he was enjoying himself. He was so much like my Henry of my time at that moment. I could hear an older Henry telling me about the stock market day after day. Had I only known how important those history lessons would be. Well, I wasn't going to brush this lesson aside, and Thomas enjoyed a willing pupil. "Although the government was required to use silver dollars, the mining industry was producing so much silver the prices fell. Banks began hoarding their gold by paying receipts owed to the government in silver dollars, but the government continued to pay for purchases in gold, meaning the gold reserves of the United States Treasury were slowly being replaced by less valuable silver."

I looked at Henry for guidance. "I don't understand. How did that cause a crash?"

"Too much of anything on the market will cause the market value to drop. That the United States might suspend gold payments, flooding the market with silver, is cause for international concern. When India announced that it would cease the coinage of silver, the international silver market crashed. The price for silver fell from eighty-three cents to sixty-two cents per ounce."

"Wow, you know a lot about silver."

"My father owned three silver mines."

"Oh. He must have lost everything."

"Not all. He was invested in local real estate, as well. When people began to come to Colorado for their health, my father recovered some of his losses."

"The sanatoriums."

"Yes. My father still owns his silver mines, but there's real concern silver will never be worth mining again."

"Didn't the war help the mines?"

"The Great War brought a need for minerals for arms production, some silver, but mostly tungsten for steel production. When tungsten was discovered near Boulder, a new railroad was built to haul minerals. The railroads brought more people to Colorado. The recently completed Moffat Tunnel will hopefully give Denver a direct rail line to California."

"And California means tourists for the ski industry," I said.

"I don't foresee that ever being of any consequence," Lillian said. "It seems perfectly silly to slide down a hill on waxed boards."

"That's how people have traveled in the north for centuries," Thomas said.

"Why, even when they have an automobile, they would choose to walk?" Lillian shook her head. "They should have more sense."

"It does seem to be catching on," I said hopefully.

"I shall believe it when it comes to pass."

I had a new idea, an idea that couldn't fail. "How expensive is land in the mountains?"

Henry looked at me, right eyebrow reaching for his hairline. "What would you ever do with such land?"

"Build a ski resort. A big fancy resort, in Aspen or Vail."

Lillian clucked her tongue. "Don't be a silly goose. There are few roads, no gas lines, and no electrical lines."

She had a good point. How could I build a resort if I couldn't even get to a good potential ski slope? "I'll have to do some research, but I think the ski industry is going to save Colorado."

Thomas considered me for a moment. "Aspen is nearly a ghost town. It was built on silver. I'm not familiar with a town called Vail."

I smiled. "Then Aspen it will be."

CHAPTER 24

It was early August and the summer had been hot and dry; the beginnings of the Dust Bowl. Time was running out, but trying to build a ski resort was categorically quite beyond my means. I had a small paycheck from the candy store, and working as a tutor and part-time nanny for the Doyles covered my housing costs, but land deals required investment, big investment.

I wasn't able to convince Thomas to pull everything out of the stock market and buy the town of Aspen, but maybe that wasn't a bad thing. I knew skiing would be huge in the eighties, but what would it look like in the next ten years? Would it be enough to feed them? Thousands of Americans would starve to death during the Great Depression and I was helpless to stop it. With any luck, I might help a family or two.

I was washing the last of the breakfast dishes when Brigid came into the kitchen.

"I've a letter from Rory," she said, spirits high. "I do hope they allowed him to return to school." She turned the letter over in her hand. "It would seem he has uprooted himself and moved once more. How will our letters find him if he can't stay still?"

August tenth, nineteen hundred and twenty-nine

Dear Mother and family,
Hope this letter finds you well. New York City is treating us suitably on this present adventure. I'm pleased to find Paul has many resources. We have been entertained on several occasions by such luminaries as Eddie Cantor, Guy Bolton, Clifford Grey, and Miss Irene Dunne. Only last week, we occasioned to attend a barbecue hosted by Harry Warner. I'm sure you know him by his motion picture company's production of the Jazz Singer last year.
The bustle of the city is so exciting. Our apartment is intimate. I found it quite enchanting with a wonderful view of Times Square. As luck would have it, Abigail and her friend have found a small parlor not five blocks away. The summers are much warmer than to what I've been accustomed, but with time I shall adapt. I have been assured by many residents that I will appreciate the warm summer after a single winter. I shall test their theory.
I have an application with Julliard, but with each passing day, it is less likely I will be called. I don't despair, as there are several opportunities for theater employment. Paul has been offered a promising engagement at the Majestic Theater, just off Broadway. He will be performing

in a new musical entitled *A Night in Venice* due to open on September the sixteenth. It is a beautiful theater, only a couple years old with seating for over fifteen thousand people. As one of the country's largest auditoriums, The Majestic attracts the foremost celebrities in the trade.

There has been much hullabaloo regarding theater over these past several years. We gladly follow the dailies as they hash over such trivialities as costume and language. The famous Mae West has caused quite a stir with her stage drama entitled *Sex*. The Catholic Church and the Society for the Suppression of Vice have lobbied for a crackdown on *Sex* and Broadway's other bawdy shows. The controversy over what constitutes art is an issue today and I don't see how a clear answer will be found anytime in the near future.

In closing, I would ask if the situation has resolved itself. Had I more time before leaving, I might have settled the matter. Do post an answer soon.

Your loving son,
Rordan W. Doyle

"I'm so pleased to hear the boys are doing well, but I so wish he could return to school," Brigid said, holding the letter to her breast.

"It sounds like they're have a good time," I said. "They're meeting influential people."

"I know my son. He would spare me any unpleasant news."

"Meeting one of the Warner brothers is great news."

She cocked her head. "Warner brothers?"

"Oh, yes. They have a movie studio in Hollywood. With their new talkies, you know the company is going to make a fortune."

"Oh, tsk. These talkies are curious today, but soon to be out of fashion."

I wanted to dispute her prediction, but how could I explain *The Dukes of Hazzard* or *Blazing Saddles* to someone who had never seen a television. "Didn't I read about the company buying a theater chain?"

"Companies buy and sell property every day. I'm quite certain Connor would be investing in the studio if it was a promising venture."

I was so frustrated. I couldn't seem to affect a single decision regarding the stock market. I couldn't convince anyone that Hitler and Stalin were going to murder millions of people or that, in a few short years, the national pastime would be television. *How would I ever get home if I couldn't effect any change?*

Later that week, while eating dinner, Connor was criticizing the recently opened Denver Municipal Airport. Here was another opportunity to invest well. Land around the airport should fill in quickly.

"I see no purpose," Connor said, "in having hardworking taxpayers spend good money for a rich man's sport."

Brigid passed the corn to her husband. "Mayor Stapleton has reached considerably with this latest gambit. I was speaking with Lillian just the other day. It would seem there are those who might wish to recall him."

"I've come to understand," Connor said as he dished green beans in a heavy cream sauce onto his plate, "the bankers who financed this project owned a good deal of the land. That land is high desert, not good for farming. Even so, a recall is hard to undertake and rarely successful."

Brigid clucked her tongue. "Air travel will never be useful for the common man, and were that to change, this boondoggle is too far from the city to be of good use."

I hesitated to say anything since she and Connor both agreed the airport was a bad idea, but there I sat, trying to remember how advanced air travel was in 1929. "Airplanes," I said, "are a fairly recent invention. If automobiles are any indication, air travel will be common in the near future. Lindbergh proved you could fly to Paris. Wouldn't that be much better than five or six days on a boat?"

Brigid pursed her lips. "My dear girl, wherever do you get these ideas?"

They had enough trouble seeing regular air travel, I wouldn't tell them one day we would walk on the moon. "I just know things change very fast. One day you're using wood to heat the house, and the next day they're piping gas straight to your furnace."

Connor's hand stopped halfway to his mouth. "You are never coy with your opinions are you, Miss Oxford? I should pity the man who weds you. One does so at his peril."

"Connor! Hush. Jett would be a delightful wife."

He laughed and pressed Brigid's fingers to his lips. "I adore you when you are angry."

"I'm not angry, but Miss Oxford should be."

"It's okay," I said. "I don't intend to marry."

"Now don't be brash," Brigid said to me. "You are well suited to marriage."

Connor grinned. "Provided the groom has an iron constitution. I should know well. My wife can be utterly emphatic in her opinions."

She snatched her hand away but smiled at him. Respectfully, she turned to me. "Now, Jett, it was our daughter's last wish that you find happiness."

"I am happy," I said quickly. Time to change the subject. "Warner Brothers Motion Picture Company has just patented the Vitaphone for talking pictures. Maybe you should pick up some stock."

"All of our stocks are doing well," Connor said. "You need not counsel me on my investments."

Brigid dished up bread pudding for Connor. "I understand Hoover has backed the water rights compact on the Colorado River. Black Canyon will build a dam now. That should help the farmers out east. It's been particularly dry this year."

"That," Connor said, "along with the Farm Act."

We spent the rest of dinner talking about farming while I drafted a letter in my head to Rory. It was obvious I would never convince Connor to move his money to safer stocks. I was going to have to try drastic measures if I wanted to save these people and go home.

Dear Rory,

I hope things are going well. I love that you got to meet Harry Warner. He could play a big part in your future.

I know this is going to sound crazy, but you must convince your father to sell his stocks while the market is high and all of his margins are covered. He stands to lose everything when the market crashes. I can't tell you how I know this, but it will crash in October. Millions of people are going to go broke and some will starve to death.

  If you can, try to land work with Warner Brothers Motion Picture Company. Move to Hollywood! New York is going to be a very hard place to find work in the coming years.

  I promise you; I'm not a lunatic; things really are going to get bad. Please do this for me.

  Your good friend,
  Jett
  P.S. Don't show this letter to anyone.

I was a wreck the entire month of September. The harder I tried to convince Connor or Thomas to pull out of the market, the less they seemed to listen. Henry teased me, nicknaming me Chicken Little.

It was the second of October when Dr. Mortenson called on me at home once more, a situation I found unsettling. I thought after speaking with his detective friend he would stop ragging on me. I found the doctor's constant questions totally irritating.

I had just settled into a comfortable chair to finish mending Kevin's sleeping gown (the four-year-old was an absolute terror on clothes) when Sean brought the doctor into the parlor.

"I see you have settled into your new life." He pulled out the usual instruments of torture. "You're looking fit."

"I feel fine. Must we keep doing this?"

"I only seek to give you the best care. With my daughter away, I don't have a reliable source of gossip." He smiled, but it felt threatening rather than friendly.

Once satisfied with my physical state, he sat in the chair across from me and opened a leather-bound book. "Has any more of your memory returned?" he asked without looking up.

"I still have blank spots."

"Aw, yes. Do you remember your parents?"

"I told you before, I'm an orphan."

"And where did you live before the accident?"

"In Colorado Springs. I was living on the streets. No one knows me. I lived in Hawaii before that." *Must we do this every time?* "I came to Denver looking for work."

He nodded and wrote something in his little book. "Yes. It would seem you found gainful employment."

"I love working at the candy store."

"The Doyles are of substantial means."

"They are." I was getting angry. It was a point he'd made many times.

"And they have taken you in as a nanny for their young ones?"

"Yes, Mother Doyle is wonderful. I tutor the four little ones in the evenings."

"I believe Guadalupe and Maria still take care of the domestic duties and watch the children."

"I watch the kids when they need a day off and I'm not working at the store."

"I see. For a few hours of tutoring, the Doyles," he looked meaningfully at the new cotton dress I was wearing, "supply you with an allowance, a private room, and all the clothing you might need."

"What are you implying, Doctor? And I share a room with Caitlin and Fiona. It's anything but private."

"Miss Oxford, you present yourself as uneducated and unassuming, but I think you're quite intelligent. Somehow you have managed to take care of yourself for many years without doing a hard day's work." He looked at my hands. "Apparently, this job requires more than your last line of employment."

I sat there in the Morris chair not knowing what to say.

"A woman suffering the anguish of grief may wish so hard to believe what she wishes were true that she can't see reality. Are you an acquaintance of the spiritual medium Grace Elizabeth Lobach? I understand she is often recognized as Gracie."

"Who? No, I never heard of her."

"Are you a member of the Temple of the Brotherhood?"

"No. Why are you asking about this?"

"Fantastical superstition will infest humankind as long as there are people who dwell in grief and sadness. Mediums purportedly mediate communication between spirits of the dead and other human beings. Anguish interferes with a person's sense of reason."

"Do you think I'm some kind of medium? I just like working at the candy store and teaching Brigid's children how to read and write."

"Tell me true, Miss Oxford, do you believe you can predict the future?"

I pricked my finger with the needle. I was so stunned by the question, I didn't answer.

In a scathing tone that chilled me, Dr. Mortenson continued, "After first look, the lion's share of this bunk—from Ouija boards to channeling—is poppycock. These charlatans often employ simple techniques used by stage magicians. If it is your game to liberate these good people of their fortunes with false hopes, I *will* have you arrested."

Suddenly aware of the danger I was facing, I scrambled to cover my ass. "I can't predict the future. No one can. The future is determined by free will." I was shaking, and doctor could see my terror. It's one thing to have someone think you're a little crazy, it's quite another to have them think you're some kind of rip-off artist.

"I'm aware that on several occasions you have instructed both the Doyles and the Watsons to sell their investments, have you not?"

"Yes, I think it's a good idea. The market is high right now. It can't stay that way forever."

"What would you have them do with the money?"

"I don't know; buy land out east or around Golden. Denver's still growing. Land will only go up in value."

"Do you know anyone who owns land, Miss Oxford?"

"Hell no! I can count the number of people I know on both hands."

He looked unbelieving.

"Look," I said, putting down the gown. "Our actions shape our destiny for better or for worse. I only want what's best for those I love.

I have nothing to gain from this. If you want me to go back to the orphanage I will."

"You will be nineteen in a few weeks if what you told me is true."

I nodded.

"Perhaps a husband would keep you out of mischief."

"I don't want to get married."

"Would you actually turn down an offer from Rordan Doyle, Miss Oxford?"

"Rory would never ask me to marry him."

The doctor slipped on his coat. "I've searched the city and have found no others who have the surname Oxford. Tell me, did you make that up when you saw the grand hotel upon your arrival?"

He was remarkably close to the truth, though I'd taken the names years before, because that was where I was found. "No, sir. My name has been Oxford for all of my life."

"You are a mystery to me. I can't seem to verify much of what you say, but I have no evidence to dispute it. There must be someone who remembers bringing you to Denver. I might like to place a notice in the dailies, but that is better left up to the police, I think." He donned his hat and opened the door. "Good day, Miss Oxford."

After the doctor left I had time to think about what had just happened. I came to the conclusion Rory had shared my letter with Abigail. It angered me, but I could also understand. I must have sounded nuts. I worried now that he thought I was some kind of swindler, out to hurt his family. My threat to keep his secret might be perceived as blackmail. If only I could talk to him, explain myself. I knew then, only the actual crash of the stock market would prove me to be telling the truth. If I couldn't effect change, I would never get home again. If I made waves here and someone noticed, I'd be locked up in the psych ward or jail.

CHAPTER 25

In October, the market started to fluctuate. Then I knew for certain this was the year of the crash. Connor held fast in his belief that it was temporary, and I kept my mouth shut. The last thing I needed was for someone to tell Dr. Mortenson I was trying to mess with either the Watsons' or the Doyles' money again.

Thomas sat beside the new gas stove reading his morning paper as he usually did once the morning's pastries were out. I poured him another cup of coffee and asked how the markets were doing that day.

"Good land! The market is absurd anymore. It bounces one hundred points or more on any day. It usually settles down by the close of business, but I'm ever grateful not to be one of those boys on the trading floor."

Henry came in carrying a box of canning jars. "The numbers are more volatile than last spring. Marine Bancorporation was at thirty-two dollars a share only yesterday."

Thomas nodded without looking up from his paper. "I've moved most of my money to Diamond Match and Mengel Co. I also bought shares of Procter and Gamble. I always thought that company put out a good product." He slowly turned a page. "I paid off the store last summer, but the taxes are quite another matter. You don't ever truly own anything."

Henry's right brow raised a fraction. "How did you afford it? I thought it was mortgaged in excess of a thousand dollars."

"I sold the Ford stock I held. After the market had such heavy corrections last March, I thought it might be a good time to invest in my own business. The truth of it is, it's exceedingly hard to watch the market. Ford is doing well today."

"Jett, would you put the cream in the icebox?" Henry asked, handing me the heavy jar.

"Sure," I said as I made room in the refrigerator and went back to the pastry table where Henry was laying out vegetables.

"That is the true nature of playing the market," Henry said, "knowing when to buy and when to sell."

"It is, son, and knowing the bank can't take my store makes it worthwhile."

"Let me wrap the last of the Benson order," I said. "Then we can start cleaning the sweet corn for canning."

As Henry and I were prepping vegetables, I suggested banks might be a poor place to keep money. "What if they lose all their cash in the market?"

Henry's brow rose. "And where, pray tell, would you keep money if not in the bank?"

"Think about it like this," I said. "A bank is a business like any other business. They make money by lending their members' money to other people and collecting interest."

"Yes," Henry said as he snapped the ends of green beans. "That's no secret."

"So, let's say stock prices fall and brokers start calling in their margins. Now lots of people have to go to the bank to get their money out to pay the broker, but guess what, the bank doesn't have the money because it's all loaned out."

Henry stared at me, unbelieving. "But they have to give it to me, it's my money."

"They don't have it. Some farmer has bought cows with it, or housewife bought a new stove, or salesman bought a new car." I was feeling sorry for him. "That's the business they're in, loaning your money to other people."

"If they didn't know they'd get the money back, they wouldn't make the loan."

"Oh, they all think they'll get it back, until it all comes crashing down."

"Jett, you can be such a depressing Chicken Little."

I smiled and kissed him on the cheek. "Just don't keep all your eggs in one basket."

All during the week of my birthday I felt a familiar anxiety. Last year's gift had been Josie coming home to die. Although I was grateful for those last weeks with her, I couldn't help feeling the twenty-third of October was cursed. The Doyle family was despondent all week and I'm sure it was the memory of Josie and the now silent rooms that once carried the sound of her laughter that held their hearts hostage. I had hoped to get away to the candy store and spend time with Lillian and Henry, but Thomas was a major bummer to be around.

He sat by the stove each morning looking over the business section of the *Denver Post*, grumbling louder with every page he turned. On Monday, the twenty-first of October, the *New York Times* read "Watson Asks Speed on Tariff as Vital to Stable Business," and Thomas couldn't stop talking about the Smoot-Hawley Tariff bill and how it had bloated the market.

"The leader of the Senate, James E. Watson of Indiana, claims businessmen are hesitating to make heavy commitments until economic conditions are stabilized by a new tariff law. If this fails, and it seems it might, the markets will be slow to recover last week's losses. However," he said boldly as he turned the page, "if this passes, other nations will have no choice but to raise their tariffs. Where will we be then, I ask you? Without international trade, who will buy all the many cars coming out of Detroit? Where is President Hoover on this? He must see the danger here."

I was exhausted by the time I got home to the bustling Doyle house. It wasn't too late for Connor to get out of the market, although several of his investments were well below the price he'd paid for them. The crash was coming and it would only get worse. *Black Tuesday. Will tomorrow be Black Tuesday? Will the Great World Depression begin on Wednesday, on my birthday? How could I have not seen this?* Over dinner I mentioned the Smoot-Hawley Tariff Act in hopes of swaying Connor to call his broker, but where Thomas was filled with despair over the fluctuating markets, Connor was in complete denial.

"Miss Oxford, you are not truly an economist, hiding under crinolines. Did Thomas put you up to this? He has been nothing short of a Sour Sam of late."

"I understand," I said without meeting his eyes, "the Dow Jones Industrial Average is down several points."

"Joseph Grundy won't let the Senate be so foolish. The bill will pass."

"Joe who?"

"See there it is, as I had imagined. You know little about the state of economics yet propose to know so much. Joseph R. Grundy is the head of the Pennsylvania Manufacturing Association. He will hold President Hoover to his promises."

Tuesday was even worse as the *New York Times* reported "Senate Firmly Bars Farm Tariff Limit."

"Without higher tariffs, manufacturing is going to see prices falling quickly. That will have a negative effect on the stock market over the next few months. Lillian, do we have a seltzer? I have a ghastly headache." Sighing, Thomas laid the paper across his lap. "The market wouldn't have had so far too fall if that ridiculous bill hadn't passed the House last June."

By the time I left the store, I fully expected to see homeless people begging for handouts along Colfax. Henry chose to walk me home because I wouldn't let him drive me, and the sun was low in the western sky before we reached Pennsylvania Avenue.

"Your birthday is tomorrow. Would you like me to come for you in the morning? We can surely splurge a bit for such an auspicious occasion."

"You should save your gas. There'll be plenty of mornings that I won't feel like trudging through the snow."

"I have saved for this reason. Will you consider it a gift?"

"Whatever."

"*What ever?*"

"If you insist. I'll accept."

He brightened visibly. "I do insist. I shall see you at quarter past five, then?"

"Whatever."

"Good night. Sleep well."

"You, too. See you in the morning."

As he walked away I wondered, would I see him in the morning as I had seen him this night, or would he be seventy years old the next time we met?

The morning of the twenty-third I'd expected to find my world forever changed once more, but the morning was just like any other morning in the crowded Doyle household. The smell of toasting bread and frying bacon drifted up the stairs to my room where I was putting on my cotton stockings. Guadalupe always tried to send me off to work with at least a small breakfast. In the bed next to me Fiona rolled over and opened her eyes. "Is it time to get up?"

"It's only five. Henry's picking me up in a few minutes, but you can probably sleep until at least six."

"No, I'd better get up. Mum has plans."

She sat up and placed her foot against the side of Caitlin's bed, giving it a steady shake. "Get the little ones up and I'll start breakfast."

In her long robe, Fiona followed me to the kitchen.

"Good morning," Guadalupe said cheerfully. "There's toast and jam, Miss Oxford. Bacon will be a few more minutes."

"Thank you. I hope I didn't get you up too early. Henry is giving me a ride to work today."

Fiona pulled out a massive griddle. "A birthday treat, is it?"

"Something like that."

Cries of "I don't want to," "He's touching me," and "She hit me," found their way from the chilly hallway on the second floor and into the warm kitchen.

"Go and help your sister," Brigid said as she came into the room. "I'll start the hot cakes. Oh, and Sean and Liam might need a bit more coaxing. They were up most of the night studying the new Sears catalog. I'm on pins and needles waiting to see this year's Christmas list."

As promised, there was a tooting horn at quarter past the hour. Momentarily feeling guilty leaving Caitlyn and Fiona to rally the troops around the breakfast table to eat, I grabbed a piece of toast and called up the stairs, "I'm off now."

"Happy birthday!" they shouted in return.

Slipping my coat on, I said, "Thanks for breakfast. See you all tonight," and closed the front door behind me.

The air was crisp but not cold, and there was Henry, as handsome as ever, holding the car door open. My immense relief, seeing him still young and virile, surprised me. For a moment, I believed this was where I belonged, in this time; in this place. Even the smell of wood smoke seemed natural.

"Hi," I said as I slid into the seat.

"Good morning." He walked around the car and got in. "I have a gift for you."

"You didn't need to do that."

He gave me a hurt look. "It's small." Handing me a book wrapped with a white ribbon, he said, "Really, nothing at all."

The little book was called *The House at Pooh Corner*. I smiled.

"It is the second volume of stories about Winnie-the-Pooh," he said. "I should think you would like to read these to the children. It's written by Milne and beautifully illustrated by E. H. Shepard."

"I had no idea you were a fan of children's stories."

"They are stories about friends, and I do so love my friends."

"Thank you. I will cherish it all my life."

"Mother has a treat for you."

"Lemon cake, I hope."

He laughed. "Yes, that as well."

When we arrived at the store I could tell most of the daily orders had been filled. "I should've been here earlier."

Lillian shook her head. "We hoped to spend most of the day away from the shop." She wrapped a package for delivery and handed it to me. "We'll leave when Henry returns."

"Where are we going?" I asked, placing the wrapped parcel in Henry's delivery box.

"With all this late season warm weather and heavy summer rain, the mountain aspen trees are in full glory. We thought a drive to the Rocky Mountain Park would do us all a good turn."

The thought of a trip to the mountains made me smile, but I couldn't help but be reminded of the coming Dust Bowl. The weather reports claimed Colorado had seen the wettest years on record and farmers were producing record crops. The overproduction of crops meant falling prices. If I had somehow stumbled into an alternate timeline, it was surprisingly similar to what I knew of history.

As promised the drive was beautiful. There was nothing quite like looking across a mountain valley filled with gold aspens and dark green pines, in any timeline. We saw several herds of elk and deer. Grazing lazily alongside of a hill stood six large bighorn sheep. At the sound of our rumbling car, they looked up and slowly climbed to safer ground.

Near the lake, Thomas pulled the car over near a grassy clearing. "We'll have lunch here, if I hear no objections."

The lake and meadow were beautiful. The small town of Estes Park, a few hundred yards in the distance, was quaint, not at all what I remembered from the one time I'd been there when I was ten. A grand hotel sat on a hill overlooking the lake. "That's the Stanley Hotel," Lillian said as she unwrapped our lunch. "Isn't it magnificent?"

The white clapboard siding and bright red roof stood out boldly from the gray rock and green trees of the mountain behind it. Remembering the movie *The Shining*, I wondered if it was already haunted. "Very nice. Have you ever stayed there?"

"Dear me, no. We haven't the finances to enjoy such sport."

After eating a couple pieces of fried chicken, Thomas and Henry grabbed their fishing poles and headed toward the water. "Do they usually catch anything?" I asked, enjoying a thick slice of lemon cake.

"Quite often, but I'm not sure that's the point of it." She drizzled a topping made from butter, lemon, and honey over her own slice of cake. "Thomas has been upset over the state of the market these past few days. Fortunately, he's here and unable to fret in front of the radio."

"Is it still bad?" I knew it was, but she seemed to want to talk about it.

"The eastern farmers have been struggling for a couple of years now. I'm beside myself with worry. We are frightfully dependent on them."

A fox darted out from the trees and crossed the road. He had a small ground squirrel in his mouth. He would be fine over the coming years; it would be the more intelligent animals, those who believed they could manipulate nature, who would suffer the most. Thomas had been railing against Congress for trying to control the economy since she'd first met him. In the years to come, Henry would do the same.

Tired of fishing, Henry asked if I'd like to go for a walk. We hiked up the mountainside, reveling in the autumn flowers.

"Let's climb that rock," I said. "I bet the view from there is fabulous."

"But your dress. How shall you climb?"

I hiked it up to my knees and tied a knot in the side. "That should do it. Come on."

Henry stared at me. "Is something wrong?" I asked.

"No. I wish . . ."

"What is it, Henry? You haven't been yourself all day."

He took my hand in his and studied it. Looking up, he smiled that darling half smile. "You are a wonder to behold. Should I never meet another such as you I will not be taken by surprise."

We climbed the rock and the view was everything we had hoped it would be. Sitting up there, gazing across the valley, I felt so alive. Evidently, Henry did too because when I turned to speak, he leaned over and kissed me.

Like I was standing over a precipice, sudden vertigo swept through my head and I thought I would faint. Henry took my momentary limpness to increase the intensity of the kiss, wrapping his arms around my waist.

I pulled back. Tears stung my eyes. I wanted nothing more in the world at that moment than to continue what he started, but something inside me screamed in fear.

"Henry . . ."

"I'm so sorry. I shouldn't have forced myself on you, but you are so beautiful."

"I don't know what to say."

"I'm like a schoolboy with you. Forgive me."

"It's fine. In fact, it was nice. But we should get back now."

"Yes," he said helping me to my feet.

As we walked in silence, my heart was breaking. I was going to hurt him when my time here was done. He would never understand my sudden disappearance. And that could happen any day or night. Would he think I ran away from him? What had the man of eighty thought when I disappeared? Had three years passed for him too, or had time stood still, waiting for my return?

The drive home was as beautiful as the drive up, but all I could think about was Henry's kiss. When we reached the store, Henry offered to give me a ride home, as a gift.

"Sure," I said. "Thank you, Mother Watson. It was a lovely day." Handing Thomas the wrapped fish he'd caught, I added, "And thank you, too. I wish I could stay for dinner. I love trout."

"We'll save some for lunch tomorrow." He kissed me on the forehead and walked through the back door into the kitchen. I felt a warm glow spread over my cheeks.

Henry was quiet on the drive and wordlessly escorted me to the door. Once back at the Doyle house, we were both welcomed inside, and I was showered with gifts. Caitlin gave me a new hat, and Brigid had made a beautiful new quilt for my bed. There were presents of colored pictures and wooden soldiers from the younger children, while Tara surprised me with a pretty green rock.

Brigid asked Henry to stay to dinner. "I shan't stay," he replied, "Mother is expecting me. I only wanted to see Jett home."

"Very well, young man. Please give my regards to your mother and tell her I expect her to tea next Friday. The Ladies Club annual meeting is at four."

"I'll remind her. Jett, can we speak before I go?"

"Sure, I'll be right back to help with dinner, Mother Doyle."

"Take your time. Fiona, help Erin set the table. I'm afraid she's going to drop those plates."

Henry and I slipped out to the porch and sat on the swing. I was thinking about the Dust Bowl, and soup kitchens, and bread lines while Henry was on a completely different track.

"You have spoiled me, and make no mistake. I don't expect to find another like you."

It took a second for his words to register. "What are you saying, Henry?"

"I wish for you to be my wife."

"I, uh . . ."

"I've asked Father Doyle. He's in agreement."

"Uh, but . . ."

"My parents have assured me this is a good match. What do you say?"

"Henry, you are my dearest friend." In another life, I would jump at the chance, but here, I don't know what would happen if I said yes. "I need some time," was all I could manage to say.

CHAPTER 26

We usually listened to the news on KOA while baking in the mornings. Sometimes the static was louder than the program, but it was comforting to know what was happening in other parts of the country.

On Friday, the man on the radio with the stern-sounding voice said: Much of the selling of the last few days, brokers feel, was induced by mass hysteria. The views of all of the brokers we've interviewed agree there is nothing disturbing to the general market situation. This is a market correction.

I wanted desperately to believe the announcer. Not knowing much about the actual crash, the hope the news programs filled us with each day was pretty convincing. In the back of my mind, I prayed that somehow, when Josie died, I'd been thrown into a completely different timeline where the Wall Street crash never happened. At the Doyle household, Connor assured Brigid there was nothing to worry about. "Stocks fluctuate. You're better off not watching them every day. In fact, we should take the children for a motorcar ride. I've come to understand Spencer Penrose has opened a zoological park. A couple days at the Broadmoor Hotel will quell our restlessness."

"I should enjoy a day of shopping. With the holidays upon us, Caitlin and Fiona will both need new gowns."

And they did. As a family, they packed up and took a trip to Colorado Springs for the weekend. Having to work on Saturday meant I'd be staying at home with Maria while Guadalupe traveled with the family. It was a quiet and relaxing weekend, and maybe the short vacation would help calm Connor if his margins were called.

On Monday morning, the man on the radio tried to keep investors from full-scale panic as the financial district claimed the largest banks in the city were prepared to exert their organized power that morning to prevent further disaster. Thomas paced the kitchen.

Rolling out pastry dough, I tried not to meet his eyes. The stocks rallied and crashed, and rallied again. After the stock market came crashing down once again in a spate of hysterical liquidation, the newsman reported that John D. Rockefeller said that there was no need to destroy values, and to show his faith in the market, he and his son, John D. Rockefeller Jr., would continue to be buyers of stocks for investment as they had for the last few days and would buy at present prices.

"He would buy at rock-bottom prices," grumbled Thomas into his morning coffee. "Like a magpie picking up road kill."

Lillian rubbed his shoulders. "I'm sure he's just trying to bolster the market before everyone tries to sell out."

"Everyone is selling out. I'm glad I invested with Lehman Corp. It's a hallmark of good investment management. It doesn't leverage the stocks, keeping it stable. I watched the numbers last March."

"We should hold on to what we have," Henry said. "There's enough money in the bank to cover us until the market comes back. It always comes back."

From across the table, Thomas's eyes met mine. "The banks are heavily invested in the stock market. I should pull my money out now."

I nodded, afraid to voice my fear that the banks had already closed their doors. Thomas left without even putting on his hat and coat.

When it was time to go home, Henry offered to drive. "No," I said. "I can walk and you need to save the gas."

"We have plenty."

"Maybe today, but if thousands of people have lost their fortunes, jobs will be the next casualty."

"You confound me. Why do you believe people are going to lose their jobs? The stock market only affects investors."

"You can walk with me," I said as I slipped on my street shoes and took my coat off the hook. "Lots of the biggest investors are banks and, if they lose their money, they can't return the money their clients have deposited with them." Henry helped me slip my coat on and I slid the big hatpin through my cloche.

"If everyday people can't get to their money to buy things," Henry said, pulling the door closed behind us, "then the plants will have to slow production and lay off workers."

"Exactly. As more people get laid off, more plants will have to close."

Henry was quiet as we walked up Seventeenth Street. I hesitated to go into more detail that might prompt questions I couldn't answer. The wind had come up, forcing me to wrap my coat tighter. I had expected to see panic in the streets, but most everyone was going about his life as if nothing had changed.

After several blocks Henry asked, "Where were you educated in economics?"

"I had a dear friend teach me everything he knew. I wish I would have listened better."

We turned on Broadway and passed the capitol, its shiny gold dome a signature of the country's prosperity. A crowd had gathered on the west steps, although we were too far away to hear what they were discussing.

Henry pulled his own coat tighter. "I have listened carefully to you over these years since we met."

I wasn't sure how to react. "And?" I said as unassumingly as possible.

"You have a logic about you that's undeniable. I should hope more people would look at the world through your eyes."

We remained quiet for the next two blocks. Suddenly, he stopped, took my hand, and turned me to face him. "You know how much I loved Josie, don't you?"

"Of course. I loved her, too."

"You're different. Where Josie was like a playful kitten, sweet and loving, you are like a mountain lioness: gracefully meticulous in your movements and thoughts. I am fascinated. From the first day we met I felt a connection I could not shake. When Father employed you at the store it was as if you needed no training. You belong there."

"Thank you, Henry. I love working there."

Without releasing my hand, he continued walking, but there was the weight of responses unsaid in the air. I wanted to change the subject.

"Have you heard from Rory?" I asked.

"What? No. I've not had a post in some weeks. Jett, I've been wanting to ask you . . . "

"Look, there's Tara. What is she doing outside alone?" I raced away to the gate of the Doyle home just as Caitlin grabbed Tara by the hand.

"Tara's a bad girl," Caitlin said with undisguised relief.

"Jate," the little one cried when she saw me. "I wanna see Jate." She wriggled loose from her sister's grasp.

I opened the gate and the toddler ran to me. "How's my favorite little girl?" I said, picking her up in my arms. "Are you giving your big sister trouble?"

Tara giggled and hid her face in my shoulder.

"She slipped out while I was cleaning the lamp globes," Caitlin said. "She was right there handing me rags one minute, and the next she was nowhere to be found. How was your work today?"

"It was pretty good. Everything okay here?"

Caitlin cocked her head. "Have you been listening to the news programs? I can't tear Father away. Is it as bad as it feels?"

Henry held the side door open for us. "I have faith," he said, "things will turn out fine."

The Doyles had many beautiful things in their large home, like the Radiola 103, with its tapestry speaker. It was an elegant metal mantle clock shape that sounded clear. Like the radio, they had the latest in gas appliances and, what I truly loved, a wringer washer. It wasn't as good as the electric washers and dryers I used to use at Smiley's Laundromat on Colfax, but it was a huge improvement over the washboards at the orphanage. Tuesday was laundry day, and being quiet days at the store, I was usually home before noon, so I often helped wash bedding.

Throughout the day, the news programs reported already depressed farm prices were continuing to fall. The world news seemed a bit slow today and I found myself contemplating the coming war as I pulled sheets from the wringer of the washer and put them in a basket for Caitlin and Maria to take outside to hang.

Lost in my thoughts, I was surprised to hear Henry's voice coming from the parlor. "Is Connor here?" His voice sounded stressed, like something had happened. Wiping my wet hands on my apron, I headed up the stairs.

"He went to the bank first thing today," Brigid replied. "He was so upset about the morning papers."

"Father was as well," Henry said. "He went to seven banks yesterday and got the same news. Banks are limiting how much a person can withdraw."

Brigid sat heavily on the sofa. "We don't keep money on hand."

"Do you know which bank he is visiting?"

"What's happened?" I asked, sitting on the couch next to Brigid.

She handed me a telegram. It was from Rory in New York.


```
WESTERN UNION
October 29, 1929
As doors opened, people crowded into brokers'
offices with New York Exchange stock ticker tapes
or quotation boards. Investors rushed to sell
stocks, prices plummeted to new lows. New York Stock
Exchange overwhelmed, fortunes lost. Thousands
fill streets. Riots. Banks closed.
```


Stunned, I laid the telegram on the coffee table. It was actually happening. I'd almost convinced myself it wouldn't. Taking Brigid's hand, I said, "We're going to get through this. It's only a setback, not the end of the world."

For the next few days, the city was buzzing with the news, but nothing earth-shattering happened. Connor took stock of his finances, and after a long evening meeting with Uncle Paddy, it was determined the family was truly broke. The carefully guarded trust fund had been wiped out and the margin calls on several investments Connor held ate up every dollar he could get from the bank. Paddy and Laoise left their generous accommodations downtown and moved into the tiny room on the third floor where Josie had spent her last days.

By Thanksgiving week, there was no money for extras. Brigid was a good homemaker and the cellar was well stocked, but items like soap would be harder to come by. Connor was doubly frustrated as winter was, by nature, a difficult time for a man to find construction work. Caitlin took over minding the younger children as the family could no longer afford the services of Maria and Guadalupe. There were many tears because the family would miss them, but also because we knew they would not be able to provide for their own families without the regular income the Doyles had provided.

"The mortgage is thirty-five dollars a month," Connor said, his voice carrying from the master suite. "I haven't had as much as a five dollar bill since the first of November."

"The children are going to be so disappointed in Christmas," Brigid said. "They're too young to understand."

"Then the time is now to grow up. If I can't get the mortgage paid, we'll be sleeping on the streets. Merry Christmas to us."

I tiptoed past their door on my way to work. I'd told the Watsons to reduce my pay if they needed to, but Thomas said their finances would be adequate for the foreseeable future. I'd been a miser since my arrival and had saved a small amount of money. As long as the Doyles continued to house me, my needs were few.

When I reached the kitchen, Caitlin was already starting breakfast for the family. "I couldn't sleep," she said. "Mum and Dada are arguing almost every night."

"They're worried. This is a big family to care for."

"Yes, and there are lots of hands to help. Uncle Paddy is carving a wooden corral with horses and cows for Finigan and Roark. He has a couple dolls and a three-car train. I don't understand why Mum is so worried."

"I think it's more than Christmas."

"It's the masquerade. Dada won't let her host the party."

I swallowed a bite of toast. "At times like this, celebrating friendship is important." I had exactly $113.28 to my name. It could keep the family in groceries for most of the year or it could pay the mortgage for just over three months. "Let me handle this," I said. "I think we can have a pretty good Christmas. I have to leave for work now. Last day before Thanksgiving, I'm sure we'll be busy."

"Remind Lillian that Mum and Laoise are having Ladies Tea next Saturday the seventh of December instead of Friday on account of the holidays."

"Sure thing."

As I walked to work under the predawn sky I couldn't help but wonder how Brigid and Connor would take my gift. They were a proud people. Although I wasn't given a salary for tutoring, they did give me board and room. I was surprised and thankful I wasn't let go when Maria and Guadalupe were dismissed. The two housekeepers didn't leave empty-handed. Through her tears, Brigid had piled clothing and canned goods in a box to give them before Connor drove them home for the last time.

I met the milkman as I walked up to the door of the shop. "Top o' the morn' to ya, ma'am."

"Good morning," I said. "How are things with you?"

"Had better days, better days. They say Wall Street crashed. Lot o' folk in a tizzy, they are. Glad to have me job."

"Me, too. You have a nice Thanksgiving, now."

I slipped inside to find Lillian elbow deep in dough. "Morning," I said, taking off my hat and coat. "What are we making today?"

"The standard fare: rolls, croissants, fruit bars. I also want to make some extra cookies to take to the Denver orphanage. It feels like I've been neglecting them."

After changing out of my street shoes and donning my apron I asked, "I know it's none of my business, but how are you and Thomas doing with the market being down so badly?"

"We're fine. Thomas is pretty savvy when it comes to investment."

"I'm worried about the Doyles."

Lillian turned the dough onto a floured marble table. "I'm not sure what to do. I truly wish to help."

"I have enough money to pay the mortgage for three months."

Lillian shook her head. "They won't take charity. They're too proud."

"They may not want to use it, but I believe I can get them to give it away."

She looked up from her kneading. "Whatever do you mean?"

"They have that huge house. Brigid is an excellent seamstress and so many people need clothing. To suit her giving nature, she could sell the clothing for less than the department stores. Laoise and Caitlin can teach music for a few pennies to ensure the young women of society don't lose their poise. Connor and Paddy can teach engineering. The boys can do handyman chores. If they rent out a couple of rooms. I think we can make enough to pay the utilities and groceries."

Lillian rolled out the dough and began cutting it into triangles. "How are you planning to pay the mortgage? Will you sprinkle these with chocolate and the ones over there with orange peel?"

I opened the box of grated chocolate. "I was hoping that between us, we could pay the mortgage until Connor can get back on his feet. He'll find work when the weather breaks." I sprinkled the chocolate onto the dough and then rolled the triangles, making dainty crescents. "We can tell them it's a loan to get their school started."

From the doorway, Henry said, "If one cannot afford food, how is he to pay for music lessons?"

I slid the full baking tray into the oven and began prepping the orange crescents. "Lunch would be included in the lesson."

"Yes, now I understand," Lillian said, smiling. "Many of our friends who neither garden nor can foods will need to provide for their children and will save face by giving them sewing and music lessons."

"Yes," I said. "And by keeping the price low, Brigid will be helping the community, as she's always done."

"You're brilliant," Henry said. "If the cinnamon rolls are ready, I can take them over to the hotel now."

"Almost," I said. "I just have to wrap this last batch. So, my next dilemma is how to announce the new school. I thought, if we help Brigid and Connor host their yearly masquerade, they can tell all their friends about it at the party, maybe even get some donations to help get it started."

Henry packed the last of the rolls in a wooden box. "Parties are expensive."

"Think of it as an investment. We won't have servers, will do it buffet style. If you can find a friend or two to help with the music, Caitlin and I will make the food."

"Count me in," Lillian said from the wash sink. "I know we can donate pastries and rolls, I'll even throw in some candy for the children's stockings."

I hugged her. "Oh, thank you. They've been so worried this last month."

By the doorway Henry asked, "Do you think Father will agree to this?"

Lillian smiled. "You let me worry about your father."

Later that day I heard the tinkle of the bell over the front door. Dusting flour off my hands, I stepped into the showroom to help our customer.

"Oh my gawd! Rory, is that you?" The shabbily dressed man was thin and dirty from head to toe. His soft ginger curls were matted under a stocking cap that had seen better days. "Come on back." I grabbed him by the hand and led him to the back room. "Let me get you a bowl of soup."

"I would be grateful. I haven't eaten since we were in Tennessee."

"Is Paul with you?" I peered into the showroom.

"We got separated in Saint Louis. Rail travel is ever so inconvenient if you can't afford a ticket." He washed his hands and face at the sink while I turned up the fire under his soup. The two rolls on the table were devoured before the soup came to room temperature. "Let me grab Henry, he's out back loading the truck."

Before I went to get Henry I called upstairs to Lillian. "Rory's come home! He just got off the train."

"Rory?" I heard her say as I went out the back door.

"So good to see you!" Henry said, grabbing his friend in both arms. "You're a sight for sore eyes."

"It's good to be home. Thank you for the soup. I was so hungry."

Lillian filled his cup again. "You're always welcome to anything we have."

"It was good to get away from New York. Paul lost his position and I'd been having some difficulties before Wall Street fell into disarray. We had no savings and couldn't make the weekly rent on our room. Abigail, the dear, is employed with Macy's Department Store and she graciously paid our rent that first week."

"I'm sorry things got so tough on you," I said, handing Rory another roll.

"You did warn me."

"Let's get you home! I know your family will be so excited you'll be here for the holiday."

"Yes. I do want to go home. Thank you again, Mother Watson, for the lunch."

I grabbed my coat and hat. "We can walk if it's alright with you?" I asked Rory.

Henry shook his head. "I'll drive. And I won't be talked out of it."

I worried Rory would mention the letter in front of Henry, but I would have been an ogre to make him walk home after his long trek across the country. "Oh, my, I haven't finished the bread stuffing. I just got so excited."

"Don't fuss," Lillian said. "I'll finish. I'll see you tomorrow for dinner. Take these loaves of bread to Brigid and tell her we'll be there at noon. Oh, and here's a sack of broken cookies for the children."

As we drove, Rory told us stories about what goes on behind the scenes of some of Broadway's biggest shows. His stories were light and charming, considering the hardship he endured getting back to Colorado. I was surprised by the number of famous people he'd already met.

"It's a rather small community. Most of the extras work for multiple people. The music scene is much like being an extra: everybody needs us, but no one knows who we are."

"You shall be bored to tears," Henry said, "with only the likes of us to entertain you now."

"And very thankful for the boredom. I've had quite enough adventure for a while, although I wouldn't mind having one more dinner with Miss Anita Paige. She is such an angel with a face to match. Paul and I were having dinner at Lindy's one night when she stumbled in. She was obviously alone and tired from a long day of work. Imagine our surprise when she agreed to let us buy dinner for her. By the by, they make a wonderful dessert they call cheesecake. You really must get the recipe."

My heart fell into my stomach when, upon arriving, I saw Dr. Mortenson's car parked out front. This could only mean bad news.

CHAPTER 27

Luckily, Rory's arrival seemed to make everyone forget the doctor was there. After looking Rory over, the doctor pronounced him to be in reasonably good health. "Nothing a few good meals wouldn't fix."

I was about to slip away to my room when Dr. Mortenson asked to have a word.

"Have a seat in the music room while I make us some tea," I said, needing a moment to calm my nerves. The Doyles had lost almost everything and I was sure the doctor and Rory were going to blame me. Pouring the boiling water into the teapot, I realized how much at home I felt here. I'd never let anything or anyone take this away from me. I'd done nothing wrong. *Everything I ever told them was to help them through these next ten years.*

When I returned, the doctor was sitting on the piano bench running his hands over the highly polished wood. "Would you like sweet cream?" I asked, pouring two cups of tea.

"No, black is fine."

I sat on a chair by the window. "What can I do for you?"

"My daughter is far away from home."

"Yes, I believe Rory said she was working at Macy's Department Store in New York City."

"Should I tell her to come home?"

Startled, I nearly spilled my tea. "I don't know the answer to that, sir."

"You told Rory he should leave New York."

So, Rory *had* shared the letter with Abigail. "I can't predict the future, sir. Macy's is a good company, and Abigail is a smart girl. As long as she can afford to stay, I'm sure New York is as good as Denver. Of course, if she were to be laid off, it would be a good idea to have her train fare available. No city is good for a girl on the streets."

He looked as if he was going to say one thing but changed his mind. "The dailies tell us this will pass quickly. I didn't play the markets. I saved my money and tried to provide a good life for my family." He turned his hat over and over in his hand. "I can't draw out my savings and most of my patients can't pay their bills."

"This is a time for sharing. You should barter for what you need and forgive when you can. Let's pray it's only for a month or two, but prepare for the possibility it could last many years."

"Years? We can't last years without money."

"I think a person can last a lifetime with the love of good friends."

He looked frightened as I walked him to the door. "How did you know?" he asked.

"I only guessed at what I thought made good financial sense. Warner Brothers is a quickly growing company. I truly believed Paul and Rory had a better chance working in Hollywood than they had in New York."

As he shrugged into his overcoat I wasn't sure I'd convinced him of anything. "Doctor Mortenson," I said, "I never did thank you for everything you did for me when I was hurt. It couldn't have been easy."

He smiled gently. "You were an extraordinarily interesting case, my dear." He took my hand and turned it over in his. "Yes, an extraordinary case."

Later that day, Rory asked me to meet him in the carriage house. When I arrived he was there, leaning against the car, smoking a cigarette. He clothes were clean, and he looked much like the Rory we'd put on the train to New York only months before.

"Hey. Glad to see you had a chance to clean up. Are you feeling better?"

"I've been distraught ever since I heard the doctor's allegations. I'm so dreadfully sorry to have breached your confidence. You must forgive me."

I nodded and sat down on the wide running board.

He began to pace. "When I read your post I was, at first, confused. That you wanted Paul and I to go to California was clear. The reason for going wasn't to be understood. I regret that I asked Abigail for guidance."

"I assumed you had told her when her father came to see me."

"Then it was—it was on account of me." Rory said, his cheeks pinking. "Abigail claimed you were pretending to be a mystic, someone who tells the future. In her mind, you were trying to induce my parents to invest in some intrigue to make you wealthy. She claimed her father would have you arrested."

"I know it sounded crazy. I never meant for anyone to give anything to me, least of all money. I just wanted you all to be safe."

"Abigail still insists you're a charlatan. My mind was hopeless of change, until on the arrival of November, I was confronted by the truth. You knew what no other person knew. Father has lost everything in the market. The bank holds the title to the house, but without employment, he can't make the mortgage payments."

I rubbed my eyes and stared at the floor.

"Jett." He lifted my face toward his. "Who are you? How did you know Wall Street would fall? If you know things that can save my family, you must tell me."

"I have a good head for business. I'll do what I can to help all my friends, but you have to trust me."

"I want to know more."

"Rory, you wouldn't believe me."

He stood there for a long time before nodding. "Someday, I shall know your secret."

I could hear Sean calling for us to come in to dinner. "Someday, I promise to tell you everything, but for now, let's go eat."

"Gladly!"

The next day was Thanksgiving. You wouldn't have known money was tight by the smell of freshly baked bread and roasted turkey. Just as we were about to sit down at the table there was a rap on the front door.

"I'll get it," I said, making my way to the front door. Through the glass I could see him. "Paul! I'm so glad you made it." I kissed his whiskery cheek when he came into the foyer.

Rory was at my side before the last word dropped. He hugged his friend as if they hadn't seen each other in years. "You made it. I worried so."

"You didn't wait."

"I didn't like to leave, of course, till you did come, as long as you'd said nothing of your plans when you left me there on the track."

"But you didn't wait for me to get back." He looked stern but happy to be at the home of his closest friend.

Rory looked admonished. "It was five days, Paul."

"I ran into some trouble picking carrots and beets from a farmer's field. I was allowed to keep what I picked as long as I worked the hogs for a week. I had no way to get word to you."

"Well, you're both here now," Brigid said from the hall. "Go wash up and join us at the table. We can wait five minutes if Rory can wait five days."

I wasn't there when Lillian convinced Thomas to go along with our plans for the school, but it must not have been that easy as it was the following Wednesday before she mentioned it.

"Thomas hesitated, but only because he thought Connor would be offended. He assures me we have plenty to share, our friends will never want for anything."

"Great. I can't wait to tell Brigid."

"As a grown woman, I think you should come with me to tea on Saturday and present your plan to the Ladies Group. I was thinking we might elect Brigid as the chair of the new Women's Endowment Committee."

"Oh, I love the name. This is going to be awesome—*wonderful*, I mean—this will be wonderful."

I was nervous on Saturday morning. Having never attended a formal tea and never proposed any kind of plan, I was afraid of how the ladies would take it. I changed my skirt twice and my blouse three times.

"What has you so atwitter?" Caitlin asked.

"I'm going to the Ladies Tea today."

"Oh, how wonderful. I would love to go. They always look so proper in their fancy hats."

"Oh, no. What can I do for a hat? I don't have anything but my plain woolen cloche."

"Come with me," Caitlin said as she pulled me toward the attic. "All we need are some velvet flowers and some feathers and you'll be in the fashion."

She opened a door to a large closet filled with what had to be Brigid's sewing stash. There were laces and beading and ribbons flowing out of boxes. Rolls of silks and satins stacked upright in a corner like colorful soldiers. On a large worktable, vases held a rainbow of feathers. "How fun!" I shouted. "I had no idea your mother had all this cool stuff."

Caitlin cocked her head, and then nodded. "She likes to keep her hand in it. She always says the way a woman speaks and dresses says more about her character than any pedigree."

"Very true."

We spent the morning decorating my little hat to match my skirt and blouse. I felt absolutely fabulous when I met Lillian at the door.

Although Brigid, Lillian, and I arrived at the Brown Palace at exactly noon, most of the other ladies were already seated in the grand lobby. I knew Mimi, of course, and her mother, Madeline, I had met at holiday parties. Laoise was there as well as Clarabelle, Jay's cousin. Opel and Ester were two women I was meeting for the first time.

As the waiter brought our tea and sandwiches, Lillian opened the informal meeting with a brief discussion about the state of the economy.

"Things are just ghastly," Clarabelle said. "Our savings have been all but depleted. I should think this will be my last tea for some time."

Opel nodded. "For me as well. Although you know how much this time with my lady friends means to me."

Mimi sipped her tea and watched as each of the women stressed the difficulties they were facing. "I know as hard as it is for me," she said timidly, "it is so very much harder on other families."

This was my lead-in. My voice shook for a moment as I began. "As women of means, I think it's our duty to keep the civility alive in the community. It would be easy for a family with little or no money to forget themselves."

All heads nodded in agreement and I felt sudden relief. I didn't know what I'd been so afraid of, but their willingness to listen bolstered my confidence. "I have an idea how we might help everyone who has been troubled by the falling markets and poor farm prices. Young women and young men will always need to have a proper education in mathematics, music, and the arts. The Doyle household has several rooms that could become classrooms. We all have talents to share. Each lesson should include a hot lunch, or if we wish to expand, we could have early morning classes with breakfast. We'll ask only a small donation to help further our work."

Madeline frowned. "How will the poorest pay even a modest fee?"

"Everyone has to eat," I said. "Most of your homes have especially large gardens. If a client can't pay, they can help in the community garden. The food can be shared, and those who would go hungry would have at least one good meal a day."

"Under the guise of private tutoring," Lillian said.

Olga sipped her tea, contemplating. "Our friends would save face while their children would receive an excellent education."

"I think that's a first-rate plan," Ester said. "What do you think, Brigid? Is your home available?"

"Well, I must speak with Connor, and as dreadful as this sounds, I'm not sure how long we can keep the bank at bay."

"I was hoping," I said, "we could start our new charity with a small treasury. I have a hundred thirteen dollars to begin our mission." By the gasps I heard, I knew they were impressed by my donation.

"We cannot! That's all your savings, child," Brigid said aghast.

"And I can't think of a better way to spend it. You have taken me in as one of your own."

Brigid looked thoughtful. "You have been a blessing to my home. The children love you."

Each of the other women promised smaller amounts to bankroll the project.

"We should choose a name," Lillian said. "How about, the Women's Endowment for the Poor?"

"I hate to call people out for being poor," I said. "How about the Women's Endowment for the Arts? We'll stress music, sewing, cooking, and if we can convince Connor, drawing and engineering."

"We can teach ballroom dancing and party planning as well," Brigid said. "All ladies of influence should be trained in the art of event hosting."

As it turned out, Laoise was elected chairwoman, and the rest of the afternoon was spent planning the curriculum for the first semester, to be announced at the Doyles' masquerade.

As the holiday season progressed, money became tighter. Both Connor and Thomas gave up smoking and Brigid gave up fresh flowers at every meal. Caitlin made a beautiful centerpiece from the holly hedge growing under the southern windows that lasted for several weeks. Lillian still sent pastries home with me each day, but they were now only the day-old or damaged samplings.

During the second week of December, Brigid's younger sister, Rose, showed up with her husband and their two children. They'd been evicted from their home in Philadelphia and had nowhere else to turn. They arrived tired and hungry but in good spirits, the family resemblance going deeper than mere appearances.

Two days later, Connor's mother and father stood on the doorstep, hat in hand.

Rory, Paul, Sean, Liam, and Caleb worked for days turning the carriage house into additional sleeping rooms, the car being parked outside on the street until further notice. Boxes of old knickknacks and livery tools were removed from the hayloft and disposed of as necessary, many of them becoming gifts for friends and family. An old wood stove was moved in to keep away the worst of the chill, and what little furniture family had brought with them helped to outfit the additional eight bedrooms. Making a trip to the eastern farmlands, Connor and Paddy were able to acquire enough straw for sleeping pallets where the family was short a bed or two.

Christmas morning proved to be like any other Christmas morning with children's laughter and pleasant family conversation. Somehow enough money was found for simple gifts for all the kids. The hand-carved toys were particularly well received, and Caitlin was delighted over the new ball gown her mother and aunt had made for her. I was equally thrilled over the dress they had made for me. The workmanship was exquisite; a jade damask with chartreuse lace trim at the cuffs and neckline.

"Your new gown matches your eyes utterly," Henry said as he handed me a small package wrapped in red paper with a white bow. "You will surely be the most enchanting woman at the masquerade."

"Thank you, Henry." I tugged at the ribbon and unwrapped the paper to find a round, brushed aluminum musical jewelry box with a tiny sculptured blue jay on the lid. The bird was of a gold metal with its perky crest, wings, and back painted in blue enamel trimmed with black and the breast in white.

"It made me think of you," he said. "Blue jays are known for their intelligence and tight family bonds."

I gave him a Waterman's Fountain Pen. "For all your accounting in the years to come."

"It's a splendid gift."

I was glad he liked it, but I didn't think it compared to the music box he'd given me. I turned the box over and wound the little key. It played *Let Me Call You Sweetheart* and was the most endearing gift I'd ever received.

As I'd imagined, the big holiday masquerade of 1929 was one of the most joyful events of my life. There was something magical about family and friends coming together, sharing what little each had, that taught me to appreciate the smallest things in life, like the sweet voice of a fifteen-year-old girl confiding a crush, the laughter of little children vying for the attention of their elders, and the warmth of a wood fire and hot cocoa.

I was sad to learn Julianne wouldn't be performing for us this year. Rumor had it she had left town suddenly, while Link was making a name for himself in the bootlegging business. I would miss her beautiful voice. But it was a joy to hear Rory, Paul, and Henry play together once more.

The announcement of the Women's Endowment for the Arts was very well received. In fact, on the first day of school, there was a line halfway around the block. As it turned out, there were many more people in need than we had anticipated and we were forced to limit the number of students we could take on.

CHAPTER 28

The spring of 1930 came and went in a rush of activity. Between the school, the shop, and helping Rory and Paul plan their next move, I hardly noticed the budding of the trees.

"We are all proud of you," Henry said as he toasted with iced tea the latest adventure of Paul and Rory. "I know you will be as well received in Hollywood as you were in New York."

Paul laughed. "Let us hope it turns out better than New York." He rocked back and forth on the porch swing.

"We shall see," Rory said. "Mum can use the extra space now that the school is educating most of Denver these days. I wonder if she plans to let her students out for the summer?"

"Yes and no," I said. "She has most of them planting the garden this week. I'm betting she'll keep them all summer to water and pull weeds."

"Liam finished the henhouse yesterday. Mum should be moving the chicks from the carriage house this week."

"That should make your Aunt Rose happy," I said, taking a seat next to him on the porch swing. "I felt so bad for Tara. The poor girl loved two of the baby chicks to death. She came in, crying about how they wouldn't wake up."

Paul nodded. "I think she knew why they wouldn't move, but I don't think she was prepared for her father's wrath."

"Caitlin should have been aware," Rory said.

"Caitlin can't be everywhere at once," I said. "She could really use some help from the likes of you."

Henry's brow lifted. "The likes of us?"

"You know what I mean. It wouldn't hurt for you guys to take the little ones to the park now and then so Caitlin can get her housework done, unless of course you would rather do laundry."

Henry tucked a curl behind my ear. "As you wish."

"I'm serious. She's supposed to be teaching music lessons."

Rory shrugged. "I've been teaching them."

"I know, but now you and Paul are leaving and Caitlin hasn't had any practice teaching."

"I'll help her," Rory said. "We'll be here for another week. Sean and Liam are old enough to take the little ones for the day."

Paul, having been a city boy all his life, asked, "When will the chicks start laying eggs?"

Henry answered, "Hens start laying when they're eighteen to twenty-six weeks old. I've spent a few summers working on my grandparents' farm out by Fort Lupton."

"I didn't know you had family here," I said, not knowing why I should have been told. I guess it was a surprise because they never came to visit.

Henry shook his head. "They lost the farm in twenty-five. My father's eldest brother is a farm implement dealer in Scottsbluff, and my grandparents moved there to help. Granddaddy is a blacksmith by trade."

"All the same," Paul said, "it doesn't sound like we'll have fresh eggs before we leave."

"The eggs we've been getting from the market are only a couple days old," Rory said. "The Miller farm brings eggs in every three days."

"But I've never had an egg still warm from the chicken."

"Why, Paul," Henry said, laughing. "I think we should take you out to the Miller farm and let you collect your own eggs."

"Why is that funny?" I asked, having never collected eggs myself.

"Not all hens are happy to give up their babies," Rory said. "I've been pecked my share."

"Back to work now, boys," I said getting up. "The chicken run isn't going to build itself. Connor put a roll of chicken wire in the rumble seat of the car. Why don't one of you go get it?"

"I'll go. I need to get my tools," Henry said. "Jett, will you help me?"

Paul rolled his eyes. "Just tell her you want to talk to her, no need to be a man of mystery."

I followed Henry to his car where he kept a box of hand tools. He opened the door and rummaged through the wooden box until he found his hammer. "I've left off the subject," he said, "for quite some time, but with Paul and Rory leaving soon, I'd hoped to receive an answer." He turned to face me. "Have you considered my offer?"

I couldn't meet his eyes. I drug my foot back and forth, making designs in the dirt of the driveway. "I've thought about it," I said. In fact, I'd thought of little else since the day he asked.

He lifted my chin to meet his beautiful blue eyes. "You know how I feel, how I have felt. Of all people, you know Josephine would understand."

Before I could answer, Caleb came looking for us. "Henry, Mum wants to know if you're joining us for dinner? She said if you were, please to ring your mother and let her know."

Henry nodded. "I'll ring her," he said. "She and Father are traveling to Nebraska in the morning." He turned to me after Caleb wandered away. "We will have to run the store ourselves for the next few days. I hope this won't be an inconvenience."

"No, of course not. I would like to get an early start on the rolls though."

"I'll pick you up at four."

"Sure," I agreed as we walked back toward the chicken house, "but I hate to see you waste the gas."

"You could always return home with me tonight. I would sleep on the chaise and you may have my room."

It was very tempting. "I don't think that would look right. Best if I stay here."

"We could make it right."

"I know," I said. "I haven't forgotten your offer." By then we were back with the rest of the family, stringing chicken wire to keep the new laying hens from running out in the street.

The next couple of days at the store went smoothly. Without his parents around, Henry was more daring in his choice of recipes. He was a joy to work with and didn't bring up the question of marriage except to grin when I mentioned having to walk home at the end of each day.

"What is that?" I asked when I found him stirring brown sugar into molasses.

"I'm trying to make a new caramel." He added cream. "I wanted a sweet coating to help preserve apples."

I smiled, knowing one day he would make the best caramel apples in all of Denver.

The next day I was in the kitchen and Henry was out making deliveries. The number of standing orders had dropped over the past year, but Watson's bakery was still doing a fairly brisk business. Just as I slid a sheet cake into the oven, I heard the tinkling of the bell over the front door. I wiped my hands and entered the showroom where a middle-aged couple were perusing the display cases.

"Can I help you?" I asked.

The woman looked up with green eyes the same color and shape as my own. I would know them anywhere, having spent years looking at photographs in search of my parents. This woman had eyes very much like mine, but her hair was red, turning to gray, while mine was jet black. They were both pasty white, Irish.

She stared at me for a moment and then asked, "How old are ye, m'dear?"

"Nineteen. Ma'am."

"And ye name? What's ye name?"

"Jett," I said. "Jett Oxford. Do you know me?"

The woman burst into tears and ran from the store. The portly red-haired man blinked at me a few times and mumbled an apology for the woman. "Please forgive me sister. She had a newborn babe stolen from her nineteen years ago while we was staying at that thar' hotel across the street. Hasn't been herself since I told her we was to be returnin' to Denver."

She must have seen the resemblance and been reminded of her stolen child. He followed the woman outside, and I watched them through the plate glass window as he tried to comfort her. A few minutes later, he returned to the store.

"I'm not sure how to ask ye this," he said quietly. "My sister thar' would like to meet ye parents iffin' she could."

"I'm sorry?"

"She would ask iffin it should be feasible to meet ye mother."

"I, uh." I was trying to make sense of what this woman was asking without giving away too much information. Telling them I was orphaned, not here, but in the 1960s wasn't an option.

"And ye father? Could we be meetin' him as well?"

"I grew up in Colorado Springs. My parents have long moved away—to Hawaii. I rarely see them. Why do you ask?"

"Don't fret, child, but if ye should change ye mind about the introductions, here's me number." He scribbled an address on the back of a card. Caine R. O'Leary was a cattle buyer from Kansas City.

I tucked the card in my pocket and walked him to the door. "What is her name, your sister?"

"Margret. Margret Elizabeth O'Leary."

Never married. In this day an unwed mother was rare, very rare. It wouldn't be unusual for someone to take her child away. I wanted to help her, but there was nothing I could do. I watched them walk down the street. A shiver started at my toes and ran up my spine until the top of my head began to tingle. I had the overwhelming feeling I might have met my mother, but that was crazy. I would have to have been born in 1910. Would that be so much crazier than getting hit in the head and waking up in 1927? Maybe I never lived in the seventies and eighties. Could it all have been a bizarre dream? No, I was found in a dumpster in 1965. I know this. I couldn't have imagined television, computers, and rock and roll.

"Jett," Henry said, holding me up by the waist. "Are you unwell? You're pale as ice."

I hadn't realized my knees had buckled. "I'll be okay. I just need a moment. I didn't hear you come in."

"What did he do to you? Do you know him?"

"Nothing and, no, I don't know him. I think I should have eaten breakfast."

He led me to a chair, where I sat, trying to clear my head.

"What did he say? Something has you terribly upset and I'll know the truth of it."

"Henry," I said, steeling myself for the reaction he would have to my words. "I'm not sure if you can understand this, but I'm not from here."

"Yes, you said you lived in Colorado Springs, but you've been here in the city for some time now. Is that someone you knew before coming to Denver?"

"I've never met him before, or the woman," I repeated, staring blankly at the front window where the couple had recently stood engaged in conversation. "She looked a lot like me, but with red hair."

"Shall I go get them? Maybe they know who you are. Could they be your parents, perhaps an aunt?"

"It was a man and his sister, but there is no way she could be my mother."

"How can you be sure?"

"I know, Henry. Trust me, I just know."

Henry shook his head and tucked a curl behind my ear. "My little one, how you confound me. You can't possibly know all these things."

"I'm going upstairs to lay down. I just need a few minutes."

He helped me up. "I'll watch the store. Take what rest you need."

As I walked up the stairs I chided myself for not having the courage to tell him the truth. He loved me, this I knew with all my heart. Over the past year he'd become my best friend and I loved him. It was May of 1930 and I hadn't gone anywhere in more than two and a half years. Could it be possible that I would stay here forever? Of course, I lived in the future for sixteen years before coming to this time. *Or did I?*

I toyed with the idea of calling the O'Learys. There could be no confirmation the woman was my mother. DNA testing wouldn't be available until long after the woman was dead and I had overwhelming evidence I had come from the future. Knowing about DNA testing and microwave ovens was proof of my world, proof I had lived in a distant future not even imagined yet. I knew the stock market would crash. I even knew it would start in October.

I spent the day changing my mind a hundred times about whether or not to contact the O'Learys. If somehow I *had* been born in this time, what could I tell them of where I'd been for all those years? Is it possible that I had traveled not once, but twice through time?

Henry took me home early because he thought I was still out of sorts. I allowed him to drive the car, knowing the gas was expensive. My knees were still weak and my mind was filled to overflowing with contradictory possibilities. Henry respected my silence, but the look in his eyes told me he was worried. I kissed him on the cheek, thanked him for bringing me home, and then let myself out of the car.

Opening the outer porch door, I heard Brigid talking. "I should like to let you know how important sliced bread is to the morale and saneness of this household. We are all in a rush during and after breakfast. You are not even risen from bed by the time the meal is on the table. Without ready-sliced bread I must do the slicing for toast— two pieces for each one—that's eighteen not counting your father and me. That's twenty-two slices of bread to be cut in a hurry! And your father's lunch requires four more slices for two sandwiches."

"Mother Doyle," Paul said. "It just seems a silly extravagance, this presliced bread."

"I assure you, it is not."

Rory turned to me as I walked into the kitchen. "Tell me truly, Jett. What do you think of this? Is it a fancy that will pass in a moment?"

I stopped and stared at the bread on the table. It had some pins holding it together, not at all what I'd remembered Wonder Bread looking like. "Uh. I don't know."

Rory took me by the hand and led me out the back door. "Last summer, when you were complaining about carrying wood, you said the gas stove was the best thing since sliced bread. And here it is. How did you know about this? Be square with me."

Crap, good memory! "I must have heard about it."

He grabbed my chin, forcing me to meet his eyes. "You said the stove was the best invention since sliced bread. Today, you don't know if it is a great invention?"

"Rory . . . " I pulled away and sat heavily on the arbor swing.

"No, Jett. You will tell me. You think I'm a fool?"

"I don't."

"Tell me."

"Promise not to tell anyone—I mean, not ANYONE. You can't even tell Henry, or I swear, I'll tell the world about you and Paul."

Rory stepped back. "You would do that?"

I put my head in my hands. "No, of course not. Rory, I'd never hurt you, but you don't know what you're asking of me."

"I would not hurt you, Jett. You're like a sister to me."

"Then let this go."

"You're a mystic, as Abigail claims. She thinks you're a fraud, but I now know you are not. You can see the future."

I was surprised how easily the lie came. "Yes, Rory," I said cautiously. "I have a special gift, but it scares people. People think I'm faking my gift because I can't see everything. They would lock me away if they knew about it. You can't say anything." *Was being a seer any less ridiculous than traveling from the future?*

"Caitlin said a Detective Bell came to see you. Does he believe you're a fraud?"

"He doesn't know about that. He's trying to find the man who attacked me the day I lost my memory."

"She was hoping the detective would visit again."

I smiled. "He was pretty good-looking. He called again last night and asked me to come down to the station to look at some mug shots. I'll take her with me."

Over the next few weeks, Rory dropped the subject of "my gift" for the most part. But one day while we were working in the garden, Rory asked me whether or not he and Paul would be successful in Hollywood. He was disappointed when I said I couldn't see individual futures. I wished that I had better news, but in my world the names Doyle and Bachmeier never made history. Although I did encourage him to try their luck writing musicals.

"I know about Stalin and Hitler because they're going to have a huge impact on the world. The likes of the everyday person is well under my radar."

"Your what?"

Shaking my head, I shoved the spade into the soil. *When did they invent radar?* It was insane how many commonly used words hadn't been invented in 1930. "Never mind," I said. "I can only predict really big world events."

I didn't need a crystal ball to see Caitlin's heart. Even as shy as she was, she never missed a chance to be with me when Detective Bell called.

"He's just the dreamiest, isn't he?" She said one night as we were getting ready for bed.

"Who?" I asked.

"Martin Bell." She sighed and sprawled across the bed.

"I suppose I could drag out this investigation a few more months so you can get to know him a little better."

"Oh, would you?" She sat straight up, eyes as round a saucers.

I laughed. "I guess it will be a little longer since I didn't recognize any of his mug shots."

Although Henry rarely mentioned the subject of marriage, I could see the frustration in his eyes. When I would be quiet for long periods he would prod me for answers, accusing me of keeping secrets. I would try to make a joke of taking time to memorize recipes, but I believe he saw through me. Only once did he actually ask me what confection had me so enthralled. I told him I missed canned cream of mushroom soup, the bases for every casserole recipe I knew.

"Soup? You miss a can of soup?"

"No, I was just thinking aloud. We should make a hot-dish casserole. All you have to do is mix a can of cream of mushroom soup into cooked ground beef, add some corn and pour it in a pan lined with tater-tots. Bake it in the oven for about twenty minutes or until the tater-tots are golden brown and crunchy on top."

Henry's eyes were wide, looking at me like I'd lost my mind. And maybe I had. I was homesick, but try as I might, I couldn't put my finger on anything I really missed that much about the future. At times, it was Jay, or Penny, or even an older, comforting Henry. I didn't miss hiding from the crazy bikers or Social Services, maybe because I had others in this time just as dogged. When it came right down to it, what I really missed was being able to relax and not having to filter everything I said for odd words and references that had no history. I had changed over the years to the point I wasn't sure if I would fit in in the eighties any better than I was fitting in here in the twenties. My slang had nearly ceased to exist, but my cooking skill had grown exponentially. It was incredible how many shortcuts in cooking would be invented in the next fifty years.

Paul and Rory left for California in June. They had no friends there, and I worried about how hard it would be for them to find work. It seemed everyone was moving to the west in search of the golden dream. They were talented men, both musically and socially. The film industry needed musicians to write movie scores. All they needed was one little break.

That week Brigid decided to clean the attic. "Not everyone is poor in these times," she said. "There are families who have made good decisions these past ten years. That we had only been so wise." She opened a dusty trunk. "Most of these curios belonged to my mother. I've never had a use for them." Wooden picture frames and porcelain bowls sat among faded quilts and doilies. "We will hold a sale at the next endowment meeting. Several ladies are bringing items to help raise money for school supplies."

I set aside the objects she indicated. "Will this be an auction?"

"Yes. There is a small side table and a mirror under that sheet. Will you take them to the carriage house?"

"Sure." I worked my way between boxes to the mound of cloth-covered furniture. The table was delicate, probably French. I pulled the sheet off the mirror and my knees buckled. It was a large round mirror with beveled edges, heavy, and about two and a half feet in diameter. Was it the same mirror I would buy—no, the mirror I did buy—on my yard sale trip with Bambi? I could almost see her wearing the felt cloche over her fully permed, bleach-blond hair in the mirror's reflection. My own reflection showed a pale and frightened girl. I began to panic. I hadn't considered the mirror before. Bambi and I had played dress up in twenties clothes in front of this mirror the day we found it. Could the mirror have been the vehicle that brought me here, like Alice and her looking glass? How could I use it to go back? There were no eighties clothes to be found. I would have to make some. And what would I go home to if I did? Jay was gone.

"Are you well?" Brigid asked, coming to my side. "You must lie down before you fall."

She wrapped her arm around me, and tears filled my eyes. As much as I wanted to go home at that moment, I never wanted to leave Brigid.

She brushed my hair away from my face. "My dear girl, you look as if you've seen a ghost."

I had. I had seen the ghost of myself, and the ghost of a future that may never exist.

I mentally pulled myself together and picked up the mirror. "I'm fine. Probably need to eat some lunch."

"We can take a break. Leave that for now."

I set it back down and followed her from the attic.

Over the next week I struggled with the idea of buying the mirror. Once it was gone, my link to the eighties might be gone as well. I had a little money, but not as much as the woman who was bidding against me. The mirror was sold at the auction that weekend for twenty dollars. Seeing it carried away was like giving up the last connection to my other life. Oddly, the woman who bought the mirror was Detective Bell's mother.

Dr. Mortenson stopped by one day in late July to see how I was doing. I was nervous and had a hard time sitting still as he asked me questions.

"I can see Brigid Doyle's Endowment for the Arts is doing well. Connor seems to be an excellent fundraiser."

"He's a well-spoken man and the Endowment is helping lots of people." I handed the doctor a cup of tea and took the chair across from him.

"Yes," he said. "I understand you were the one to propose the charity."

I swallowed hard. Where did he get his information? Abigail was still in New York. "Well, it was really Lillian Watson and I who came up with the idea."

"Abby tells me the charity has grown to help more than one hundred families."

"Abby said this?"

"Oh, she is quite close with Mimi these months."

"Ah, yes. Mimi is the treasurer. She would know exactly how well we're doing."

"Your name is on the board as a full member. You hold an equal share of the treasury, do you not?"

"I suppose I do."

"And you have an imposing voice in how the monies are invested?"

I was getting uncomfortable again. I paid little attention to most of the charity's business. Even the chickens were Ester's idea, although it was brilliant. "We do our best to keep the bills paid. We expanded the garden and added the chickens so we could feed more people."

The doctor studied his hat. "Did you know Abby was moving to California?"

"No, I hadn't heard that. What about her job at Macy's?"

"She wishes to be a movie star."

"You're kidding me."

He looked at me out of the corner of his eye. "She had an offer from a director she met while working the perfume counter at Macy's. They've asked her to do a screen test."

"That's wonderful! She has a great face for movies, like Jean Harlow or Constance Bennett."

"I don't get out to the pictures much."

"Trust me, Abigail has the look."

"I feel much better now that I've spoken with you. I miss her greatly, but I want her to have the best chance life has to offer."

I wasn't sure if he thought I had some inside track on the movie industry or he just wanted to grill me about the charity's finances.

He turned his hat over in his hands. "The market has been brutal over these past months. I was assured it would soon return to full value by my broker."

"I wouldn't count on it." From the window I could hear squabbling children.

"You wouldn't?" he asked with sudden interest.

"I don't know. It's just a feeling. Better safe than sorry, I say." An extremely upset Tara burst into the room. "JATE! Cai'lin won't let me hold the chickies."

"Oh, darling," I said as she crawled into my lap. "The chicks can't take all that handling. It scares them."

"But I wanna hold 'em. Kevin gets to go in the pen."

"You'll have to excuse me, Doctor. I have a bit of a crisis here."

He smiled for the first time that day. "I understand. Thank you for speaking with me."

I stood, coddling the child in my arms. *Like I had a choice.*

"Come with me," I said to a teary face. "I'll teach you how to feed and water them, but you must not touch them. Do you understand?"

She nodded and blinked back tears. By the end of the summer the chicks were chickens and not cute enough to hold anymore, but Tara continued to help me water and feed them every day.

A week later, Rory wrote to tell us Abigail landed a walk-on part in a new movie to be produced by Paramount. He and Paul had worked on the score. Her screen test had gone well, and she was added at the last minute.

On August twenty-ninth, along with a crowd of thousands, we gathered in the streets in front of the Paramount Theatre to celebrate the Grand Opening showing of *Let's Go Native*. Tickets were expensive, but Dr. Mortenson insisted that I attend the premier along with Brigid and Connor. The show's opening-night excitement rivaled the glamorous Hollywood premiers reported in the movie magazines. Rave reviews and widespread public awe immediately established the Paramount as Denver's leading theater.

The movie score was wonderful and the comedy timeless. The moment Abigail appeared, I saw the doctor reach for his wife's hand. We all took pleasure in knowing someone who appeared on the silver screen, no matter how short the clip.

In September, news came from Los Angeles. Abigail had been given a movie contract and both Rory and Paul were working steadily at Warner Brothers Pictures. I was feeling good about everyone I knew. Even Dr. Mortenson had taken a trip to visit his daughter and came home raving about the beautiful home she had near the ocean.

The Watsons' store was struggling, but surviving. Money was tight for everyone. The Doyles had managed to meet their mortgage each month and usually had money for the utilities. Things seemed to have settled into a steady rhythm of living.

My chores were done and four o'clock came early, so I went to my room to read for a while. The book couldn't hold my attention. As I lay on my bed, staring at the ceiling, I couldn't help wondering, *why was I still here?* Did I still have something to complete? Was this going to be my life? I missed television. I missed the microwave oven. I wound the key on the dainty music box Henry had given me and let the song play.

Let me call you Sweetheart.
I'm in love with you.
Let me hear you whisper,
That you love me too.

I sat up and looked at myself in the mirror. *What was I doing?* I should marry him. If I went back, then I went back. Why was I living for a far-off future when my life was right here? I had to stop looking for my family and accept that I'd found them. Suddenly, I couldn't wait to tell Henry.

I grabbed my hat and raced down the stairs.

"Where are we off to in such a hurry?" Brigid asked as I passed the dining room.

"I need to speak to Henry. I've decided to say yes."

For a moment I wasn't sure if she was unhappy or just confused. Suddenly, she swept me into her arms. "I knew you would come to your senses one day. Lillian is going to be so happy."

"I needed to be sure."

"Of course, dear. Marriage is a big step. Now, you aren't going to see him like that, are you?"

I looked down at my cotton dress, still dusted with flour from the morning's baking. "I, uh, I guess not."

"Follow me," she said as she turned to go up the back stairway. "I know just the thing."

In the corner of the sewing room was a dressmaker's mannequin decked out in white brocade. From the table nearby, Brigid grabbed a sapphire skirt and jacket. "I think this will fit. You can change behind that screen."

I did as I was instructed. The outfit fit pretty well. The waist was a smidgen big and it seemed a tad bit long. I came out to show her.

"Take it off, that will never do."

I changed back into my cotton dress and handed her the suit. "This will only take a moment," she said, clearing fabric off the sewing machine. "Wait right here." I was impressed. It took only a minute to remove the waistband of the skirt. As I waited, I went over to look at the brocade dress. It had a delicate lace bodice. There was a necklace hanging just above the low-cut neckline. Tiny, intricate silver filigree holding a radiant cut clear crystal. It was beautiful. The last time I'd seen it, Josie was wearing it. I wanted to cry, I missed her so much at that moment. I couldn't understand how time had altered, but this would be my life. *I miss you, my friend. It should have been you standing here. Forgive me.*

Brigid finished the alterations. "My goodness, child. You look as if you've seen a ghost. Haven't changed our mind now, have we?"

"No. I haven't changed my mind. I just hope I'm doing the right thing."

"You are. I haven't had a doubt in months now."

"Thank you for fixing the suit."

"Hurry now, I'll have Connor take you in the automobile."

"Henry isn't home yet. At least I don't think so. He went to Brighton with his father."

"Well, you'll just be pretty as picture sitting there when he gets home."

CHAPTER 29

I was sitting at the Watsons' dining room table. Brigid had called Lillian before I'd even closed the car door. "Henry is a wonderful man," I said. "I should have seen it sooner."

"I feared you would never give him an answer," Lillian said. "The boy moped about for days neverending."

"I have nothing to offer him. I have no family."

"Oh fiddlesticks. You have a family with the Doyles, and now, a family with us." She patted my hand. "You were made to work in this store. I can see it in your face when you mix a batch of cookies or decorate a birthday cake."

"I do love it."

"We should plan your wedding cake."

"Shouldn't we see what Henry says first?"

"We will, but let us not give him too many choices."

It was dark before I heard the truck pull up behind the store. Suddenly, my palms were sweating. I dried them on my skirt. The back door opened and Thomas came in.

"Are you alright?" he asked me with concern. "You look pale as a sheet."

"I'm fine." I said. "Is Henry with you?"

"Yes. He's getting some dry goods from the truck. Are you sure you're alright? You don't look well."

"Hush, Thomas, she looks beautiful."

Henry came in with a sack of flour over his shoulder. He was strong and handsome.

"Hello. I didn't expect to see you here. Is everything alright?"

"Yes," I said standing. "I wanted to talk to you."

"Could it not have waited until morning?"

"No. I might have lost my nerve."

He set the sack down beside the flour bin. "Well. What is it, then?"

I looked around the room where Lillian and Thomas were making themselves busy and trying not to be too obvious. "Can we go for a drive?"

"Let me put these things away."

"Nonsense," Lillian said, pushing us toward the door. "Your father and I will take care of this. You go, now."

Henry looked confused, but nodded. He handed me my hat and helped me into my coat. Opening the car door, he asked, "Has something happened? You're frightfully skittish."

"I've been doing a lot of thinking."

He smiled as he slid behind the wheel. "I hope you haven't hurt yourself."

I gave him a playful jab in the ribs as the car rattled down the street toward the river.

"You look beautiful tonight," he said. "Where would you like to go?"

"This is fine, just pull over."

He parked the car on a side street and turned to look at me. "Something has you upset."

"Henry, you have to listen to me. You're going to think I'm crazy and, if you don't want to marry me after what I tell you, I'll understand."

"You want to marry me?"

"Yes, I do, but not until you know me."

"I know you." He tucked a curl behind my ear. "I've studied your every move since the day we met. I've watched you bake, I've watched you clean, and I've watched you with the children. I love you."

"You don't know where I came from, Henry. I'm not from this time."

He didn't even blink, and I figured he hadn't heard me. I braced myself and said, "I was born in 1965. A maid found me in a dumpster behind the Oxford Hotel on October twenty-third." I stopped to give my words a chance to sink in. "I met you and Jay—Josephine—for the first time in 1981. I came to work for you at the very same candy store your parents own today." I wracked my brain to think of something that might make my words sound less crazy. I rambled on. "There was a fire in the kitchen in 1982. Josephine was trapped under a beam. You and I, we tried to move it, but it was too heavy. Something hit me in the head and I woke up at the hospital, but not in 1982. I woke up in 1927."

I waited for a response. He was silent.

"Do you know what I'm telling you? She made me promise to take care of you, Henry." I was crying now. "Somehow I ended up here, thirty-eight years before I was born. But I couldn't take care of her."

"How can that happen?" He looked skeptical.

"I don't know. I've been trying to figure it out for the past three years. It just happened, Henry."

It was Sunday night, the seventh of September. He looked out the window at the full moon, low on the eastern horizon. "I don't understand. Why are you here, now?"

"Henry, I wish I knew. I was afraid to marry you because I always thought I'd go back to 1982. I was afraid I would leave you, end up in some other time. When Josephine died, I should have disappeared. I don't know how I can come to work for the two of you if she isn't there when I turn sixteen."

Henry stared out the window of the car until I thought I would die of apprehension. I wanted him to say something, anything. *Call me crazy, tell me you don't believe me, ask me to get out of the car.*

The silence lingered on for an interminably long time before he started the car and headed toward the Doyle home. My stomach hurt. He was quiet until we stopped in front of the house. Turning to me, he said, "I don't understand what you're trying to tell me. How can one travel through time?"

"I don't know how or why it's happened, but I'm telling you the truth."

He opened the door and got out. I waited for him to open my door. Stepping out, I said, "Henry, I love you, but I had to tell you where I came from, why I've done and said so many strange things."

He nodded, surely recounting the times I'd acted peculiar. We walked up the front steps in silence. At the door, he took my hand and raised it to his lips, barely brushing across my fingers.

"Good night," he said, distracted.

My heart caught in my throat, keeping me from commenting as he turned to leave. I watched him climb into the car and drive away. I should have expected the truth would be too bizarre. Maybe I should have told him the same lie I'd told Rory.

I opened the door as quietly as I could. I didn't want to face Brigid with my dismal news. The parlor was dark, and I was surprised to hear Caitlin's voice.

"You're home earlier than I should have expected." She stepped into the hall where the nightlight revealed my face.

"Oh, no!" she cried, wrapping her arms around me. "How could he refuse you?"

"He . . . " I had no words.

"I'll make you some hot cocoa."

Numbly, I followed her to the kitchen, where we talked about the day's classes, the garden, and trivial things I no longer remember.

The following morning I telephoned Lillian to tell her I wouldn't be at the store that day. I couldn't face them. Caitlin brought breakfast to me as I hid in our bedroom. She seemed understanding beyond her fifteen years.

"I hope you don't mind," she said. "We didn't have bread for toast today."

"Thank you for bringing this upstairs. I feel like a slug."

She sat on the bed across from me. "Do you want to talk about what happened?"

"I think it's pretty obvious that he didn't say yes."

"Did he say no? Maybe he wanted to be the one to propose."

"He has. Numerous times."

She busied herself straightening up the bedroom. "He loves you. Of that much, I am certain. Give him time."

"I would give him until 1980 if that's what it would take." *I have nothing but time.*

Tara opened the door. "Is Jate here?"

"Yes, moppet," I said, putting on my best happy face.

She wondered over to my breakfast plate and wrinkled her nose. "I don't like eggs."

"Well. I won't make you eat them."

"Mum says I have to eat eggs."

"Not these, you don't. Caitlin brought them for me."

She curled her finger in her hair. "Are you sick?"

"No, just tired."

"You won't go away like Josie?"

I pulled her up on the bed beside me. "No. I'm going to be around a long time."

"Good." She hugged me and jumped down.

Caitlin stopped her at the door. "Why were you looking for Jett?"

"'Cause Henry is downstairs."

I scrambled to get dressed. "Tell him I'll meet him under the arbor."

Caitlin smiled. "I knew he would come to his senses."

"This doesn't mean anything. He just wants to talk. Maybe he didn't believe I was sick today and is checking up on me."

"Maybe this, or maybe that." She handed me a hairbrush. "Either comb it or put a hat on; you'll frighten the chickens."

I looked in the mirror. Dark circles and puffy eyes greeted me. My hair was a mess and for a brief moment, I missed the hair products of the future. I settled for the hat.

After powdering away the dark circles under my eyes the best I could, I went to meet Henry.

"Fifty-four years," he said quietly. "That's a long time from now. Tell me, what is the world like in 1982?"

I wasn't sure if he was testing me or teasing me. "Well, you don't have to work as hard."

His eyebrow jumped up.

"And," I said, "we have seriously cool kitchen gadgets like automatic dishwashers and air-conditioning." I told him about television and how radios were mostly for music. I described as best as I could the latest model cars and air travel. "You know, we sent a man to walk on the moon in 1969."

He rocked the swing back and forth. "Why?"

"Why, what?"

"Why would we go to the moon?"

"I guess it was to prove we can."

"You claim that you worked for Josephine and me at the store, and that we were old."

"Yes," I said. My gut was churning. "You're going to be a charming old man."

"Did Josie know about this?"

"No. I haven't told anyone until you. The doctors would lock me away and no one would believe me if I tried to explain."

"I don't know what to believe. Do you remember when Rory left for New York, and you suggested I play music at the Baxter Hotel?"

"Yes." Vaguely.

"You called it the Rossonian. The Baxter Hotel changed names a year after you called it by that name."

I felt the hairs rise on the back of my neck. What else did he remember?

He shook his head. "If what you say is true . . . "

"It is, Henry. I promise. It's all true."

"I don't know how this can be."

"I don't know either and it scares me. I've been alone with this secret for so long. I really need a friend, someone I can trust completely."

"I love you, Miss Oxford. Of course I'll marry you." He reached over and took me into his arms. "It was, after all, my idea. I'm not saying I understand any of this, but it does explain how you knew enough to tell Paul and Rory to get out of New York."

"They told you?"

"After Rory came home last November, he showed your letter to me."

I gulped. The letter would have sounded crazy.

He stared into my eyes. "I read an article only today about a wonderful new medicine called penicillin. You asked Paul to search for this medicine when Josie was ill. I've been trying to learn more about it." He studied my face. "You know things I can't explain."

"In the future there will be vaccines and antibiotics. Children won't get small pox, polio, or scarlet fever. Children will grow up. It's a wonderful future."

"Any future with you will be wonderful." He pulled me closer and kissed me.

We set our wedding date for Saturday, November first. I only had to get passed my twentieth birthday. If I was still here . . .

The next two months were a blur of anticipation. The closer the date came, the more excited I got. Brigid and Lillian helped me choose a menu of chicken and potatoes because we had them. We had beef and pork at the butcher shop because Connor was able to pick up a hog and a cow for pennies on the dollar. Unfortunately, because the family had scarce few dollars, that meat would be sold at a profit to help keep the mortgage paid.

We decided Tara should be my flower girl, Kevin the ring bearer, and Caitlin was to be my maid of honor. She was my dearest friend and little sister, now.

Upstairs in the sewing room where Brigid had so expertly altered my suit, she asked me what I wanted to be married in.

"I don't know. I have the red velvet dress I wore at the masquerade."

Brigid shook her head. "I think you should wear that one." She pointed to the dress I'd seen on the mannequin the day she altered my suit.

"Oh, but I can't. Surely that dress is for Caitlin or Fiona."

Brigid ran a hand over the bodice. "Josephine was having this made for you. She swore to me that you would marry before you turned twenty."

I stared, my mouth open.

"She said it should be white lace and crystal beads." Brigid pulled out the delicate sleeve and turned the cuff over to inspect the crystal buttons. "She had me purchase these the week she came home from Agnes Memorial."

I couldn't believe what I was hearing. "How did she know?"

"My Josephine has much in common with you. She had a gift for reading a person's intentions. Much like you and your economics. It hasn't been lost on Connor and I, that had we listened, we might not have lost everything."

"I'm so sorry."

"You needn't be. We're going to be fine and you, my lovely little daughter, are going to make me so proud. I admire a woman who isn't afraid to speak her mind."

"Thank you, Brigid. It's been so wonderful living here."

"Call me Mum, and let's see if the dress fits."

I slipped the dress over my shoulders and let it fall gracefully to the floor. "What's left to be done?" I asked. "It looks perfect."

"I have a small train to add and some more beading at the waist. Would you like to help?"

"I would love to."

We spent the afternoon working on my dress. I'd learned to hand stitch and how to hem. I'd learned how to crochet lace and how to take in a waistline. I wasn't a woman of the twenties, but I was comfortable here.

I was so busy between the store and the wedding plans I'd nearly forgotten to be wary of my upcoming birthday.

Henry, Lillian, and Thomas had joined us for dinner. It was only when we sat down, and Caitlin said, "I have a birthday surprise for you, Jett," that I felt that familiar quiver of fear run down my neck.

"It was hard to keep it from you, but . . ." The front door opened and in strolled Rory, Paul, and Abigail.

"Oh my gawd!" I said, getting up to greet them with hugs.

"You didn't think we'd miss the wedding?" Paul squeezed me tight.

Setting his suitcase down, Rory said, "I thought the poor man would never talk you into it."

Brigid came from the dining room. "Come on now, we're just sitting down to dinner. Caitlin said you would be here on time, but she didn't want to give the surprise away by setting your dinner plates. Come, come, it's getting cold."

I helped Caitlin grab the extra place settings as Rory and Paul told us about their exciting jobs working at the movie studio.

"Abigail," Rory said, "has won a feature roll in a war drama. We're so proud of her."

The girl had the grace to blush, and I found myself liking her just a little bit.

After dinner, Brigid brought out a lovely cake with a candle. I couldn't remember ever having candles on my cake.

"You must make a wish," she said as she set the cake before me. "Wish for a special gift because dreams can come true."

I closed my eyes and blew out the candle. Everyone cheered. A moment later, Brigid handed me a brightly wrapped box. "I've wanted to give this to you for the wedding. It goes so well with your dress."

I tugged the ribbon off and unwrapped the box. Inside was a necklace. Tiny, intricate silver filigree held a radiant cut clear crystal. It was the necklace I'd seen Jay wear every day. Henry took it and I lifted up my jet-black curls so he could fasten it about my neck. In the dining-room window, I caught my reflection and finally understood everything. For sixteen years I had drifted from foster home to foster home, never feeling like I belonged anywhere. Now I could see the answer had been there all along. A shiver ran down my back as I reached up to fondle the necklace. *This is home. I'm really home at last.*

"What's wrong, my little blue jay?" Henry asked. "You look so pale."

"I'm okay," I said. "For the first time in my life, I'm really okay." I shook my head. "What did you just call me?"

"Forgive me, I called you 'my little blue jay'. Is it not acceptable? You know how I love blue jays."

Looking at my reflection once more, I laughed. "Yes, Henry, it's wonderful. I suppose it was only a matter of time."

EPILOGUE

Once we were married, I moved into Henry's room, above the candy store. Because the store usually closed at four in the afternoon, I was able to spend many evenings at the Doyle home tutoring the children, much as I had done since the summer of 1928. Whenever he could, Henry would join me and teach music as well. Lillian and Brigid would make simple biscuits and watered tea for us, and together we would chat until the sun went down behind the Rockies. Connor and Thomas spent many of those summers during the early thirties working on eastern farms to help cover the expenses, often leaving Lillian, Brigid, and the children home alone for weeks at a time. The weather was dry and many farms went under, bringing more mouths to feed to the city.

When the political landscape began to intensify in Europe, Rory convinced Paul I could see important changes in the future. Several families pooled their money together to help bring Paul's family, three grandparents and two maiden aunts, to the States in early 1932. By 1935 Paul had decided Stalin was also a terrible leader and began preaching the merits of capitalism to anyone who would listen. By 1950 he had embraced the teachings of Ayn Rand. The Depression had varying effects on everyone, but none so much as Paul.

1936 produced the coldest winter on record and the hottest summer. The dry winds blew mile-wide dust storms from North Dakota to Oklahoma. Every window had to be covered with wet sheets to help keep the dust from sifting in. Dishes were washed and then placed upside-down on the table and covered with a sheet to help keep the dust out. The summer dust storms made cooking particularly difficult, not to mention how hot it was to have the oven going when it was over one hundred degrees outside.

The majority of the country was in a tailspin economically, but Denver seemed to be limping along better than most of the eastern cities and was far better off than the Midwestern farmers of Kansas and Nebraska. The candy store made enough money to pay the taxes, keep us in groceries, and help fund the Endowment for the Arts. We had no extra money for clothes, so we patched and repatched what we had. We saved flour sacks to make dresses and shirts. During those cold winters, we cut cardboard to put in our shoes when the soles began to give out, and through most of the summer we all went barefoot whenever we could. When household goods broke or furniture gave out, we didn't buy new. We fixed everything the best we could, including our car.

Henry's father, Thomas, died the summer of 1936. Heat stroke or heart failure; it was hard to know the difference. Lillian took the loss in stride, and I could see where Henry got his strength. I was proud to be his wife.

My birthdays passed almost unnoticed until 1937, when I gave birth to a beautiful ginger-haired daughter. We named her Margret Josephine. She was the love and laughter of our lives. Two years later, Josie was followed by a brother, Thomas Henry Watson the Third.

As much as I tried, I couldn't stop the rise of Hitler or prevent the country from going to war and, in 1939, Roark and Finigan flew to England to help the cause. A young man of seventeen, Kevin joined his older brothers in 1940.

We lost Roark in '43, and Finigan in '45. Kevin came home from the war, but forever lost was the little boy who used to cling to my leg when he was frightened.

In 1936, three of the brothers, Sean, Liam, and Caleb, joined the Civilian Conservation Corps to work on a project that would become the greatest outdoor amphitheater in the world, and then went on to open an architectural engineering firm with Connor in 1943.

Roisin married a local farmer, while her older sister Erin married a soldier and moved to Maryland.

Caitlin married detective Martin Bell in 1932 and moved in to his mother's house on Ogden Street. The mirror she bought that day at auction hung above the fireplace mantel. Whenever I chanced to visit, the mirror always gave me a sense of vertigo.

Of course, Detective Bell never did find the man who attacked me on that fateful day. After several years, I convinced him to stop looking. Caitlin and Martin still live in that big house on Ogden Street, although most of the rooms have now been turned into law offices or apartments.

When Tara turned sixteen, she came to work at the candy store until a charming young ski instructor whisked her off to live in Aspen. I talked Henry into buying a little cabin nearby and we usually spend Christmas with Tara, Bob, and their five children. I still like to read *Winnie the Pooh* to the little ones.

Rory and Paul live in Los Angeles, making good money writing movie scores. Although Abigail acted only for a few years, she went on to be a successful producer and still shares a house with Rory and Paul on Doheny Road in Beverly Hills. Fiona joined them in 1950 and married a banker in 1953. She currently works on Rodeo Drive as a fashion consultant.

Happily, as the years slid past, I forgot about the future until October of 1966 when I was momentarily tempted to see if there was a new orphan at the Denver Children's Home. What would I say or do if she was or wasn't there? No, I decided. My life had turned out well. The only thing I *will* do to affect any change is put a help wanted sign in the window of Watson's Candies on the morning of October twenty-third 1982.

I wonder if she'll come in?

Michele Poague is a special events planner, an accomplished political activist and author of the multiple-award-winning trilogy, *The Healing Crystal*.

Praise for *The Healing Crystal*

Great characters, an interesting and realistic plot. This book wasn't about space. It wasn't about religion. It wasn't about science. (Ok, it was a little...) What this book really examined was humanity and if it could ever really change.

Rebecca, The Library Canary

The Healing Crystal, Book One, *Heir to Power*, Book Two, *Fall of Eden*, and Book Three, *Ransom* are available through your favorite book dealer.

For more information regarding Ms. Poague, *The Healing Crystal* trilogy, and her works-in-process visit **michelepoague.com**.